The Fires of Windameir

by Niel Hancock

WARNER BOOKS

A Warner Communications Company

FOR SMITH AND WENDY:
Who taught an old dog new tricks

WARNER BOOKS EDITION

Cover design by Don Puckey

Warner Books, Inc.
666 Fifth Avenue
New York, N.Y. 10103

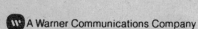 A Warner Communications Company

Printed in the United States of America

First Printing: February, 1985

10 9 8 7 6 5 4 3 2 1

Contents

caused the bound man to draw back in fear.

"The Red Fleet is awake and . . .
on "it is the Age from the past . . .
"not . . . a sea"

THE RUNES
OF DESTINY

Spring Storms

In the spring of the year, the winds and rain came and the river reached floodtide twice in a week, forcing the settlement to move to higher ground until the water receded. The winds had ruined much of the thatch on all the roofs, and many of the dwellings were left open to the endless march of blustery rain squalls that seemed to come in ceaseless storms from beyond the twin peaks of the Bitter Roots.

Stretched along the hills above the water-soaked settlement, the tents of the villagers were pitched, along with a larger canvas-and-wood shelter which housed the meeting hall, and which was the gathering place for all the various holidays and dances, or just the usual nightly exchange of news and gossip.

It had been a long winter, and there weren't many visitors up or down river, even when it was clear of ice; they had heard nothing of any other settlement, either along the Roaring Sea or further away toward the mountains, which was unusual, but nothing to unduly alarm them. Their settlement was a large one, and well protected from the normal run of winter, except for the current one, which showed them they would have to move their dwellings further back from the water's edge in the future. It was the first time in all the years they had lived there that the floods had been so severe or the winter so long.

There were those who sat by the fire in the great hall at night over their tea or ale, and told frightening stories about the old days, although there were but few who were old enough to remember much. Mostly the townsmen were of a younger generation, the descendents of those whom the stories were told of, the Old Ones who had become the legends and myths of their long distant kin.

On this particular evening, there were two ancient men who sat at table, sipping at their mulled ale, and listening with obvious relish as the storm outside pelted the canvas roof with large raindrops, and the wind blew sparks about in the open-faced stoves.

Both of the men were dressed in the same fashion, long gray capes that covered them from head to foot, and tall riding boots that were old and worn, but well made, and showing the signs of much hard use. At the side of both hung swords of an antique design, undecorated in any but the most simple fashion, and sheathed in a blue scabbard with only a single marking, a small round rune that ran around the top of the sheath, next to the hilt of the sword. Their knapsacks were leather, and beside each was a quiver and bow, which was taller than a man, and would seem impossible to draw.

These strange old travelers sat staring at the fire, oblivious to the whispered chatter and speculations of the locals.

One of the men looked up to order food, and was met by the earnest gaze of a young man who was slightly built, with a shock of light brown hair that trailed carelessly across his forehead.

"Oh-ho, what have we here, Gillerman? Look! A tad who thinks he's seen a ghost!"

The second traveler stirred his thoughts from the blazing fire behind the stove grate long enough to study the object in question.

"So it is," he agreed. "I think, Wallach, that we have here the genuine article in the flesh."

"Genuine what, sir?" asked the lad, drawing back.

"A genuine, dyed-in-the-wool curious tom, who is waiting to ask old Tom Gillerman and Simson Wallach who they are and where they're bound."

"Oh, nor sir, not at all. I was trying to see what it says on the scabbard hilt you're wearing. I've never seen blades fashioned quite like that before."

"He's never seen blades like these, Wallach," repeated

Gillerman. "The lad says he's not seen steel like this before now."

"Isn't likely to have ever run across anything at all in the nature of these blades," agreed his friend.

"What do you think they're made of?" asked the first.

"Why, steel, sir," replied the youth. "What all swords are made of. But I was looking at the sign on your holster. What hand is it?"

The old travelers looked at each other in silence for a time, making nodding motions with their heads, and casting their eyes about as though trying to detect if they would be overheard when they made their answer.

"The runes are not those of any human hand," whispered Gillerman, in a voice so low the boy had to creep nearer to hear the words.

"And no eyes ever saw fairer work, nor sturdier steel," added Wallach. "When these blades were forged, the world was younger then, and a terrible danger stalked every single living thing that drew breath."

"You mean the time the raiders came to Sweet Rock?" asked the lad eagerly.

"A lifetime before anything you would know or hear of," corrected Wallach. "This was in a time when your river was but a stream, and the forests here were but saplings."

There were others in the crude shelter that had slowly gravitated to the pair of timeworn travelers, and they all now drew up their chairs to hear the conversation, and ask questions of their own.

"Here, here, friends! What stories are you giving our young Owen here? You'll have him dreaming of distant towns and seas, and he'll run off to a life on the ocean and break his poor mother's heart."

"That's it, Juliun, that's it. The poor tad will be took with all this hooly-hoop, and the next thing you know, he'll be out living under the stars without a roof to ever call his again."

"His mother won't thank you for stirring up his imagination. She's already had no end of trouble all along, trying to keep him at home, and attending to his studies."

Gillerman turned to his friend, speaking so the others

couldn't hear. "What's this? No secrets here, friends," cried another man, sitting beside the youth.

"I'm trying to find out what my friend wants for his supper, citizen. I think you'll find that no secret."

"What is more of a secret to me is how you two old goats managed to get through to Sweet Rock here in all this storm. We haven't had news or traffic with anyone this whole winter, and now here you two sit, as pretty as you please. That's the secret I'd like to know about."

The speaker was a surly man in his early sixties, with close cropped hair and a bristly beard.

"Pay no attention to Bristlebeard," apologized the boy. "He's always suspicious of anything or anyone."

"With good reason, lad, always with good reason. I'd like to hear the tale these two old gaffers have to spin."

There was a rumble of consent from the gathered crowd, which had swelled in ranks as the afternoon grew on into dusk.

"You can come home with me," said the lad, looking around at the peering curious faces that surrounded the two old men, now looking frail and outnumbered in the flickering light of the rushlamps and lanterns.

"You can see to our horses, my young friend. Make sure they've got themselves a dry spot out of this weather."

Gillerman reached into the folds of his cloak and withdrew a small leather pouch, and took out a coin to give to the boy.

"I'll look to your mounts, sir, but I don't need pay. I wouldn't leave any animal left untended in a storm like this. I'm sure my mother and father would be happy for the visit."

Wallach motioned for the young man to go ahead with his chore of minding the horses, turning back as he did to face the increasing unease of the crowd in the shelter.

"I have a small word for you, friend, and that's tact. You seem to lack a great deal of it. Especially toward strangers who come seeking a shelter and food, who've been long on the road and are weary. Perhaps when we're fed and rested, we'll tell you of what has befallen us, and where we're bound, perhaps not. This is the first time in many a day that we've been among company, and I'm not so sure that I don't prefer solitude."

Gillerman nodded agreement, even as a ragged note of disapproval made the rounds of the group gathered about the fire.

"You've got no right to a high-handed attitude with us, stranger. We're a peaceful settlement here at Sweet Rock, and we give no one any cause to complain of our treatment to travelers."

"Well said, Hiat. We've given these two no reason to insult our hospitality, or to bring a black mark against our good manners."

The man with the bristly beard stood up and approached the small table where the two old friends sat. Spreading his legs apart in a battle stance, he picked up the tankards of the mulled ale there and called loudly for them to be taken away.

"We don't need your likes in Sweet Rock," snarled the man. "We have a well-ordered, peaceful settlement here, and we don't have any use for armed tramps with salty tongues."

A hush fell over the makeshift room, as all there waited to see what the ancient strangers would do.

Gillerman broke the tension first by announcing that they had to get on anyhow, that there was a fire awaiting them, and old friends who were eager for their news.

The bearded man laughed, revealing an ugly smile.

"What friends have you here, vagabond? All here are decent folk, who wouldn't have cause for your acquaintance."

"There are some of the old clans still sprinkled throughout these lands," said Wallach, his voice guarded.

"Old clans? What of the old clans? What would you two tramps know of the clans?"

"A tale that might cause your tongue to sing a sweeter tune," returned Gillerman.

There was a commotion at the door and all heads turned

to see who was making such a noisy entrance, and what news was brought that created such a furor outdoors.

The center of the storm was a balding man, with a large droopy mustache that still carried some part of his last meal in it.

"The Westerlin folk are on the road here! The river has carried away the settlement!"

"Quickly, then, me hearties! Get the others gathered, good Nehman. We shall have need of all the spare shelters we have, and all the foodstuffs as well. How many are there left, messenger?"

The man addressed wrung his hands and shook his head. "Not above two dozen, sir."

This news startled all present.

"Two dozen? Out of all the Westerlin?" questioned a man near the bald messenger.

"Those that weren't lost in the flood were taken by the raiders. The filth came out of the darkness on the night of the water. No alarm, no warning, just there!"

This last piece of news chilled the gathered locals, causing a loud moan that might have come from one man.

There was another call for ale all around, and in the disturbance, the two strangers, Wallach and Gillerman, were forgotten for the moment, and the two friends sat back down at their table to see what was to occur next.

The youngster burst back in and ran to the strangers, breathless. "I tried to take your horses to shelter, but they wouldn't go," he gasped. "And one of them told me that I should come back and tell you that there are dangers afoot!" The lad's eyes were wide and unbelieving.

"What's taken the boy? What does he speak of? A talking horse?"

"That's it," cried another. "Poor chap didn't ever have too many wits about him anyhow, always hanging about in the woods with his mother. I wouldn't put it past the likes of her to be filling the lad's ears with such tales as walking trees and talking horses."

A sudden light went on in the strangers' eyes, and they looked quickly at each other.

"Who do them talking horses belong to now, I wonder?" asked Bristlebeard. "Aren't they just fit for each other, I ask you? Tramps and horses that give you news about your enemies!"

"Maybe they're in league with the raiders," roared an angry voice. "How come them to be here so easy like, when we haven't had any travelers through our parts in all this long winter or spring?"

A low rumble of agreement shook the room.

"Maybe they're waiting to give the signal to the others they're with, so they can fall on Sweet Rock like they did Westerlin," went on another voice, standing next to the messenger from the doomed community.

"Maybe they are," put in Bristlebeard. "We haven't forgotten how to handle sneaking vermin like that, have we, lads?"

A booming "No" filled the room, and more than one of the crowd edged forward to lay hold of the travelworn strangers.

"Hold your tongue," ordered Gillerman. "Stand off, you fools! Have you been locked away in this backwater settlement so long you've taken leave of your good senses?"

"I don't think they can tell their left from their right, or up from down," agreed Wallach. "Much less a friend from an enemy."

"Your smooth talk holds no sway here. We'll be the ones to decide who our enemies and friends are."

Two brawny locals moved forward again, and one of the men grabbed Gillerman roughly by the shoulder to drag him away.

"Come along you! We'll throw you into a cooler until we decide what's to be done."

"Call a general court! Let the settlement hear the evidence. And get all the men to arms," ordered Bristlebeard, taking over easily.

"Wait!" cried the boy. "These men are friends! They haven't come to harm us! My father should decide this, not you!"

"Out of the way, whelp," snarled Bristlebeard, knocking

the boy roughly aside. "Come on, chaps! Let's put these two pigs in a poke!"

Before the two old friends could make a struggle of it, they were hastily bound hand and foot and hauled away to be locked in a root cellar at the back of the shelter.

"Let's see if they have any more friends skulking about," suggested a man at the front of the mob. "The lad said the horses were talking, but we know better. There must be others here about! Come on, lads, to arms!"

It took another few minutes of hunting and calling out loudly among themselves to conclude that there were no others to be found outside, or anywhere in the vicinity.

The young boy, Owen, who had spoken in their defense, was upset that the remarkable talking horses were gone, and wondered where they could be, or who could have taken them.

Bristlebeard and a dozen others took torches and scoured the entire woods surrounding the crude shelter converted into their gathering hall, but there was not so much as a hoofprint or bent twig to signify that anyone had ever been there at all.

"A ill-omen, this," predicted an aging local, counting his prayer beads as he spoke. "This is like them times my pappy told me of when we was all up at arms with them vile things from underneath the borders."

"It smacks of it, indeed, Clem. I don't want to even think of what it means."

"What it means is that we've got to get ourselves armed," snapped Bristlebeard. "Hop to it! Ring the alarm bell there, whelp! Make yourself useful for once! Your father shall hear of your behavior here tonight!"

The boy, seeing that he would be beaten if he did not do as he was told, slowly went down the hill to where the settlement's great bell was, and with a heavy and troubled heart, began to strike the notes that would call the settlement of Sweet Rock to arms.

Mystic Steeds

A hard southerly wind whipped the trees into a brisk dance, and sent gray-black clouds scudding across the night sky. Patches of stars showed here and there, but the shadows on the wood crept back and forth as the wind tossed the limbs of the trees, and it was hard to keep to the beaten track that lay like a lighter-colored trace through the skittering night.

There were strange noises above the wind that startled the boy as he made his way homeward, and he jumped at every other step, clutching his thorn cudgel and imagining all sorts of terrible figures lurking in the eaves of the forest, waiting to ambush him.

He thought of the two ancient strangers, and wished that they were there with him. No one believed that their horses had talked, but he had heard them as plainly as any of the men speaking in the meeting hall. He smiled to remember how polite they had been to each other, and how they had used their proper names in speaking.

"I never would have thought it," he said half aloud, trying to cheer himself up, and take his mind off the looming forms and shadows that were darting to and fro all about him. He was on the verge of being encouraged somewhat, when another noise somewhere in front of him made him stop dead in his tracks, and steal as silently as he could off the path.

There were more sounds then, plain above the howl of the wind and creak of trees—horses, moving through the wood, and the clink and rattle of steel against steel, and harness straps squeaking under load.

The lad drew further back into the protective cover of the wood, and holding his breath, tried to make out the nature of these late-night travelers who moved about under the dark blanket of night. He felt a great need to hide himself from the new intruders, whoever they were; his flesh crawled and he broke out in a cold sweat, and his heart hammered so loudly he was sure anyone nearby could hear it.

Hoofbeats sounded almost at his elbow, and the dark form of a mounted rider crashed by so close to him he could have reached out and touched the saddle. The rider was shrouded in a cloak that covered his head and trailed all the way down over the knees and lay over the rump of the horse; without warning, the rider suddenly reined in and sat still a moment, as if he were listening intently to some suspicious sound.

At first, the boy thought hopefully it might be the two ancient men at the meeting hall and their talking horses, but when the animal in front of him turned so that he could see him clearly, Owen saw only the baleful glance of dumb brute eyes.

He was terrified for a brief second that the beast was going to give him away. His heart thudded explosively beneath his shirt, and a bead of sweat found its way down his eyebrow onto the bridge of his nose; still the horse and rider stood immobile.

After another heartbeat, they were joined by another rider, and the two of them crashed away, and were soon lost among the other sounds of the windy forest, which moaned and sighed like a live thing.

The boy lay still for a long time after the sounds of the ominous intruders were gone, and there was nothing left to hear but the footfall of the wind in the high boughs of the trees. Each black shadow became a dangerous enemy, and each unknown sound became the signal that he was discovered and lost.

After a long while, he at last dared to creep out of his hiding place, and begin again his interrupted journey.

As he moved forward once more, he suddenly thought of his mother and father, and that they must be warned about this band of raiders that were full upon them. He quickly forgot his fear then, and the pounding of his heart hammered through his pulse as he raced away toward the simple dwelling that had been his home for all those past seasons, warm and cheerful, and always full of the family friends and neighbors.

"I can't let them down," he said aloud, through gritted teeth, but the wind swept his words away.

He had not gone more than another few paces ahead, when he drew up short and stood staring in amazement at the sight before him. He rubbed his eyes and blinked, but the apparitions were still there, and he could not take his gaze away.

"Come, lad! Don't be fuddled by all this business. It was the quickest way we could get to you."

The animal before him was the horse that belonged to the man called Wallach, and beside him was the mount of Gillerman.

"This is all a bit of a shock to you, I'm sure," said the latter. "It was something of a surprise to us as well, I can assure you. But there was no one left across the Boundary that would come back to take care of this last bit of business except us. We owned we'd do it, because we have a few friends about in these parts we wanted to look in on."

"We never expected all this to-do, though," interrupted the other. "It was supposed to be a simple messenger's job, back, hop-quick. I never would have been tempted if I'd known all this blatherskite was still making such a muddle of things."

The boy tried to find his voice, although without success.

"Here, you've frightened him out of his wits," said the first horse, seeing the plight of the young lad.

"The woods are full of those raiders you were trying to warn the others about," Owen managed at least. "And no one would believe that you talked."

"We most certainly do," agreed the dark chestnut-colored

animal. "I think it would be a good deal more unusual if we didn't."

"What do they call you, lad? What name do you go by?"

"Owen Helwin, sir," replied the boy, looking from one animal to the other.

"By Windameir's spur straps, the very thing! Here we thought we were to be in for a fuss of it, and the next thing you know, here is the lad that Wallach and Gillerman were looking for right before our eyes."

"A pretty jest." His friend laughed. "I was ready to have to carry those slugs to scour one end of this strip of the Boundary to the other."

"Excuse me," said Owen softly. "But what are you speaking of? I haven't been able to make heads or tails of anything since I met your two gentlemen at the gathering hall."

"Gentlemen! Hear that, Gitel, he calls those two louts of ours gentlemen!"

Gitel snickered a long whuffling sound through his muzzle.

"Brave Gillerman has never been addressed as such, to my knowledge. I dare say Wallach would shift in his traces if he were ever called as much to his face."

"Oh, no offense," hastened Owen. "I didn't mean to offend you."

"You haven't, lad. We carry on this way so much we forget that a stranger might not understand our jesting. We have to have help to get those two louts out of that ratnest they've been locked into. Can your parents help us?"

"That's just where I was on my way to," replied Owen. "I know they would help us."

"Good, good lad. Climb up and tell me the way."

"But we'll run into those others who were just by here."

"We'll be to where we're going without anyone knowing any the better."

Owen struggled up into the tall stirrup, and told the huge animal the directions to his shelter. He was amazed at the ease with which the horse moved, and soon he was unable to separate the wind from their motion, and in another blink of the eye, they were standing in the front garden of Owen's small, tidy dwelling.

"I'll tell them we're here," he cried, leaping down and racing to the door. "Mother! Father! Come quick and see my friends!"

The house was dark and Owen's first thought was that his mother and father had gone to bed already, but then he remembered the raiders in the woods, and dashed through the door, holding his breath. He lit a candle and raced through the small shelter with it held aloft, but there were no signs of struggle or violence, or any other clue as to what might have become of the occupants.

"They're gone!" cried Owen, coming back to the horses.

"They may have made their way to the gathering hall," concluded the horse called Gitel. "Wallach and Gillerman must have called them."

"But how could they do that?" asked Owen, confused and very near tears.

"There are a lot of our ways that you may find strange, Owen. Has no one ever spoken to you of your grand heritage, or the exploits of your mother and father?"

"Or the great battles that were waged in the olden days, when we were but colts?" Seravan went on, his dark gray coat shiny in the shadowy darkness.

"You speak of the bleak years," answered Owen. "That was a time long before the Middle Islands, or the meeting of the Four Elders of Atlanton."

"See!" said Seravan. "The lad does have some idea of his history. But it was before that, Owen. Your parents were in the last of the fracas. They are held in great regard in the place we have come from."

"And where is that, sir?" asked Owen. "I know of almost all the lands about here, but I have never heard of one which had horses who spoke."

"You will find out more about that presently, my boy. Come up, and let's find your father and mother. And we have to get those two lumps free before they do something foolish. It wouldn't be wise to reveal our hand just yet. We have urgent news of an old friend of theirs they must have before the night is out."

Owen was beginning to protest, but he was taken up by an unseen hand and held in a viselike grip in the saddle of Gitel.

"Come along, lad. Quickly! We don't want these other chaps to beat us to the settlement. They're a nasty lot. I've thought all along they'd prove to be troublesome one of these days."

"Always the optimist, Seravan," scolded Gitel. "Anything that has a dark side, leave it for you to find it."

"I know human nature, that's all," returned his friend shortly. "I've been at all this business long enough to know bad seeds when I see them."

"That's neither here nor there. To work now! We must go down to the edge of the river, and then across the bridge that leads by the old mill road."

"Lead on, then. Keep a sharp eye for those chaps, Owen."

"We shouldn't let them off so easy. We might leave a little surprise for them."

"Not now. Perhaps when we've seen to our business and gotten Wallach and Gillerman back, and found the lad's parents."

Seravan struck out in the lead then, and held his course at a steady pace through the windy forest, making ever toward the flooded banks of the Line River, and the settlement hall at Sweet Rock.

They had gone on but a few miles when another sound began to make itself heard over the howling of the wind and the broken chatter of the trees; it was a distinct sound, and one that spread a sense of dread in all their hearts.

"Fire," breathed Seravan under his breath, although he need not have spoken.

Owen was down and running toward the sound before either of the animals could move to stop him. "We have to hurry! They've fired the settlement hall, and your friends are in the cellar."

"Get down!" shouted a vaguely familiar voice, just as a volley of arrows sang past his head. There were loud shouts and cursing then, and three mounted horsemen cut off the boy, preparing to ride him down.

Owen leaped aside at the last instant, and felt the hot stab of pain on his cheek as the blade of a sword flashed past him, an inch away from splitting his skull in two. He rolled away, falling into the prickly thorns of the underbrush at the edge of the road.

There were more cries then, and another shower of arrows that landed harmlessly all about him; his head reeled, and he gritted his teeth and clenched his fists in a helpless rage as he watched the flames eating at the roof of the meeting hall. Shadows of riders circled in the fiery outskirts of the fire, cursing and shouting to each other in a language that was faintly familiar, although he could not quite make out all the words. His brain raced as he watched, and it was another heartbeat before he made out that the raiders were looking for survivors, and were combing the surrounding woods to find them. There were no faces he knew, no sign of Bristlebeard or the mob that had been present earlier, and Owen felt all hope go out of him.

A voice right at his ear almost caused him to faint, but it was the old man, Gillerman, tugging at his sleeve. "Quickly, lad! We have to get you away from here. The others have all escaped into the woods for now, but these louts outnumber us, and we have to reach safe quarters."

"We thought you must be roasted by now," cried Owen. "Where is your friend?"

"Wallach wasn't born to be fried in a root cellar. He's safely away now. Hurry! We must fly!"

As he spoke, he whistled a short tune, and immediately at his side was the horse, Gitel.

"We must fly these parts, my friend. Wallach and Seravan are away already."

The huge animal neighed and stood still while the old man and boy mounted, his nostrils flaring and his ears laid back. "They are coming," he warned his rider. "There are three of them heading this way."

"Hang on, lad," shouted Gillerman, and in an instant, his gleaming blade had sprung from the simple scabbard, striking sparks into the night. The edge of the weapon glowed a faint silver that wavered and shimmered, slowly turning a blazing white that almost blinded Owen to see it.

Out of the stinging smoke and flames, there were suddenly the looming forms of mounted riders, bearing straight down upon them. One of the shadowy figures put a horn to his lips and blew a harsh note, and they came on, swords drawn. Owen clung tightly to Gillerman's back, and his mind clouded with fear. He was sure he would never see his mother or father again, or even the light of day.

The old man smelled of forests and rivers, and something else that Owen could not quite decide on, but before he could think of it further, the horse's back bunched, and the animal seemed to spring into the air. He felt the bone-jarring clash of steel, and heard the deadly thin ring of swords clanging and then the groan of a man. In two more swift blows, they were away, lifting into a rush of wind and stars that flashed past so suddenly the boy thought he must have fainted or been wounded. There were whirlpools of moons that spun in circles of flame about his head, and there were voices calling to him in faraway sounds; there was his mother next, and a faded sunset that looked like all the sunsets he had seen in his short life, yet upon looking again, the morning was blazing up from beneath the curve of the sea, and faint blue stars still lit a part of heaven just above him, held in place by a wind that smelled of pine and ash and oak.

"Good morning, my young friend," said a voice, coming from a long way away. "You've certainly had a nap."

"Is he all right?" asked another voice, worried and close in his ear. There was a warm touch on his cheek then, and he knew it was his mother's voice.

"Hush, Linne. Your son is too much for a mere scratch to keep down for more than the time it takes him to blink. That lot back there in Sweet Rock wasn't warned about us, thanks to our lucky stars, and the sensible decision to lock us in the root cellar. It would have gone a lot harder on us if they had known we would be there."

"Is Famhart safe?"

"On his way to gather the rest of the settlement. We'll be joining him soon."

"Where are Wallach and Seravan?" asked Owen sleepily. "Was I hurt?"

"You helped me fend off that raider, or don't you remember?" Gillerman chuckled. "He made a play at pulling me out of the saddle, but you grabbed him by the arm and wouldn't let go. Good thing, too, or I'd have been in a dash of trouble. Gitel got us away clean, though, and here we are, safe and sound."

"I thought we had seen the end of all this." Owen's mother suddenly sounded very tired. "Was it just a dream we had when we were in the Middle Islands?"

"No, my dear, it was no mere dream. And you have had a time to rest and gather your strength. It was said then that the fight would go on."

"I thought Owen would be spared. He's still a lad yet."

"I know how you must feel, Linne. It is never a promising thought to discover that we all have our own ends to meet, and our own lives to lead, no matter what else comes of it."

"You don't know anything about a mother's heart! You're like all the rest. It's all still excitement to you, and a chance to play your silly childish games!"

Gillerman laughed softly. "You hear that, Wallach?" he asked his friend, who had just that moment entered the room.

"I don't mind telling you that it was no idea of mine to recross the Boundary and come back down to all this, my dear. I was pleasantly occupied with a small portion of a meadow without a single stump to remove, and fresh water, and a cow or two to graze. There wasn't even anything in the way of a wasp or a fly to pester me."

"You speak riddles, good sir. I don't follow your meaning."

"No need to confuse anyone any further, Wallach. We may as well spell out our errand here, and the less muddy we make the water, the better off we'll be."

Linne moved to gather Owen in her arms. "Have you come with these two?"

"I met them at the gathering hall. Bristlebeard and the others thought they were raiders and locked them in the root cellar, but they escaped. Gillerman saved me. And their horses talk as plainly as we do."

The words tumbled out of his mouth, and he drew breath to go on.

"Pull up, lad. Your mother will never get the drift if you keep on in that gallop," said Gillerman. "What we need here is a direct order of march, from the beginning to the end, first, middle, and finish."

"Exactly," agreed Wallach. "That's what I've said all along, but no one ever thinks to listen to an old boot like me."

"Will you gentlemen tell me what you know of my husband? And who the raiders were who attacked us at the settlement?"

Linne held Owen closed to her, and tried to remember her old courage, wondering if it had gone in all the peaceful times, or if she had mislaid it somewhere in her day-to-day chores she had been busy with all these last years of her life.

It had come as a shock when the arrows snapped by her head as she fled across the road toward the woods, and then the memories had all come flooding back to her, all too quickly, it seemed.

"Famhart is safe enough for the moment," soothed Wallach. "We shall say what we have to say quickly, then trouble you no more for now. There are others we have to find before this plague of ills is spread too much farther. A vast cauldron of trouble is brewing in the Channels and beyond, and we must gather the ones together who will strike the blow to stop it."

"What my friend means is this," Gillerman went on. "We have come to deliver these charts and this weapon, and to warn you of an impending danger that has begun to grow among even those of you who yet dwell here."

"That has become obvious," replied Linne.

"There is worse yet than just this riffraff who've raided Sweet Rock."

"The Darkness?" asked Linne, thoughts of an older time returning in powerful waves.

"Not the Black Death, my dear. Not yet. This danger comes in the form of one who dwells under the shadows of the South Channels. He is known to you, Linne, and I fear that his memory may not be the most pleasant."

"A traitor?" breathed Owen.

"No, lad, a misguided soul who has forgotten the simple fact that there is only one King of Windameir."

"Then how can he still be thought of as not a part of the plot and scheme of the Darkness?"

"The hand of the Dark One is heavy on him, but his own folly is his worst crime yet! It is easy to be snared by the web of greed and power the Dark One spins."

"But what can we do about such a man as that?" asked Linne. "That would be better left to healers or teachers." Her heart contracted in a strange way, and there was a faint echo of an old sadness welling up there.

"Exactly. But you must be the messenger who carries this word. You are the one he will seek out, and the one who might yet reach him. Your life is known to him, for your lines go back to the road to the Middle Islands. You and Famhart are both familiar with him. There is another from your old days, but we shall see to him ourselves."

"Then who are these raiders who have struck Sweet Rock tonight? Are they from this man you speak of?"

"These are more than bandits, my dear. They are not anything near the danger they will be if they join forces with this man. He is very dangerous. These louts are but small fry in the picture of this riddle, but they are to be reckoned as dangerous, too."

"It's as easy to be skewered by a small fry as a large one," observed Gillerman. "Although I think this lot is led by a very ambitious chap who is proving to be more of a sticker in our path than we have dared consider."

"He has certainly done a good job of creating this little inconvenience," said Wallach. "I had thought we would have been able to have completed our errand here without all this to-do."

"Still, we shall have to deliver these charts and this weapon, and get on with it quickly. Gitel says we need to be on our way before dawn."

As he spoke, Gillerman pulled a gray bag from beneath his cloak and empited the contents on a small campaign table.

"This chart will guide you over the Silver Mist, in the South Channels. This blade will be your badge of proof for those who would doubt you."

As the old man talked on, a ray of light spun in dazzling circles outward from his form, and Owen felt himself caught up once more in the whirlpool of stars and suns that flashed past him in blinding colors of blue and gold and green.

"Good-bye," called Gillerman over the storm of speed and sounds, "Good-bye, fare ye well. We shall meet again in the South Channels."

Without further warning, Owen found himself in the windy wood not far from his burning settlement, holding tightly to his mother's hand.

It was all as though nothing had happened, yet everything had changed. In his hand was the longsword the ancient stranger had given him, and slung over his shoulder was the gray bag.

They had no more time to inspect them, because the next instant was full of arrows, flying from both sides of the wood, and the two, mother and son, had to make for cover near the river's edge to avoid being trampled by a company of the settlement's men, charging hard into the raiders' flanks.

Rumors and Omens

There had been rumors from time to time of troubles brewing in the vast mountains along the coast on both sides of them; Owen had heard his father and mother speak of the events often over the supper table, but he had never given any serious thought to the eventual consequences of it, and never in his wildest dreams had it occurred to him that it would one day find him living under an umbrella of stars in the forest, and flying for his very life.

Linne had tired, and they lay hidden beneath a grove of ancient oaks, not far from the settlement meeting hall. There were distant shouts and cries, and the occasional sound of a skirmish, although it sounded far away, and moving in a direction that ran toward the road to the sea.

Just before dawn, he roused his mother, and the two of them cautiously made their way to the meeting hall, and met stragglers from every point of the compass, who had come fleeing from the raiders.

Owen met one such young man in the course of their short journey, and he questioned him eagerly for news of what had been going on beyond the small expanse of their own quiet life.

"What name do you go by, stranger?" asked the youth, holding out his hand. "My name is Darek."

"I'm called Owen Helwin. My mother is Linne. My father is Famhart, but he is gone with the others to drive off the raiders."

Darek lowered his gaze and spoke in a softer tone. "I don't know what's happened to my mother and father. I haven't heard word of them since the raiders came."

"I'm sorry to hear that," said Linne, reaching out a hand to soothe the lad. "Perhaps there will be news today. We are on our way to the gathering hall to call our people together, and to see what we must do to face these troubles that have come on us."

"I shall join you," replied Darek. "I'm old enough now."

"And I shall, too," echoed Owen. "I have my own sword."

He proudly drew the ancient blade that the two strangers had left with him, remembering as he did the mysterious sights and sounds from the night before.

"Where did you get that?" asked Darek, wide-eyed.

Owen was on the verge of saying, but thought better of mentioning it, and looked away to study the sun, setting the distant mountain peaks ablaze with a golden fire.

"It was given to me by Gillerman and Wallach," he said at last, although he did not mention the talking horses.

"Are they kinsmen?"

"Not exactly," replied Owen, unsure of what answer to make. "Friends."

"You're lucky, then. I have no weapons but my cudgel."

"If you stay with us, my father will see to it that you have the proper arms, won't he, mother?"

Linne looked alarmed, but quickly hid it. "Of course. We shall try to find out about your family first, then we shall see to it that you have everything you need. You'll be perfectly safe with us."

"Thank you, ma'am. I can earn my keep, and I'm handy with gathering wood and making fires."

"What was your father's craft?" asked Linne, hoping to turn the talk to more peaceful subjects.

Darek seemed uneasy and at a loss to reply, but after a short time spoke softly, looking at his feet. "He is a potter."

"I should think we'll have a great need of his trade before this is all over with. Our shelter is burned, and I doubt we have a single bowl left unbroken."

"Don't forget all the other things we've lost," reminded

Owen. "It's not likely we'll have need of anything but bows and swords until all this business is properly taken care of."

His voice cracked as he finished, which embarrassed him, so he slipped his sword in and out of its sheath to make his point.

Linne was painfully aware that her little boy was not so small that he hid behind her skirts anymore, and she was at once amused and saddened by his efforts to appear more grown up than his years warranted.

"Do you think we'll chase the raiders back into the mountains?" asked Darek. "I've never seen that part of the country before."

"If they are as strong as we have heard, that will prove quite a chore," replied Linne. "We have had tales now for ever so long. There are stories about a clan that is led by one from my husband's old country, Boghatia."

"Bog Hats," said Darek. "I've read about them."

"My father's father was one," exclaimed Owen. "And he was one of the worst."

"Shush, Owen," scolded Linne. "There's no need to keep remembering things that are better left alone."

"But he was terrible, mother! You said so yourself."

"He was a misguided, ignorant man who never had a chance to learn any better, or to mend his ways," said Linne, a finality in her voice that told Owen the subject was better left alone.

"I'd hate to meet one," said Darek. "They say they have fangs for teeth, and yellow eyes."

"That's the Worlughs, or the Gorgolacs," corrected Owen. "But they don't exist anymore."

"I wouldn't be too sure. I've heard news of just that kind of thing, away up toward the Lost Falls. No one goes up there anymore because of it."

"Who would want to go up there?" asked Owen.

"Anyone looking for the pass over the mountains," said Darek.

"The pass to where?"

"To the country beyond the Edges."

"What?"

"The country beyond the Edges," repeated Darek. "The Sea of Islands. Haven't you heard of it?"

Owen looked at his mother. "Do you know of that country?"

Linne nodded. "I have heard of it. When I was a little girl, I thought it was a story that had a very sad ending, so I never told it to you."

"Sad? How, mother?"

"The story that I heard as a little girl was very sad. It always broke my heart to hear it. My brother, my poor unfortunate brother, knew it upset me, so he always made it his favorite. I heard it all my life, until I met your father and things ended as they did."

Linne had grown very distant, and there was a faraway look in her eyes that silenced all the questions of Owen and Darek. She looked very beautiful then, and much younger. It would have been difficult to tell her from the two youths who were there, if it had not been for the silver gray threads that ran through her long hair.

"Was it really so sad?" asked Darek. "I only heard the promises that were given to anyone who should ever find the secret of where the waterfolk went when they left this life."

Linne smiled and turned her face away to brush back the tears. "I'm sure you heard right, Darek. There was a mention of promises to anyone who should find the Three Trees. It is said those leaves grow with maps to those havens. All I ever heard, I'm afraid, are the lost souls who perished trying to find the country where the Three Trees are hidden."

"Did someone you know go in search for them and die?" asked Darek solemnly.

"My father went," replied Linne, resolutely promising herself not to cry. She exerted all her power of self-control, and managed to hold her chin steady.

It had been a long time since she had thought of her father and her poor, misguided brother. Since she had been in the new settlement with Famhart, and had her son, she had filled her life with all the endless things that had kept her busy and happy; in the early years, the infant that demanded all her attention, and her young husband, with all

his plans and dreams. There were a number of years, full
and happy, although fraught with danger and filled with
numerous moves, when they had crossed the Plain of Reeds
and settled in Sweet Rock. After her son had gotten older
and began to experience life more on his own, she had still
found no reason to dwell on the past, or remember those
long forgotten pains and regrets she had left behind in her
childhood and early adult years.

As they moved swiftly along toward the meeting hall, the
smell of smoke from the burning shelters, and the sight of
slain men, who had ridden with the raiders, brought back
many agonizing memories with all the force of a bolt from a
bow.

And now it was beginning again, just when her son was
old enough to be affected by it all.

A rider approached just at that moment, and Owen was
proud and confident when he brandished the longsword of
Gillerman and Wallach. It felt awkward and clumsy in his
hand, but the look in his new friend's eye as he stood poised
before them, made him forget for a moment that he would
not have known what to do had the rider been a foe instead
of an old family acquaintance.

"Holla, Linne. Come aboard here. We shall have to hurry
if we are to catch Famhart. He was just at your place
searching for you and the whelp here."

"Holla, Jacob. We were on our way to the meeting hall.
Are the others already back?"

"We've rounded up all the stragglers from the outskirts in
the settlement. Famhart and I are to head a party to make
sure the woods are clear of this vermin that came on us last
night."

"Did Bristlebeard go out?" asked Owen. "He almost hurt
my two friends."

"Those with the talking horses?" Jacob laughed.

"Yes," replied Owen, coloring and putting away his
sword. "They gave me this," he went on more resolutely.

"Be careful that you don't slice off a finger with it,"
teased Jacob. "And don't drag it behind you like it was a

farm plough. You'll have its point rusted through, if you do."

"Don't nag him so, Jacob. We've had a long night."

"You don't have to stand up for me, mother. Jacob speaks the truth."

"Aye, Jacob does. That fancy sticker will get you into a heap of hot water if you don't learn about using it before you go around flashing it about like that. One of the blokes who were at work last night would have made short shift of you, I'm afraid. Your father is going to have to give you a few lessons with what to do with that."

"And me, too," added Darek. "I shall have to learn as well."

Jacob laughed good-humoredly and vowed to the new youngster, "And you, too, young master, whoever you are."

"This is Darek," offered Owen. "He was riding to find safety last night when the raiders came."

"So!" said Jacob, his manner more serious. "And from where, good Darek? Is there another settlement on the move toward us?"

"Only the stragglers, sir," replied the boy. "All those with me were slain. I'm the only one that got away."

"Then you are welcome here, lad. We shall search for any others that might have gotten away as well."

Linne put an arm around the small shoulders of the boy. "He has come through a lot, Jacob. Is there food and a place to sleep at the hall?"

"Along with everything else you'll need, Linne. Put the two lads up there with you. I'll walk back from here. I want to check something over at the shallow ford near the old shepherd's den. Tell whoever is on their way after me that I shall be there."

"All right. Come on, you two! See if you can get up."

Owen and Darek mounted behind Linne, and the three of them set off for the meeting hall, leaving Jacob afoot, and disappearing toward the river. The two lads waved, and were gladdened to see the man raise his arm in a parting salute.

Soon they were among a crowd of others from the settlement making their way there as well, and shortly after were dismounting in the square, where Owen paraded about like a small peacock, in spite of the warning he had gotten from his friend on the road.

A Mother's Sadness

Famhart found Linne in the throng and gave her a strong hug. "I see you two have managed all right," he chided her. "And you've picked up another one for our ranks as well."

"This is Darek, father. He has lost his kin and is going to stay with us now."

"And here! What's this, young man? Where come you by that longsword?"

Owen blushed under his father's look, and put his hand on the hilt of the sword. "Gillerman and Wallach gave it to me, father."

"The two strangers who Bristlebeard told me of?"

"Bristlebeard doesn't know who they are," persisted Owen. "He is a harsh man."

"He is a brave and respected warrior from our ranks in the old days. He may not have such smooth edges, but he is a fair judge of humankind."

"He has mistaken his judgment if he thinks those two are our enemies," interrupted Linne. She had always felt the man in question was coarse and vulgar, and reminded her of all the undesirable qualities of the Bog Hats.

Owen squeezed his mother's hand, and thanked her silently for coming to his defense.

"So! You've met these two, have you? Bristlebeard only told me of the circumstances that took place last night, just before the raiders struck. It would have certainly been easy to mistake the strangers' intentions upon the face of what happened, and the strangers' odd manners."

Famhart's face darkened. "Has anyone had word of them after they escaped? Perhaps they were with these bandits."

"They're gone. Did Bristlebeard tell you they had horses that talked, father? They did! I heard them myself. They're named Gitel and Seravan."

His father scrutinized his son's face to see if he were jesting.

"Linne? Did you know of this unusual faculty of the horses the strangers rode?"

"I believe Owen," she replied shortly. "If he says the animals spoke, I have no reason to doubt his word. I have heard more than a few animals with speech myself."

Famhart looked a question at her, but chose not to engage her any further.

"I have never encountered talking horses, so I wouldn't know," he said, looking perplexed. "It is indeed an odd thing, but I guess there are many more things that I have no knowledge of."

"I wish I had heard them," said Darek, trembling with excitement. "I have often dreamed of dogs or geese speaking. It must be a wonderful thing."

"It was just like you and I speak, Darek. It was so natural, I first thought it was two men who were watering their mounts."

"But there was no one there?" asked Famhart. "Are you sure you weren't tricked by some ruse? Bristlebeard said the two strangers reminded him of some of the magicians from the old clans."

"They were strange, father, but not because of what Bristlebeard said. They were getting ready to leave because the men were going to lock them in the root cellar."

"We shall question the others about this later. First we have to see what we must attend to with this bunch from the boundaries. Come, Linne, let's round up the news. You two try to keep yourselves out of trouble, and lend your ears to any gossip you can."

Famhart gave his son a short hug, and clasped hands with

Darek. "And don't wear such long faces. We shall get to the bottom of all these matters before long."

He looked more kindly at Darek. "And don't fret, my young friend. We shall have reports soon, from all our scouts. Perhaps there will be word of some of your family or friends. It you were on your road to us, we shall be sure to hear the news from any quarter."

Looking up at Famhart, the young lad tried hard to control his tears, but without much success. "Thank you, sir. I was afraid for a while that I might not find any settlement left that would take me in."

"You come along with us, son, and we'll make sure you're fed and armed."

Famhart caught the frown of disapproval that lingered in Linne's eyes, and quickly changed the subject away from arms or the threat of another war with the new tide of raiders from the Wastes of Leech and beyond.

"Let's all get our news straight and come to order," cried Famhart aloud, then blew a high, clear note on the silver horn that hung by his side. "Everyone fall to, and let's share our news by rank. Gerlich, give us what you know of the numbers and particulars of the raiders."

A large-boned man with a terrible scar down the side of his face took up his place on the stump which stood in front of the settlement hall, which all the locals called the Throne. It was four feet across, and had once been a living giant, but was felled by a lightning storm some years before. The trunk of that tree had provided the settlement with building material and firewood for the first year or two they had been in that place, and even after all that time, there was still a great indentation in the earth a foot or more deep, where the giant tree had crashed to the ground in its death throes.

There were some in the settlement who thought the tree was one of the last remnants of the Shrane Fal Wood and the Sorodun, but Linne, who had known one of that number and had heard him speak, knew that this giant was a mere tree, and not one of the lost mystical beings who moved about from time to time, and which had the powers to change forms if they chose. And it was the same mystical beings she knew that were mentioned in the legends of the country of the Three Trees of which Darek spoke.

Gerlich clambered upon the stump and cleared his throat a number of times to get the attention of the restless crowd, and when that failed, he took a small, curved horn from beneath his cloak and blew a shrill on it.

"Enough, good citizens, enough! Gather round, and let Gerlich spill his noodle so that you'll all know what he knows, and be that much the richer for it."

"We'll find it hard to spend that treasure," teased a brawny man dressed in tanned leather, standing beside Gerlich, and leaning on a tall bow that reached another foot above the man's head.

"Hush, Stearborn! You shall have your turn next."

"We wouldn't miss anything if we started with me now," replied Stearborn, shuffling the bow from hand to hand, and making clucking noises in his throat, a strange sound that came as a result of an old arrow wound in the days when Linne and Famhart were young marrieds, and before the birth of Owen.

"Be quiet, Stearborn. Let Gerlich speak," cautioned Famhart, a faint flicker of a deeper fire burning in his eyes. That small display silenced the heckler, and the rest of the crowd soon followed suit and fell into a suitable posture of listening.

"I've come from the back river near the Ledges," reported Gerlich. "There were plenty of the raiders that crossed there, but they're gone now. There was a hundred or more, by the signs on the riverbanks."

"Stearborn!" called Famhart. "What of you?"

"The same," replied the man, his voice sounding like a leaky valve letting air escape after every word. "They burned the shelters at Crossing Fence, and the keeper of the herd beyond Rolling Ford is gone, dead or run away."

Linne had searched through the crowd gathered at the Throne, looking for familiar faces. It all had a sad feel to it, although she had not remembered much of it for a long time; many of the old ghosts were awakened by the arrival of Darek, the frightened youngster from another settlement, who had lost his parents and friends, much as she had lost her own long ago.

She tried not to be a clinging mother to Owen, and to let her young son grow as he would, but this orphaned boy who had been delivered to their doorstep broke her heart, and try as she would, she could not help planning to keep Owen closer to home, and out of harm's way.

Linne found herself detesting the idea of Owen's having the longsword that the two travelers had entrusted to him, and she began to clearly remember their words, come from that half-waking dream, when they had all seemed to be swept away on a burning wind, and delivered into a snug, small study somewhere at the backporch of the sunset.

One after another of the settlement's inhabitants made their reports, adding whatever information they each had, and drawing upon the reserves of food and arms to resupply themselves for the best defense they could devise to protect their borders.

Almost at the last, Jacob, leading a bound and bleeding man, made his appearance before the Thorne, and raising his voice so that he might be heard, called out, "Friends and worthy neighbors, hear me out quickly! I have come from the crossing at Sheep's Head, and have brought this raider with me to bear out my story. I have overheard some distressing news, and tidings which do not bode well for us."

"Speak, Jacob," urged Famhart, moving to stand beside his friend. "What news do you have?"

The captive struggled against his bonds, and made as though he would lunge at his captor.

"This is Medor, from the mountains of the South Channels. His governor was known to us once! Hear what he has to say of our treaty now! He has talked to one who has made promises to him that they will have all our lands and goods before the fall comes again."

A dull, stubborn roar went up from the crowd, which caused the bound man to draw back in fear.

"The Red Bear is awake and abroad again," Jacob went on. "It is the sign from the past that tells us our time of peace and plenty is over!"

Jacob, dazed and weakened from a wound he had gotten in the struggle to capture his prisoner, raised his bow above his head and shook it feebly.

"It is on us, neighbors! They have been slayed in the outer settlements! The omens are coming to pass!"

Linne's heart had stopped as her old friend spoke, and her blood ran cold at the talk of the omens, those signs of old that they had been cautioned to keep a strict watch for, all those years ago when the young Keepers of the Light had at last crossed the Boundaries, and left the responsibility to those remaining behind to carry on the task.

Famhart met her troubled gaze over the heads of the crowd, and just for a moment, Linne thought she saw her young husband as he was in those years, handsome and brave, and devoted to the service of Windameir; and in the next instant, she saw her son standing next to his father, his very image in many ways, and her breath came in shallow gulps.

"We had best call a council meeting for this night," said Famhart, raising a hand to silence the crowd. "This will mean that we need the Coda read, and to draw lots as to who will lead the parties, and who will stay behind to protect our homes."

"Bring up the prisoner! Let him say why we should not put him to a swift death!" cried a man at the edge of the crowd nearest the bound captive.

"Aye!" echoed others. "Give him the court of law, and then explain to us why he deserves to live another hour longer."

"And let us have the Feast of the Red Bear," shouted a grizzled old warrior right at Owen's elbow.

Like a spark in a dry field, the call was taken up and shouted on all sides, and there was the sound of swords rattled on scabbards, and war horns blown. Owen had never heard the men of the settlement in such a violent mood, and was quite shocked to see that even his father's old friend, Stearborn, had raised his sword above his head, calling out with all the rest.

Darek moved closer to him, trying to make himself heard over the din. "What is this feast?" he shouted in Owen's ear.

"I've only heard of it," cried Owen. "I don't know exactly."

"Come on," called his friend. "Let's get back where we can hear."

Darek made for a hole in the crowd, closely followed by Owen, and soon they were free of the tumult and roar of the settlement, sitting beside the river and splashing their faces with the icy cold water from the high mountains away to the west.

"Here's my mother! She can tell us what it means."

Linne had seen the two boys break away from the crowd and followed them. Her face was ashen and she had been crying, but she tried to collect herself as she came up to where the two youths sat.

"Will you tell us what the Feast of the Red Bear is, mother? Why does everyone get so ugly when they speak of it?"

"The others may have seen one before," said Linne, brushing back the hair from her face. "I have seen one, long ago, when we first came from the old countries beyond the Diamond Swamps. We traveled then with the Keepers, and it was a grand time."

"Who were the Keepers?" asked Darek, his eyes wide.

"There was Borim Bruinthor, and Olthar Olthlinden, and the dwarf called Roundhat, but better known as Brian Brandigore. It was a time of trials and defeat, and bitter losses in the Middle Islands, until the end came, and the hosts of Windameir ruled the day."

"You mean you were there with these Keepers? You and your people?"

"Yes, Darek, some of them. We stumbled onto that grand stage as innocents. None of us ever dared to think of it as anything but ordinary. It was not a big affair to sit at table with Olthar and Jahn Spray, or share a simple supper with Borim beside a woodland fire."

"I have never heard you speak like this, mother," said

Owen, surprise and amazement in his voice. "You've barely mentioned those times before."

"I always said there would be a time when we would need to speak of them again," replied Linne. "I have been quite selfish, I know. Some of the memories I wanted to keep for my old age, and not share them with any but Famhart. Sometimes it is cruel to stir old ghosts that linger on in the safety of your mind, far from the light of day."

"But you'll tell us more, mother? We would know of all the exploits and all the dangers," insisted Owen, clasping the hilt of his sword resolutely.

"Yes, my funny one. The time has come that we shall have to sit down to a fire and spin out all the old yarns, and gather together our strength for these troubled times that seem to have found us out again."

"Will you let me go with you?" asked Darek timidly. "I know I don't warrant the honor, but I would serve in any capacity. I could cook, or carry wood, or tend your horses."

"You shall do no such thing, my good Darek. Wherever we shall find our fortunes, that's where you shall be, too. We have all been made wanderers once more, and all of us shall have to bind ourselves closer together as never before, if we are to see the end of these times that are upon us."

"Could Gillerman and Wallach be with the Keepers? They certainly acted oddly enough. I can still hardly believe my own eyes and ears."

"We mustn't speak of them again, Owen, except among our most trusted friends. There are those who would not welcome news of such doings, and to find that the Keepers are once more being recalled together to contain the dark tide that's flowing."

"Will I learn to ride and use a longsword?" asked Darek. "And to go with the men of the Line?"

Linne reached out a gentle hand. "I am sure everyone your age will be called upon to do those very things, Darek. A mother always knows, and always dreads the day that shall come, when she shall see her sons take up the call and march away to war. I never thought I would fall victim to it, but I have."

Owen hugged his mother tightly, torn between his feelings of pride at wearing the longsword the two masters had given him, and sorrow at knowing he was the cause of his mother's sadness.

OVERLORDS
OF THE
CHANNELS

A Ghost from the Past

Around the late fire, Linne and Famhart sat, watching the two young lads dozing beside the cheerful warmth, stirring occasionally as a twig snapped and crackled into a thousand bright sparks that showered the gloom about the flames with fiery red trails. They had been asleep for an hour or more, but were reluctant to give up their new status as grown-ups, and continued on, nodding with their heads leaned on their hands.

"Here we have the two newest warriors of the clan," teased Famhart, looking toward his son and the orphaned lad who had in a short space of time become a part of their family.

"Don't," said Linne quietly. "I'm having a hard enough time as it is. Let's not talk of it tonight."

Her husband gently pulled her to him and hugged her, stroking back the long hair from her eyes. "You were never this giddy about action before. I remember a certain young lady who was even ready to go so far as to take her own life rather than surrender herself to a lout that claimed to be my father."

"You know that was different."

"But you were younger then, you say? I don't recall that that stubborn streak has lessened any over the years."

Linne drew away halfheartedly. "You're terrible sometimes. I don't think you worry at all that something will happen that will take Owen away from us."

"He has been taken away from us since he was able to reach the door latch in the shelter, Linne. We can only watch him grow, and try to give him the things he will need to live in his world, whatever it may turn out to be."

"And poor Darek! Look at him! So young, and all alone now."

"I know what you're thinking, my sweet. It could just as easily be Owen in his place, if anything were to happen to us. Let's just hope that there would be others like us out there who would take him in and care for him, and to make sure he had a chance at growing to be a contented old man, full of tales and memories enought to last him a lifetime."

Linne shook her head stubbornly. "That's not what I meant. It would be easier dealing with our own deaths! I just can't bear to think of him carrying around that ridiculous sword, and falling right into the old patterns that we all know are so painful, and lead to such grief."

"Here, here, we'll have no talk of anyone dying as yet. I certainly don't intend to end it all so soon, and you know I'm not going to let Owen go off into something that's dangerous without teaching him everything he needs to know to defend himself."

"That's what I'm talking about," pursued Linne. "It never changes. Here we are with a fire and a blanket again, just like it was when we started. I hate this life, leaving one place and wandering on to somewhere else, always on the run to somewhere, and never knowing where it all ends or begins."

Famhart studied the fire for a while in silence, listening to the crackling and watching the sparks fly away into the darkness. He brushed away a live ember that had landed on Owen's riding cloak, and stroked the sleeping lad's head.

The night about them was cool, and a high band of stars stood gleaming brightly between the leaves of the tall aspen and pine grove where they had camped. Around them, but at some little distance, the other watchfires of the settlement glowed in dim echoes of the stars.

"It does seem as though we've done all this before," he said at last, his voice husky. "But then I guess it was different, with the Keepers being with us, and all the wonderful things that were always at hand."

He looked beseechingly at his wife. "You have to admit that some of it was glorious fun. I had almost hoped that maybe the story of the talking horses might have something to do with the old ones. Those were grand days."

Famhart's voice trailed away, and he gazed with shining eyes at the memories he found in the flames.

Linne drew him back abruptly. "There were some good times, husband, but that was long ago, and now we're not dealing with the Keepers or their like. This is simply a man-made border war that promises to be long and ugly, and the celebrating of the Feast of the Red Bear won't make it anything other than what it is."

Owen's eyelids fluttered at the mention of the Red Bear, but he kept his eyes tightly shut and pretended to sleep on.

"You and I know that, Linne. The others want to try to get the steam up with practicing the old rites, and that may be what they need. These aren't the best of times now. There are none of the Keepers here with us to keep everyone's spirits up, or to give us much to cling to. They left us with the idea that it was all over when they crossed the Boundaries again. I don't think any of us expected anything else to happen."

"I didn't," agreed Linne. "I have to admit that when Owen was born, I honestly thought that he'd be able to grow and prosper in peace, without ever having to learn about all the harsh edges that life has. I had enough foolish youth left in me to think that once the Middle Islands were reached, that would be an end to the Darkness, and all that went with it."

Owen wanted to ask a question of his mother, but he dared not breathe any louder. He felt Darek moving about uneasily next to him, and thought he would surely attract his parents' attention, but they were joined at that moment by the old warrior, Stearborn, who gruffly greeted them, and poured himself a mug of mulled ale.

"Help yourself to the stew, you old war horse," invited Famhart.

"These are more like the old times, eh?" grunted Stearborn, dishing himself up a heaping plate of the hot stew. The steam rose before him as he placed the bowl to his lips, giving his scarred face a grotesque appearance by the flickering firelight.

"We've certainly traded our lot of tales around campfires like this, old friend."

Stearborn ate noisily and quickly, then washed his food down with the mulled ale. He had watched Linne carefully the whole time.

"Your stew is beyond the words of an old fish like me to compliment," he said politely, his voice raspy and hissing from the old wound.

"You are always a willing victim for my cooking," returned Linne.

"When you've done for yourself for as many seasons as I have, you learn to take your pleasures when and where you can. That's one of the rules of the game." He paused and looked at the two youngsters. "Another is that you play the hand as you see it fall, my lady. Sometimes we have a choice of the matter, other times not. We get our greatest hurts from not knowing when to fight, and when to walk away."

"Your parables don't reach me tonight," said Linne irritably. "I don't follow your line of thought at all."

"Oh, there is no line of thought to it," chuckled Stearborn in his croaky, hissing way. "I'm merely saying that you've lost any hold you have over the whelp, and too much interference at this point will make him buck-shy."

Stearborn left the rest unsaid, and finished his ale at a draught.

Owen was awake now, and cleared his throat unsurely, so that his voice would not crack as he spoke. "What Stearborn says is true, mother. I'm old enough to be following my father now. The settlement has seen the last of the boy that I was. I have to learn the craft of war to protect you and all the rest of our friends."

He lowered his eyes and spoke more softly then, but there was an intensity to his voice that struck Linne.

"And you are married to Famhart. My father is the leader of the settlement, and they are all waiting to see if I measure up to my father's mark. I must grow up now, mother, or it would be the worst possible thing for me.

Others half my age have been instructed in all the ways of the bow and sword and horses, and look upon me as a sickly lad more at home about the camp than at a watchfire. I have to do these things."

Darek, who had awakened in time to hear Owen speak, sat silently, watching the lad with a strange expression that escaped the others.

Stearborn laughed a gruff laugh, even though Linne was raising her voice to object.

"You four have me outnumbered and at a disadvantage," she managed. "There are not other mothers here now to take my side, but I shall give you reason to thank me for that. If there were others here with me, we could give you an ocean of tears that have been caused by your silly codes and rituals. If it were only a game, that could be overlooked and indulged, but it's a matter of young lives at stake here. Blood shall be spilled, and for what? Because someone else wants a piece of land or a horse? Small matters to slay one another over!"

"Small matters, indeed," countered Famhart. "There could be nothing closer to the truth, and yet if that is allowed, the killing goes on, until at last you have a long string of bloodshed that grows to such proportions that the weight of it is staggering."

"Another way to put it is this, my lady," interrupted Stearborn. "If we let the raiders off with a handslap, they shall be back in a fortnight with twice this number, and twice as many of our folk will be slain. But if we catch the wolf when he comes in among the sheep, that's an end of it, and the flock has no more worries for its safety."

Stearborn made his point by hacking off the end of a log in the fire with his longsword, and stamping it out beneath his boot heel. "You may have a loss of life, but it is a calculated loss, and is nothing like the cost if you let the aggression go unchecked."

"Men!" snorted Linne. "I wish for once women could set the stage and direct the action. There would be a definite shift in the shape of things, I dare say."

"I dare say," agreed Famhart, "yet things have been

going on in this manner for as long as there has been humankind about to grace this small world of ours. And it's not only us, but all kinds as well, whether of the sea, or air, or earth."

Stearborn had poured himself another ale, and seeing Owen sitting next to him at the fire, he offered the lad a drink from the large mug. Owen refused at first, fearing a reprimand from his mother, but she looked away in disgust, so he eased the vessel to his mouth and drank a small amount, choking as he did so, but managing to keep it all down.

The grizzled old warrior laughed his ragged laugh and clapped him heartily on the back, which almost brought the warm ale up again. "Good lad! You'll learn to take life as it comes, and not fear any man or beast or creed, and live free, as we were meant to."

"Hear, hear," piped in Darek, tasting the contents of the mug, and spewing it back out immediately, making horrible faces.

"You've got to learn what to do with it, lad," scolded Stearborn. "That's good, honest ale, and not meant to be spit upon the ground."

"Go easy on him, you old wart," chided Famhart. "You've grown calloused in your age. The lad is but a sapling. He needs more from us than chastisement."

Stearborn clapped Darek's shoulder and reached into his cloak, where he rummaged around for a time, at last withdrawing a small knife with its own sheath, and a fine carved ivory handle. "That there came from the battle at Two Flower Well. Hold to it, and you'll never have trouble with anything of a nature to harm you."

"It was said to have cut a leaf from the Three Trees," added Famhart. "It's said it is one of the blades of the world which can do that feat."

Owen looked longingly at the small, perfectly shaped knife. "I'll let you hold my sword if you'll let me see your knife," he offered.

Darek held his prize close to his chest, gazing lovingly at

every small detail of the intricately shaped and delicately formed blade.

"It is Darek's," reminded Famhart.

"I know, father. I only wanted to see it."

Stearborn clapped Owen on the back again, laughing. "You'll get your turn at it, my lad. Come, here's Jacob! Come on, you rough-hided old goat, sit with us and tell us how it fares with the questioning of the border rat."

Jacob sat down heavily and took up a plate of stew. He ate hungrily for a time, staring into the fire, then turned to Famhart.

"He knew of you and Linne," he said finally, shifting his weight to get more comfortable, and stoking up the fire until it blazed fiercely.

"How came he by that information?"

"He said that this was a special message from his governor to you, and that it was for you alone. I took it from him before the others had a chance to search him."

"Is he alive?"

"Yes, for now. I don't give his chances much thought of more than an even roll. The citizens are not in a forgiving mood."

"They'll calm down," said Stearborn. "After they have their reckoning at the feast and blow off some steam, they'll be happy enough to send the prisoner to do their labor for them."

"We'll see, my good Stearborn. I don't know that I would agree with you there. Perhaps if the raiders had not come, that might be the way of it."

"What is it that the man sent?" asked Linne, her curiosity getting the better of her.

"Strange," mused Famhart. "I can't make heads nor tails of this." He held the small object out before him, studying it by the uncertain glow of the fire.

"It almost looks like a brooch," observed Linne. "It's fashioned like some old pieces I have seen in books, from the ancient Boghatians."

She took the object and gazed at it for a long while, then

gave a little cry of surprise. "Here! It is a brooch! See the clasp? It's hidden here in the fine web of the metal."

"Something from my great-great-grandmother's day, by the looks of it," ventured Stearborn.

"Or older," added Famhart. "There's something written here, but I can't make it out."

Owen and Darek joined the adults in trying to decipher the tiny runes that seemed to flicker about in the fiery shadows like flames on a misty lake, and no one noticed that the same reflection came from the longsword that the two ancient men had given Owen.

Linne tired of trying to read the seemingly illegible writing. "I can't make anything of the words, but it would be pretty piece to close my cloak with," she said, holding it up to her throat to show Famhart how it would look.

"You ladies always have an eye for a sparkle," chided Stearborn. "I've never known it to fail where the fairer set is concerned."

"Bosh, you old goat! What would you know of any of that?"

"You might not think it to look at me, Jacob, but I've been married nine times in my life. My last wife threw me out two winters ago because she claimed she couldn't recall whether it was me she was wedded to or not, for she hadn't seen me in so long."

Famhart had laughed at his friend's reply, and was turning to speak to his wife, when Linne turned an ashen color, clutched wildly at her throat, and fell in a senseless heap at his feet.

The men at first looked about in every direction, thinking they had come under an attack by an unseen assailant, but they soon discovered that their perimeter was secure, and returned their attention to Famhart's stricken wife.

"She can't breathe," snapped Famhart, his jaw set tight, "Loosen her cloak, son!"

Owen did as he was told, although his hands felt like awkward claws, and he had to struggle to undo the brooch that Linne had fastened her cape with.

"I can't get it undone," he complained, growing frantic in his efforts.

Stearborn leaped up and moved the lad aside. "I smell a dead fish in all this," he cried, and took the brooch between his strong fingers and put all his strength to the task of opening the reluctant fastener. Try as he might, he could not budge the clasp, and in a last ditch effort to release it, he took the knife he had given to Darek and used the small blade as a pry bar to force open the lock.

There was a faint pop, and the brooch fell away, leaving Linne still unconscious, but some color began to return to her face.

"The devil's locket," snarled Famhart, and flung the offending thing into the fire. A great hiss of steam shot out of the flames, and a towering green cloud hung over them all for a moment before drifting away into the waiting night.

"Quickly, son, get us a blanket and the healer. Run!"

Owen flew as though pursued by a demon, followed closely by Darek.

Stearborn and Jacob covered Linne with her cloak, and Famhart tried to make her comfortable, and patted her hands in an effort to revive her.

"This is foul work," growled Jacob. "And my fault! I shall never forgive myself if anything should happen to Linne."

"Hush, Jacob! She will be fine. You did nothing amiss. She's not able to get her breath, that's all. She'll be fine in a moment."

Owen returned breathless and wild-eyed, followed by an older, balding man who wore the dark green cloak of a healer. They parted to let the man in, and watched anxiously as he examined the fallen Linne.

"What has she had that smells of flowers?" he asked at last. "A tea?"

"Nothing, Burnell. She had nothing! She was all right one minute, then she just grabbed at her throat and fell, just as you see her."

"The brooch! Where is it?" asked Jacob. "I thought I smelled flowers as she put it on the cloak."

He raked a stick through the fire until he found the object he desired, then flicked it deftly out of the flames.

"Let it cool, then let me see it," ordered Burnell.

"What was it the prisoner said about it, Jacob? That it was for me?"

"From his governor, and that you would understand."

"Did he say who his governor was?"

"A man called Largo."

As the name echoed shallowly about his head, Famhart sank slowly to his knees beside his wife, and took her unfeeling hand in his.

"It is not yet finished," he muttered to himself. "We never thought of this."

"What, father? What is unfinished?"

"Your mother had a brother, Owen, who turned to the Darkness. We thought he had been dead all these years."

Owen was about to question his father further, when the men came to set up the shelter for Linne, and in the ensuing activity, Famhart was called upon to address the others, as well as direct his lieutenants in the following day's marching orders.

Owen crept back to the tent where his mother lay and held her hand close to his heart, saying all the prayers he knew over and over again, and trying to imagine why anyone would harm her. He had never heard anything of her brother, except that he was a poor unfortunate lad, who never seemed to be able to do anything right, and who finally came to a bad end.

Except that now his mother was stricken with an odd illness, and would not open her eyes, and it was her own brother who was somehow at fault.

"I shall find him and kill him for this," he vowed, and in swearing his oath, he pulled his longsword from its scabbard, and held it aloft over his head.

As Owen spoke, a pale glimmering white fire seemed to flow out of the blade and down his hand, until his whole body was alight with it, and as quickly as it had begun, it was over, except that a firm voice came, as distinct as if

Gillerman had been standing beside him, speaking into his ear.

"You must bring a leaf from the Three Trees, Owen. It is the only thing that will help your mother."

"But how?" cried the boy. "I don't know how to reach there."

"You must find the country of the Three Trees. We await you there."

Owen was poised to ask another question, when the air about him moved as though someone were brushing by him in the dark, and he was left alone in the tent with his mother, who tossed about uneasily, lost in the chambers of a deep and troubling dream.

The Men of the South Channels

In the early morning light of the high pass, the snow was still silver white against the gray rocks that had begun to show through. The hooded figure of the man moved slowly along, picking his way carefully, leading his horse while walking gingerly on before. He was tall and dark, with long curls of thick hair hanging outside the cowl of his cape. His horse was a handsome roan animal, with fine tack and a heavily ornamented saddle.

At intervals, the man stopped to gaze out over the valley floor far below, faintly gold and pale green at the lower altitudes, with a silver thread of a river running along the western edge of the forest, which went on into the hazy clouds that marked the beginning of the coast of the Sea of Roaring.

The horse champed anxiously at his bit, and lifted a hoof to stamp nervously on the frozen ground.

"We're almost there, horse. Don't give yourself fits now. We'll be there in an easy ride before this day is finished."

The animal shook his mane and flared his nostrils, his breath still coming in soft white clouds from the high cold of the dawn.

After another long pause to study the valley, the man went on, slowly and cautiously, picking his way along the narrow trail that had almost imperceptibly begun to lead downward. Small streams of water collected under the horse's hooves at every step, then collected into larger rivulets, all running faster, gathering speed as they went, until a few hundred feet further down the trail, the man saw the first of the small falls that cascaded over a forty foot drop; from there, it filled a large pool, which in turn fed a bubbling brook, icy to the touch, and growing ever wider and faster as it continued on into the distant valley.

Horse and rider followed along beside the infant river until it fell away into a gorge hundreds of feet deep, roaring and tumbling and making a noise so great it seemed to fill the very air with its thunder. The man rode on from that point, picking another branch of the trail which skirted the river in its deep channel, and crossed a rocky outcrop, then dropped downward very slowly until the tops of the first trees came into view, and announced that the worst of the high pass was over, and that the going would be much easier.

The man was riding at barely a walking pace, his head nodding along as if he were dozing in the saddle, and paying no attention to his surroundings. Twice the horse snorted and turned its ears about this way and that, as if it had heard something that spooked it, but the man never moved a muscle, or took any notice of his mount's giddiness.

There were small knots of trees along the crude path the man followed, and as they got into lower altitudes, the small clumps became groves, then larger still, until at last they were in the top-most edge of the great green vault that covered the valley floor.

There were oak and elm and ash now, and taller, deep red trees that had trunks larger around than five men could circle with their outspread arms. These were not new to the man, who had once been to the ancient country where lived the mystical Three Trees. He had stolen a leaf then, and it had given him the powers he needed to carry on his mission of revenge, to pay back all those who were against him, and left him for dead long ago, during the monstrous siege of the Middle Islands, when all the infidels had overthrown the true ruler of the Lower Boundaries.

And here he was at the next step of his plan, to gather together the most awesome army yet left on Atlanton, to strike a blow while the opportunity presented itself, when the lands were free of the dreaded Keepers. In all the countries the man had traveled, he had found only traces of his hated enemies, but no sign of their immediate return. Since he had taken the human form, he had been able to travel freely, and to pass among all kinds without notice or alarm, and he had begun to find that he had many compatriots for the asking, who seemed eager to join with his forces for the promise of booty and adventure.

As he rode thinking of all the pleasant moments he would have to savor when victory would be his, and he would be able to cast all those who had opposed him into the sea, a long, yellow-feathered shaft buried itself in a tree next to his head, followed shortly by two more. The horse reared and whirled about, but the man was an expert rider and kept his seat, spurring his mount on to outdistance his unseen assailants.

"He's breaking for it," shouted a voice from his right. "Head him off at the crosstrail."

A horn blew wildly, and there were others that answered, and the hiss and angry crackle of the arrows as they snapped past his ears. He drew his longsword and thrust his arm through the leather loops of his shield, which hung at his saddle horn, and put the reins between his teeth to leave his arms free to defend himself.

There were cries and shouts, and the snap of arrows, but they all missed their mark, except one, which struck the man's shoulder, but glanced away, for he was wearing an old elfin mail shirt from the armies of the Shanoliel.

Thundering along at full gallop, he came head-on with a mounted rider who attempted to block his way on the narrow path, but the enemy was not as quick or as powerful, and was ridden down, losing his seat in the process. Another appeared, then another, and both met the same fate, and were overthrown by the swift strokes of the dark man.

The horns were further behind him now, so he slowed his pace, and tried to muster his thoughts. He had not planned to announce his arrival in so bold a way, and had hoped to be able to scout about in the valley before the inhabitants knew of his whereabouts or business. He had hoped that he would find settlements that were of his own sentiments regarding the Keepers, and all who followed them, and he smiled to himself to find the natives to be so ready to kill first and question later. They would have no way of knowing his intentions, or whether he were of a friendly nature or otherwise. This cheered him greatly, and he could not have received a warmer welcome had there been musicians and fools to lighten his way.

He reined in his lathered horse and dismounted, walking slowly along to cool the animal.

"Perhaps they will catch up with us, horse, and we shall clap an eye to their features, be they fair or foul. I hope foul! But not those imbecile Worlughs, or the grotesque Gorgolacs. I hope there are simple folks, who look as akin to another as bread and jam. Those are the ones I have most need of now. It was a wretched fool mistake to loose that filth before. One look at those creatures from the northernlands, and all joined against them. No, horse, what I have in mind is a more daring deed than simply lining up beasts to attack the Keepers and their pawns. We shall be the new order, and the first to return to the true law, which says that the strong shall survive, and the weaklings shall serve their masters."

The horse raised his head and shook his mane, blowing and breathing heavily.

"Even you, horse, are fooled. If you knew my true nature, you'd have shied away and been gone long ago, and never accepted me as your master upon your back."

Here the man threw his head back and laughed a short, barking laugh. "If you only knew, horse, that you were carrying me, you'd bolt away from me this moment, and never allow me near you again."

As the man walked on, he threw back his cloak and hood, and shook out all the long dark hair, which fell down to his shoulders, which were broad and powerful.

"I'm glad that I found man-shape that was of the proper stature. I grew tired of my runtness. But no one shall ever ridicule me for that again. I shall not take up that form again until I have come face to face with my old tormentors."

He was prepared to go on, but at that moment, he heard movement close behind him.

"Come, friends! I have not come to rob or plunder your settlement! I seek allies to band together to drive the infidel out. You can see I am but a simple man."

"Who be you, stranger?" asked a curt voice from behind a thick oak. "What trade have you in the South Channels? Speak up!"

"I am here because I have heard there are settlements here which welcome all comers who have sworn a blood oath against the infidels which rule by the power of the Keepers."

A silence fell as his words trailed off into the forest, and for a brief moment, he felt a pang of fear that he had revealed himself to the wrong side, and that his information was in error about the South Channel Mountains and the wild clans that lived there.

Without warning, a gray-bearded man clad in a deep green cloak and knee-boots stood before him. The stranger was as large as the man, and had pale blue piercing eyes, like the eyes of a bird, or a snake.

"You speak boldly for a man who has just crossed the lines into the South Channels. There are none here to speak for you, or to save you if we don't take a cotton to you. What say you to that, lowlander?"

"I am no lowlander, friend. I have come from over the Malignes, and crossed the Silver Mist Pass. I have been in all the lands between, collecting all those who will ride with me against the lowland infidels."

"Mighty large talk for one that appears to be in a heap of hot water, Arnault. We could string him up by his ears if we liked, and there wouldn't be a lot he could do to stop it."

"I could do quite a lot that you wouldn't care for, my friend. But we waste our time here gabbing in the wood. Surely you must have a governor, or elder, who makes such decisions as these. Let's go before him, and I can present my case in a proper fashion."

"I am an elder," replied the man called Arnault coldly. "I make these decisions."

"Very well. Then I shall address you, my good man, and put it to you as quickly as I can. Spare me, and you spare yourselves. Join me, and you shall share in all the lands and goods of all we take. We shall drive the Keepers' stewards from their lands, and rule once more for ourselves."

"We already do that," said Arnault, who motioned to an unseen figure behind him, and there came forth another green-clad figure with a long bow, who was taking aim at the man's heart.

At the precise instant the arrow was released, the man whirled once and raised a hand, which the dart hit, and fell shattered to the ground.

"You cannot harm me, my friends. I tell you I am Bern the Red, come from death and murder to avenge my betrayal. You would be wise to join with me here, for I can call upon more powers to convince you."

"Did you see that? He struck my dart down! And it was fair shot!"

"Hold," ordered Arnault. "We'll hear you out, stranger. If you be who you say you are, then you've come to the right place. None of us here hold, or ever held with the Keepers. They may have been all right for the louts who believed all that palaver, but those of us who wanted the truth, and to follow the law as we saw it for ourselves, never went along with the good-rights like them."

"Wisely said, master. I can be a good ally, or a terrible enemy. It's for you to decide which it shall be."

"If you have any way of teaching us how to bat down darts like that, then I'd say we'd have a fair chance of taming these mountains, and the Valley of the Lost Weir as well."

"Our goals will go on to include much more than that, good Arnault. I have a plan that will sweep away all the infidels below the boundary, and I shall sit in state over all of it. Those who swear their service to me shall be well rewarded for their efforts."

"We may or may not swear service to you, stranger. That remains to be seen. There's more to it all than a little sleight of hand. We've long lived here in these mountains, and we're not so anxious to take our leave of them. We might be of some aid to you here, if you have an army, as you say you do."

"If he had one, why isn't it here with him?" asked the man who shot the arrow, eyeing Bern suspiciously.

There were grunts of agreement from several others who had crowded in closer to their leader.

"My armies have grown in strength, and multiply every day. I have been on the move these past years, enlisting those I find trustworthy. It has been a slow and tedious job. There are still agents of the Keepers who watch for those of our kind, but I've been clever, and they have never suspected my presence."

"But where are these armies? Do they follow you about at such a distance that we can't see them?"

"I have done my best to explain it to you, friend. They await word from me. They are armed and ready to move at a moment's notice. When I send the signal, they shall arise as one force and smite down the infidel with one sure, final blow."

Bern paced as he spoke, spinning around on his heel so suddenly that he startled the leader, Arnault, who had been walking beside him.

"And the fools don't even know that the word that shall call my army together will be the very celebration that they have been holding for themselves. A feast in my name, good Arnault! The very thing. It is too sweet to think of."

"The Feast of the Red Bear," repeated the gray-bearded man. "We have heard of it, but only in old tales. I can't recall why we don't have it ourselves."

"It is still celebrated by the lowlanders, friend. They have cause to hold it every so often, to keep the blood boiling and the swords honed. They will have cause to remember it well now, for the Feast of the Red Bear will bathe them in blood and finish up the fools once for all. I have suffered all that I have suffered gladly, to be able to be there at the finish, so they will know who it is who has won. It will indeed be sweet!"

"You speak as one who has held a long grudge, brother," said Arnault. "We, too, have known the sting of defeat and loss. We are an old clan here in the South Channels, but we have all we can do to keep open our borders. The lowlanders went to war with us and have kept us at bay here in the South Channels for a long time, but we are beginning to tire them with our raids. They never know when or where we'll strike, and they have grown lax these past seasons."

"If it is the valley that you want returned to you, or if you have a debt to settle with someone for an injustice done to you, it will be made right for you if you agree to follow Bern the Red. We shall cast down all those fools who have opposed the natural law. There is no room for the retiring or weak. The law reads that he who is the fittest shall conquer all."

"Hear, hear," shouted a voice, then was joined by another.

"We'll have a bit of that," added a third.

"Come along, Bern. We shall introduce you to the others of the settlement. They shall be glad to know of your ideas. Life here in the South Channels hasn't been the easiest existence."

Bern swung smoothly into his saddle. "I'm sorry to have been so rough with you fellows back there. I wasn't sure that you weren't from the other side."

"That's a joker pot if I ever heard it," laughed the bowman who had shot at Bern. "The bloke was worried that the good-rights might have gotten him. What a fate!"

"If they had known who I was when I was among them, it would have set off a stir that I dare say you would have heard about, even living off out of the beaten track as you do."

"You speak mighty big for a fellow that's out of his territory. Even if you know some small trick to fool the common riffraff hereabouts, there is more to be said about it than what we can chat over here. We shall talk at length about this when we're home."

Arnault blew a short signal on a curved stag horn, and the woods about the men became alive with motion. Armed riders appeared from every direction, and the entire procession followed their leader off in a general course that wound downward on the faint path, and more riders joined them as they went along.

"You seem to have a good following, friend," said Bern after a time. "This is well, for I have a need of large, well-armed parties. There shall be fine rewards for all who agree to ride with Bern the Red."

"You shall have to explain yourself at greater lengths than that," replied Arnault. "Just because we live in this isolated part of the world doesn't make us easy to dupe. We come from a long line of high-blooded ancestors. If we find we don't have a use for you, or your high-flown plans, there are ways of dealing with you when we arrive at that bridge."

Bern cursed under his breath, but this was not an opportune moment to demonstrate any of the other illusions that he had mastered while he was a guest in the country of the Mystic Trees.

There was a short ride through the thickening forest, then Arnault dismounted and led the way to a seemingly solid wall of thorns and vines that marked the end of the path. There was a moment of silence, then very slowly the wall parted, revealing a wide lane that ran between even lawns and neat dwellings, each one painted a matching green or brown to blend in with their surroundings.

Bern had not seen anything at all from his vantage point high in the Silver Mist Pass, and was quite amazed at the number of shelters, and the crowds of people that thronged about their leader, eyeing the newcomer with open distrust.

He had some misgivings about his plans then, but his fear made him desperate, and he vowed to himself to return to his old form if necessary to properly convince his new acquaintances. They were much more adept at many things than Bern had expected, and did not seem easily daunted by a few sleight of hand tricks.

If the worst happened, he knew he could rely on his old form to throw them off their guard, and he would take that opportunity to make good his escape.

"There must be a soft spot to this fellow," Bern whispered to himself, trying to gain his confidence back. "And when I find it, I shall work on that until I have them all eating out of my hand."

Promising himself this, he unloosed the cloak from his shoulders, and rode taller in his saddle, deciding to put on the best face he could, and to see what he could of the settlement and its folk. Somewhere there, he knew, was the one flaw he would need to bring these strangers to their knees, and to put them at his beck and call.

Kegin in Command

It was very early and still dark beneath the morning sky, when Famhart took Owen and Darek aside, careful to move out of earshot of Linne, although they knew she could not hear. Burnell had stayed by her side in the travel shelter all night, but had no good news to report.

"You and Darek must stay here to take care of Linne while I go to try to find help. There must surely be some of the Keepers left somewhere in one settlement or other.

Burnell said there might be one in Red Point, so that's where I'll try first. It's their help we need now. We can do nothing for this kind of illness. I see an omen in it that doesn't bode well for any of us."

"But who will teach us if you're gone, father? You said you'd teach us the sword and bow!"

"I will, son. I must first find someone to guide us."

"Gillerman and Wallach told me where to go," said Owen. He had hesitated to mention his dream, but now when it looked as though they were to be left behind, he spoke up.

"Who are they?" asked Famhart, his fair features aged by the worry over his stricken wife.

"The two who gave me the sword, father. And who had the horses who talked."

Famhart nodded absently, then turned to call to a man standing next to the watchfire in front of the shelter where Linne lay. "Kegin, come here! I want you to tell these two that you will show them all there is to know of the longsword and bow! You are my finest soldier and instructor of the tender art of arms. I leave these two under your charge."

Darek smiled, but Owen spoke up again. "Father, I tell you I know which way to go to find the help my mother needs. And then you can teach us our lessons yourself."

"I'm sure your two friends were fine fellows, but I have need of a Keeper. I rue the day I didn't protest when the last of them began to leave. I should have known better than to think this business was finished."

Kegin, standing next to his commander, turned and studied the growing sunrise. "What of this Largo? Surely we can't leave the camp unprotected with him at large. If he found us once at Sweet Rock, it would only follow that he would be able to find us again."

"Of course, Kegin," agreed Famhart. "That's why I propose to take a band to seek help from the Keepers, and to leave you in charge here. I think you should all be safe and sound if you made in a general direction of the coast. There are two or three friendly settlements left there. Then we can link up again at say White Bird, or Swan Haven."

"I'm at your service, Famhart. Whatever you wish. We shall say White Bird, or Swan Haven."

"But father," complained Owen. "That's the wrong direction! Gillerman and Wallach said we need to get a leaf from the Three Trees, and that's away toward the South Channels."

The two older men shook their heads.

"The South Channels would be the last place to seek help for Linne, son. Those parts have been full of the worst outcasts since the call to the Middle Islands. Those there that aren't outright renegades are on the borderline of it, and the others just follow their own rules and live as they please with no thoughts of others. I can't say that they're evil, or turned to the Darkness, but they certainly have no interest in us or our concerns."

"But that's where Gillerman and Wallach said we would find the help mother needs. We have to at least try!" Owen was rapidly nearing tears, so he clinched his fists tightly to keep control.

"We have no proof that those two can be counted as friends, Owen," said Famhart evenly. "I hope so, but there was no proof. If I could speak to them, I could find out soon enough if they were of the right sort, but they seem to have disappeared."

"They said they would be in the South Channels, father. I know they would explain it all if you could talk to them."

Famhart's lieutenant bent closer and whispered into his ear.

"It's true, Kegin! You're right as rain. That's where that lout of a brother is hiding." Famhart slapped his gloves viciously against his palm and began to pace. "He knew where to find our settlement and how to be as devious and treacherous as he always was. Time, nor a return from the dead, has done nothing to reform him."

"Then we'll go there, father?" asked Owen. "We might find out what sort of spell was on the brooch."

"We shall go to the South Channels, son, but not until I've gotten help for Linne. Burnell said she is in no danger now, just in a deep trance. He said if nothing's done, she could be

this way forever. So we shall have to have her mended first
of all, before we tend to any other matters, no matter how
pressing."

Owen was prepared to argue further, but saw the look in
his father's eye, of deep pain and an old sorrow.

"You and Darek will stay here with Kegin to learn your
proper arms, and by that time I shall be back with help.
Then we'll plan our foray into the South Channels."

Famhart went into the shelter and was gone some time.
When he returned, Owen saw his father had been weeping,
but tried hard not to show it.

"Come along, you two can help us gather the lads. I've
called a party together to set out for Red Point. Burnell says
there is a healer there who may be able to help us."

A large party stirred about their mounts in the center of
the camp, and there was all the last-minute activity that
took his father's attention away. There were orders to give,
and last-minute inspections of gear and mounts, and a dozen
other details to see to. Owen and Darek wandered among
the men, watching with envy as they prepared for their
journey.

"We could take horses and join up without anyone knowing," suggested Darek. "There are so many here, they
wouldn't notice two more."

"My father would," disagreed Owen. "He already knows
how many are here, and who they are. We wouldn't make it
a mile."

"Would he be very angry?" asked Darek.

"I don't want to find out," said Owen. "My father has
always been very fair, but I have found him to be a man who
follows his word."

"Did he beat you?"

"When I deserved it," returned Owen, then laughed.
"When I remember it now, I earned all the lashings I got."

"My father never whipped me," said Darek. "I don't
think I've ever seen my father angry."

"What is your father's name, Darek?"

"Morgan Alynn," replied the lad. "He was handsome and

brave, and was trying to save the settlement when he was lost."

"What was the name of your settlement?"

"Clover Hill," answered the lad, looking away.

"Are you sure your father was slain in the fighting? Maybe he was like you, lost in the battle, and is trying to find you somewhere right this moment."

Darek's eyes shone, and his voice was paper thin and fragile. "I only dare hope that it is so. I'm afraid to think of it."

Owen gave him a brisk pat of reassurance. "You stick with me. If we can find Gillerman and Wallach, they will be able to help us. If your father or mother are anywhere to be found, those will be the two who can do it."

"Did their horses really talk, Owen? Just like you or I?"

"As plainly as we're speaking now," said Owen. "I wanted to ask them some questions, but they seemed so serious and all, I forgot. And then the raiders came."

"I hope I can see them someday."

"You shall, Darek. We shall see them together."

"Promise me," said Darek, clutching Owen's hand.

"I promise! Stick with me, and we shall see and do things together that will make us heroes, Darek. We shall be in all the tales, and everyone will know of our deeds."

"Oh, good, Owen. You make it all sound grand. We shall do all those things and more. Owen and Darek, Riders of the Line. Do you think there are any more of the flying snakes? It would be good to be able to slay one of them."

Owen shook his head. "I don't think so, Darek. My mother and father fought them once, but I think they're all gone now." Remembering his mother, Owen turned his steps toward the shelter where she lay. "Come on! I promised my father I'd look after her. Kegin can show us what we need to know for now. There may be a way I can call Gillerman and Wallach here. My sword got all full of light and too bright to look at when Gillerman's voice came. Maybe I can find some way to talk to him."

"Your sword?"

"Yes. It got very bright, and there was a white light that ran all over it, and right down my arm."

Owen wasn't sure if talking about the exceptional qualities of the sword was permissible, but he trusted his new friend Darek, and knew that it was safe to speak before him.

They had reached the shelter, and found Kegin posted guard in front.

"Your father will be here to give you his farewells," he said. "They will be going out the Green Road. Do you have anything to give him for luck, Owen?"

The lad had completely forgotten the ancient custom, and had to hurry to his mother's side to find the small locket she kept there at her throat. He hastily undid it, and clasped it gently in his hand.

"He'll be back safe, mother, and bring help as well. We shall not rest until you're better than new."

Owen kissed her quickly on the cheek, and emerged just as Famhart and his troop rode up. There were a hundred bowmen with him, and the party wore the gray cloaks woven of a fine thread that the elves had given to Famhart and Linne as a wedding present long ago. It had the power to make those who wore the cloth almost invisible to any but the sharpest eye, and was said to have wonderful qualities which would keep the wearer from hunger and fatigue for days.

"You're in time, Kegin. Keep a stout heart, and teach my two young wards there the meaning of respect for the longsword and bow. I shall test them on your prowess as teacher when I return."

"Of course, Famhart. You may count on me," Kegin said, bowing low to his friend. "You may be surprised, for your son could well outdo you!"

"Ever the rogue, Kegin. Since you bested me once at archery, I have not heard an end of it."

Famhart grasped his friend in a tight bear hug, and went alone into the shelter for a last good-bye to his wife. His party waited nervously, eager to be off, with their mounts stamping and edging about, and Owen smelled the excitement in the air. The sunlight looked brighter and more golden than it had in a long, dreary time, and the men were dashing and young, their eager faces boyish and carefree. They called back and forth to one another as if they were on a lark with nothing more than a picnic to look forward to at the end.

Kegin strode over to a youth who rode a tall white horse with a black mane. "You lads mind yourselves! You're not off on a ride through the woods today. Famhart will regret this, I fear, leaving behind all his old guard, and taking you whelps to season you."

"Aha, Kegin! You're jealous that your students get to prove their mettle at last, while you stay behind to stir the soup at camp. We all get old! There's no disgrace in that. The world is made for those who don't have joints that creak and groan and eyes that blur. You stay home and make the plans, Kegin! Us young bucks will carry them out!"

"Fairly said, Dorcet."

"We have earned the right," said another, mounted on a prancing roan.

"I never said you hadn't," replied Kegin shortly. "Just be sure you bear up as well to our enemies as you have to your old teacher. If it comes to that, then I'll be satisfied I've done my job properly."

"You've done it well enough, Kegin. Most of us here can outshoot you now. You've taught us all you know."

"No, I haven't." Kegin laughed. "I'm still breathing in my old age, and you lads haven't survived your youth yet. When that occurs, you'll be well seasoned, and remember the trouble you've given me."

He laughed again, and turned away. Owen saw that the smile was forced, and that there was a heavy sadness behind Kegin's clear blue eyes.

"Come on, my bucks, let's you and I see your daddy off properly. Give him the token, and we'll send our arrows out over his head to lead them safely there and back."

The two lads helped Kegin string the stout longbows, and he showed them how to notch the arrow and hold it with the left hand to guide the shaft. Darek had trouble drawing the heavy pull of his bow, so Kegin got him a smaller one, which fit him better. Owen had difficulty as well, but he put all his strength into it, and the great bow finally bent.

Famhart emerged from the shelter pale and unsettled, but quickly composed himself, and took the parting gift from Owen. Kegin handed up a stirrup cup of strong, hot mulled ale from the fire, which Famhart touched to his lips, and handed on to the rider next to him, who passed it on, until each of the men had had a farewell sip.

With another nod of his head, Famhart undid the horn from beneath his cloak, and blew two short notes, followed by a longer, higher call, pure and sweet, that set the birds in the wood into song.

All in a rush the horsemen sprang forward, and the air resounded with their hoofbeats, and the chink and jingle of the harness of horse and rider, metal and leather.

At the signal, Kegin raised his bow to let fly a flashing red shaft with green feathers, then Darek let fly his, and last was Owen's; his shot flew higher and further than the others, and as the shaft arched into the high sunlight above the trees, a tiny rainbow burst into view, glittering and falling away into the woods below like broken starlight.

"Well shot!" cried Kegin, marveling at the sight.

"It was a sign from my friends," said Owen, amazed at himself. "Look! Below the shaft! It's the South Channels."

Kegin followed his pointing hand, and there framed by the eaves of the forest, showing clearly in the sky beyond the camp, were the glittering white domes of the distant mountains called the South Channels.

Kegin turned back to speak to Owen, but the lad had gone inside the shelter to be beside Linne. His mother was the only one who had believed in Gillerman and Wallach, and he felt that it would be through her that he would get his answers as to what to do.

There was a faint ebbing glow of light from the sword at his side, and Owen removed it and placed it down next to the silent form of Linne. Burnell looked in for a moment, but left quietly when he saw the boy. The sword gathered more light, and a soft hum began, low and vibrating the ground where it lay. Owen tried to pick the blade up, for fear it would disturb his mother, but it was hot to the touch and throbbing.

"Is that you, Gillerman?" breathed Owen. "I don't know how to turn this thing off."

There was no answer, but the light grew brighter, with flashing golden beams that pulsed across the shadows in the darkened shelter.

Darek came in at that moment, and the lights and motion faded quickly away.

"What was all that?" he asked, looking about, and blinking in the sudden gloom of the shelter.

"I think my sword has tried to contact me, but it quit. I have a feeling it's Gillerman."

"Oh, good," said Darek. "I want to see it."

Owen looked at his friend evenly. "It stopped when you came in. Maybe it only works when I'm here with it alone."

"Then I'll go away and let you try again," said Darek, trying not to sound rejected.

"It's nothing against you, Darek, it just never seems to work except when I am alone. It worked when my mother was there, though."

"I'll go out and you see if it works again," said his friend, rising to go. "Then you'll tell me about it, all right?"

"All right. We'll see what happens. Tell Kegin to wait outside, too."

The younger lad left, and Owen put the sword at his mother's side again, waiting. He turned it this way and that, and called out to Gillerman and Wallach, but the blade remained silent and cold.

After a long time of trying, Owen finally gave up and lay down exhausted to rest, and in doing so he noticed a shadow near the wall of the shelter where he had tried to work the spell of the sword. It wasn't moving, and Owen felt it had been there for a long while, which perhaps was why the sword had shown no sign of life.

As quietly as he could, Owen stole to the front of the shelter and peered outside, but there was no one anywhere near, except Kegin and Darek, sitting beside the watchfire making tea.

The Line Stewards

Four heavily armed riders watched as the river of refugees flooded past, their flocks and livestock herded before them. The people rode or walked, and, if they had anything left from the raiders' attacks, they carried their belongings on their backs or in wagons, their faces drawn and gaunt. The women and children were carried in the carts whenever it was possible, along with the wounded, but the roads, where there were roads, were sometimes dangerous and impassable, and all those who could were forced to walk over the treacherous spots. These were people who were fleeing from the older settlements above Swan Haven, which had been called Olson's Well, before the raiders came, but all the settlement that had not been slain was driven out, and forced to flee for their lives. On the main highways such as the Green Road, the crowds began to gather together for protection, and there were some tearful reunions among those there. As the four riders looked on at the spectacle from a slight rise above the road, one of the men pointed and spoke.

"Look, Chellin! I believe it's Gruning and the Brothers! We haven't clapped our blinkers to their ugly hides in a long season or two."

The man addressed as Chellin was clad in a brown cloak that draped him from head to toe, and covered most of his horse's neck and rump as well. He had a bushy brown beard

66

flecked with gray, and sensitive blue eyes that sparkled with a ready humor and a great experience at travel and war.

"Holla, good ruffians!" called Chellin Duchin. "Come out of the road here and give us the news! Are you removing all of Lake Fork today?"

"Hail, Chellin! Good speed, Jeremy! I don't believe I have the honor of knowing the mugs of these other two."

"Hamlin and Judge, at your service," replied Chellin. "They have only been with me these past months. They never came up as far as Lake Fork or Olson's Well before."

"No Lake Fork or Olson's Well left," growled a gruff, aging man, dressed as Chellin, and as heavily armed. His duplicate sat beside him on a horse that matched.

"The Brothers speak the sad fact of the matter," said Gruning. "We saw the great hall torched and the millhouse sacked, and we were lucky to get off with the flocks or herds from the upper pastures. The whole forest was swarming with this new breed of trash we've been seeing of late."

"I thought they were random bandits from the Tybo campaign, but I've changed my tune now," replied Chellin, dismounting and stretching his limbs from the long hours in the saddle. He sat then, and took off a boot to search for a stone.

"What I think we're dealing with here is something everyone said wouldn't happen, and that is that these fellows have found a leader who has organized them, and has begun to make war on all of us in earnest."

"Why not?" grumbled the twin called Port. "There's nothing to stop the ransacking of any one of the settlements along our entire border. It's been so long since half these folks had to do anything except mind their farm or flock or fish, that they hardly know the answer to a threat of force is to arm and repel it."

He looked to his brother as he spoke, and they both nodded agreement many times, and kept muttering "well said," until Chellin raised a hand to quiet them.

"I hear your words, Port. We've grown old in the duty of border steward, and we know the worst of almost any situation that comes along. We've given up home and family long ago to pursue our duty as we see it, and it's easy for us to watch what's been happening. Yet I haven't felt this uneasy in a long time! Look at that." He waved an arm at the throng of people passing by in a seemingly endless line.

"They are from settlements as far away as the Great Bend, and all have the same tale to tell, of armed raiders coming in greater numbers out of the South Channels, and fire and destruction. I've called up every reserve I can count on, but we haven't confronted any of these lads from the other side yet. We get rumors and see a slain raider now and again, but we've got nothng solid to go on. We don't know who we're really up against, and as long as everyone keeps striking their colors and high-tailing it further from the trouble, we'll keep on seeing exactly what we have here."

"Confusion and terror! That's the way of it," agreed Gruning. "The old stewards have done their job well all these years, and then when we're finally called on to deliver, they desert us cold and take a hike. There's not much we can do without cooperation from the citizenry."

"Why don't you and your bunch join us when we camp tonight," suggested Chellin. "I think we need to put our noggins to the task of trying to find some sort of plan for all this. Uncharted waters are risky business."

"I see your point, Chellin. The Brothers and I will round up the scoundrels that are with our lot, and we'll lock up with your lads tonight. Shall we signal, or do you have a spot in mind?"

"I think about as far as these folks can make it by dark is the old ford by Ten Elms. We'll see you there!"

"Ten Elms it is then. Keep a weather eye!"

Gruning reined his mount about and cantered off to rejoin another armed party on the far side of the long line of the procession that had been filing by as they talked. The twin brothers, Port and Starboard, lifted their hands in salute, and were gone as well.

"Those two are a pair," Jeremy laughed. "I have known them for as long as I can remember, and I don't think I've ever seen them any farther apart than a bow shot."

"Their mother was one of the Moon Children of Trew,"

said Chellin. "I've never met any of them but her, but that was enough to chill my bones. They never speak plainly about anything, and they only prepare meals after dark. She lived in a deserted settlement near the Darien Mounds until her husband died, and then she brought the two boys to North Brook to give them to a family there. I think she disappeared with her husband's body, and no one saw her again. It must have done something to the lads, because as you say, Jeremy, they haven't been far apart from each other since then."

"What a strange tale," mused Hamlin. "I thought almost everyone in these coastal settlements had become fairly tame, but I can see I overlooked a few."

"They're tame enough along the coast, lad," replied Chellin. "The ones who still cling to the old ways and the outlawed rituals mostly live out their lives a little nearer the old border counties, that run beside the old boundaries."

"Do you think all this is something more than an uprising in the South Channels?" asked Judge, who was the youngest of the companions.

"I don't know," answered Chellin. "I've been at this game long enough to be a fair thinker on these matters, but I don't quite know what to make of all this latest business. There were the usual raiders that have found their way to us, and think they'll have easy pickings, but they are easy enough to frighten off, once they get the idea that we have patrols that serve the settlements."

"That wouldn't account for all these folk," said Hamlin. "This is something I've never seen before. It's enough to set off our worst doubts about being able to contain that pestilence that's pouring out of the mountains now."

"We are going to have to find a way to scout them out," said Chellin, stroking his beard thoughtfully, then remounting quickly.

"I'm not sure how we shall go about it yet, but that is a plan we shall have to perfect if we're to continue to be effective here."

"We shall have to be quick about it, Chellin. Look at the

numbers on the road here! If this keeps up much longer, the
Line will be nothing more than a deserted land."

"The Line shall never be deserted," said Chellin grimly.
"Not while Chellin Duchin draws breath. These hills and
woods have been my home since I was a tyke, and no upstart
renegades from the South Channels shall drive me away."

"I hope you're right," said Jeremy. "I have no heart for a
move, but I can't see staying in an overrun land to be
captured by the likes of these lads we've had the privilege of
running into. They're a nasty lot."

"Only because they don't seem to have any center," said
Chellin. "I don't know what's gotten into them up there.
You'd think the air was too thin to support good thinking."

"They don't seem to have any love for anything except
killing," agreed Judge. "It's strange to fight someone who
looks so much like one of us, yet there's something missing
from their thinking. I've seen them destroy shelters and
crops and slay innocents as though they were having a cup
of mulled ale after their supper. It chills me to my marrow
to think about them coming in any great numbers. There
aren't enough good men from the Line to stand up to a
crowd like that, especially if they're organized and ready to
fight."

"That's why we've been at our posts all these years,
Judge. I tried to tell you about all this when you came to us
to join our ranks. I knew your mother didn't want you to
throw your life away on what she considered a useless folly.
She wasn't alone in that way of thought, either. Until all
this began again, there were meetings of settlement councils
called to stop our wages, and calls to disband the stewards."

"It's a wise thing they didn't," said Hamlin, "or we would
all be in the soup by now. If it hadn't been for the Line
Stewards, there wouldn't be any place of safety left anywhere on this side of the Roaring."

"That may be carrying it a bit far, but we would be in a
deal of trouble if we hadn't had a reserve ready to tap these
past few days. If we can regroup tonight and tomorrow and
call in all our inactives that are with the citizens on the road

there, we may just have a chance to reshape our borders, and clear this rabble out."

"Who were you thinking of sending as scout into the South Channels?" asked Judge. "Are there any in our camp who know the area well enough to risk going there alone?"

"I have no thoughts as to who would go," replied Chellin. "We'll find out tonight if there is anyone among our lot who has a knowledge of the area."

"Famhart of Sweet Rock has spent time there, I hear," offered Hamlin. "He and his lady were with the Keepers at the Middle Islands. He would know the area as well as anyone."

"Aye, Famhart, the Rod of Truth. He is well known in all the settlements of the Line. We shall see if he is with us tonight, and if he would be willing to make such a journey."

The four men had rejoined the flowing column of humanity, and paced themselves at a slow walk on the right flank of the march. The wood had thinned until a large meadow surrounded them on all sides. A shallow lake at its center reflected back the bright blue late afternoon sky.

"This looks as though it must have been settled once," said Judge. "What a perfect place for dwellings."

"Bugs," replied Hamlin curtly. "Plenty of bugs, and too much humidity."

"But there are ways past all that," went on Judge, ignoring his friend's remarks.

"It was settled once," confirmed Chellin. "In my youth, there was a thriving community here, but it disappeared at the Celebration of the Crown of Winter somewhere along the way. I can't remember what year it was, but it was cold and bitter. No one ever heard anything more of the souls who lived here."

"Where are the dwellings? I can't see anything man-made here."

"You wouldn't," said Chellin. "These were people from a long line that went all the way back to the waterfolk. They built their shelters so cleverly you wouldn't be able to see them at all until you were right on them."

"Who were the waterfolk?" asked Judge, studying the terrain carefully.

"There are two ways of thinking on that," replied Chellin. "There were the waterfolk from the old folklore, the elfin clans that used to roam these parts. I don't know whether you believe in that sort of thing or not anymore. Times have changed, it seems. The others were the Boghatians, where Famhart comes from. An old line long since forgotten, I dare say, just like the elves. The Boghatians weren't so lovable toward the end, but they started as a high-blooded lot. I don't know what happened to them. I think they began to believe all the things folks had said about how wise they were, and how advanced their thinking was. That always seems to bring about a fall as quickly as walking a log with moss on its back."

"There doesn't seem to be anything left about to show for all their wisdom and hard work," persisted Judge.

"Come on, then," said Chellin, turning his horse aside and striking out for the small lake, which was not a great distance from the roadway.

The younger man followed his leader until they were at the edge of the lake, where something caught Chellin's eye, and he dismounted hurriedly and knelt down in the churned mire of the lakeshore.

"What is it, Chellin? What have you found?"

"Trouble, by the looks of it," growled the older man. "Trouble plagues this poor, ghost-ridden hole, it seems, and nothing has happened to change that even after all these years."

Judge dismounted and knelt in the mire next to his commander.

"What signs do you read in this muck, Chellin? I can see nothing but the mud we've churned up here with our horses."

"You've always been blind as a bat to the obvious, you thick-headed whelp. May the High King have mercy on our poor lost souls if we ever come to depend on your quickness to detect an enemy among us, or to seek a friend's advice. Look!" Chellin held up a small clump of what appeared to be water reeds woven together. "This is the work of some lads I haven't heard tell of in a season or two. I would have thought they would have been long gone."

"That?" asked Judge. "That's only some reeds!"

"Look, dunderhead! See the woven work here, and here? The fellows who did this were here not so long ago, and were disturbed before they finished."

Chellin stooped and began searching all about the area, pulling aside rush and water lily, and ploughing the wet earth with his ungloved hand.

"Finished what?"

"That's what I intend to find out, my buck. Come along here and help! No, better yet, you mount up and go fetch Hamlin. I don't want you tromping around here with those clumsy feet of yours."

Judge withdrew in hurt silence.

Chellin scooped up handfuls of mud and water, sifting it carefully through his hand, and knelt for a long time beside a large lily pad that caught and held his interest. When Judge returned with Hamlin, Chellin had shed his cloak and mail shirt, and stripped to the waist, he waded into the lake to a distance where the water was almost over his shoulders.

"Have you lost your senses, Chellin?" shouted Hamlin, raising himself in his saddle as he did so. "You can't swim!"

The older man made no reply, but went on a few paces farther, then suddenly disappeared beneath the placid surface of the lake.

"Quickly! Quickly, here, Judge, hold my horse! The old man has drowned himself!" Hamlin leaped from his mount and threw off his clothing as he went, already waist deep in water. "Fetch a rope if you can!" he shouted over his shoulder, laying forward and beginning a slow and methodic crawling stroke toward the spot where Chellin had disappeared.

He had gone no more than a few feet when Chellin's head broke the surface, and he began to struggle toward shore, pulling something along behind him.

"Chellin! Are you all right?"

"Here, lad, help me!"

Hamlin felt as though his limbs were moving in slow motion as he struggled to reach his leader, but he was at last beside him, reaching for the object that Chellin was pulling from the secret recesses of the small tarn.

The Edges of Trew

The settlement was small, nestled against the high banks of the creek that ran through the open eave of the wood and across the clearing, to disappear again in the deep gloom of the forest beyond. Looking for any sign of life here was confusing, for the dwellings were out of sight, almost half submerged by the water at floodtide in the spring. It was difficult to pick out the shelters from the water's edge, and the rider who reined in his mount to survey the scene did not immediately see the four figures standing beneath the shadow of the larger trees at the edge of the clearing.

"This is the heart of Trew, outsider! What want you here?"

The mounted man was startled badly at first, and had difficulty picking out who spoke to him.

"My name is Argent Largo. I am no enemy to any who dwell here."

"Trew has only enemies. It is spoken by the Lord Trew himself. We have no friends from beyond our hearthfires."

"May my horse drink from your stream? We have come a long way today."

"We deny water to no one, man or animal. Drink your fill, and then we shall hear what your tale is. If it suits, we shall see you to the Edges."

"The what?" asked the rider. He could make out nothing

but dark shapes on the border of the wood, and couldn't decide which of the men was speaking.

"The Edges! The ends of Trew."

"What is this riddle you speak of? I am a stranger to these parts."

"Trew! You are within the Edges of Trew! And you must be on your way quickly, if it is true what you have said about not knowing where you are. Strangers are dealt with harshly here."

"Argent Largo is no knave that you escort to your borders. I would speak to your king!"

"You cannot have audience with Lord Trew. He is beyond the world's end at the moment, and will not return for a time beyond count."

"Are you daft, man? What game do you play me? Speak plainly, so that I may understand you!"

"I speak as plainly as the smallest child, stranger. You cannot have audience with Lord Trew."

"But you might speak with the Lady, if you wish it," added a second voice, softer and less strident.

"The Lady of Trew sometimes holds converse with outlanders. You might speak with her if you'll follow us to her court."

"Then by all means, let us go to seek this Lady," insisted the man. "I would make more of this puzzle than your confused tongues tell me."

"This is Trew, sir. The Lord is away and shall count the nine north stars and seek the wilds of black meadows at the back of the moon, but he won't talk of it to strangers."

"That he won't," concluded the softer voice, "but his wife speaks in plainer speech than most, and she might tell you of where you travel, and why the road has been so harsh to your fortunes."

"Harsh enough, my simple friend. There are things I have endured that would turn your blood to ice. I am seeking to find a way to avenge myself on those who have wronged me."

"The Wastelands will take the bitterness from your heart, stranger. Stay but a time, and you'll find that the cruelest cut of all will be but a small pain. The Lady of Trew can help you forget your worst fears, and bring you peace."

"I have no need of such medicine, yet I might have news of such neighbors as you have hereabouts, or enlist your arms to my cause, which is just, and cries out for vengeance."

"There are no arms borne in Trew, my good cousin. They were outlawed long ago, before the Lord left. He hated the thought of senseless killing and war."

The man had fallen in beside the four strange humans, and rode slowly by their side while they talked. Each of the four wore long hoods that covered their features, and had silver belts that circled their waists in a series of links, each finely carved and wound together in an intricate fashion. The cloaks were a dark greenish black, and smelled slightly of flowers.

"How long shall we be in reaching this Lady you speak of?" asked the man, reining in his mount.

"Not long, by our reckoning. A year perhaps, or three," replied the first figure, who seemed to be the spokesman for the group.

"A year! You jest, surely?" snapped the man. "There is no trip so far as to take that long."

"Not if we travel but to a place on this plane, brother. Our journey is of a different nature. The realms we seek are far beyond the reach of your noble animal there, or the stretch of mind that believes we live in a box of time."

"I begin to think I have fallen in with fools," said the man, pulling up suddenly and dismounting.

"Show yourselves to me at once! What sort of oaf do you take me for that you should speak in such witless banter as this?"

"We shall show ourselves to you soon enough, wise one. It is against the Code to remove our cloaks while we yet stand in the open fields of these lower planes."

"Do you expect me to believe any of this? I begin to doubt that there is a Lord or Lady at all. Farewell, poor fools. I shall find my own way back from here."

"Oh, you can't find your way back to where we were, good

soldier. There was no way to warn you that you had crossed the Edges of Trew. Once here, you shall have to join us, I fear, until we can guide you back to the outside. And even then, there may be no way back for you now."

"Unless the Lady wills it," added the second, softer voice, which the stranger now recognized as that of a woman.

"You'll carry this jest too far, I warn you. All I ask is the way to Darien Mounds. I seek one there who has been pledged to help me."

A soft laugh filled the air.

"You wish to find your road to the place of all places that we despise the most, oh traveler. Those are parts that are loathed above all others in Trew."

"Why, good lady?" asked the stranger. "I have never heard ill spoken of the place."

"It may be true that you have never heard ill spoken of those death mounds, but I tell you for truth that the place is a bane to all things living. No one ever returns from there, and there are new and terrible tales we have heard about that ghastly place. Be wise, and stay here with us, pilgrim. We shall make you one of us, who shall one day join our Lord on his journey to the forgotten backyards of the stars. It is safe there."

"I'm sure it is, my good lady, but I have other pressing business that I must attend to before I depart this world."

The stanger turned his horse so suddenly that he almost trampled the two closest to him, and without a word of farewell, spurred his mount into a gallop.

"Come back! Stop! You are going the wrong way!" cried the four cloaked forms, waving their arms and shouting in a vain attempt to call the man back.

"Come back, indeed," snorted the rider to himself. "I'm lucky to have escaped those fools, if fools they are. I have no time to be wandering about with dolts such as those. I am lucky to be rid of them."

He rode faster as he spoke, needing to confirm his own wits, and to help him calm his spirit after the strange encounter.

Dealing with the four had disturbed him greatly, and he

was reminded of his own narrow escape from the hands of the band who had held him captive after he survived the terrible time of the Purge, when the dragons of doom were abroad.

"It has not been easy," he went on aloud, addressing only his horse. "They thought they had turned me around, but I showed them, just like I shall show that blasted, accursed sister of mine. She shall not escape, or elude me much longer. And that miserable husband of hers shall wish he had never seen the day that he met one so marked for misery."

He laughed aloud, a harsh, cruel laugh that held no humor, and he urged his horse on to an even greater pace.

"Argent Largo has been born again, and he shall find all those who betrayed him, and the day will come when his banner shall fly over the finest of all settlements on the Roaring Sea, and all will come to him to pay him their respects and vow him service."

He laughed again, and spurred his horse unmercifully, his riding cloak flying out behind him as he plunged headlong down the faint path through the trees. Faster and faster he sped, until at last he had ridden away the horrible burden that burned his heart and caused his teeth to gnash in mad fury.

As he slowed to a walk he noticed his surroundings again, and pulled his mount up short in front of an odd-shaped structure, which looked almost as though it had been fashioned by one of the woodland animals, except for the entrance, which was tall and framed by a door that was obviously man-made.

"Holla," cried Largo. "Is there anyone abroad? I need water for my horse, and food for the stomach of a hungry traveler."

There was no immediate reply, so Largo dismounted to examine the crude structure.

There were windows of a rough sort, with broken glass and no curtains, but the stone chimney showed signs of a recent fire, for there was still a thin, almost invisible trail of smoke rising into the unmoving air.

A strange sensation crept over Largo, and he felt his hackles crawl, as though he were being observed by unseen eyes.

He cautiously retraced his steps to his horse, and eased his longsword out of its sheath.

"That won't be necessary, my bold one," came a cackle. "You'd have a time using that thing on me."

Largo whirled, brandishing his weapon before him, but search as he might, he could see no living thing anywhere about.

"Heh-heh-heh," came the cackle again, maddeningly close to him, but still there was no one there to see. "I've come like a nighthawk to pluck out your eyes, oh mighty one, and serve up your gizzard in a stew."

Largo whirled about, slashing at the air viciously.

"See, my dears, he's no gentleman! Look at him there, swinging away as though he'd hack poor Letta's head off."

"Who are you? What do you want of me?" asked Largo, trying to locate the voice that spoke, in hopes of striking a blow by following the sound to its source.

"You are speaking to Letta, my poor dearie. No one much ever notices, because when I get through, they don't have that much interest, heh-heh. I've been low of gizzards and bonemeal for a time now, but I can say that that's all over now, thanks to you, my boldness."

The cackle came from a spot nearer to him, and Largo lunged suddenly, sweeping the blade in a large arc before him.

"You'll tire yourself out that way, my sauce. There's nothing of Letta that you can hurt with that pin. No, no, sweetness, it would take a deal more than that to harm Letta."

Largo flashed about wildly, left and right, dealing the air dreadful blows.

The cackling laughter grew in pitch until Largo's ears were ringing with the mockery of it.

"I shall call the Dark One down upon you for this," cried Largo desperately, stopping to catch his breath and look about him. "You shall pay dearly for interfering with her messenger."

"Dark One, my sassy? You don't know a Dark One until you've met Letta. She is the only power here that commands respect of all things furred or feathered or skinned."

A long cackle rent the air, then the invisible voice went on, but from a different location.

"You shall find my hospitality very warm, my pudding. I haven't had such a nice visitor for dinner in ever so long."

Another shriek of laughter set Largo at his futile attack again, slashing and swearing about in all directions.

"Here, here, that's enough of that, I think," came the voice. "I shall not have you working off an ounce of that lovely fat."

Largo found himself tangled in a web of sticky bonds that dropped over his head like a net, and struggle as he might to cut himself free, he was soon weighted down by an irresistible pressure that forced him relentlessly to the ground.

"Enough, whoever you are! I have power to bargain with you. You'll be making a terrible mistake if you kill me before I can tell you who I am."

"A dreadful mistake, my pumpkin? What a shame it would be if I can't roast you after all. I don't think I shall listen to you, my plumpness, because I might find some nasty fact or other that would make me spare you! Then where would I be?"

"Wiser, madam, much wiser. I assure you I can make it worth your while to hear me out!"

Largo kept his voice under control with an effort, although his heart was hammering wildly beneath his tunic.

He tried to reach into his cloak to grasp the necklace he wore, made of the scale of one of the great flying snakes that had carried him across the borders of death and back again, but his arm was wedged so closely to his body that he couldn't move it enough to grasp what he sought. He knew it was his only hope now, and the thought of being done out of his revenge on all those he hated gave him a strength not his own, and he strained and struggled to take hold of the object at his neck.

"I shall give you a surprise if you release me, madam. A special gift that not many in the world can claim. Or permit me to see your beauty, so that I may at least know the face of Letta."

"Letta has many faces, my dumpling, but none I think would please you. I have ruled these tombs at Darien Mounds since the end of the War of the Flying Death. They left me all I could wish here, but the crops of humans that I fancy so have started to wither away now. You're the first bit of tender meat that I've seen in a spell. I was beginning to think I might have to move to more hospitable surroundings."

"I know of places where you might have all the pleasure you could wish, Letta. Settlements full of fattened humans that would whet your appetite and keep you full for years."

Largo knew it was a desperate gamble, but the reference the unseen Letta made to the Flying Death could only mean she spoke of the great snakes, and might be persuaded to listen to him, if only he could get to the necklace he wore. The Dark One herself had bestowed it on him, in exchange for his promise to seek revenge on all those who had opposed her. She had returned him to life, and set him on the trail of a vengeance so sweet he hardly remembered the cost, or the deeper feelings he had once had.

"The Dark One would give you more powers than you have already, Letta, and help you to find a harvest that you could enjoy for a long, long time."

The laugh came again, but after a short pause, so Largo persisted.

"If you'll free me, Letta, I'll show you a sign that would prove to you that I speak the truth."

"What sign could you show Letta? You tempt me, my sumptious tart."

"Free me so that I can show you."

"I think I shall, but you won't see me, my crafty one. You just show me what you have."

As Letta's voice trailed away, Largo felt a slight release of the pressure of the unseen bonds that crushed him to the ground. As soon as he was able, he withdrew his hand from the sticky ropes and grasped the pendant securely.

"This is what I would show you, Letta," cried Largo, and he clutched the dragon scale and held it out before him, uttering the words that would call up the sleeping fire it held.

There was a hush, and then a faint sound was heard, much like the distant roar of a thuderstorm, and a hot blast of air spun round the hand that held the necklace.

"It is the dragon's hide, Letta! It can scorch your eyes out, even if I can't see to strike you myself. You should have listened to me at first. We could make powerful allies."

The scale of the dragon had begun to glow and emit harsh, screeching sounds, as though a huge iron grate had been moved across the face of heaven, and the heat began to be unbearable. There was a cloud over the sun, and a putrid aroma of burnt flesh filled the air, but still Largo held the pendant aloft before him.

"Stop your show, you bold thing. I recognize what you hold, curse the luck. I can't go about butchering those that are marked by *that* sign."

As she spoke, the one called Letta removed her spells and appeared before Largo, sitting beside her crude porch step at her shelter.

"Now you've spoiled my fun and my dinner! I hope you're happy."

The woman was slight of build, and wore a black cloak that covered her from head to foot, and although Largo could not see her face, he could feel her eyes peering out at him.

"We shall be good allies, you and I. I have so many good victims that I can hardly wait to introduce you. You won't regret this."

"I hope I shall not. I have a great hunger just now. I haven't fed for too long a time. My powers grow weaker, and I need food."

"Then we shall conduct our business quickly, and I can show you a morsel to whet your appetite, and they are not far from here."

Letta's body shivered with eagerness.

"I won't eat the flesh of your animal. It must be pure!"

"Look! See, Letta, I have brought them here for you!"

Largo pointed back down the path toward the four cloaked figures he had seen out of the corner of his eye, and who were hurrying along toward them, motioning with wild gestures and calling out something that he could not make out.

Largo was shoved backward by a violent explosion of a dirty yellow flame, and his flesh stung with a terrible wind that blinded him momentarily.

"You bungling, wretched fool! You have set them on us all. You don't know what harm you've done! Flee! Run for your life!"

The voice trailed off to a long wail, then was gone.

Largo recovered himself quickly, and put away the pendant beneath his cloak.

"You were warned, friend! We tried to catch you to keep you from this. These woods are full of those beasts. They are the last of the Rogens, the eaters of flesh."

"Why did you run away from us, pilgrim? We only tried to help," said the woman, who pulled back the cowl of her cape, revealing to Largo a beautiful, dark-haired woman of slender build.

"Why didn't you speak to me of the truth," returned Largo, "instead of telling me tales of lords who travel to the stars, and all the other nonsense you told me?"

"It was not nonsense, and we would have told you everything if you had been a bit more long-handed on patience."

"We shall have to do the rituals to return the Rogen to her mound, Elita. We have no choice now."

"Yes, Cham. You and Shal do what you must. I will take our visitor to see our Lady. He has much to explain of himself."

Largo bowed low to the beautiful stranger, and tried to conceal the confusion and bitterness he felt at being caught up again by the mysterious beings. They somehow made him feel more ill at ease than had Letta, the Rogen, whoever or whatever the Rogen were.

And it angered him to think he had been robbed of a vessel of vengeance that he might have used against his sworn enemies.

Largo smiled and bowed again, presenting his best innocent face, and kissing the hand of the one they called Elita.

The Arrival of a Minstrel

A soft harp played a haunting refrain that lingered in the night for a long time after the musician had laid his instrument aside, and the silence that followed was deeper and more profound because of the sweetness of the memory of the song.

Owen roused himself at last, and looked across the fire at the man who had played, now silent and watching the merry blaze before them. He was dressed in the clothes all musicians wore, a red tunic and green vest, with striped blue and gold trousers and red knee boots.

"How did you learn to play so well, my friend?" asked Kegin, coming out of the trancelike dream he had fallen into as he listened to the man's deft skills on his instrument.

"You could learn as well, if you wished," returned the man, pouring himself another mug of the strong tea that brewed on the firedog.

"Not that well," laughed Kegin. "That tune reminds me of something, but I can't quite lay my hand to it."

"Me, too," added Owen. "My mother used to sing a song to me when I was small that sounded something like it. She always said it was something taught to her when she was in the Middle Islands."

A memory had jogged itself in Owen's mind as he spoke, of a certain evening somewhere lost back in the dimness of his childhood. It was an evening similar to the one that had fallen about him where he sat with Kegin and Darek, and the others of the settlement who had stayed behind to await the return of Famhart.

"It might well have been played there, young man, for it comes from a line of folk who were there at that battle."

"Who were they?" asked Darek.

"The dreamers," replied the man, a minstrel known only as Emerald.

"The dreamers?" repeated Owen.

"The ones who came from the morning, and who have all gone back to the sunset," the man went on. He picked up his harp again and began another haunting melody that brought tears to Owen's eyes.

"Stop, friend," protested Kegin. "You break my heart with your songs."

The man played on, seemingly not to hear the interruption, and soon accompanied his instrument with his voice:

> "Down six long rivers and six long hills
> I've searched for my lost bride of nights gone by,
> But she's gone forever to the Hills of Trew,
> And never will be at my side,
> No, she shall never be at my side."

"Are those the Hills of Trew that we know?" asked Owen, when the man had finished his song and fallen silent.

"The same, young friend. That was a song given to me by a traveler once, when we were holed up to wait out a winter in the Mountains of Skye."

"Great Havens of Weir, you mean you've been in those parts, friend?" asked Kegin, wide-eyed.

"More than once," returned Emerald. "When you travel as I do, no one pays you much mind. I've run onto some nasty customers from time to time, but it's known to be the worst of luck to bother anyone in my line. We seem to be protected that way."

"How long have you been doing this?" asked Darek. "Is it something you learned, like I will learn my craft of arms?"

"Exactly," replied Emerald. "There were sixteen brothers in my family, and I was the youngest. By the time I came of age to apprentice to a craft, there was no place in my village that had a need of me, so I was sent away with an old man who came one winter to see if he could stop the calves in our herds from dying. They mostly all lived, and as a gift to the man, my father gave him my service until I should come of age."

"How could your father do that?" asked Owen. "He had no way of knowing whether the man was honest or not!"

"Oh, you would have known if you'd ever met him. There was no way to think my master was anything other than honest." Emerald laughed. "No, you wouldn't think it, if ever you spent more than a passing moment in his presence."

"What name did he go by?" asked Kegin. "Perhaps we have heard of him. Sometimes minstrels come through to entertain us, and spin us yarns of faraway places."

"I doubt my master ever reached these parts, kind sir, but he went in those days by the name of Gillerman."

The minstrel watched their faces closely, although nothing could be read in his eyes. Owen bolted up from where he sat. "Gillerman and Wallach! They have horses that talk and they were here! My father wouldn't listen when I told him they would help us, but we would have to go to the South Channels to find them."

"Whoa, whoa," said Kegin. "Slow down, old fellow. One thing at a time. Now what's this about Gillerman and Wallach?"

"You amaze me to say that my master has been here," said Emerald. "I have not heard word of him for more seasons than I care to count."

"He and his friend Wallach reached us the very night that Sweet Rock was attacked. The men there put them in the root cellar because they thought they were with the raiders," said Owen. "Bristlebeard said they were enemies."

"Bristlebeard tends to be on the thick-headed side, but I don't think he's bad at heart," offered Kegin. "I've known him for a long time, and he's always been true to our lot, and a good soldier."

"When did you say you saw my master?" asked Emerald, his excitement showing in his eyes. "If it was not too long past, I might be able to catch him somewhere along my road."

He clasped his instrument and struck a chord on it.

"That would be a fine thing, indeed! It would make my heart as light as a sparrow."

Emerald lapsed into another song, and the tune gladdened all who heard, and Owen even hoped that his mother, although she showed no signs of being aware of her surroundings, could hear and feel the special music of this minstrel.

"When was it, Owen, that your two friends escaped?" asked Kegin. "I was on a scouting party, and only heard about these two mystical blokes when I got back."

"It couldn't be more than a few days past," answered the lad. "Everything has gone so fast, I can hardly place events. It seems a long time by one account, and hardly any time at all on the other. And with my mother like she is, and my father gone, and the settlement ruined, I can hardly keep track of my thoughts."

Kegin patted the lad gently on the shoulder. "I know, old fellow. Times like these are always rough to handle."

"Can you remember if he did or said anything that struck you as unusual?" asked Emerald, leaning closer to Owen. "Was he acting in any way upset, or like he carried a great load about?"

Owen shook his head, trying to think of anything that was unusual about the two men, Wallach and Gillerman. "I was so taken with them, I hardly know how they acted, or really anything they said. And then when I went outside and heard their horses, that was the best thing of all."

Owen stoked the fire and put on another small log, trying to recall something that Gillerman had said in the strange dream, when they had given him the longsword.

"I wonder," said Emerald, jumping lightly to his feet and

pacing about. "If this has begun to happen so suddenly, then there must be more afoot than I was led to believe."

"What suspicions have you minstrel?" asked Kegin. "In your travels, have you seen something which would help us piece this puzzle together? First there were the raiders, then Linne, the wife of our elder, was struck down by a sinister blow that's left her in a death trance. What news have you that would help us?"

"No news, good sir, that would return the fair lady to herself. That is the realm of my master. I have seen cases such as hers before, but it was Gillerman who tended to them. He knows the magic from the Country of the Three Trees, and has healed many who were given up for dead."

"See, Kegin? I told you I heard Gillerman! He spoke to me through the sword! That's what he said, to go to the South Channels, for a leaf from the Three Trees."

Kegin shook his head and raised a hand to motion Owen to slow down. "What are these riddles? What means the Three Trees? And who spoke to you through your sword? What nonsense is that? Steel can't speak!"

"Gillerman," returned the youth. "You are as bad as Bristlebeard. This longsword that he gave me does something when he tries to speak to me. It goes all full of light, and starts to hum."

Kegin raised his eyebrows skeptically. "Light? What sort of light?"

"Like a molten fire that's blue and white and gold?" asked Emerald.

"Yes! Have you seen it?" shot Owen.

"I've seen master use that sword, or one like it. The light ran down the blade to his arm until his whole body was surrounded with the light, and you couldn't keep your eyes on him anymore."

"That's it," cried Owen, relieved that someone else had seen and believed.

"But what are the Three Trees, and what have they to do with the South Channels?" asked Kegin, looking in confusion from Emerald to Owen.

"Stearborn gave me a knife which can cut a leaf from one

of them," put in Darek. "That was what we used to cut the poisoned brooch away from Linne's cloak."

The lad took out his prize and held it out before him as he spoke. "Stearborn said that this was one of the few blades there are that can take a leaf from the Three Trees."

Emerald looked closely at the youth and the small, finely crafted object he held. "I have seen that somewhere," he said slowly, scratching his head in an effort to remember something that eluded him.

"Stearborn gave it to me," repeated Darek.

"Yes, whoever he may be. Yet I've seen that knife in the hands of someone else. It was a long time ago."

"You can ask Stearborn if you like, friend. I can send for him. I'm sure he can tell you how he came by it."

Kegin rose from the fire and called out to a sentry, who quickly came and hurried away to do as he was bidden.

"So the Three Trees actually exist?" asked Kegin, returning to his place and pouring himself another mug of tea. He slowly stirred in a spoon of honey and put the bowl back on the small camp table.

"Exist? I don't know if they exist or not, at least as we think of things," said Emerald, "but my master spoke of them just as though they were as real as the honey you just put in your tea."

"Truly, Emerald? And do you believe in them?"

"I do," said Owen firmly. "Gillerman said that we needed a leaf to help my mother, and if there is a tree somewhere that has the powers to help my mother, I shall find it."

"But there is no help at all in knowing of the Three Trees, but not knowing which road to travel to get there," cautioned Kegin. "That's why Famhart has taken the road he's taken."

Owen looked steadily at his father's trusted friend.

"We could find Gillerman and Wallach in the South Channels. They know the way to where we need to go. And if we left soon, we could quite possibly be gone and back by the time my father returns, Kegin. They gave me a chart that I'd forgotten. Here!"

Owen unslung the gray bag that he wore, and hastily searched for the map the ancient man had shown him.

They spread the small chart out in front of the fire, and Kegin held a rushlamp over it so they could make out the strange markings.

"What do you make of it, Emerald?" asked Kegin. "Does any of it look familiar to you?"

The minstrel frowned as he studied the map, but shook his head.

"I don't recognize any of the markings. But here, this may be the Silver River, and there must be the Edges. That's Silver Mist Pass, I'd wager."

Emerald put a finger on the map, pointing out what he spoke of. "And these must be the South Channel Mountains."

"But it shows more, further beyond the South Channels," said Kegin. "None of our charts went any further than the Bitter Roots."

"Maybe that's the country of the Three Trees," said Darek, peering over Owen's shoulder.

"And there's another sea there," added Owen. "Look!"

"What does it say?" asked Kegin.

"The Sea of Islands," replied Emerald.

"I never heard of any but the Roaring," said Kegin.

"Neither have I, but that doesn't mean it doesn't exist," said Emerald.

Kegin laughed, and stirred up the fire. "You would enjoy seeing me explaining to Famhart what we were doing leaving against orders, eh? If you have ever tried that, you'll know why we shall do no such thing, and that we'll wait right here until we have word to do something different, even if we have a map."

The tone of voice which Kegin used reminded Owen of his father, and it seemed to draw down the curtain on any further hope of convincing him.

"I'm interested in these trees you speak of, good minstrel, especially if they were of any use to help Linne, but I don't lay any of my gold on their existence, even with this chart, which says nothing for certain. If they exist, why haven't others found them?"

"They have," replied Emerald. "They are sung about in a dozen old songs, and written of in the stories we hear around the campfire."

"Maybe I've been at the wrong fires," laughed Kegin. "I don't recall any such stories."

"You are too much the bread-and-butter man, then," replied Emerald.

"Perhaps that is so. Perhaps I have never allowed myself the luxury of daydreaming."

"I believe the stories," interrupted Owen. "I never thought anything of them before, but now I remember my mother once telling me about someone she met a long time ago. He was a tree!"

"That's nothing but a tale to put you to sleep with, Owen. You and I know that trees can't talk, or move, or do anything except grow leaves and be whatever it is that trees are."

"She wasn't talking about a tree, exactly," explained Emerald. "I don't really know what the word is. They are beings, but not human or animal, or plant, or anything else. They can change their shapes, according to the tales I've heard, and have powers that are far beyond anything anyone can tell of."

"I like your company, minstrel, and I think you are amusing. That's what these tales are for, to distract and entertain the poor folk who labor at ordinary lives day in and day out. That's why there are minstrels. I would be highly disappointed if you were any other way."

"Oh, Kegin, you sound like Bristlebeard! That's what he said to Gillerman and Wallach when they were at the meeting hall. He wouldn't believe their horses talked. He's too thick to think things might be any other way than what he's used to." Owen's anger was barely concealed as he spoke, and he could feel his cheeks burning. He folded the small chart and returned it to the gray bag Gillerman had given him.

"You need not rile yourself, good lad," soothed Emerald.

"I am a minstrel, and see this often. I am a singer of songs, and a spinner of yarns, that's true. My lessons have been in other areas of life, and I know not much of how people get on day by day, with their drab lives tied about their necks like stones dragging them down to despair. I like to think that there is more to it all than that. My lot isn't what you think of as highly regarded, but I don't spend my life looking for a reason to go on getting up in the morning."

"I meant no offense, minstrel! I am not a man who doesn't like to think that perhaps there is more to all of this than meets the eye, it's just that I've lived long enough to see how matters are. The gray light of reason comes up with the dawn every day, and I rise early enough to see it and know it's true."

"There are things far beyond your logic or reason, good citizen. Most of our lives are lived in the dark of disbelief! We don't know how to see the truth sometimes!"

Emerald paced restlessly as he spoke, the firelight glistening in bright patterns off his shiny costume.

"Come, sing us another song, like a good fellow! Have an ale and don't let us quarrel. We have the need of all the cheer we can gather to ourselves in these troubled times."

The minstrel gave no answer, but took his harp into his lap and began to play. It was a plaintive melody, full of sad endings and soft partings, but as it went on, there was a note of hope that entered, and as the musician finished the piece, the hearts of all who had heard were stirred and strengthened.

"What was that?" asked Owen. "It seems so familiar."

"It was from the court songs of the Keepers, when they yet dwelled below the Boundaries," answered Emerald. "My master taught me all their songs."

"Who were they?" asked Darek. "Were they kings?"

"Not kings, my lad, but masters. They came to help us all in a time of need."

"My mother and father were there with them at the Middle Islands," said Owen proudly. "They were friends of Borim Bruinthor and Olthar Olthlinden, and the dwarf Brandigore."

Emerald held out a thin reed pipe to Owen. "This once belonged to Olthar. It is one of his own pipes. Listen."

He placed it to his lips and blew a slow air that sounded at first like a summer wind through willows at the water's edge, then like bubbles bursting above a lily pond.

"If you have all these ways of traveling about good minstrel, perhaps I should commission you to do us the service of becoming a scout. We need all the information we can get from all the other settlements. You said yourself you seem to be able to travel without great fear from anyone."

"Anyone except this new breed that has begun to flow into our world. Things seem to be changing. I'm not sure my status as minstrel holds any water with them. Those lads in the South Channels seem to have broken with all the old ways."

"You need have nothing to do with them, except tell us about where you spot them. The rest is up to our stewards to make sure the woods and rivers remain free of the invaders."

"It is not so simple as you think, citizen. I can tell you that you aren't safe as you may imagine. I saw things that have given me pause for thought. I haven't feared to travel anywhere on the Line since I began my work, but these past days have seen a marked change for the worst."

"Tell us, Emerald, where you saw these things! We'll send a party to rid the woods of anyone who is an enemy of the folk of the Line."

"Raiders aren't the worst, citizen. I have come through settlements where the talk has been more frightening than meeting unfriendly troops in the wildest part of the woods."

"What do you speak of, friend?" asked Kegin. "Even for a minstrel, you begin to sound more and more like a mystic, or a fool."

"I play all parts equally well," replied Emerald. "That is all part of my office. It is the only way I can speak out on matters that weigh perhaps too heavily with some."

"What is it you spoke of? Come, old fellow, you have no need to mince words here."

"I know I don't. I speak only as a friend when I say those

things. There are not many who are prepared to hear me. I knew when I came upon the first of the signs that they are holding the Feast of the Red Bear that I had reached a time when I had better find myself a place to go, or a settlement to be with. The signs are all there."

"The Feast of the Red Bear! So other settlements have held it, too? We were not the only ones?"

"Once that feast has been held, there will be no more peace in our lifetimes, citizen, or even in the lifetimes of these young ones here."

Owen looked from one to the other, waiting for something further. "They have held the feast here," he said slowly. "We weren't allowed to go."

Darek nodded agreement. "Famhart said it was no place for us."

"There are strange stories that have been riding the skirts of that tale," said the minstrel. "From one end of the Line to the other, and from further north as well, I've heard it said that the feast is the omen that marks the onset of the troubles."

"Where have you heard these tales, minstrel? Who are your sources?" asked Kegin, feeling uneasy, even though he was reluctant to take Emerald seriously.

"From the South Channels, and from the Moon Children of Trew, and others."

"The Moon Children of Trew! Surely you place no substance to anything they might have told you?"

"I hear everything, from all sources. Some I believe, some I don't, it depends. When there is a spark of truth, Emerald listens."

The minstrel looked evenly at Kegin before going on, then pointed to the tent where Linne lay.

"I know where the blow came from that struck your elder's wife! It came from Trew, by one there who goes by the name of Argent Largo."

Kegin had risen in a rush, and was prepared to fall on the musician, but Owen was between them in a flash and held his father's friend back.

"If you know this, then you must be in league with that devil," said Kegin through clenched teeth.

"Not in league, citizen, nor anything else. And this young lad here is right about what it will take to save his mother! I heard as much from the Lady of Trew."

"How come you to move so freely there? No one comes or goes there anymore! The Rogen have come back, and the borders have been closed to travelers for more than a half dozen turnings."

"Emerald goes many places where others can't. And he is here to tell you that you're in grave danger if you remain where you are. The one who calls himself Argent Largo is gathering a following to capture your lady, even as we speak."

"Great Havens of Weir, why didn't you say so, man?" blurted Kegin, tugging at a signal horn that was tangled in his cloak.

"There's no need for that, my good citizen. There is time. I've come to warn you in plenty of time to take action."

"Shall we go toward the South Channels, Emerald? Will we try for the leaf of the Three Trees, and to try to find Gillerman and Wallach there?"

"We shall indeed, my lad! I was to hold my tongue until I found a sign, and when I saw the longsword, I knew I was home. That was the very weapon that my master wore for all the time we were together. I know we can find our way back to him now."

"Hold up, friend! No one said anything about galavanting off toward those pestholes of mountains. There's only one way to reach the South Channels, and that runs through Trew, and across the Edges. There's no one in his right mind would try that now, and no way to say for sure one could get over the Silver Mist Pass, even if they succeeded that far."

"I've done it," replied Emerald calmly. "It can be done. And it's the only way you will ever reach the country of the Three Trees."

Kegin was opening his mouth to protest, when the sword at Owen's side began to glow a brilliant blue-white, and a faint, faraway sound of the sea began to grow in the clearing about the fire, which shot great flames upward into the night in all directions, bringing the camp out into a state of general alarm, and causing a frantic call to arms.

Soon the darkness was ablaze with the watchfires all along the Line River, and a council of war was begun in earnest, led by Kegin and Emerald the minstrel, and the two young friends, Owen and the orphan Darek.

Chellin Duchin

It took all their strength to get the water-logged basket ashore and to dry land where they could study it more closely. Chellin and Judge sat exhausted by the lakeside, breathing in great gulps of air, and coughing up water they had swallowed.

"I thought you'd lost the last of your wit there," gasped Judge. "I know you never learned to swim from all the teasing the other stewards rag you with."

"No need to try to do something a fish likes," growled Chellin, between a coughing bout. "A waste of good time well spent elsewhere."

"A fine thing that would have been to carve on your funeral stone," chided Judge. "Here is Chellin Duchin, too stiff-necked to learn to swim. Drowned."

"It would have given a great deal of pleasure to more than a few I could name," said Chellin, standing up and gathering his discarded mail and cloak.

"There won't be any such luck for the raiders this day, Chellin. But what is this that has almost drowned us both to drag it off this lake bottom? I don't think I've ever seen anything quite like it."

"I was trying to show you some of the craftwork that went

into this earlier, Judge. You said it looked like a knot of vines."

"It still does. Were there lake people who used to use this way of cording reeds together?"

"After a way of thinking, my dull dog. But you are looking at something that goes back even further than the dwellers here before. You are looking at the burial shroud of an ancient race, and this one in particular is one of high station, if I'm not mistaken."

The two were joined by the others as they spoke, and soon were surrounded at the lakeshore by their party.

"What is it?" asked Hamlin, leaning closer to the reed basket.

"Chellin says it's a funeral basket," replied Judge, "for one of an ancient race."

"What ancient race are you speaking of?" asked Jeremy.

"The dreamers," replied Chellin. "The elves."

"Elves!" echoed Hamlin and Jeremy together.

"The same. Have your ears gone so bad you can't trust them?" grumbled Chellin, carefully pulling away the outer layer of thatched reeds to reach the watertight compartment which lay beneath the rough outer surface.

"How did you ever spot this, Chellin? It looks just like the rest of the reed banks here."

"The story is all in the mud along the shore here. It didn't take too much to piece together what had happened." Chellin looked up from the burial cask and studied the distant sky. "There was a small party here who came ashore from the lake, and were surprised by someone ashore. That much I can make out. What puzzles me now is what happened to this fellows' friends, and how they escaped."

"What are you talking about? How did who escape?"

"The others from the lake, Jeremy. There were five or six of them. I can't imagine what errand they had been on to be in these parts, or how they came to be set upon. These lads aren't the easiest to come on by surprise, and I don't think those louts from the South Channels are so good that they would be capable of doing it."

"They evidently found a way to do it, Chellin. Here's the proof."

The gruff face of the commander softened when he pulled back the scented cloth that covered the elf's features.

"He was of high rank, by the look of it," said Jeremy. "And see how young he was."

"Don't let their looks deceive you, lad. This poor fellow is older by a score of years than all of us here put together. There's something in the makeup of these folk that keeps them looking like youngsters even after they've lived a hundred turnings or so."

"But how could that be? No one could live so long and not show it," argued Hamlin.

"These are questions you shall have to ask someone who knows, my buck. I have an idea that we may be stumbling into some of the chaps returning to retrieve their friend."

"Why would they do that?" asked Judge. "They've done the best for him they could."

"I'm surprised to find they left him behind at all. It's not their way. They must have been hard pressed to have gone without him."

"They stayed long enough to bury him. It must have taken some time to weave that casket!"

"They're handy at that, Hamlin. And I wonder at this! Look!" Chellin had been examining the inside of the burial robe as he talked, and had withdrawn a small packet that had been concealed inside the elf's shirt.

"Can you make any of that out?" asked Judge, peering intently over Hamlin's shoulder, trying to read the strange markings. "And what kind of marking paper is that? I've never seen the likes of it."

"Sometimes they would use this for building settlements, Judge. It's paper, but it folds like cloth, and is as hard as a plank. It can't be soaked or burned, and I've heard tales of some of the waterfolk who built boats out of it."

"Can you read what it says?"

Chellin held up the packet to try to study it by the fading afternoon light. "We'll look into it tonight when we have more time. Now let's get this poor fellow hidden again. I don't like the feel of being out here in the open like this."

"Is there anything else in there? Shouldn't we check?"

"There's nothing else, Hamlin. I feel like a bandit taking this packet, but it may tell us something of who this chap was, and where he came from, and perhaps what happened to him and his mates. We need to know all we can now. We're dealing with a dangerous enemy here. They've grown bolder and stronger, and we don't seem to have any real clue as to where they've come from, or who is behind them."

"The South Channels," said Judge. "That's where the raiders have always come from."

"Aye, the South Channels," snorted Chellin. "A good whipping post to lay the blame on. The rebels and outcasts have always lived there because of the wilderness of the mountains, but there were old families there once, and grand clans that were powerful and respected."

"You must jest, Chellin! There has never been a decent soul come out of the South Channels!"

Chellin Duchin looked away from Jeremy and studied the sky. "You are a very young man, my buck, and haven't had much in the way of education, what with always being away at duty as a steward of the Line. I am as much to blame as anyone, I suppose. There were always times that I intended to set aside so that you and Hamlin and Judge could get a proper education, and learn your books as well as you had learned to look to your longswords, and be like the rest of the lads in the other settlements. That was always my idea, and I guess I kept it until one day I looked about me, and you and the rest of the mongrels were grown. I don't know when it happened, but it did. And now I suffer for it, to hear you make statements like 'there was never a decent soul from the South Channels.' I can understand your ignorance, and forgive you for it, but I won't tolerate it to go on any further. I shall have to make sure I keep my promise to have the books taught to you the first time we cross the track of one of the loremasters."

Jeremy and Hamlin squirmed and groaned aloud.

"You've threatened us with that fate for as long as we've

been with you. It begins to lose its sting, Chellin. I don't think there are any of the old loremasters left."

"We shall find one, if I have to search him out of the Rogen Woods. It won't do for grown men of the Line to be so misinformed as to their proper history. Some of your own ancestors came from lines that go all the way back to their birthplaces in the South Channels."

"I never heard that," said Hamlin, whistling his unbelief.

"You will hear it from those who know. When we reach camp tonight, we will speak to Port and Starboard. Their mother was of the clans of Trew, and was said to know many things. There were tales spread once that she could see the future with a cup of leaves."

"You know the clans of Trew are all mad! What nonsense, Chellin! No one can do those things."

"Remember this, Judge, that you were one who would not believe me if I told you of an elf, if you hadn't laid eyes on him yourself."

The young man nodded slowly. "That's true enough, Chellin. I would never have given much weight to a story of that clan, if clan they are. They have always been spoken of in the same way as all the other stories we tell about the fire to entertain our young ones."

"That's why I should have kept my promise to have you all taught the books. It isn't right to be brought up without the right ways of looking at what goes on around us. It can be a sad thing to have no sense of belonging, or understanding of how it all fits together."

"You sound like my old father, Chellin. He was forever threatening me with doom and destruction if I didn't see to my education and give up all my daft ideas of joining the stewards of the Line."

"Your sire was right in his concern, Hamlin. Look at you now! You sit at the very funeral cask of one of the forgotten clans, a race so old that there are no stories that were ever told when there were none of them around, and if it weren't for that race, you'd have no idea of what it means, or what it holds for our future travels."

"It spells trouble, however you look at it," snapped Jeremy. "Whoever attacked the elves can't be far removed from here, and now we have an added mystery in finding out how the assailants, whoever or whatever they were, could stage an assault on someone you say are good soldiers."

"More than soldiers, Jeremy. They are masters at silence, and getting about unnoticed. They are clever with cloth and thread, and have secrets that we could never dream of. Some speak of the dreamers as being able to become invisible, and their weapons are among the very best that have ever been cast or forged or hewn."

"None of that helped this poor fellow," said Hamlin. "And I don't see any fancy arms here."

"No," agreed Chellin. "And that struck me as passing odd. I begin to think that maybe he wasn't armed at all, which is even stranger."

"Who would travel in these times without arms?" asked Judge. "Surely no one who was familiar with the countryside would be so careless as to try to journey outside his own yard without proper weapons."

Chellin had fallen silent and withdrawn, and stood lost in thought, idly handling the small packet he had taken from the elf's burial casket.

Hamlin and Judge looked at each other with puzzled glances, but their commander paid no attention to them, and squatted down and laid out the contents of the packet on the soft ground.

"I can't make this out, blast it to blazes. It looks like a date, but it can't be right."

"What are you talking of, Chellin? What date?"

"The date of death! See there, at the edge! The rest of the writing looks to be names. Probably his sire and dame, and a whole family log. Sometimes they put the marriages and births in as well." Chellin paused, holding the document he was studying up to the light. "There's no mistake here. The date of death is over a hundred years ago! It's beyond me."

"How could that be?" asked Jeremy. "They only just buried him recently!"

"It escapes me," confessed Chellin. "I thought I had read the scene in the mud right, but maybe I'm losing my touch."

He shook his head wearily. "The signs were all there for a fight at the water's edge, and then when I saw the cask, I thought I understood how it was."

"You read the cask right enough," said Hamlin. "How you saw it there I'll never know. And how did you learn all this other lore? I would never have thought of you as a book man, Chellin."

"You'll find I'm more things than meet the eye, my buck, even if I do misread signs once in a great while. You don't know half the things that lie up old Chellin Duchin's cloak-sleeve."

"I'm beginning to believe it," grumbled Judge. "I thought this was all to be a regular tour of duty with the Line Stewards, but I'm beginning to believe that it might all be better handled by a loremaster or juggler or one of the wandering actors who used to come in the old days."

"Aye, and you might be a deal more suited for that part, you worthless hound," scolded Chellin, but without anger. "All of you together astound me sometimes. It's more than old Chellin can bear! I just hope there will be some help for me tonight when we tie up with Gruenig and his crew."

"You wouldn't be happy if you couldn't complain of something, Chellin! I think your heart would break if you didn't have something to find us at fault for!"

"Right you are, Jeremy! My blood would grow thin and weak if I didn't have you onion-heads to amuse me with your antics. I can't think of a man in the stewards of the Line who has more to endure than does poor Chellin Duchin."

Chellin had risen and rolled the elfin packet up and put it safely inside his cloak. He studied the flat surface of the lake a moment, then turned his attention to where the woods began again, which was at some distance from where he stood. It was already dark under the eave of the forest, and a faint breeze had begun to come up, stirring the tops of the taller trees. There were other sounds there, of the knots of refugees traveling slowly along the road, and a large fly buzzing somewhere nearer to hand, but the gruff old warrior seemed intent on listening for another sound. His face was drawn and puzzled. "Can you hear that, Hamlin? Judge? Any of you?"

"What? I hear only the fly, and the voices from the settlers," replied Judge.

"No, not those sounds! This is something else. It's like music!"

"Music!" chorused Jeremy and Judge.

"Yes, listen closer. There are pipers, and drums as well. I'm sure it's music now."

"Your ears have been filled with lake water, Chellin! That must make them ring. There is no sound of pipes or drums," said Judge.

"There are pipes," argued Chellin. "I can hear them plainly now. What's come of your ears, lads, that you can't hear this?"

Hamlin shrugged his shoulders. "We can't hear what's not there, Chellin! Maybe you've lost your hearing from being in the water. Jeremy is right there, it must have had some affect on you."

Chellin shook his head, a strange look crossing his grizzled features. "There is nothing wrong with my hearing, lads. It's like nothing I've ever heard before."

Jeremy and his companions exchanged worried glances, and were at a loss as to what to do next.

"Perhaps we can get him to a healer tonight when we camp," suggested Hamlin. "They must know something to do."

"For arrows or swordstrokes, or broken bones," said Judge. "I don't think they would know what to do for someone who has come loose of his senses."

Chellin looked sternly at his young charges. "You lads are the ones who've come off your senses. If you can't hear these pipes and drums, you're all as deaf as rocks!"

Jeremy was at the point of thinking of trying to subdue his leader, when a ripple crossed the lake in a long slender silver motion, and behind it came a wind that was not a wind, but rather a breath from a hushed note from a pipe, high up and far away.

Dumbfounded, the friends fell back and gazed at the

water, watching in awe as a sleek golden craft appeared from a white mist that had sprung up from the ripple, and glided silently to the edge of the small lake, At first they could see no one aboard, but another note was blown from the unseen pipe, and a figure, all clad in dazzling green and gold, stepped off the boat onto shore, directly in front of Chellin.

Jeremy and Judge and Hamlin fell to one knee in a sweeping bow, and Hamlin grabbed off his cap and clutched it tightly before him.

"Our greetings, Stewards of the Line. May your roads go on in safety, and your beards grow gray in front of friendly fires."

Chellin found his voice, and beginning to detect a glimmer of what was happening, he replied in kind. "Our greetings, clan of the troubled dreams. May you ever have the sea to sail, and a fair wind to drive you."

Hamlin was shocked to hear his leader addressing the imposing stranger in such a familiar manner, but he held his peace, unable to utter a word.

There were others there in the silver mist that surrounded the delicately shaped craft, but they remained behind their leader, and did not show their features.

The one who had spoken was a living replica of the elf they had seen in the funeral cask, but with a fine white beard that ran to his waist.

"We have come to retrieve one we have lost, citizen. You have called us from our rest when you disturbed his sleep."

"We did so not knowing," said Chellin, bowing. "We have not seen nor heard from the clans who dream in many seasons. I was trying to piece together the puzzle by these means. We meant no harm to you or yours."

"I know that, citizen. We have ways of knowing the heart. We read no blackness in-yours. But we must take our fallen, and his belongings. They are not to be left behind."

"Can you tell me what has happened, oh dreamer? What has occurred here that caused the death of your friend?"

"Our brother was not slain, as you know it, citizen. He was betrayed and poisoned by the folk of Trew, that crafty lot who have long been our bane. We have come to fetch him, and to give him the leaf of breath from the Tree Who Walks."

"You mean to say that you're going to make him live again?" asked Judge. "That's impossible!"

"He is not dead, good citizen. He merely sleeps the sleep of silence."

"What is that, except death?" asked Jeremy.

"I see you are not schooled in the ways of our clans," replied the elf. "But no matter. It is for another time, perhaps. Let it be known that there are deaths, and then there are deaths. We each experience many before we are through, and seek the Last Havens."

Jeremy was on the verge of questioning the elf further, when the air about them filled with the sound and light that had come before, and a party of six hooded elves disembarked and gently picked up the funeral cask, and carried it back aboard the shimmering form of the golden craft.

"We must ask you to return that which you removed from our kinsman's cask, friend. It must return with him when we leave for our journey. Nothing must remain behind which would pull him back."

Chellin reached into his cloak and withdrew the small packet. "You have explained much, sir, but you leave many questions unanswered that I had hoped to discover with this."

"Your answers will come in time, citizen. You are on the verge of all you desire to know."

"Wait!" cried Judge. "You can't slip away like this! We would have more of an answer than your vague ramblings!"

Chellin bowed low to the elf, apologizing. "You must forgive my hotheaded young companion, sir. He has never been raised in much of the way of manners. He is well meaning, though, and has a stout heart."

"No offense taken, citizen. We must go now. There are many others of our clans who must be found and taken from their waiting. Farewell, good pilgrims. May your roads lead you on to freedom."

As the elf finished speaking, the pipe music grew, stirring

the air about the friends into a gale of light and sound, whirling ever faster, and causing their horses to rear up and neigh in wild-eyed terror.

Almost as soon as it had begun, there was a total silence, and the waters of the small lake again became placid and smooth. Nothing moved, and there was no sound except the nervous trembling of their mounts, and the slow procession of refugees on the roadway to their right. A large bee hummed and lazily landed on the hilt of Chellin's sword, drawing him back from the deep thought he had fallen into. The others seemed to come to their senses at the same time, and all tried to speak at once.

"What on earth?" began Jeremy, but his voice trailed away when he couldn't find words to express himself.

"Now you have made the acquaintance of the dreamers," said Chellin quietly. "The fair ones who wait for the last call to sound so they may return to their homes for good."

"Where is that?" asked Hamlin.

"Beyond any maps or charts we know of," replied Chellin.

"They certainly don't stand much on civility," muttered Judge. "We could use their help."

"They have matters of their own to attend to, it seems," said Hamlin. "And I don't miss my mark when I say their hasty exit was a sign of proof that they aren't overly fond of the human animal."

"They may resemble us in some ways, but never think they are like us," corrected Chellin. "I don't know so much of their kind or their past, but I do know that after the Middle Islands, they chose to leave this world as we know it, for wherever it is they call home."

"They sound like a very strange lot," said Hamlin. "And seeing how they make their presence known, or take their leave, I can do as well without them. It isn't natural."

Chellin Duchin laughed. "They are some of the least disturbing of the lads I've crossed trails with, my bucks. There are fellows that would make your hair fair stand out on end, and I wager we'll meet some of them before this little errand sees its end. Running into these chaps has convinced me that there is much more afoot than a simple border skirmish. The stewards of the Line may not be enough to turn the tide this time. This is bigger than anything I've ever dealt with."

The grizzled leader folded his arms behind him and walked back and forth in deep thought, pausing briefly to stare away at the horizon where the beginning of the taller mountains raised their white towers toward the deep blue of the late afternoon sky.

"We have much to look into when we camp tonight," he said at last, taking a long breath and looking sadly about him. "Let's see to our heels, lads. We have a way to go to catch up to our good companions. They'll be there long before us at this rate, and I dare say the soup will be cold to boot."

Hamlin and Jeremy were full of more questions, but they had seen their leader in his thoughtful state before, and knew not to pursue anything further.

Chellin was distracted again as they mounted and prepared to join the others at the rendezvous, and got down once more to walk about on the edge of the lake, peering intently at certain objects here and there, at places the others could find nothing unusual that stood out, or that would warrant such attention.

Jeremy saw Chellin stoop one last time, and thought it distinctly odd that he had carefully picked up what appeared to be a small brown leaf, and put it gingerly away in a leather wallet he carried at his belt.

The lad made a point to remind himself to question his commander as soon as they arrived at their destination for the night.

RIPPLES
ON THE
RIVER

Secret Plans

From far and wide the vast host came, lured by the promises of great rewards offered by the man who called himself the Red Bear. The hills of the Bitter Roots, and the Wastes of Leech spewed forth legions of soldiers who sought out the warrior who spoke of booty and spoils and land for the taking. They were not disappointed when they arrived in the settlements of the South Channels and saw the huge gatherings of an army that would retreat from nothing, and which grew more powerful with every passing day.

There were all manner of arms and mounts and armor, and many bands and clans who mingled there in the early spring of the year, playing at their rough sports that prepared them for war, or tending to their mounts and gear. Great camps sprang up wherever the armies gathered, and thriving populations followed the soldiers, making numerous settlements bulge with the new numbers, and founding other settlements where there had been none before.

The one who called himself the Red Bear had discovered early that there were icons in all the main squares of the settlements of the South Channels, and in the gathering halls as well, and those icons had given him the clue to the weakness he had been searching for when he was first brought before the elder of the Order of the South Channels.

These people who he wished to enlist in his campaign of revenge were taken with bears! He had not believed his good fortune when he first saw the small statues in the village square, when he was brought in as no more than an odd captive, who proved to be entertaining, and as such, would be kept alive accordingly. The citizens he had met did not seem overly awed by his small magical illusions, and it was becoming alarmingly clear to him that the dwellers of the South Channels were not ignorant peasants who would be taken in out of fear or intimidation.

They were powerful enemies, and would be quite capable of slaying him, unless he could succeed in calling back the spirits of the flying snakes. Those dark beings had carried him away from his final resting place in the Sea of Roaring, when he had been stunned by the dreadful fury of the storm of white light that had erupted after he had touched the Horn of Bruinthor that his infidel brother had carried.

Now he sat at the crown of strength overlooking his gathering armies, alive and in command, and on the move to claim his rightful place, while his miserable brother was long gone over the Boundaries, swept away into eternity by the same wind that had brought him to power.

That thought gave Bern much pleasure as he sat watching his invincible army daily build in strength.

"Does this please you, Lord Bern?" asked a voice at his side. "You seem fond of looking out your window and seeing all this show of force."

"It pleases me well enough, Arnault. I like the thought of being able to strike a swift and fatal blow with the first thrust. It is in my bear code that that is so."

Bern looked sternly at the man, a cold, deadly gaze that turned Arnault's heart to ice, although he did not show it.

"I meant nothing but that it seems the time grows near to sound the call for flowing out of our homelands to avenge the wrongs done you. We need no longer fear any force that might be thrown up against us. We have the most powerful armies now. Even the stewards of the Line are matched above their strength when compared to us."

"That's well and good," replied Bern, pacing back to the window overlooking the broad square, now filled with smithies and craftsmen who traded in the wares of war. "Yet when I strike, I want nothing left to counter me. This blow must be placed at the enemy's heart, and fall so suddenly there is no other course open."

"Look for yourself," soothed Arnault. "There is no stronger army anywhere in the South Channels. You have called all the old factions and warring clans back together with your promises."

Arnault paused, smiling slyly. "I hope you are prepared to deliver all you say you shall. These are rough lads, these hillmen. They don't cotton well to strangers. I've never seen them take to anyone the way they have to you. I would hate to see it end badly."

Bern laughed.

"Your smooth talk covers nothing of your malicious heart, good elder. I know you hold no great affection for me, and haven't from the first. I have a use for you, and shall continue to endure your company, even though it galls me. Just pray your use to me continues, Arnault! Heed my advice, and goad me no further. Send in the scouts and the charts. I have much to do this afternoon."

Arnault bowed low, mumbling under his breath as he did so, secretly planning a fitting end for the upstart who had come into his settlement and seized control of all the other members of the council, and of the other settlements that thrived in the South Channels as well.

He had seen the mysterious transfiguration of the man into the form of a bear, and had not been able to spot the illusion, or figure how the ruse had been worked. It had been done well, he knew, and it had duped the others of the settlement into elevating the stranger to his present high command, but Arnault knew there was a key to the trick somewhere, and when he found it, he would expose the imposter and have him slain.

Those thoughts cheered Arnault as he set out to find the scouts Bern wanted, and the chartmasters who busied themselves all day every day deep in the recesses of the dark shops, toiling away at marking and detailing the geography of the lands around them. No one was quite sure when the chartmasters had started their work, or exactly why it had been begun, but now they had a new purpose to serve under the Master Bern, and they strutted about grandly in their newfound favor with the strange leader who was known to be able to take on the form of the Sacred Bear.

"Fat leeches, all of them," grumbled Arnault, watching them hurry away to their appointment. "They never had any real use before, except to show the kippers at their lessons where they lived, and what was beyond our own front doors. I hope the lot of them get what's coming to them when this whole affair is shown up for what it really is."

Arnault hurried along to finish his errand, and met his friend Morghen on his way.

"I see you have been to see the mighty Bern this afternoon," he said, raising his eyebrows and making a pompous face.

"Hush, you idiot. Don't let anyone hear you talking like that. You know how everyone is awestruck since that show of his in the square."

"I believed it," said Morghen, nodding sagely. "Until he started in on the stories of the treasure. I don't think there is anything like he says in any of the lowland settlements. The riffraff he convinced, but I know what I know well enough, and I say he went a bit too far out on a limb with all those tales."

"Look at the fools pour in, though! I never thought there were so many lamebrains in the South Channels."

"More coming in everyday."

"I think Master Bern may be giving himself enough rope to hoist himself here, Morghen. With all this mob that's coming in now, there's bound to be someone who may have known him before, or have heard of him. I know he claims that his true form is that of a bear, and all that rot, but I don't swallow it. The son of Mother Arnault was not born a blathering idiot, and I say we just bide our time and wait for him to make a slip."

"Speaking of which, you'd better keep out of his way. There's talk among the council at how you bait the great Bern. You and I have always had our enemies among the council, Arnault. This new tyrant has taken their eyes off us for the moment, but they are treacherous dogs, and bite without warning."

"I know them well enough, Morghen. And I think this bloke is a stroke of fortune for us, in spite of it all. If we play our hand right here, we will be rid of this imposter, as well as all those who have opposed us all these turnings. We'll have the South Channels for ourselves yet, and be rid of the yellow gizzards who have long held our purposes at bay."

"That will be a fine thing. We have waited long for the return to power."

"I see our time approaching, my trusted friend. Long have we been held in check by Daghen and his cross-and-shield banner! Sit and wait won't be our policy, Morghen! We shall annex all the South Channels, and the Edges as well!"

"Those are the dreams of our fathers, Arnault. That was always said to be the way of it, and it was the destiny of our clans to head all the others beneath us."

"Come along then. We have to send the last of the scouts. I want to have a talk with this fellow. He's one of ours, and I want to instruct him on his report to Master Bern, the Almighty."

The two men wound through the throngs on the busy street of the hidden settlement of Atholade, seeking the scout who was loyal to Arnault. The crowds were boisterous and the newly arrived soldiers of the various settlements boasted aloud to each other, and called loudly for ale and cheese at the tents that had sprung up to tend to the needs of the growing army.

At last, in one of the older sections of the settlement, Arnault found the man he was seeking, and the three of them sat for a time, speaking in voices lowered to bare whispers.

"You will tell Master Bern that our best path lies not over the Silver Mist Pass, but through the lower passes of the Edges, and on across the Hills of Trew. With all this mob, we'll never be able to stay together unless we go that way."

The scout, called Trabe, looked puzzled.

"That was the way our great-grandsires came to the

Channels! Wasn't there a story of all the hardships and loss they suffered there? The Rogen Keep is across that trail!"

Arnault lowered his voice further still, and his eyes were narrowed until they were mere slits.

"Now don't you think that this Master Bern will be able to deal with those folk at the Edges? Rogen Keep will be nothing to our new leader. He says he can outdo anyone, so we shall see how true to his word he'll be. If he defeats the Rogen, and wins through for us to go through that way, our passes will be open and free of that filth that have closed our western borders for so long. And if he fails, then we won't have lost anything at all, except to be rid of an outsider who has no ties to our cause or our kind."

Trabe and Morghen puckered their lips and looked wide-eyed at their leader.

"That's a plan!" whistled Trabe. "Two strokes at one, and it won't cost us anything, even if it goes awry!"

"But you must argue well for the plan of going through the Edges instead of over the Silver Mist. That way is dangerous enough as it is, and it might be done, but we'll lose our advantage there, and this upstart is the one who would gain if an invasion succeeded by that route."

"I'll do my best," said Trabe, rising to go.

Arnault grabbed the man's wrist in a viselike hold, looking coldly through a threatening scowl.

"You'll do more than your best, Trabe! You'll convince our good leader of the merits of going through the Edges. You will be greatly rewarded for your efforts, of course."

"And if I fail to sway him, Arnault?" asked the scout, disengaging himself uncomfortably.

"We shall see. I don't wish to contemplate a failure! We will go on with our plans as though everything were in order. Do your duty bravely, Trabe, and we shall see it through together!"

Arnault smiled then, a thin shadow of menace creeping through.

Trabe went without further word, leaving the two men at the table.

"He is a good man, Arnault. If anyone can convince the

lowlander that the plan to invade the colonies should be through the Edges, Trabe is the chap to do it."

"I hope so, my friend. I hate it when I must cajole or use a threat to make someone see reason. My arguments have always been of a logical sort, and I have never understood those who have opposed me. Sheer poor judgment on their part, and envy, I suppose!"

"They are just angry because they haven't come from a long line of Channel blood like you, Arnault. We've become so crossed and mixed now, it's rare to find a Channelite whose family goes back further than a generation."

"We must cling to our roots, Morghen, or we shall all be lost. Mark my words, my friend."

Arnault slapped an open hand down on the tabletop to emphasize his words, then rose hurriedly and followed the direction Trabe had taken to find Bern.

A great war cry had gone up from somewhere in the distance, and the sounds of chanting caused Morghen to hurry along behind Arnault, to seek out the source of this great new disturbance.

A Troubled Sleep

Emerald sat at the dying fire, watching the embers glowing against the night shadows of the camp. It had been raining hard earlier, so a shelter had been spread about the friends, and a rhythmic patter of the drizzle still sounded, lulling the sleepy mind, and making it hard to stay awake. Owen and Darek were at his side, wrapped in their cloaks, sleeping soundly, and next to them was Kegin, nodding off occasionally into a shallow state of half-waking dreams.

He was snapped awake again by a noisy explosion of the

crackling fire. "Hello! Are we attacked?" he asked, stuggling to get to his feet. "Is it Famhart?"

"Easy, good Kegin, it is nothing but the green wood in the fire. We are secure here," replied Emerald in a low voice.

His companion rubbed his eyes, blinking in confusion. "I was having a dream, I guess. Strange men had set on-us, and we had no weapons to defend ourselves."

"I've had those dreams," said the minstrel. "It always seems to happen when I'm overtired, or anxious about something."

Kegin, fully awake now, looked evenly into Emerald's steady gaze. "You are a soothsayer as well, minstrel. You read me well. You're right! If Famhart should return before us, I will have much to explain to him."

"You didn't have to come along, then. I told you I'd lead the lads through to the South Channels. I'm sure we shall find my old master."

"I couldn't let Owen go without me. That would be worse than leaving Linne, and I didn't fancy my choice."

"She would have joined us, had she been able. You said as much yourself."

"And I think she would have. I only worry about leaving her behind. The fiend who struck her down with treachery is still loose somewhere. He could strike again while she's helpless."

"Not likely," argued Emerald. "Besides your own camp, there are a dozen others there now, so there is more than enough of a party to guard against an attack. Your being absent could make no difference, my friend."

"Except that Famhart left me in charge," Kegin went on.

"You have heard my stories of my master, and the stories Owen tells of him. He has said that they sent word to him to meet them. I'm surprised that Famhart would have failed to heed that sign."

"I was too, to tell you truly. He and Linne were at the Middle Islands with the Keepers, and I know they were friends with some of them."

Owen stretched and yawned, sitting up and rubbing his eyes.

"Sorry," said Kegin. "We didn't mean to wake you."

"I heard you saying something about my father. I thought for a minute he'd returned."

"No. There is no one here but us Owen. Go on and try to get some sleep. We'll wake you when we're ready to leave in the morning," said Emerald.

"I'm too awake now. I think I want to sit here and watch the fire awhile."

"Here, have what's left of the tea, lad," offered Kegin. "This will help you sleep."

"I keep having the same dream over and over, Kegin. It's like Gillerman is trying to tell me something, but I can never remember it all when I wake up."

"What sort of dream?" asked Emerald. "You know there are those who have the power to do that, to speak to you in dreams."

"That's what this seems like, only I can't remember all of it, and it slips away before I can call it back."

"Try to tell yourself that you'll remember it all before you go to sleep again, lad. That will do it sometimes."

Kegin stirred the last of the fire and offered what was left of the mulled ale to Emerald.

"No thanks, I'm fine now. Any more and I'd have to leave this shelter in the middle of the night to find a place to relieve myself."

"That's reason enough to forgo it," agreed Kegin. "It seems awfully early for a storm like this."

"It gets stranger the further we go toward the South Channels," said Emerald. "I've seen snow on the Silver Mist Pass in the hottest part of July."

Owen sat with his longsword laid across his lap, and as he moved about to make himself more comfortable, he noticed a faint golden white glow emitting from the scabbard. There was also a humming noise, as though someone were singing a note low in their throat, so he eased the blade out a bit, and was astounded by the light that flooded the shelter, blinding them all a moment with its brillance.

Darek awakened with a start, and stared wild-eyed about

him, making little stuttering noises until at last he found his voice and called out to Owen.

"I'm here, Darek. I don't know what's happened."

Kegin and Emerald had leaped to their feet, but stood transfixed, unable to move further.

A wavering form appeared above the blade, and as the companions watched, another appeared, then another, followed by a voice that seemed to come from everywhere at once.

"You are on the right road, my good Owen. We have come to give you this warning, for tomorrow you will enter the old settlement of Clover Hill. There is danger there, and you must be wary. There are assassins who will set on you. Be ever wakeful, and keep to the path toward us."

"Wait!" cried Owen, trying to see the wavering, ghostly forms more clearly, but they had already begun to fade. In another few moments, the shelter was again lit by only the pale red flames from the watchfire, and the one voice that was heard was that of Darek, who sobbed incontrollably beneath his cloak.

"What is it, lad?" asked Kegin. "Have you been hurt?"

Darek was unable to answer, and cried more violently than before.

"He must have been frightened by all this," said Emerald. "I dare say it was jolt enough to wake from a dead sleep to all that."

Owen ran his hand along the sword from the tip of the blade to the hilt, feeling the keenness of its edge, and marveling at the fact that it still felt warm to the touch.

A faint flicker of the golden white light still flared deep within the dark steel, and as Owen peered closer, another outline appeared, followed by Gillerman's voice, which seemed to come from beside his ear, and was whispered, as though no one else was to hear.

"You have one among you who is not what he seems! You must keep to the path, lad, and not be swayed by surprises. Keep on toward the Channels."

The figure in the pale light within the blade brightened a moment, then dimmed, then was gone altogether.

Owen was vaguely disturbed as he gazed into the depths of the blade, for there was an outline of a faintly familiar face beneath the hood of a cloak, but it was gone before he could recognize it.

An uneasy feeling swept over Owen then, and he scrutinized the faces of his three companions who sat with him beneath the shelter, listening to the soft patter of the rain.

"What was it?" asked Kegin at last, finally able to muster his thoughts. "I've heard of ghosts and spirits, but I always thought they were just tales told to the young!"

"This wasn't ghosts or spirits, my good fellow," replied Emerald. "I haven't seen the likes of it since I was at my old master's table, but I'm not likely to forget this kind of show. He was always at it, one way or another, he and his friends."

"You mean there are those who bandy with the likes of all that?"

"And more, Kegin. This was but a taste."

Darek had sobbed loudly throughout the friends' conversation, and Owen was at his side, trying to calm the lad. Kegin and Emerald stirred up the fire and mulled another pot of tea, talking all the while in soothing tones to try to quiet the distraught boy.

"It was nothing to be frightened of, lad! This sort of fireworks is of a good cause. It only seems to be so startling at first when it comes on you by surprise. You'll get used to it."

"You mean there's to be more?" asked Kegin doubtfully.

"Oh, to be sure. Since Owen has the sword, there's an easy way for the master to reach him. He could even without it, but it helps to have a familiar to focus on."

"A familiar?"

"Yes, something that you've touched or handled. Something that isn't hard for you to imagine."

"But how does that help?"

"If you were at the sea, Kegin, and I were here, and you wanted to think of something about me, what would it be? What would you think of first?"

"Why, your musical toy there," replied Kegin. "It's almost as though it's a part of you."

"Exactly. And if you had learned the simple techniques of being able to speak within your mind, all it would be necessary for you to do would be think of my harp, and imagine it until it was clear in your thoughts. Then you could speak to me almost as clearly as you should if you were actually in front of me."

"That's all mullet stew to me, Emerald. I prefer to do my talking to you the way things are, with me here and you there. I like to have my two good peepers on something flesh and bone when I talk."

The minstrel laughed, handing Owen a cup of the steaming tea to give Darek, who had stopped sobbing, but still shivered beneath his cloak, as though he were chilled beyond warmth.

"There's nothing so mysterious about it all when you learn the workings, my friend. If I were to hand you my harp and tell you to play, you wouldn't be able to do it because you haven't learned the way of it. But if I were to teach you the steps, in time you'd be able to play and sing along without even thinking of how you did it."

"Did Gillerman teach you how to talk like that?" asked Owen. "If you were with him all that time, did he teach you those things?"

"What I learned was that you can't reply on unnatural acts to get you by in this world, lad. My master taught truth and service. He always said that to believe a thing without working at it as well was worse than not believing at all, or lying about it to others. And I was constantly at my lessons."

"You mean how to handle arms or horses?"

"No, Owen, although I have had my fair share of that. I was taught that to be truly strong, you must be able to keep a foe from making a mistake and attacking. If I appear unbeatable to you, you will never go to weapons against me, and I shall never have to resort to arms to drive you away. It is a mistake some make, but my master always tried to show that by his example, that war was not by law a warrior's trade."

Darek had calmed considerably, but still shivered and chattered beneath the folds of his cloak.

"Do you feel ill, lad?" asked Kegin. "Should we find a healer for you?"

"N-n-n-ooo," stuttered Darek. "I'm all right. It's just that Clover Hill is near my old settlement, and where my father and mother were lost——I——."

The young man could not continue, and broke off into heaving sobs that wracked his small shoulders.

"Here, here, old fellow," consoled Kegin. "The first rule of the march is that a soldier has to be brave!"

Darek cried harder at the warrior's words.

"There's no harm in tears," said Emerald, taking his instrument out of the leather sack at his side. "Listen to these words that a very old soldier sang a long time ago, at the battle of the Middle Islands."

As the minstrel tuned his harp, Darek quieted and wiped his eyes.

> "Once was a mighty wind
>   blew from sea to sea,
>   and it was said that
>   all the men
>   would find a road to glory,
>   but then the still night came
>   that followed morning's call
>   and all who rode the winds of war
>   were lost one and all,
>   oh the dragon high came with fire
>   and the darkness brought the ice,
>   while the silver horns of Windameir
>   sounded hopes of wounded dreams,
>   of silence and serenity,
>   among the lands of plenty
>   while with golden hands of kindness,
>   sought to soothe the empty hearts
>   of those who bent the bow
>   and toiled at swordstroke,
>   until another dawning brought

the light of love at last,
    and the sweet memory of forgiveness
  and forgotten pain grew as a hope of peace
    winging with the tiny bird
      to find a heart to dwell in,
      oh a heart to dwell in."

Emerald strummed the harp twice in a chord that wrenched the heart in an odd, sad way.

"We must look to our tomorrows," he said, laying down the instrument. "It may look like we're small and without help, but if we can reach my master, we shall have a key to the Keepers. They must be called again to stem this tide."

"Why can't they foresee all this, if they're so wise and all knowing?" asked Kegin sharply. "Surely if they're so aware of happenings anywhere, they'd know we could use all the help we can get."

"Oh, they know," answered Emerald. "Yet sometimes there is nothing for them to do but wait. There will come a time in all this when we'll see the point of it."

Kegin snorted.

"Now that promise would almost make me want to stick around long enough to see what reason there was to it all."

"We are going to find Gillerman," said Owen resolutely. "Gillerman will help us find the leaf that my mother needs. If there is nothing else other than that I can do, it is goal enough. She needs the help of all of us."

"Of course, Owen! We were never in doubt of trying to do all we can for Linne. There is no one among us who would doubt that!"

Owen thought he saw a moment of uneasiness flicker across Darek's face, but he cursed himself for being stupid, remembering that his young friend was still suffering from the shock of losing his mother and father in the battle that set the settlements of the Line into motion to escape the relentless invaders who beset them on every side.

With that thought, he resolved to himself to do everything in his power to seek out the two powerful men in the South Channels, and to bring aid to his mother as quick as mortal man could possibly do it. Kegin gave him a reassuring clap on his back, but there was a faint, knowing look in Emerald's eyes that disturbed him. It could have been a reflection from the fire, but it forced him to recall a half-forgotten memory of a tale that his mother had told him long ago, of friendships and betrayals, and death.

It was not a pretty thought, and it took Owen a long time to fall into a troubled sleep.

A Renegade Squadron

Inside the small confines of the travel shelter, Stearborn's large frame seemed to dwarf the kettle that sang on the camp stove. The others sat restlessly, looking from the door to Stearborn, and back at the door again.

"This visit of mine was a bit unlooked for, was it?" The big man laughed. "Not often that you get waked up from a snooze on the dead watch to come in for a pot of tea, eh, lads?"

Stearborn's rough laughter erupted again, causing a fresh wave of unease among the gathered sentries.

Outside, the sound of horses and men were confused, and it seemed that a great commotion was taking place beyond the shelter walls.

"They had warned us of tricks like these, but I had hoped my old eyes would never see it," said Stearborn, shaking his head sadly. "What has come over the world, I don't wonder. The next thing I'll hear is that we have lost our way so completely that you'll give me a perfectly reasonable story as why two hundred of our best bowmen are on the road to Trew without orders, and no real way to explain their behavior, except to speak the truth, which tells me that you and your squadron were defecting."

The huge man spoke so softly, in a voice so devoid of inflection, that he might have been reciting a long forgotten love poem.

In front of him, a burly man with dark circles under his eyes, and a black, bristling mustache, stood up.

"You've got the picture all wrong, Stearborn. The lads and I were pursuing a band of raiders these past few days, and we had lost them just before you came on us. If we are near the Edges of Trew, it's news to us, and no good news at that! I know the old stories of what happens to those who enter Trew."

"I like your steel, Nashet! Pure and simple, and down to it! Simple story, and it would fit with all the facts we have, except that I've been in these woods long enough to know there hasn't been a raiding party anywhere near here since the night Sweet Rock was attacked."

"These are slippery felons, Stearborn. These aren't the old raiders you and I have been used to dealing with all these years. I have never seen the likes of these blokes! They fair turn your blood to ice, they do."

Stearborn barked a short, gruff laugh, or what passed for it.

"Mud doesn't lie, Nashet. My men and I have covered every direction from here for half-a-day's march, and there's nothing at all in the way of raiders, real or imagined. But that leaves a lot in the way of explaining how I come to find a full squadron of the Line, fully armed, fed, and on the march, without orders, and in the direction of a known enemy stronghold."

"Trew is no enemy stronghold, Stearborn! Never has been! Nothing more for it, but a place to avoid when traveling."

"Perhaps that has been so in the past, good Nashet, but now there are those nasty rumors that keep reaching old Stearborn's ears about a rebel upstart who offers gold and glory to any and all who come to join him wage a fight against the order of the Lower Meadows."

Nashet shook his head stubbornly.

"I've never heard tell of anything near a tale like that.

You have no way to prove it, either, Stearborn. You have lingered too long in the twilight of your reputation to begin to think you would be able to make your insulting accusations hold up before a clan council."

The older man tugged his beard thoughtfully, as if pondering some dark and puzzling object on the small camp stove.

"You're right about one thing, Nashet. I have lived too long in the twilight of my past reputation. I'd begun to be a bit set in my ways, I can see. I've also lost touch with how things stand with my watch commanders. Most frightening, indeed, to suddenly be drawn up short like this."

Nashet made no reply, but studied his commander behind half-shut eyes.

Stearborn moved to the table where a map of the Line was spread out.

"It's not far from here. Another two hours' march and you would have been gone."

"I don't know what you're speaking of. You can ask any of my men, and you'll find the same answer. We were pursuing a force of the enemy, but they had given us the slip. We were simply trying to make contact again."

Stearborn pulled up the stool from beneath the table and sat down, sighing as he did so.

"I have half a mind to wash my hands of you. It would be a simpler thing than the fal-tra-do this will cause if I pursue it."

Nashet's eyes registered surprise at first, then a gleam of hope.

"That's it, Stearborn! You have no proof at all, and you know it wouldn't sit well now, not with all the trouble abroad. One more thing to burden the council with would be a serious mistake."

The old commander froze his lieutenant with a gaze that seemed to bore straight through the younger man.

"I have made no mistake here, Nashet. I can see what's clearly afoot, yet I know not how best to deal with it. It's a problem I have never been faced with in all my years as a

steward of the Line. I am sorry to have lived so long as to
have to see a time like this arrive."

"There's no sense in making a high issue out of nothing,
commander. You'll find there may come a time when an
apology might be in order."

Nashet sensed a change in the charged atmosphere of the
shelter, and had begun to breathe a sigh of relief.

"Too soon, I suppose," said Stearborn. "I have always
been accused of impetuous actions. Perhaps my hand would
have been played differently, had I slowed myself until you
had crossed over into the Edges."

"You would have had to have been slow, indeed. You are
the one who issued the order to not pursue any enemy force
into Trew. There are stories there that would turn any
decent man's heart to ice!"

"A problem you wouldn't be forced to deal with, Nashet.
I've watched and hoped all these years since you took over
your father's command, that you would fill his shoes in some
small degree. It is better he's dead and gone and can't
witness this shame on the bright honor of his name."

Nashet's nostrils flared and he flushed a deep crimson; his
hand flirted with the hilt of his longsword, but he turned his
back on Stearborn instead, shoulders heaving, as though he
were having difficulty in controlling his breathing.

"My father's good name is nothing to me, Stearborn. He
is a relic, like you, only you're still alive. These are changed
times that have done this! You refuse to see what has
happened to the Line, and the rest of the settlements."

"It's a changed world, aye, lad, but no much for the
better. There was a time when kinship and loyalty meant
something. There was a time when honor and right were
words that meant more than a pretty sounding way of
working treason."

"That's your old way of thinking, Stearborn! These are
new times, awaiting any bold enough to dare dream of how
it can be, not only here, but all across the settlements,
wherever they are."

Stearborn narrowed his eyes in a worried frown. "You

have been listening to the wild talk from that upstart in Trew! Hasn't it occurred to you yet what he's about?"

"I would say he's about talking the truth, for a change. We have grown up with the idea that the rightful king has been victorious in all his battles against those who would overthrow the standing order, but now at last, we find that trickery and deceit have kept the truth from all those of us who never knew the real nature of how power keeps its own school, and might is right, no matter what."

"You are a fool, Nashet, all the worse for you. I can think of no good reason to stand here arguing with you about the rebel loose in Trew. He is known to me, and to all who follow Windameir. Your own elder's wife has been struck down by this man you say you will follow. I have no more words for you, except be careful of your hide when next we meet, my boy. My heart aches with the sorrow of this, but I will hold my hand only this once. If I hear you've crossed the Edges into Trew, by the Goat of Elmarda, I'll see you gutted like a mountain trout."

"A good show, coming from one so long in favor with the powers that be, my commander. We shall see what we shall, but you haven't seen me do any such thing as you have accused me of. I will ask for an apology from you next council session."

"You shall have it, Nashet, if I see you there. I shall announce to one and all what I suspected, and offer you my public apology for casting a shadow across your good character."

The older man looked at his lieutenant with an intensity that caused Nashet to drop his eyes and stand up suddenly, moving away from the table. He paused at the door, looking away into the gathering darkness. "It will be a bit light tonight for moving about with raiders nearby. Why don't you have your men bivouac with us? It would drive off anyone who might be holding on to an idea of attacking tonight."

"My camp is already made at the Crossing of Garret's Slide. We are expected there before the moon is down."

"Then don't let me keep you, good Stearborn. We both

have our men to look to, and a picket to set out. But don't say I didn't warn you about the raiders, if you run into trouble. It was a large party, and I dare say they would give even you a run for your hide. These are no fresh lambs that are crossing the borders now."

"I'll take your warning to heart, Nashet. I sense in it more than enough ill-will to keep me properly at my guard."

"It's only a fair warning, commander. My father didn't go completely wrong when he raised me."

Stearborn moved swiftly to the shelter door, pulling at his cloak as he did so. He withdrew his signal horn and sent three sharp notes up into the still air of the settling evening, which called all his men to their saddles.

"Off, lads! Up, me bucks, we've got clearer business elsewhere in the Line tonight. Get me out of this accursed pesthole, so that I may breathe freely again!"

The huge commander mounted in the blink of an eye, and had spurred his mount away from the shelter of Nashet, causing a knot of men who had been lingering there to scatter before him, like leaves before an autumn wind.

"Good riddance," Nashet called out, shaking his fist after the retreating form of the horseman, who was followed into the gathering gloom by his men.

"That was bad timing, Nashet. We can't have covered our tracks so well if all this end of the wood has heard of the offers this Largo fellow is making. We're lucky Stearborn didn't cleave all our heads."

"You're a bright one, Laron, always on the damp side of an issue. Don't you think he would if he really had any proof?"

"Where he caught us would be a fair clue as to our intent."

"Our intent was to run down a raiding party. We lost them and had to scout about for a new trail."

"Do you think he bought that cock-lolly story? Stearborn has been around for a long time."

"He knew my father. That may have helped us. According to the commander of the Line, I'm a disgrace and a blight on my father's good name."

"Said that, did he?" asked Laron, stoking up the fire to boil water for tea.

"That and more. I've stood still for all the maudlin stories about my father that I'm going to stand. Living in the dead past has gotten none of us anywhere, and day by day the odds against us grow longer. When we heard of this fellow that's operating in Trew, I first gave it no mind, but after Silam and Orvis spoke to him, I'm curious to talk with him myself. There is a ring of truth to what he has said about Famhart and the others."

"Treason! You're dealing treason, Nashet. We had best be sure of our road before we cut our bridges. If this fellow has a leg to stand on, we might do ourselves well by siding with him. I have no great love for Stearborn, or any of the other commanders of the stewards of the Line, but I want to make sure the ground I'm taking a stand on isn't quicksand. We'd be finished chop-quick if we go over to this Largo, and find out that he had lied."

"Does it sound to you like a lie? Come, come, Laron, the man has braved everything to be able to retake what was wrongfully stolen from him. I trust a man who has revenge as his master! And his own sister sold him out! Linne, the proper Linne, so pure and above reproach, tried to have her own brother murdered so she would be the next in step to take over her father's eldership."

"I don't make too much of that story, Nashet. I'm not saying it might not be true, but I'd rather find the real cause of all this bad blood. The reasons this fellow has don't concern me so much as his chances of success in his ambitions."

"Always the realist, eh, Laron? That's why I've always taken such a liking to that warped brain of yours. You always cut through the emotional tripe to get to the real core of a matter. Cut it to the bone and see what makes it turn! That's not a bad philosophy these days, my friend. I shall be wise to keep my eye turned to those strange visions that you see."

"I don't think you'll do yourself any harm in pursuing

that policy, Nashet. I may have my little faults, but failure isn't one of them."

The two men laughed.

"That's it, Laron! We shall have our tea now, and see to our troops. We'll wait long enough here to give the good commander of the Line long enough to be clear of our perimeters, then we shall set our lads back to the task at hand."

"Preparing to trail those raiders, even if it means crossing the Edges to catch them! Stout Nashet! Brave squadron! Bully good lads!"

"Sound out the muster, Laron! Let's see what our fortunes are waiting to reveal across the Edges. We have long lived in the shadows of a past that has died and left us long ago. If there is to be anything for us, any glory, let us step for it boldly, and throw our lots with the new dawn of Argent!"

"Hear, hear, Nashet. If all that be true, our fortunes are well made. No more dreary duty and forever eating from our stirrups riding with the Stearborns and his likes."

Laron laughed an off-key, disagreeable laugh and stepped out of the shelter to call the troops gathered about to muster. He was known to be a prudent man, and not given to excesses, which he prided himself on, but he had begun to feel in his later years that he was undervalued and overlooked when it came time for promotions and honors. Time and time again, he had been overlooked or ignored, and as he grew into mature adulthood, he saw the other stewards of the Line rise up in stature among the ranks, and a small burr of resentment had grown and grown, until he found no guilt in doing whatever he could to turn the tide of lost opportunity to his favor.

He blew the notes of muster, and went back into the shelter to finish his tea and help Nashet lay out their line of march into Trew, which made him feel somewhat apprehensive. There were old tales of that country, and none of them were pretty, but Orvis and Silam had scouted the area, and even met with the new leader that had come to free them all from a past history that doomed them to forever riding the bleak borders of the Line, from youth to old age, without so much as a thank-you handshake from the order of elders who had ruled from ancient times until the present.

"Old orders, old ideas," muttered Laron to himself.

"What's that?" asked Nashet.

"Just promises to ourselves, Nashet! We shall shake these fetters they've held us with for all these years. All we need is the right timing."

"And a good headstart," added Nashet. "Send out a scout to see if Stearborn is away. He's a sly old boot. I wouldn't put it past him to be lurking about out there to see what we're up to. Once we know it's clear, then we shall see to ourselves."

There was a short commotion then, and a rider was dispatched. Camp was broken, and the shelter was struck, and the squadron of Nashet prepared to resume their march.

It wasn't a long wait for the scout to return with the all clear, and in another short space of time, the riders were mounted and lost in the darker eaves of the wood, which bordered the outer regions of Trew.

The Bow and Harp

From the top of the tree he had climbed to get a better picture of his surroundings, Kegin searched the wood for any sign of intruders. An eerie silence had fallen since their journey had begun at dawn, and there were no signs of animals or birds, which disturbed Emerald.

"What do you make of it?" Owen called up, in a guarded whisper.

Kegin motioned for the lad to be quiet, and went on with

his search of the woods. A strong sense of danger kept tickling the hair on the nape of his neck.

"Can you see the markers for the Edges?" whispered Emerald. "We should be nearing them now. I've tried to keep our bearings marked as well as I can on Owen's chart, and according to what I remember of this wood, we should be very near the crossing for Trew."

Owen put a hand on Emerald's sleeve.

"We can't lose our way now, Emerald! My mother's life depends on us!"

"Hush, lad! Old Emerald never gets lost. We may not know where we are for a bit, but you can't lose a trail once you're on it. You have to remember that when it seems the darkest."

"I don't know what that has to do with losing our trail, or finding Gillerman and Wallach, but I know if we fail, my mother will stay the way she is. We can't fail her!"

"No need to fret over a failure that hasn't happened, Owen. Think of it only as that we haven't succeeded yet."

"We've been wandering about like this for a week now. If Trew is so hard to find, it may be because we haven't gone far enough yet."

Darek had been standing quietly beside Owen, drawing figures on the floor of the forest with a long stick.

"It might be that the map you have is wrong," he suggested. "None of the landmarks appear anywhere in the wood like they are on that map."

"That is an old chart, Darek," said Emerald. "That was drawn up in a time when there were bigger settlements in all parts of the country, from the coast to the mountains. Time will have put a different face on a lot of old landmarks."

"But we would see something that would give us a clue," persisted the youth.

"My master does not leave important matters to chance. If he has given this chart to Owen, it was with purpose. It is simply a matter of us finding our way to where it is this map shows the likeness of. Trew was never well known to many, and I don't recall it being mapped in any great detail. What may have happened, is that we might have crossed the

Edges already, without knowing it, and be in Trew, instead of trying to find it."

Owen's eyes widened. "I hadn't thought of that! That would explain the absence of any of the landmarks that would be on the map, but not in truth. No one travels here, so we could have passed the borders back there somewhere and not known it."

Emerald whistled Kegin down, and the comrades spread Gillerman's chart before them on the fragrant forest floor.

"None of it makes any sense, I tell you," insisted Kegin. "I'm familiar enough with my own borders to know whether or not I've crossed them."

"No doubt, Kegin. If we were traveling in the lower part of the Line, I should imagine there would be no problem. I haven't been up this way in a long while, and I can see the country has suffered from the invaders' hand all these years. It could be that the forest has simply reclaimed its own."

"Nothing would grow so fast that you couldn't tell a new stand of timber," argued Kegin.

"Perhaps not in an ordinary time or place, but we are talking of Trew now. Once you pass Lost Falls, everything changes. I've never been sure of what exactly it was, but I could always tell I was in a different place. It made my hackles creep, just like they are now."

"You've felt it, too?" asked Kegin, looking about the close wall of the forest. "I've been feeling it now for a while. It's very slow to come to your attention."

Owen and Darek nodded agreement.

"I wasn't sure what it was at first, but I definitely feel it now. I wish we could find a way out of this wood."

"We'll be out soon enough, Darek. Even if we've strayed into Trew, and are in the Edges, we'll come out sooner or later, and near where we need to be."

"You're an odd fish, Emerald. Doesn't any of this upset you?"

"No sense in getting into a froth over being lost, Kegin. We shall have to come out of this wood sooner or later, and when we do, we shall know how true this chart really is. All we have to do is find someplace or something that would be evident, so that we can locate it squarely on the map."

Kegin squatted down next to the chart, studying it closely. "All I can make out of any of it, is that if we get near those places we're likely to recognize, we may be in a bit of trouble. Look! See this? Rogen Keep." Kegin looked at Emerald evenly. "Those are things that I'm sure you must have heard of?"

"The Rogen? Of course."

"What do you speak of?" asked Owen, his eyes wandering over the map.

"Here," said Kegin, pointing out a small spot on the unrolled chart. "Rogen Keep. It is said to be guarded by souls without bodies that drink the blood of the living."

"I've never heard that," said Darek. "Where did these things come from?"

"They are supposed to be the slaves of the doom-snakes. They were the poor unfortunate souls that were captured by the Purge."

"But there are no more dragons," said Owen. "How could someone stay a slave of those monsters after they were destroyed?"

Emerald began rolling the chart up as he spoke.

"The Purge, or doom-snakes, disappeared, Owen. What happened to them, no one can be sure, but they weren't destroyed. They were called back, perhaps, but the fear of them is hidden deep in the hearts of all men. It's like a sickness. If it is unchecked, it can grow into a physical thing. The Rogen were given great powers by the Purge, and never did surrender them when all was lost after the Middle Islands."

"You mean when my mother and father were there?" asked Owen.

"Exactly. Somehow there is still a splinter of Darkness that has kept the Rogen locked into that black night they live in. They have remained that way for so long, they must destroy other living things so they won't feel the pain of that living death they lead."

"Is that anything like the story of the Red Bear?" asked

Darek. "Linne said she would explain about that, but she got sick before she could."

"Do you know about that, Owen?" asked Emerald.

"Only that there is a feast, and everyone gets up in arms, and it seems to make everyone very angry."

"That's a part of it. It goes back to a tale told of the brother of Borim Bruinthor, one of the Keepers. It was said that every season, there would be a feast held in honor of those who had fallen in with the Darkness, to help guide those poor lost ones back to the Light of Windameir."

"It is not that way now," snapped Kegin. "The Red Bear is a sign of war, and a way to rally everyone to arms."

"That's the way of it in these times, Kegin, but it was a sad day to celebrate in the beginning of it. Even Borim's own half brother was lost to the Darkness. It was a day to call out to all those forgotten ones to come back to the true Light."

"Was Borim the bear king?" asked Darek.

"Yes, my young friend, he was the mightiest of all. The Bruinthor that lives in a hundred songs, from one country to the next. A Keeper of the highest order."

"Do you know any of those songs?" asked Owen. "I think my mother may have sung some of them for me when I was small."

"I know all of them." Emerald laughed. "And when we get somewhere I think is safe enough, I'll treat you to all of them."

The minstrel patted the case that carried his harp, and put it back beside the quiver of arrows for his longbow.

"We may have more need for the bow that the harp," said Kegin, in a tone of voice that alerted the others. "I'm not so sure who our visitors are, but I know they're out there."

"Do you see anything?" breathed Owen, peering into the dense wood that seemed to have crept slowly closer to them.

"I don't like this," went on Kegin, moving to rise. "Chart or no chart, we're lost, and I don't like the feel of this wood."

"I think we may as well go on. There's nothing to be gained by staying here any longer. If there are spies about, there's no need to go secretly. Whoever our friends are, we're no news to them now."

Emerald began to remount, then thought better of it.

"Maybe we should walk the animals for a while. They could use a breather."

"I could use a breather from this confounded silence," complained Kegin. "It's enough to drive you daft."

"When we reach the end of the Edges, I'm sure we'll find our way easier."

"*If* we reach the end of the Edges, Emerald. We have yet to confirm that we're even there yet."

"Oh, I think we're here. Look at Owen's sword! See how it's beginning to put off that light! Pull it out, lad! Let's see what news we have from Gillerman."

Owen had begun to feel a faint pulsing hum from his side, then when he looked down, he saw that the sword had indeed begun to emit the same blue-white light he had seen before. As Emerald spoke, he had drawn it from the simple scabbard, but had to turn his eyes aside from the dazzling white brilliance that flickered and leaped along the keen blade.

A harsh scream tore through the curtain of silence like a knife, causing the companions to start badly. The mounts tried to bolt, almost jerking the reins from Owen's hand.

"Acccch, put out that accursed sticker!" snarled a voice, which fell off into a whining growl.

"Put it out, we say! Put it out, or we can't be liable for what we shall have to do!" came a second voice, very close to Owen's side.

He whirled, holding aloft the pulsing, white-hot blade. "Gillerman?" cried the lad, not knowing how to address the odd strangers, or whether he was merely talking to the empty air.

"Strike! Strike, Owen!" shouted Kegin. "Stand to, lad, like I showed you!"

In a moment, Emerald was with Owen, his own sword drawn. There was a fire in the minstrel's eye that reflected the white flame in the depths of the sword, which caused the youth to wonder at the seemingly gentle singer.

At once, a half dozen figures lunged out of the heavy undergrowth beneath the tall trees, shrieking and howling in guttural animal sounds.

Darek tripped and fell at Kegin's feet, which caused the seasoned veteran to fall heavily just as two wildly swinging attackers reached him.

"Blast you, lad! Look to it," he cried, rolling away to his left to avoid the vicious swordstrokes, which fell harmlessly on a fallen log.

Emerald engaged three of their assailants, driving them back with a furious flurry of strokes, and as he fell back to Owen's side, a horn was heard away in the wood, blowing shrilly, in short, urgent notes.

"Recall! Recall!" cried a voice, and as quickly as the small company had been set on, they were left alone again, and the same, dripping silence that had been before began to return.

"What do you make of all that?" asked Kegin, dusting himself off, and making sure Darek was unharmed.

"I don't know, but look! Owen's sword has gone still!" said Emerald, pointing to the blade in the youth's hand.

"What strange thing is this marvelous weapon?" asked Kegin, coming to inspect the sword. "I think it frightened those bounders away. I was almost blinded by it, myself."

"So was I," put in Darek. "I couldn't see where I was stepping."

Kegin turned a serious face to his young student. "You could have been my death, sprout. I shall have to teach you better footwork before any of the others see you. I'd never live it down if any of my other aspiring soldiers heard that Kegin had stooped so low as to allow one of his students to cause his head to be split up like cord wood."

"I'm s-sorry," stammered Darek. "I just couldn't see for a bit there when he pulled the sword out. The light blinded me."

"It's of no matter now," said Emerald. "Whoever our good friends were, they're gone. Now we need to see to our own stirrups. I don't think they're gone so far as to not have to worry about them."

"Look, Kegin. There where you're standing! One of them must have dropped it!"

Owen bent and picked up a small dagger that lay at Kegin's feet.

"What strange markings," mused Kegin. "And I don't recall seeing any weapons shaped like this in a long life of wearing a sword in the duty of Line Steward."

Emerald took the dagger from Owen and examined it carefully, going over the blade and handle with extreme caution.

"A good thing you weren't knicked with this, Kegin! This has been dipped in something, and I'd wager you my life that it's poison, or a drug of some sort to stun an enemy."

"What sort are we dealing with here?" Kegin whistled. "First we've got a sword that plays at lantern, then a wood full of blighters that carry pricks with poison. I don't think I like these parts any too much. The quicker we get through them, the better."

Subdued by Kegin's outburst, Darek sat down wearily in the fragrant smelling leaves. He was playing with a large pine cone, when Emerald whirled and flung himself across the lad's body.

As the two crashed flat into the soft earth, the distant whisper of a small shaft sighed through the silence, and Owen saw the dart bury itself in a tree behind where the two had fallen.

"Emerald! Darek! Are you all right?"

"I'm sorry, Darek," apologized the minstrel. "When you were playing with that cone there, I saw the trip beneath the leaves. It is a clever and deadly device I've seen before. They have a small crossbow set there, behind that tree, aimed at a point on the trail so that a horse or man would trigger it. Cruel little piece of business. No doubt the bolt is tipped with poison, too."

"I like this less as time goes on, Emerald. We've got Famhart's son here, and I'm responsible if anything should happen to us."

"I'm s-scared," stuttered Darek. "I want to get away from here."

"Easy, old man," soothed Emerald. "We just have to take it easy. Now that we know this place is full of this little trick we've seen, and that whoever attacked us had to get out the same way we will, all we have to do is snoop around and follow that lead."

"Great," snorted Kegin. "I didn't happen to see anyone leaving any markers on the trail for us, or scattering any invitations to follow them."

"Maybe the sword would work again to lead us," suggested Owen. "If it lit up like that to warn us about the attack, maybe it would warn us about traps!"

"It's worth a try, Owen. We can also keep our eyes to where we put our feet. Anything at all that looks unnatural, or like someone has disturbed anything, just stop and point it out."

"What about those cutthroats? Do you think they were really frightened off? It sounded more like someone signaled to break off."

"I think you're right on both accounts, Kegin. Whoever signaled may have seen the sword as well."

"I'd feel better if we had a few days travel already between us and this unhealthy place. I never thought I'd be a one to spurn the sight of trees, but I could distinctly use a little wide open space now."

"It doesn't seem so bad when I think about the wood around Sweet Rock," agreed Owen. "This place almost suffocates you."

"Single file, lads," ordered Emerald. "We're going to see if we can't find our way out of here. Owen, come up here with me on my horse, and keep Gillerman's blade out. We might have noticed something sooner, if we had been paying attention to our business."

"Come up behind me, Darek. If we're going on this way, it might be better to have you where you can't get into too much trouble."

"I'm sorry, Kegin. I really couldn't see." The lad began to tremble, fighting hard to hold back the tears.

"Here, lad! It's all past now. I know you didn't mean it. I'll just have to work all the harder to make sure I teach you the proper way of handling yourself when the going gets a bit sticky."

"We'll get to that when we're out of this pickle, Kegin. It's something to look forward to, lad, so don't fret yourself about it too much. I once caused my old teacher to lose a tooth by my clumsiness."

"You, Emerald?" asked Owen, incredulous.

"Myself, indeed. It wasn't an easy thing to live down, I can assure you. I shall most likely be reminded of it again, when next we cross the trail of our friend Gillerman."

"I wish he was here with us now," said Owen wistfully. "I'd feel a lot better about everything. I'm still worried about my mother, and I don't know where my father is, or if he's well and safe."

"Don't worry yourself on Famhart's account, sprout," assured Kegin. "This sort of thing is as easy as breathing to him. There's nothing he or Stearborn likes any better than a good rousing campaign."

"I wish Stearborn was with us, too," added Owen. "And I wish we were already in the country where the Three Trees are, so we could get a leaf to bring back to my mother."

Emerald gave the lad a long, searching look. "It shall come to pass, my small fry, if we keep steady to our course, and don't fall to the wayside because of faint hearts."

Owen couldn't be sure of the meaning of the remark, and was on the verge of questioning him about it further, but a new and more ominous sound had begun in the woods ahead of them. In a slow and steady fashion, the minstrel guided his mount along the faint trail, watching for signs of danger ahead and alongside, while keeping his eye trained for any change in the longsword that his young companion held out before them, like a lamp to guide them safely through the danger-ridden woods that had swallowed the afternoon, and left them going forward in nothing more than a dim twilight, which was rapidly fading.

The cries and calls came at the same instant that Owen noticed the sword begin to flicker and flare in the gloom.

"Steady, lad," cautioned Emerald, and he spurred the

horse on, leading Kegin and Darek on into the darker reaches of the lost wilderness that was the Edges, on the borders of Trew.

Baiting a Trap

The march had been long and exhausting, and Famhart had driven the men relentlessly, although they had not complained. Linne was considered one of the first heroes of the Line, and none of the soldiers considered it anything other than a great honor to be among those Famhart had handpicked to try to find aid for his stricken wife.

Famhart had at first followed along the Green Road toward White Bird, in hopes of finding one of the healers that resided there. To their disappointment, they were told that the old man in question had followed a band of soldiers earlier, who were marching along the edge of the Wastes of Leech, on their way to the Tybo River Valley.

No one could offer any more specific clue than that, and amid all the refugees that were making their way further away from the threatened borders, Famhart could discover no one who could give him reason for any of the Line Stewards to be sent off on a mission so impossible or dangerous as the Tybo River Valley, or suggest why an expedition had been mounted without having consulted Famhart at Sweet Rock, who headed one of the strongest squadrons of all in the defense of the Line.

"It doesn't make any sense at all, Alac. What sort of tale is all this?"

"I don't know, sir. None of the people we questioned could offer anything other than what they told you."

"Do you have any scouts set out?"

"Three, sir. One has gone down the coast to Swan Haven, and one is off up the Tybo to see if those customers left anything behind that we might read, and one is scouting down the other way on the coast, to the west, to see if there's anything we overlooked there."

Famhart nodded absently, looking away across the flat blue surface of the South Roaring. "It's like a lake today," he said at last, startling his subaltern.

"Sir?"

"A lake. It looks like a lake today. But I have seen it otherwise."

"I'm sure you have, sir."

"When Linne and I crossed to the Middle Islands, we saw a storm that sent waves higher than an oak. I never thought I'd stand ashore on solid ground again."

"How did you escape?"

"By the luck of Windameir, and the seamanship of great sailors, lad. And we were aboard vessels that were laid by skilled hands."

"And luck, sir?" asked Alac.

Famhart laughed. "Aye, and some luck, Alac. Luck of the sort that comes from hard work and a right cause. There were cruel things afoot then, that I doubt I've seen the last of. Sometimes you can put memories away for a time, but there is always a place somewhere down the line where they reach back out and touch you."

"Like how, sir?" questioned the lad.

"Sometimes it might be sitting at table with your family, and it's no more than the way someone asks you to pass the bread. That's all it takes." Famhart paused, smiling. "Or it might be like this, lad, sitting here as I've so often done, talking with my lieutenant."

"What was it like in the Middle Islands? Was Kegin there?"

Famhart shook his head. "No, but he has been with the stewards since they were formed in Sweet Rock, and seen more action than he would have agreed to."

"Do they really come out of the air at you, sir, breathing fire?"

"Do what come out of the air?" asked Famhart.

"The doom-snakes, sir. Everyone always said you and your lady fought one of the Purge."

"It was the worst thing I have ever had to face, Alac. If it hadn't been for Borim and Olthar, and Trianion, and the key of Brian, the world as we know it would have perished away and been no more."

"Were they as brave as the stories say?"

"Braver, my lad, by tenfold. You don't know the meaning of courage until you have stood beside the likes of those four."

Famhart's tale was interrupted by a thin man dressed in a riding cloak that was wet and torn.

"Standin, what is it? Speak up, man, what news?"

"I've got a piece of information that won't sit well, Alac. I've just come back from up the Tybo a few miles, and there's a staging up there for transporting anyone who wants to go upriver."

"Up the Tybo? But that's a road that would run you straight up into the Bitter Roots, and the Plains of Grief, or the South Channels!"

"Aye, that it is, sir. The word is that there's a fee waiting for any able-bodied man of the squadrons of the Line who will make his way up there to join a blighter calling himself Argent Largo."

"Where did you come by all this? Quickly, man!"

"It's pretty widespread, sir. I had begun hearing bits of it this morning when we questioned the refugees about the healer. Some of the blokes said he went of his own doing, and there was another side said he was forced against his will."

"You mean they took him prisoner?" asked Alac.

"It begins to look that way, sir. There was a special bounty to be paid for all healers and loremasters and such."

Famhart slapped his hand with his riding crop. "A new twist to this devil's web! Now we begin to see what lies in store for us. Go on, man, what else have you learned?"

"Only that some of the squadrons have been at it tooth

and nail, and there are stories that some of them have deserted and gone over."

"Treason," breathed Alac softly.

"They said they were only returning to their true origins. This fellow up there claims to have been the rightful heir to the throne long ago abandoned, when the South Channels was ruled by the Lord of Eight."

"What rubbish is that? Did they say who this Lord of Eight was?" questioned Famhart.

"He was a king that had come in search of the Three Trees, and stayed on in the South Channels on his way home. His son and daughter were left behind, but when he tried to send for them, the daughter plotted to kill her brother, and rule alone as heiress to the throne."

"What a pack of lies Largo has come up with," said Famhart, pacing furiously up and back beside the small fire they had used to brew their tea.

A fly had landed on the lid of the honey jar, and become stuck in the sweet, dark streaks.

"There is a lesson to be had there, Alac," said Famhart, directing the attention of his two companions to the plight of the trapped insect.

"Sir?"

"Look at it. It senses food, and plenty of it. The aroma is sweet, and it promises freedom from want. All you have to do is come to the jar and get it. Now look! The poor beggar is doomed by the very thing that promised to feed him!"

"I don't see what you mean, sir. What has a fly to do with anything?"

"Nothing, lad," Famhart laughed. "It only reminded me of Largo in the South Channels, determined to avenge himself for a wrong he thought was done him. Only now it all begins to look like a giant pot of honey."

"What does, sir?"

"Revenge," said Famhart simply. "To return to the scene of a bitter defeat, and make your enemies pay."

"But who is this Argent Largo? Why has he attacked the Line? I thought only the raiders from over the borders had any interest in us."

"Largo is my wife's brother, Alac. He was thought to be lost, before the battle of the Middle Islands. But the forces of the Darkness plucked him away, and I'm sure he is a perfect tool in the plot for revenge."

"Whose revenge? I'm not so sure I understand any of this."

"You will, Standin. Kegin didn't have time to fill you in on all the lore when he was teaching you to tend your weapons."

"All we got from him were lumps and harsh words," grumbled Alac. "He is a hard taskmaster."

"But he may have given you the ability to stay alive when the going is rough."

"I would have preferred more lore-learning."

"You say that now in jest, Standin. Wait until the day comes when there will be nothing between you and whether or not there will be any lore left to carry on, when only your sword hand, or bow shot will make the difference."

"Revenge and lore, and flies in the honey! It's enough to confuse anyone," complained Alac.

"It begins to make more sense, after I've heard the news of the offers Largo has made. That has opened up an avenue I had thought closed years ago. It also is another chance to fix it. I may just go along for this all the way, and approach Largo as a lad who would come to collect the fee he has offered to any of those who would join him."

Standin and Alac were astounded, standing speechless, with their mouths open.

"You can't mean that, sir!"

"Oh, but I do! Why, it would be a chance to see some country we haven't seen before, and to put our eye to the sore spot of all this troubled wood. We'd know for certain of our enemies, and how the deck lies stacked against us."

"But what of our kin? What will they think if they hear we have gone over the Edges? I couldn't think of letting my sister and mother believe that of me! And you, sir, your wife has been struck down by this villain you say is the very one you will go to see!"

"Of course we shall get word to the settlement, and all

our kin, Standin. That would be too cruel a blow, as you say."

"But how shall we send word? One of us shall have to return to the camp, then catch back up with our party on the trail."

"Too long, Alac. It would take too long to go about this in that manner. If we ride, it will be tonight. There's no time to be lost. We shall draw up the lads, and the youngest shall go back with our intentions, so that Kegin can keep abreast of what we're up to."

"None of the lads will want to be singled out for that duty, sir. It will seem a job better left to one of the settlement's womenfolk."

"They'll get over that thinking. And I don't want to force anyone along with me who doesn't want to go. This is really a job for myself alone, but I don't think I would be able to bluff my way into Trew alone. It would seem more reasonable if I were a squadron commander come with my men to collect the fat bounty being held out as a lure."

"Then make it a draw, sir, with all of us equal. That way none of us will feel the worse for it if we have to be the one to return to bear the news of our plan."

"That trip alone won't be a dance, Alac. We have covered a good plot of ground since we left, and there are signs all about us that there are plenty of raiders loose in the Line."

"One man will be faster, and draw less attention, sir. That should prove no problem."

"Good lad! Then we shall draw lots. Sound the rest out, and muster them here."

"Aye, sir," said Alac, standing up and setting off to carry out his mission.

Famhart stirred up a small packet of the wonderful powder that Brian Brandigore had given him long ago in the Middle Islands. As he mixed it, he remembered the words the dwarf had spoken, and said them aloud to himself.

"Whenever there is weariness, or sorrow, or spirits low, drink up this draught with the blessings of Round Hat, the last of the kings underground." He lifted his cup and drank. "I shall have need of all its powers, old friend."

"What is it you're talking of, sir?" asked Standin.

"The powder, my lad. It was given to Linne and me at the battle of the Middle Islands. A dwarf by the name of Brandigore had thought to thank me by giving me this. Wonderful stuff! Mixed up by his folk in the depths of the earth for as long as they had been about."

"Dwarfs, sir? You mean the half-ones?"

"Dwarfs," corrected Famhart. "Kegin has many holes in his teachings, but I can't fault the man. I know he has had his hands full with this lot."

"They actually existed?" pursued Standin, not to be put off.

"They did, and in many places. It was a grand sight to see one of their armies there, helmets and axes a burnished sea of flame in the sunlight, glowering and looking like death itself."

Standin had never dared to ask his commander about the old times, although he heard various accounts of the veterans of the Line, who had fought in that long ago war.

"There were so many of the dwarfish clans, the boats had to make return trips all night along to land them, lad. What a sight it was."

"Was Linne there, too?" asked the young man, then wishing he hadn't when he saw the look of pain that crossed Famhart's face.

"Aye, lad. She's a fierce warrior, on any account. I met her when she was a prisoner bound for my father."

"The Bog Hat elder?"

"Aye, lad. It was a strange enough meeting, I assure you. She almost knifed me before it was all over."

Standin was unable to cover his shock, but was saved by the arrival of Alac, and the clamor of the others of the squadron gathering about.

"All present, sir. Tamlock is squaring the lots to be drawn. We'll make it so the one who goes can't be missed."

"Have you told them what we're up to?"

"Yes, sir."

"What do you think, Alac? Any ideas? Do we have any bright ones who don't want to go along with the plan?"

"Sir?" asked his young subaltern, looking confused.

"I'll find out when we draw lots, Alac. See to it we have our stores in order, and plenty of water for the march. Once we're into Trew, we'll have to be extra careful about what we pick up to eat or drink. There have always been nasty tales about poisoned water and bad meat. I've got something that will help us along that line, but no one is to eat or drink anything without first clearing it with me. Clear?"

"Aye, sir."

"Good. Let's see to our other business."

Famhart strode briskly to the center of the gathered circle, and raised his hands above his head to call for quiet. There were questions called out to him from all sides, but he finally brought the group to order, and was able to make himself heard.

"I suppose some of you don't like the new plan," he began, and had to wait until the grumbling subsided before he could continue. "We are going under wraps, lads, to the very heart of this affair. We have to find out exactly what we're up against, and who is holding the knife to our throat. You all know my wife is in a death sleep brought on by an enemy who calls himself Argent Largo. This blighter is in Trew somewhere, and that's one of the places we know the raiders are coming from. We also know that there are rumors of bounties being paid for anyone from the Line who joins with this Largo, to overthrow what's left of the settlements in all the lands below the borders that are still free."

"How do we know this fellow won't spot us for spies and have done with us?" asked a young man standing next to Alac.

"For the simple reason that I'm who I am. If I read my man right, he will relish the idea of having Famhart coming to call upon him. And I still have a fancy that somehow or other, I might yet sway him."

Famhart put his hands behind his back and paced a few steps, thinking intensely.

"No, we shall have no trouble arriving. Getting out may be another story."

"Then what good would we serve by handing ourselves

over to our enemies?" asked the youth, a clear-eyed young man not much older than Owen.

"I have no intention of turning ourselves over to the enemy. I said getting out would be another story, not impossible. We have to find out the nature of our problem before we can begin to remedy it."

"Then we'd best be drawing lots to find who is to advise Kegin and the others of what we're about," said Alac.

"Right you are, lad. Set the hat there, and have each of you pull out a marker. The cross and star shall tell the tale. Whoever gets that mark shall have a ride back to the others to keep them up on our whereabouts, and what we shall be up to."

Famhart's features softened then, and his voice was a tone more removed. "And whoever goes, be sure to look in on Linne for me, and make sure she gets this."

He had removed a ring from his left hand, and rolled it about his open palm.

The drawing began then, with a lot of complaints and protests, but it went quickly until a slender, blond young man with the faint traces of a beard, raised his hand with a groan.

"I have the blasted thing," he lamented. "Leave it to Clede to fetch out this wretched chore."

"Now you can rush back into dear Nina's embrace, you dog, while the rest of us will be facing no telling what dangers."

"He speaks the truth, Clede," went on another young warrior. "We shall come home covered with glory, only to find you've won over the hearts of all the eligible maidens who are left of the old settlement of Sweet Rock."

"That's what a steward of the Line is supposed to do," argued Clede. "Gather honor to his name, not be lolling about camp with the womenfolk."

Famhart laughed as he approached the youngster. "You have taken all Kegin's teaching to heart, Clede. I shall tell him about this when next we cross paths. He has done an admirable job."

"Hold off, sir, until we hear this all again after our first encounter. Blood runs high, until cold steel comes into play."

"And what of it, Alac? Do you think that there are those of us that won't be able to pull our weight when the time comes for it?"

"All I say is that we shall see who has done what when the first blow falls, Clede. It won't affect you in the least, though, since you shall be safe back in a snug shelter with Nina."

Clede's face flushed a bright red, and he edged forward toward Alac with clenched fists.

"You've gone far enough with your jest, Alac. This is a job that needs to be done, and there's no certainty that it is one that will be safe. We don't know who or what roams the wood between here and where we left the others. It shall take a stout heart to leave here alone and go all the way back without a single friend to ride with."

"Maybe we should send two," offered Standin. "If what you say is true, sir, then it would be foolhardy to send a man alone."

As Famhart turned the question over in his mind, Clede protested.

"To send two men to do a single job is uncalled for. Two together might keep each other company, but it wouldn't be enough of an edge to counter a force of a dozen men or more, and that's when speed is more to my liking. One can go faster, then, so let me go alone, and you'll have the extra body here, where you shall need it. I shall be perfectly safe. I know these parts, and have a shortcut in mind that will take me back quickly. I'll be home in three days time."

"You have a good point, Clede," agreed Famhart. "I follow your logic for all of it, and tend to agree with you. Take what stores you need, and get some rest. You can leave when we've watered the horses and had our meal."

The young man saluted smartly, and whirled on his heel to find his supplies and tend to his kit before departure.

Famhart led Standin and Alac to the small fire, where a quick meal had been prepared. "We'll see to our stomachs, and then to our saddles. We've got a long trail ahead of us, and we shall have to begin to act like lads that have seen it quits with the stewards of the Line. There's no way of telling whether or not we're being watched, even now."

"This is strange, coming from you, sir," said Alac.

"Not so strange, when you consider that it might serve the Line better than if we swore allegiance twelve times over every day, but could do nothing about stopping the threat which hovers unhindered beyond our borders."

Famhart took up a bowl of the hot stew then, and fell into a silence so deep that his two lieutenants were afraid to disturb him, and he remained in such a withdrawn state until Clede came to report that he was ready to leave on his mission.

The elder of Sweet Rock listened with half an ear, then put a hand on the young man's shoulder. "Don't stray from your course, Clede. We're depending on you to alert the others. You can also tell them to wait for further orders from me, as soon as we're in touch with Argent Largo. That will be the turning point of it all, I feel. Once that contact is made, then we shall be down to business in earnest."

Famhart gave Clede the ring for Linne, shook his hand and watched while he mounted and rode away, turning frequently to wave, until a denser patch of forest blocked his view.

The larger party waited for a few minutes more, listening until the last of the lone horse's hoofbeats had died away, then moved off toward the cold and inhospitable north, following the swift waters of the Lower Tybo.

Chaos at the River

From the inner depths of the domed mounds, an eerie music filled the night with soft moans and sighs, like the cries of some ancient wind, trapped beneath the dark earth. Lights moved about in the eaves of the wood that ringed the mounds, and a dim rushlamp could be seen clearly, as though an invisible hand were carrying it.

Largo stood beside the silent hooded figure in the hour after midnight, feeling for his sword beneath the long cloak.

"It is the Lord Trew's entourage," explained his companion, a pale blond woman, with startling blue eyes.

"I thought your king was dead," remarked Largo, trying to pierce the gloom to see how the mysterious figures managed their small deceptions.

"He has gone beyond the last of the world's end to count the stars," corrected the woman. "Lord Trew cannot die. None of us can."

"That is a thing I would know of, Elita. If I could but master that, all my troubles would be over."

He felt the dark heartbeat within him then, and recalled with satisfaction how he had been given back his life by the Dark One, with a promise of sweet revenge on all those who had betrayed him. His sister was the first he had struck down, with the help of the Lady Elita, the strange follower of the Lord of Trew. She had shown him the vehicle for his revenge.

"Do you have any other trinkets like the brooch you gave

me? I have taken a great fancy to that way of working my displeasure on those who are my enemies."

"Do you have other enemies who threaten you, Largo? I hope it's not so."

"My treacherous sister was my greatest danger. If she has taken the bait as you think she will have, then that is the most serious problem solved. The rest is as simple as marching with an army down below the borders to claim that country for our own."

"We have a country here, dear one. Trew is wild and lovely. There are no sorrows here. There can never be tears or partings here. The sleep of the dreamer is swift and painless, and it cannot bring fear when it visits. We shall be laid side by side one day, here where the outer doors to the mounds lead down into the hallway of the stars."

"That is a lovely thought, Lady Elita, but I don't intend to allow myself that pleasure for many years to come. I have too much to see before I can enjoy the sweet repose you speak of."

"Must you do what you say, Largo? That is all taken care of now. No one can hurt you here. Trew is unkind to her enemies."

Largo reached out and took the pale hand, smiling. "I shall count on that to be so, Elita. There are those who will find out that they have not succeeded in their treason against me, and will try to find me."

The lights in the dark wood flared up, as though an invisible breath had swept through on unseen wings. A higher keen began, from somewhere inside the mounds. Steps, carved and laid by masons, led down into the passages, and the women descended a few paces downward.

"Come with me, Largo. We shall place the Cross of Locust on the altar of my king's life. He shall be with you to protect you then. No enemy can deal with the Lord of Trew."

"Are you going down there? It sounds as though we're not wanted."

"Those are the watchers. They make that noise to frighten away any who do not belong."

"Is that all they do?" asked Largo cautiously.

"Oh no, by no means. They have powers that even I can't tell you of. They have been long at their task, and they have done it well. There has never been a single time that any of our sleeping chambers have been disturbed."

"Are these watchers controlled by you?"

"Yes, sometimes. I can speak to them. Anyone who is of Trew can."

"Could you teach me?"

"You? Why would you want to learn of this?"

"I was just curious, my lady. It seems such a fascinating idea, these watchers. I would like to see them at their work."

"I don't think it would be too pleasant a thing, Largo. There are things that aren't meant to be witnessed by eyes that are still in our poor human shapes."

"You mean they are so horrible as all that?" persisted Largo.

"Not horrible, exactly. No, I wouldn't say they are so horrible, but they take strange forms, and they have been known to drive men beyond the boundary of madness. They catch at that thin curtain we have to protect ourselves, and rip it asunder."

"Now you really have my curiosity awakened. These watchers sound as though they would be a better weapon than all the armies I could muster from mankind."

"They cannot leave Trew," said the woman simply. "I don't think they would be able to exist even beyond these shrines."

Largo's hopes fell. "Oh? Surely there must be some way they could be moved about."

"They aren't meant to be moved about, Largo. When they were brought into existence by Lord Trew, he only gave them form and shape for this job they were to do."

"Then your king knew how to call up these watchers?"

"Yes."

"Can you do that as well?"

"Why would I call up watchers? They are here, right where they're needed."

"But if they should ever be needed, Elita? Could you call them up then?"

"If Trew was in danger, I could. Any one of us could."

Largo smiled and kissed the pale hand. "The Lord of Trew would be proud of his subject, Elita. You are truly a grace to your country."

"Trew only asks that her subjects be of stout heart, and to follow the edicts of what has been the Truth and Way for all time. The Lord Trew himself has found that these are only knaves and tyrants outside our boundaries here."

"Your king was a wise man, my lady. You will be well advised to continue on with that policy. There are great armies gathering in the lands beyond, and they are as bloodthirsty and evil as the Lord Trew was kind and wise and good."

"Where are these armies coming from, Largo? You mean they intend to invade Trew?" Elita's eyes were wide, and her breath came in shallow gulps.

"Not to invade Trew, Elita! To destroy Trew, and slay all those who dwell here!"

"How do you know this, Largo? Have you been in the lands beyond?"

"Before I found safe haven here, my lady, I was pursued by the tyrants who would put me to death. I was a marked man, singled out by the underlings of my sister. When they found out that I had escaped the cowardly trap they had set for me, they marked me openly for death. It was only my good fortune that has led me to Trew, and safety."

"You shall be safe here with us, Largo. The Rogen have long guarded the Edges, and until you survived that meeting you had with one, no other soul has escaped them. That was the main reason I think the aldermen let you live."

"Just causes are always favored, my lady. When that is no longer the case, I hope I shall have no breath left to my body."

"Don't speak of that Largo! You shall have a long and full life here in Trew. I can see to it that you shall one day sit upon the Court of the Sacred Oak. You will be safe from your enemies, and we shall perhaps find our way into the lost hills behind the moon, where Lord Trew has gone."

Largo found himself falling under the spell of the deep blue eyes of the pale woman, and a part of him that had been haunted and hidden by the breath of the dragon stirred for a moment.

"It shall be as you say, my lady. You have proved yourself to be a valuable friend. In helping me deal a blow back at my sister, you have helped me strike as the very core of the enemies' strength. With her out of the way, we shall find out whether or not the precious stewards shall be able to retain control of the Line."

"Where have you sent my kinsmen? Are they all still beyond our boundaries?"

"They have done a small favor for me, my lady. They have delivered word to any and all they chance upon that Argent Largo is alive and well in Trew, and will pay a fat sum to everyone who will join him in overthrowing the rule of my tyrant sister, who robbed me of my birthright, and tried to slay me in the bargain."

Elita had pulled the cowl back from her head, and stood a pale, ghostly figure in the dim shadow of light cast from the rushlamps in the corridor. "Do you think any of these men will come?"

"They shall! I can promise you that. And we shall need to keep the Rogen at bay, at least until we sort the true from the false."

"How will you be able to tell that, Largo? Can you read the thoughts of people so easily?"

Largo laughed, although his eyes were cold and gray. "I have my own secrets, Elita. You have your ways, and so do I. It shall not fail me."

He was fingering the amulet at his neck, and as he touched the cold scale of the dragon, he felt a short, hot blast of foul breath down his back.

"Trew is not a middle ground for your battles, Largo. You have been a guest here, and we have extended our courtesy and hospitality to you without reservations. I have spoken for you in the Hall of the Alderman, and to the others who doubted your story. They accuse me of being smitten by your charm, but I can't help believe what you've told me is so. The Rogen make no mistakes, and you were a sign sent to us. No one has ever escaped the Rogen."

"I am a sign sent to you, Elita. We shall have our world to rule together, once this injustice is righted. Your people will be free once more to go and come as they please, without having to resort to such horrors as the Rogen, or the watchers, to keep their borders safe. Then we shall be at our leisure to pursue your Lord Trew, and to find the way that he's gone, and to ponder the mysteries behind the stillness of the grave."

"Come with me, Largo," whispered Elita. "Come to the Second Level. There are the singers there, who tell tales of the forgotten world."

Largo felt her hand in his, tugging him gently toward the stone vault at one end of the long, damp corridor.

The amulet had begun to grow hotter at his throat, and in the closeness of the tunnel, he was panic-stricken for a moment, being unable to breathe. "I must go up, Elita. This tunnel seems to grow in upon me. I can't stand these small places!"

He stumbled up the entryway, and stood gasping in the stillness of the open air. The starlight seemed to blind him after the gloom of the tomb.

"It's the same every time," he stammered, as Elita hurried to his side. "That was the way my sister tried to murder me, at the crypt of my father."

"How dreadful," said Elita. "You poor soul. So much has happened to turn you to this plot for revenge. I can understand more of it now."

"I don't want to burden you with any of this, my lady. It's just that sometimes I can't quiet my heart. It's like a firestorm in the forest. It burns until there is nothing left at all."

"We have healers here, Largo, who can help you. There are ways to forget all these wrongs that were done you."

"I don't want to forget, Elita! Can't you see that? I have

to make the wrongs right, or I shall never be able to rest again."

"There are other things in life than the righting of wrongs. You could live here in Trew without ever another thought of your sister. She has fallen into the death-sleep, so there is no more that you need do. It is a fitting punishment for her crime."

"But how can I be sure? If I could be certain, then I might think otherwise. When I have proof that she is indeed under the spell you told me of, then I shall look at my life in different terms."

Elita smiled hopefully.

"Then we shall wait for my kinsmen who have gone to deliver your messages. They will have all the news from beyond Trew."

"You're right, my lady. Now I want to see this Hall of the Alderman you've told me of."

"It is only for the aldermen, Largo. Even if you were a son of Trew, you wouldn't be allowed to see it until your twenty-seventh nameday."

"There would be no harm in it, Elita. No one has to know."

"But I would know! There's no harm in your asking, for you are an outsider. You don't know the Code, so you couldn't know what you ask me to do. But you know it now, so don't press me any further, I beg." Elita was crying softly, her eyes turning a more startling blue.

Largo shrugged his shoulders and grasped her hand. "Of course not, sweet lady. I did not know I was pressing you so in the matter. Where I come from, a hall of elders is just that, nothing more. Anyone is free to go or leave there as they please."

"This is Trew! There are things we do here that have always been different than others. The Lord Trew himself set that tradition when he closed the borders, and began to seal off the outside world, with all its ugliness."

"One can't stay away from things that are ugly, Elita. That is the way of this life of ours."

"Perhaps yours, Largo, but we in Trew see things in a

different light. You will too, once you have come to know us better, and understand our ways."

"Perhaps I shall, at that," he said, preferring to drop the subject for the moment, until he could try and find another approach to the tender question of the mysterious hall. Whatever was there, it might prove of use to him in his budding plans for the invasion of the lowlands.

"Come with me now, and we shall see the floating lights on the river. They are the most beautiful on nights when it is so dark."

"Lights? Like the ones we saw in the wood?"

"Very similar, but not the same. No one knows for sure why they are there. The Lord Trew tried to discover the secret for himself, but he was never able to pierce the mystery."

"There are lights on the river?"

"Yes, at certain times of the year. This is the time that we often see them the most. A week ago, the Silver was so bright, it looked as though the water was white gold, and the shorelight on both sides was as bright as noontide."

"What could cause such a thing?" asked Largo.

"There are stories from the olden days, about the dreamers, but no one ever saw them, or heard the music that clan is supposed to be so well handy with."

"Dreamers? Music? What clan do you speak of, Elita? Is it a race from beyond Trew?"

"From beyond anywhere that we know. The Lord Trew once sat fasting for twelve days and nights on the shores of the Silver, but no clues were given as to what it all meant. That was very hard for him."

"It would be hard for anyone, if it is as dazzling as you say it is. Is there no one who could explain the mysteries? Surely, someone must have an idea?"

"There are those who always have ideas of everything, but it is not always wise to speak too loudly on things that are not to be spoken of."

"Superstition, my lady, nothing more. If I see these lights you speak of, you can be assured that Argent Largo won't rest until he has an answer in his mind that fits all the questions."

Elita looked down shyly. "Have you answers to all the questions in your life?"

"That is a strange one, coming from you. How do you mean it?"

"Only that you seem so sure of everything, and yet there are things about you I see which puzzle me."

A leaden feeling of apprehension crept over Largo at that moment, and he darted a quick sideways glance at the woman.

"Why do you look at me so? It makes me feel quite strange."

"I'm sorry, my lady. For a moment I thought I heard something."

Elita held the small, finely wrought rushlamp up, and peered about apprehensively. "What could it be?"

Largo eased the longsword at his side slowly out of its scabbard, and paced a few steps out into the edge of the flickering light. "Someone who is trying to spy on our movements, no doubt. Do you have any enemies, Elita? Or suitors?" Largo turned back toward her, his mind off on a new tack.

"Trew has no enemies but the outsiders."

"What of the Rogen?"

"You saw what happened to her. They will not attack one from Trew. That is the way it has always been."

"You mean those things only feed off outlanders?"

"You were in the gravest of dangers, Largo. The fact that you escaped with your life was the one thing in favor of you being allowed to stay on in Trew."

"I don't think this was the Rogen," he went on, bending down suddenly, and picking up an object from the dew-wet ground.

"What is it?" asked Elita, trying to see the small limp object.

"It looks like a band from a quiver, my lady."

"A what?"

"A stopper for your bolts. A cloth to keep the arrows from coming out of a quiver."

The woman took the cloth from Largo's hand, holding it close to the lamp so she could see it more plainly. "I can make nothing of it. I've never heard of anything like you describe."

"Then do you recognize it for anything you're familiar with?"

"It might be a cloth from the altars at the river. When the lights appear, we set a table for whoever it might be, in case they might need food or drink. This looks like one of the cloths."

"Let's go to the river. I'd like to see what you're speaking of."

"It's not far. We can be there in a short walk. Listen! You can hear the water now. It always sounds louder the later it gets."

"I didn't notice it so much before. I'm surprised I didn't hear it."

"The trees do funny things with the sound sometimes," said Elita, holding the lamp out before them, to show the path they were following.

"I guess they do. What I would like to know now, is how this cloth got from the river to where we found it? No matter what purpose it serves, it certainly didn't get from the riverbank to where we found it by itself."

"There may be others who are out for a walk tonight. Everyone in Trew loves the nighttime. It always has been that way."

"A strange habit."

"Strange, perhaps, but true, all the same. Some say it happened when Lord Trew began to keep his hours after dark, instead of carrying on his business by day."

Largo watched the woman as she talked on, and wondered to himself if the habit of living by night caused her eyes to change to the startling blue. He had seen others of the settlement with their cowls drawn carefully over their faces, as though the light hurt their eyes, but he couldn't be sure of anything of these strange beings who had befriended him.

"It might be the Wornel," she went on, breaking in on Largo's thoughts.

"Who are they? Are they something like the Rogen?"

"Oh, no, these are the animals who dwell in Trew. They are subjects, like all of us."

"The animals?" asked Largo, walking close beside her now.

"The Wornel. They befriended Lord Trew when he banned all killing here."

"The venison we had was certainly killed by someone!"

"That wasn't venison, Largo. It tasted that way to you, but it was not an animal that was slain."

"By the breath of the Purge, what do you people do? You live by darkness, and say you don't eat animal flesh, and speak of lights on the river in the middle of the night."

Elita placed a hand on Largo's arm. "We are the Children of Trew. It is the way of things here. You must not be concerned about how strange we seem to you. And remember, you seem as strange to us!"

Largo nodded in agreement. "When I first met you, I thought I had fallen in with a company of fools."

"We knew not what to think of you. It wasn't until you survived your meeting with the Rogen that we knew you were different from all the others who live outside Trew."

"Were you leading me to the Rogen when we first met?"

Elita looked down, lowering the rushlamp. "Yes. It is our duty to take outsiders to the Rogen."

"Well, I'm glad it all came to a cheerful end, my lady. I can't blame you for doing your duty, but I'm glad things didn't work out as planned."

"So am I, Largo. That is all the more reason for you to stay with us here in Trew. There is hope here. It is gone, outside."

"How can you speak of things you know nothing of, my lady?"

"Your own story bears me out! Where is the sanity and

order in a world that allows sisters and brothers to murder each other! And for what?"

"Your point is well taken, my lady. Yet there are other things that are not quite so horrible, which are very compelling, and attract you to them, again and again."

Largo's eyes lit up in the dark as he spoke, and a strange look transformed his features into an eager mask of anticipation.

"I won't ask you further, Largo. I feel a strange attraction to you which might draw me away from my ideals as a child of Trew. I feel I have already done too much in showing you the tombs. I begin to doubt what I have been taught all my life, and that frightens me."

Largo was on the verge of speaking, when they came into a clearing that bordered the river, and the rushlamp was swallowed by the brightness of sparkling lights that danced in the clear, icy depths of the water.

There was another sound then, of music, which tore at Largo's skull, forcing him to take deep breaths to keep himself from screaming aloud in pain. The notes soared, then fell away, but they left a hard echo in his heart, which made each gulp of air seem a flaming hot iron to his lungs. The amulet at his neck became red hot next to his skin, and for a moment, he thought it would burn through his shirt and cloak.

He turned to the woman and called to her for a drink in a voice which sent her hurrying to obey his request. Elita knelt to dip a small cup into the Silver, but the fragile piece seemed to catch fire in the process, and she fell back stunned.

Largo gathered his cloak up about him then, and ran as fast as his stumbling legs would carry him, back toward the settlement of Trew, and away from the terrible roar of the chaos at the river.

THE CHALLENGE
OF THE
STEWARDS

Trial by Fire

Tiny rivers of sweat dropped off Kegin's eyebrows as he crouched waiting, and he had an overwhelming desire to sneeze. A few yards away, Emerald was poised, his bow at the ready. Owen and Darek were further along in the trees, longsword and dagger drawn.

Another horn call broke the stillness of the soggy morning, which was gray and overcast. The noise died away, but was followed quickly by answering notes from all directions. Some were flat and harsh, and others were high and clear, but they all spoke of a large party traveling through the wood, spread out in what seemed a battle line, to listen to the signals that passed among the unseen units.

There were human sounds then, and the muffled tread of horses being led, and the distinct clink and squeak of pack gear and weapons.

Owen whispered hoarsely to Emerald. "Can you see anything yet? Are any of our squadrons operating here?"

"Shhhhh," cautioned the older man, motioning with a hand to stay put and remain quiet.

"What did he say?" questioned Darek, his voice pinched with the tension.

"Shhhh," repeated Owen. "We have to stay put."

"What if it is our squadrons?" asked Darek. "They could go right past and never know we're here."

"Friend or foe, they'll both know we're here if we don't shut up our yapping."

Owen made an impatient face and turned back to his scrutiny of the trail.

Drops of rain that had fallen earlier dripped slowly down

through the thick growth overhead, making it difficult to hear the softer sounds that came from further away.

A distant rumble of thunder promised another storm was awakening in the new morning, and the knowledge did not give comfort to the companions as they lay in hiding, awaiting the arrival of the unseen army that was moving through the forest just at the first part of dawn.

Emerald had notched an arrow to his bow, and strained to see through the dense gray gloom. "Look alive, Kegin! Horsemen directly in front of us!"

Kegin nodded and eased his longsword out. His grip tightened on the hilt until he could feel the cold steel become a part of his heartbeat.

A shadowy form began to emerge from the wet green background, mounted, with a heavy riding cloak drawn up over the head, making it impossible to see the face of the rider, or the nature of his gear.

"Blast the luck," breathed Kegin. "The blighter is going to be on top of us before we can say for certain who he is."

Another figure loomed out of the wood behind the first, followed by another close on his heels.

Kegin gave the signal they had devised, should they have to fight for their lives, and the companions readied themselves for action. Emerald drew down on the lead rider, and waited for the man to get close so there would be no chance for a miss. Kegin was then to pull the man out of the saddle and set off, causing those behind to give pursuit, when Owen and Darek would stand to and draw the attention of those who followed, giving Emerald a chance of another sure shot.

The cloaked rider appeared closer now, and Owen's heart hammered in his throat, and he couldn't swallow. The sound of his breathing was so loud he was sure it would give them away, but the mounted man came on, unaware of the danger.

Just at that moment, one of the horses behind Darek snorted and gave a tentative little greeting to the stranger's mount. There was an immediate air of electric tension, and the rider had thrown back his cloak to draw his longsword.

In that brief instant, Emerald recognized the coat of arms

of an outlaw chieftan from the Wastes of Leech, and let fly with the deadly shaft in his hand. The flight of the arrow was swift and true, and the enemy rider was struck down so suddenly he never had a chance to whimper or cry out.

Kegin was on the man instantly, hauling the lifeless body from the saddle and mounting in one fluid movement. He had no need to spur the frightened horse, and was away before the other riders behind him could react to the sudden onslaught of the attack.

One of the men started to raise a horn to his lips, but Owen stood up at that moment and walked slowly toward him, the Gillerman's longsword held out before him like some religious relic.

The man's cowl was thrown back, revealing a head of dark hair, and a close-cropped beard. It was not a handsome face, but it was not what Owen had expected either, and he hesitated for an instant, unsure of what to do next.

As Emerald's second shaft flew, the man spurred his horse toward Owen, to trample the lad beneath the animal's hooves.

Owen leaped aside as the horse and rider thundered down on him, noticing as he did that the sword had begun to glow a fiery white along the edges, and the same, low hum was throbbing through the blade, making it at once hard to hold, and yet impossible to let go.

Owen wished he had had time to learn more of the skills of the weapon, but he grasped the handle resolutely with both hands, and brought it above his head to strike at the charging horseman. The heavy body of the rider bore the youth to the ground, and he was struggling wildly to escape from the suffocating weight, when his hand felt the shaft of the arrow, buried to the feathers in the man's chest. He fought to control himself to keep from crying out aloud, and pulled himself painfully from beneath the still twitching corpse.

"Here, Owen! Up lad! We still have work to do!"

Emerald was holding the shying horse's rein, trying to calm the animal so that he could mount. His face was almost serene as he worked with the horse, while Owen got to his feet with a wobbly effort, panting.

"There is another one coming," he gasped, looking over the shoulder of his friend.

"I hear him. Kegin will have a clean shot at him."

"Duck! There's one there!" cried Darek, pointing with a violent motion to his left.

An arrow hissed by, crackling as it passed, and buried itself in a tree not a foot from Emerald's head.

"Blast and dash it! Hop to, lad! Get cover! If he comes this way, slash at him from hiding."

Emerald was mounted in another flash, and had jerked the shying horse around and spurred it on.

Another arrow narrowly missed Darek, who seemed frozen in his tracks next to the body of the first horseman.

"Down, Darek! We have to come on them by surprise."

His words fell on deaf ears, and the orphaned lad continued to stare as if in a trance.

Owen heard the rider coming, and knelt behind a thick, sweet-smelling bush, his hands gripping the longsword with all the strength he could muster.

"Help!" cried Darek, sensing his danger as the rider bore down on his small figure.

As the horse came on, Owen clenched his teeth and tried to time his blow just right, waiting until the last moment and swinging the gleaming blade through a high arc, at about where he thought the mounted rider's knee would be.

There was a jarring crash that almost tore his arms from their sockets, then the scream of a horse, that was followed by cursing, and the swooshing sound of a blade being swung with great force.

Owen rolled away instinctively, and watched the rider try to regain control of his spooked mount. Blood was spurting from the man's leg, just below the boot top, and the horse reared and pawed the air, nostrils flaring and eyes wild with fear and pain.

"Jump, Darek!" cried Owen, although his voice sounded thin as a reed. He didn't think anyone could hear him, it sounded so small.

Darek remained frozen where he was, and only a lucky, glancing blow from the rearing horse's flank saved the boy from being cleaved in two by the swordstroke the rider directed at the lad's head.

After another struggle to control his mount, Owen saw the man regain his saddle and whirl about, turning away from the area where he had been ambushed, and disappear into the gray eave of the wood away to his right.

Owen ran after the retreating form, waving his useless blade, his heart sinking within him. "I've let him escape! Now Kegin and Emerald will have another one to deal with. I'm no help at all!"

He remembered Darek then, and hurried back to see if the lad was wounded.

"I'm all right, really I am," protested Darek, pulling himself up from his knees and dusting himself off. "It was a good thing his horse turned when he did, or I'd have been finished."

"Didn't you hear me yell? I tried to warn you."

"I just seemed to be glued to the spot," said Darek. "I thought I was running, but I couldn't get anything to move."

"My father said that happens when it's your first time."

"It doesn't seem like anything moves at all, and then it goes so fast you can't do anything about it."

"I couldn't get my sword high enough to strike a good blow," lamented Owen. "That fellow got away, and now Kegin and Emerald will have to deal with him before he can warn the others."

"You wounded him, Owen! I saw the blood."

"This isn't at all what I thought it was going to be like," said Owen, sitting down wearily. It felt as though his mouth were full of ashes, and his limbs all gone to stone.

Darek's eyes were still wide with excitement. "Where do you think Emerald has gotton to? And Kegin? Did they leave us?"

Owen shook his head without looking up, studying the sword in his hand. "They haven't left us, Darek. We have to get the horses now, and go on until we meet them. This place is full of danger for us."

"But if we leave now, we may get lost from Emerald and Kegin."

"We have to move, Darek. You can see we aren't safe here."

The youth looked about like a trapped animal. "They will be coming back for us. We must wait for them!"

"The others will be coming back too, and they aren't going to be pleased with anyone they find here." Owen stood shakily, testing his legs. "We'd better go over the two Emerald shot. They may have news of something we might have need of."

"You mean touch those dead things?" asked Darek, cringing at the thought of it.

"It is what a soldier of the Line is taught to do. We must find out all we can. We need to know who they are, and where they've come from, and how many they are."

"I can't touch them! It's not right."

"Right or not, I must see if they have anything about them that will help us. Come on! You don't have to do anything but stand watch for me. Can you do that?"

"Yes."

"And bring the horses. We've got to get away from this place."

Owen crossed the clearing stiffly and approached the first of the horsemen struck down by Emerald's bowshot. He was surprised at the lack of blood on the man's chest, but he recoiled when he rolled the body over, for there was the damp red pool, glistening on the soft earth.

The lad could make nothing of the manner of dress, or the insignia, and for a terrifying instant, the thought ran through his mind that they had slain one of their own, from a far distant squadron, so as to be unrecognizable in a moment of quick decision.

Owen tormented himself with that until he came upon the leather pouch at the man's waist, and the contents inside. There were vials, sealed with wax, with a skull and crossbones painted on it, and a scrap of paper which was instruction on dipping a knife, or sword, or arrow point.

The man's face, although glazed and distant in death, was

not a cruel one, which puzzled Owen. He thought it would
have been easier if this enemy had been a Gorgolac or
Worlugh warrior he had read of.

"Owen!" came a shrill cry, then another, cut off before it
was finished.

Owen looked up in time to see a dismounted man send
Darek flying from a blow of his fist. The soldier was dressed
in a cloak of the same color as his fallen comrade, and he
held a riding crop loosely in his gloved hand.

"You shoot passing well for a pair of whelps," said the
man. "I had thought we were set on by that accursed bunch
of filth from the Line."

Owen edged up from where he knelt, trying to remember
what it was that Kegin was always teaching his students
about keeping your adversary in front of you.

"We are from the Line," replied Owen, his throat dry.

The man threw back his head and scoffed. "This is what
they throw against us now, is it? T'will be easier than they
said. Whelps! Mere whelps! And I have no compunction
about drawing and quartering the both of you!"

"You might think differently if my father were here. Or
my friends."

"Friends? Friends, you say? Have you friends hereabouts
now, whelp? Speak out!"

"A hundred or more," lied Owen, hoping his voice didn't
give him away.

The man had drawn his sword, advancing on Owen.
"Then they will surely hurry to keep me from lopping off
that sassy young head of yours."

Owen drew the sword of Gillerman in an awkward move,
and tried to hold down the fear he felt.

"A cheeky whelp, I'll give you that. Your slab there is
almost as big as you." The man laughed and jumped over
his slain companion, confronting Owen. "Now, my piglet,
let me see how you propose to use that fine sticker."

He leaped at Owen, striking two broad strokes that drove
Owen backward clumsily, almost losing his footing.

"Well, they've not taught you much of how to use that
thing in the pure and upright almighty Line. Have they

forgotten their sworn outcast enemies? Do they think they can send women and children against us? Speak up, whelp! This idea sends the gorge to my head."

"We only send the stewards of the Line against our enemies, sir," replied Owen, baffled by the man's speech, and afraid of his sword.

"The stewards! What a loathsome lot! What bloodsucking leeches they have been! They have denied our countrymen all for as long as we've lived on the Leech, but we have sworn our vengeance! We shall join with the new leader in the South Channels, and drive you filth from any hideouts you may run to cower in."

"I've never heard of any injustice we have done to anyone on the Leech," protested Owen, trying to keep the man talking.

"You wouldn't, whelp. You and your kind are so almighty pure and wise, it never occurred to any of you that your upright and ironbound code might cause grief to those of us who have had to scratch out an existence on that barren land we were driven to."

"That is only where the outcasts are banished," replied Owen. "The Line is merciful. We don't execute our lawbreakers."

"Aha, you see!" screeched the man. "Only a whelp, and you already have that down-your-nose way of preaching at me!"

"Are you one of that lot who were exiled to the Leech?" asked Owen.

"A man without a decent bed to call his own, or roof to shelter him from the cruel rain. All my life I've been driven from one downfall to the next, only trying to save my poor body from perishing away from a lack of everything, and then one day I happened to run afoul of your precious stewards, curse their black hearts. All I wanted was a meal from the settlement. A dog would deserve that! But they pronounced me outcast, and rode me to the boundary of the Leech Plains, and cast me into the wilderness there, with naught but my poor horse and a day's water."

"That is the law, sir," replied Owen, hoping to forestall

another attack until he could think of another plan, or in hopes that perhaps Emerald or Kegin might come back in time.

The man stood before him, sword held like a cane, supporting himself by it as he talked. "Your pure and wise stewards didn't take into account one thing, my piglet! They never thought anyone could survive the Leech Wastes. But they have missed their mark there, for there are hundreds of us that found it to our mutual benefit to band together. We've hired out to anyone with a grudge against the Line, and now we've found the choke-hold we've been looking for in a chap up toward the Channels. Promises booty to equal our body weight, and a country to live where we don't have to skulk about."

The man stopped, shaking his head.

"And now look at poor Bozzer here, all staked down like a turkey dinner! He won't be there for the fun when we pick the Line like a ripe apple!"

"I'm sorry about your friend, sir. He was trying to kill us."

"Bozzer? Not that lad! Why, he's never harmed anyone much. Poor sad sod, always the one to take everything he got back to the missus and nipper."

The man acted as though he were drying a tear from his eye.

"Poor old Bozzer! I've got to think of his missus and nipper, so I'll thank you for that pouch back you took from him."

A slow, cruel smile spread across the man's craggy face, revealing a thin scar that split his upper lip, giving him a grotesque appearance.

Owen looked down at the leather pouch in his hand, his mind working quickly once more. "It's not much to trouble yourself over, sir."

"Hand it over!" growled the man.

"If I give you the gold, will you let me keep the pouch? It's all I ask."

"You can keep his boots, too, if you want. But I want the coin and any other hard trinkets he had about him!"

Owen opened the pouch quickly, holding the vials in his hand. It was awkward opening the wax seals, but he managed it, being careful not to touch the light brown liquid inside.

"Shall I throw the gold to you? I don't think I want to get any closer than this."

"Aye, throw it, my piglet! If there's enough there, I might even be tempted to let you live on as my slave. I have need of a good stout boot-boy like you to help me with my arms and mount. Good pay, too! A beating for you everytime I feel the urge!"

The man threw back his head and roared in triumphant laughter, which gave Owen the opening he had been waiting for.

He launched himself at the man, getting leverage from the body of the slain outcast, and as he leaped, he flung the open vials in his hand into the face of the laughing soldier, and followed on through with trying to get the sword of Gillerman up into a defensive position.

Owen's aim was true, and some of the liquid had splashed into the eyes of the man, who threw both his hands to his face, screaming in agony. His sword was flung aside, and he stumbled about blindly, finally tripping over his slain companion, and falling into a writhing heap on the ground at Owen's feet.

A voice from behind him frightened him so badly he almost jumped out of his skin.

"Finish him, Owen. That poison you struck him with will take hours to do for him. It's a terrible death! Give him the mercy of a quick end."

It was Emerald, with Kegin beside him.

"You did fine, lad. It was the only thing you could have hoped to have done against him. He was going to kill you and Darek, once he had what he wanted from you. He was toying with you."

"How long have you been here?" asked Owen.

"We saw it all, lad," replied Kegin.

"Why didn't you do something sooner?" cried Owen, in anguish. "Now I shall have to strike him!"

"It is always a terrible thing, but it has to be dealt with, Owen. The craft of a warrior is not all a playful lark. These are the things you need to learn Owen, just as surely and well as you learn your lessons at the handling of arms."

"But this! This is not what you teach, Kegin! This is a helpless man!"

The man had screamed again, and rose to his feet, ranting and pulling at his eyes in his pain. He suddenly drew a short dagger from his belt, and lunged forward, toward the voices he heard from in front of him.

Owen whirled just at the moment the man crashed heavily forward, impaling himself on the sword the mysterious old stranger had given him on that night in Sweet Rock, when none of this nightmare he was living had come to be.

The man's eyes rolled wildly once, then the thin film of death descended, leaving Owen struggling backward under the weight of the sagging body. Emerald and Kegin helped free him, and went to see to Darek, who was sitting up holding a hand to his head, taking in everything that had gone on in the small clearing. Owen tried not to look at the man, but his eyes kept being drawn back, until at last he was staring at the convulsed face, with the hand clutching at the wound his sword had made.

He was on the verge of flinging the sword away from himself, when the familiar humming started once more, and the faint voice of Gillerman sounded almost at his ear. It was so close and so real, Owen looked about him twice to make sure the old man was not somewhere about.

"This is not the first time the elfin steel has slain. It won't be the last. You are to remember that no matter how you try to judge, there is no way the innocent can suffer by this sword. It was forged in the fires of truth."

"I didn't want any of this to happen, Gillerman! It isn't like I thought it would be!"

"It never is, lad. The emptiness you feel at taking life is a sure sign that we have made no mistake in the value we place on you. You are very near help now, lad. Quickly, while the time is still there, ride on!"

There was a scene then of a lovely lake, and a strange

woman who seemed to beckon to him. When Owen looked again, the illusion of the sword was gone, and in its place were the three tired faces of his companions.

After making what sense they could of the information the outcasts of Leech had given them, and after another search of the bodies, the friends mounted and left the clearing, taking along the extra mounts, in case they should need them somewhere along the way on their journey.

Darek rode next to Owen, but he said nothing, and looked away everytime Owen turned to ask a question.

Emerald removed his harp then, and played odd tunes and sang quick little ballads to amuse them, and one by one, their thoughts turned away from the scene they had left behind, and wondered at where their wandering would take them next.

When they camped that evening, Darek wouldn't speak, and ate his food quickly. Before Owen could move to him to ask how his head was, the lad pretended to be asleep, rolled tightly in his blanket with his back to Owen and the others.

"He is not well pleased with himself, Owen. He'll get over this. It's hard to be half-man, half-boy. That is a big step to take, and he hasn't reached the time yet when he will free himself from this shame he feels."

"What shame?" asked Owen. "He has done nothing wrong."

"I know. But he feels as though there is something more he should be doing. It will pass. Being his age is more difficult than learning how to find the lost pearls of the Silent Sea."

Emerald smiled then, and played a haunting tune that made Owen sad and happy at once.

As he went to sleep that night, his dreams were of wild-eyed men in armor chasing him about, while Emerald played on his harp, and the woman beside the still lake appeared again, following him down into a troubled sleep.

Proposal for a Journey

Chellin Duchin watched the last of the river of refugees pouring into the temporary settlement, where a fire had been set ablaze to guide all the stragglers home. There were women with tiny children, and frail-looking oldsters, wandering about through the crowds, seeking the faces of lost loved ones. Starboard and Port emerged from the milling throng, and came to stand beside their friend.

"This is not a sight I had thought to ever see," said Chellin, shaking his head.

"None of us ever thought it would come to this," replied Port.

"None of us," echoed Starboard.

"Have you seen the rest of my slackards? They seem to have gotten out from under my noose."

"We saw them a moment ago, Chellin. They were asking after any of the settlement of Sweet Rock."

"Good lads. They are trying to find Famhart. He's the one we need now."

Port cracked a nut and chewed it noisily as he replied, "No Famhart. No one has news of him."

"No one at all," repeated Starboard. "It's hard to make anything out with all the ruckus going on."

"Hard to make anything out," repeated Port.

Chellin Duchin raised a weary hand. "You've given me bad news, friends. I had hoped to meet with someone here we might use to salt the tails of our fine bucks up in the Channels, or maybe down toward the Wastes of Leech."

"You've got your cronies to go with you. Why do you need to wait for any others?"

The brothers nodded in tandem, waiting for Chellin to answer.

"Aye, I've got these dunderheads with me, hard as my lot is. The lads don't have an inkling of a notion about lore, and I can't say that that fault is not my own. I've neglected their teaching for too long, I fear. They have no sense of place or background, and if the subject is anything but weapons and horses, you might as well be addressing a mule."

"They seemed the right sort, Chellin. I can't say I didn't take a cotton to them."

Port and Starboard looked to each other in agreement.

"A right decent lot of chaps."

Chellin clasped his hands behind his back and paced to and fro in front of his horse, which was grazing lazily at the moment on a patch of sweet green grass.

"They're the right sort, and a fearless bunch, but they need age to temper their hot heads. My only complaint has ever been that they're too quick to leap to a fracas before they know the where or why of it all."

"Not bad recommendations to complain of in these times," said Port.

"Not bad at all," added Starboard.

"I'd try to wrangle you two into going if I thought I could get away with it."

"Where did you have in mind, Chellin? You're making a long way around a short subject here."

"You're right. I go on sometimes, when what's needed is a straight stroke to the heart of the matter. "

"There's the sure-fire trump to a confusion," agreed Port. "Stand to and brace yourself for a hard blow, and drive her in steady, so you hold a course."

"I'm thinking of altering my patrol once I get these poor beggars safely out of harm's way. I keep thinking that our answers are going to lie back in the direction we've just come from. It's not in my nature to be leaving just when the going is getting sticky."

"You've got a duty to these folk, Chellin. It's always been a steward's sworn duty to protect any and all citizens of the Line who are in danger, or in need of aid. That's what we swore to when we raised the cup on our oath."

"There's no question of leaving the camp here before we see them safely settled, Starboard. And once that's done, then our next duty is to seek out and drive off or destroy whatever has caused the threat."

"Not so easy, in these times. No way to know which direction to strike out in first. It was easier in the old days."

"Easier, and everybody knew what to do," said Starboard.

Chellin Duchin unrolled a set of charts wrapped in a leather sheath, and spread them out on the ground. "Here's my path. I want to deliver this settlement to safety, if that's to be found anywhere, and then set my sights on the Silver. I'd like to work my way back up on the borders of the Leech Wastes, and take a look at what's been happening there. We might get an idea of what we're dealing with here, and everywhere else in the Line."

The brothers whistled, and shook their heads, casting long looks at the map.

"That's harsh country you're talking of," said Port.

"Harsh country, brother," echoed Starboard.

"It's country you know something of," went on Chellin. "Hamlin and Judge and Jeremy are too young to know anything of Leech, or the goings-on up the Silver. I have need of hands that have been at this puzzle for long enough to know a thing or two."

"How many squadrons are you taking?" asked Port, stroking his close-cropped beard, and staring at the chart.

"Only the one. The others will have to stay with the camp."

"One squadron to go up the Silver, onto the Leech Plains?" asked Starboard.

"That's all that can be spared," said Chellin. "I know it

sounds like I've been frying my head in the sun too long, but that's all I can spare for this errand."

"It's not enough to do it safely," argued Port.

"I don't care whether we do it safely or not," replied Chellin. "I've never done anything safely since I signed on in this mullhash affair. And I'm not thinking of an engagement! That would be the last thing I'd pull with such poor strength. All I'm interested in is the lay of the place, and who's been there, and what's going on. I want to have a look at both sides of the river, and a squadron is the right number for that kind of a trip."

"If everyone is sweet, and gentle, and treats you nice," grumped Port. "And I don't think you're going to find too many gents up that way that'll be inclined to cooperate."

"Not likely at all," said Starboard, slipping his dagger out and cleaning a nail with the razor-edged point. "That part of the country is like riding the edge of this blade, Chellin! It's sharp on both sides of the Silver. And the river hasn't seen a friendly face for more turnings than I care to count."

"We couldn't count that high," said Port. "When we came down the last time from seeing our mother, rest her soul, the way was almost blocked with every sort of bandit and cutthroat that was scratching a living out of poor innocents who still dwelled there. My mother tried to keep us from leaving, but we both enjoy the longshot, so here you see us."

"I wish I'd listened to her now," said Starboard.

"That's why I need you two. You have a nose for the country, and you've made the trip. I haven't been up the Silver any further than Lake Fork, and that's been some time back. I left that area mostly to Florian, bless him, and never had a complaint there until all those lads were lost at Spirit Tarn. That's when I knew it was rough up there. Those were not green fellows that could be dealt with easily."

"I remember that," said Port grimly. "It was a black day for the stewards."

"We will have our day," said Starboard. "A reckoning always comes."

"Sometimes too soon, my friends. If we were to close with our enemies now, we'd be in poor shape to deal with them. Look at it, lads! A flock of frightened sheep, and overworked, overtired squadrons that are doing well to keep to their saddles. Those that aren't tired are hungry, and the rest haven't had a breather for weeks."

"A good turnout at the camp will mend them," said Port. "It's always the same after a few days in clean linen, and hot meals to fortify your strength."

"Nothing like sleep and stew to make a new man out of you," agreed Starboard. "Puts the steel back!"

"It may take more than sleep and food this time," said Chellin. "This has been a long time coming. I've seen it in the cards, but I tried not to look at it. Something has changed over the years."

"What, Chellin? What change could there be?"

"You are one of the old school, Port. You and your brother belong to my time, and the thoughts I keep. But the newer bunch coming up isn't so sure of their ideas, or the direction they want to travel in."

"That all comes right when they reach their age," argued Starboard. "I guess we were the same when we were pups."

"Not by a long throw," said Chellin. "I'm talking about something that is as hard to find as a bat in the dark. I can't put my finger on it, but it creeps along the minute you turn your head to look the other way."

"You've been harping on this too long, Chellin. I believe you're starting to show signs of the grouch. Our mother, bless her, always said that begins to come on when you reach a certain place in turnings. The gray begins to cloud your vision."

"We've seen the best of lads come down with a case of it," agreed Starboard. "The cure is always a good rest, and a belief that everything eventually comes out straight in the end, if you're square with your maker, and fair with your friends."

Chellin let out a low chuckle, but his face remained

drawn and haggard. "You two would rag my ear off if you came along with us. I retract my call for assistance! I'm sure you're needed much more right where you are."

The brothers shook their heads in unison.

"No, Chellin, you've convinced us we're needed, and come along we will. It has been some time since we've put flowers on our mother's tomb. It will be a good thing for us to tag along with you, Chellin! If you are determined to get a squadron butchered on the Plains of Leech, or the country somewhere up the Silver, then we're the lads that want to be there to remind you that we warned you against the trip."

"You'd go to those lengths, would you?" Chellin laughed. "Then by the sea-maiden's tail, you shall get your chance. Bigger scoundrels than you two have tried to chastise old Chellin before."

They were joined at this point by Jeremy and Hamlin and Judge, who gruffly exchanged handclasps and greetings with the brothers, but with a reserved gladness.

"These two have agreed to see us try the journey up the Silver," said Chellin. "They've given me every reason there is for not going, which only convinces me all the more that the trip is necessary."

"Your logic is beyond anything I've ever heard tell of," said Port.

"It always gets him his way," offered Hamlin. "No matter what you think at the moment, Chellin can have you twisted about his little finger quicker than you could snap off a bow shot. We've watched him work. We know this rogue."

"Is it true?" asked Starboard.

"Always," said Chellin. "I gave up accepting anything else long ago. There just seemed to be no more point to it."

"That's the right outlook, lads. Just ignore the worst of this wicked time, and you can avoid any discomfort or fal-de-hoop easy as rolling off a spooky mare."

"You should know, Judge! You've lived by that rule since you were old enough to ride with the Line!"

"You're harsh, Chellin! I've always tried to follow your lead."

Chellin Duchin bantered lightheartedly with his lieutenants, but his eyes were troubled.

"Does this have something to do with the meeting we had with the waterfolk at the lake?" asked Jeremy. "You've been as closed as a clam, and you don't even chew on us as often since then."

"Does it seem so, lad?" asked Chellin, concern in his voice. "I hope I haven't fallen on such hard times that I can't hide you all with my tongue anytime the feeling moves me."

"There's no chance you've changed your ways at this late date. If there's a reason, we'll know of it in due time, and I'm sure it won't be a reason we can believe has to do with our well-being."

"On the contrary, Jeremy, it has everything to do with your welfare, as well as all the rest of us. The dreamers have always been a guarded crowd, and they were never known to have been open with mankind as we know it, except for the times of the Middle Islands. Since then, they've retired more and more from sight. It was unusual to have seen and spoken with them at the lake. That told me that something far beyond the usual ebb and tide is afoot, and that, as likely as not, will be the death of us all."

"What are you speaking of?" asked Hamlin. "I assume we're talking of the same meeting back at the lake?"

"The same."

"Then the water did shrink your reason. I can account for it no other way!"

Chellin laughed, and pounded Jeremy on the back. "The lad thought I'd gone and drowned myself back at the old mill-grinders' lake," he explained.

"You were in the lake?" asked Starboard.

"Our mother always warned us about water! It eats the dreams and turns your mind to mud," said Port.

"He doesn't even know how to swim," added Hamlin. "I thought he'd slipped his wits, and was done for sure."

"Old Chellin Duchin is a long way from slipping his wits, lads, but if ever anyone were driven to it by being surrounded by a pack of empty-headed field sparrows, I'm the man."

"What would make you go in the lake?" asked Starboard.

"That's what we all asked him," said Jeremy. "And then as pretty as you please, and right out of nowhere, we were staring at a bunch of ghosts from another time. I never saw anything like it."

"They took back the burial cask Chellin had pulled out of the lake, and disappeared in a golden boat," added Judge.

The brothers looked at each other, shrugging their shoulders.

"It was the old mill-grinders' lake," explained Chellin. "Those that used it in recent times never knew of the history, or who had dwelled there long before them. To the millers, it was convenient to the rice and grain harvest, and that was that."

Chellin paused, smiling. "They never knew of the legend that surrounds that place."

"Neither did we," complained Hamlin. "Until you went through all the motions of drowning yourself there."

"Nor of the dreamers," Chellin went on. "It was a place that I'd read of as a slip of a lad, full of the moonlore and strange people who had long ago vanished. They filled my thoughts as a young man, and I dreamed of one day searching out all the sites in the Line that I knew went back to the old days. The mill-grinders' lake was one of the first I discovered."

"But you never went into the water before, did you? How long had that burial cask been there?" asked Jeremy.

"A good question. That cask, and a shore full of tales, confused me at first. I couldn't make out what was what at the start, but as I read it afterward, I saw what had begun to happen."

"Now you open up," grumbled Judge. "You were as silent as that cask when we tried to find out about it then."

"I was thinking, my boy. It's a habit you should become better acquainted with. It might sit well with that impatient head of yours."

"What were the signs on the shore, Chellin?" asked Starboard, doggedly pursuing his friend for an answer.

Chellin Duchin sighed heavily, and sat down, laying his shoulder back against his saddle. "We've been chasing one band of renegades or another for all our lives, yet never really knowing any more than that they are raiders from one of our borders or another, and that they have been outcasts from civilized older communities, or some of the ancient invaders from the wilder countries beyond the Malignes. That satisfied me for the first turnings I was a steward, but as time grew on, and changes began, I looked backward to the loremasters to try to find answers to some of my questions."

"Questions about what?"

"Questions about the clues to the riddle, Port. Questions as to where the Darkness had gone after the battle of the Middle Islands, and why there had never been any word of where those who had fought there were."

"You mean what happended to the other races who fought for the High King?"

Chellin nodded, his eyes seeing nothing of his surroundings. "My own father had spoken of seeing a host of elfin horsemen once, so dazzling to the eye he couldn't stand to watch them full on. They had swept over a hill in the Middle Islands that was afire by the terrible beauty of the fair ones."

"I've never heard you talk like this, Chellin," said Hamlin. "All this time we've been together, I always thought you were just a pig-headed old relic who liked the duty of Line Steward because it was lonely work, and you could spend your time away from the settlements and crowds."

"Those are reasons enough to encourage the job, my boy, but you've come a deal closer to understanding the true nature of Chellin Duchin. I've always read the old books and followed the old ways."

"Aye," agreed Port, looking to his brother for agreement. "You've got two more in us that follow that Line. Maybe our old dame who bread-and-buttered us had it right when she said that we would one day come back to our roots in Trew."

"She used to tell us tales of wonderful mines that lay in the Channels, full of gemstones that stored sunlight, and could burn in the Darkness for a lifetime."

"She also spoke of the small ones who mined them, and how ugly and evil they were. The Draghers, she called them. They never saw much of the light above ground."

"Those clans were mentioned in my books, Starboard. They were not an evil race, although they didn't have much traffic with humans."

"Our mother said they tried to seal off the Watchers of Lord Trew, and they closed the lower tombs in the burial mounds by flooding them with an underground river."

"No one can understand what drove those clans," said Chellin. "We have to remember that no matter what they've done, they fought on the side of the High King at the Middle Islands."

"But no one has anything to say of them since," persisted Port. "I think our mother came as close to understanding the nature of the small clans as anyone."

"Was your mother from Trew?" asked Judge, astonished at the fact.

"Aye. A child of Trew. So are we, Port and I. You can tell in the way we can see in the dark, and by this." Starboard drew up the folds of his cloak and bared a powerful forearm. "You see this?" he asked, pointing to a small crescent-shaped figure just below his wrist, between his thumb and forefinger.

Judge and Hamlin and Jeremy crowded closer to look.

"The same as I have," said Port. "And so does everyone else who is a native child of Trew. It is a mark that has been with us for as long as Trew has existed."

"You mean everyone has one of those marks?" asked Judge.

"Everyone who is of Trew," replied Port. "It was a mark in the old days, so we could come and go without fear of the Rogen."

"What on earth is a rogent?" asked Judge, still marveling at the intricate detail of the tiny design on the hands of the odd twin brothers.

"It is Rogen, friend, and they are the doorkeepers of Trew, or were. I think something has happened somewhere that has turned them into something horrible."

"Doorkeeps? What do you mean? Are they guards of shelters?"

"More, by a yard or two. They were brought about in the history of Trew by our father and keeper, the Lord Trew, Flame of the Hills of Trew."

Starboard continued the story: "When the world was at open combat, the Lord Trew called up the Rogen from a book he had from one of the Sisters of Skye. It was supposed to be a spell that would protect Trew from all enemies, and keep outsiders from invading."

Jeremy looked at Chellin Duchin, his eyes wide. "And you say you want to take a squadron up through Trew to reach the Channels? Even Famhart, if we could find him, would argue against going through such hostile country."

"No one knows what happened," went on Port. "Somewhere the Line was crossed, and the Rogen not only kept outsiders from entering Trew, but they began to not allow those in Trew to leave. We were smuggled out by our mother, but the price was high. She fell into poor health after the effort, and I don't think she ever was the same afterward."

"Did your mother tell you about the Rogen?" asked Hamlin.

"She told us about everything that had to do with Trew. She told us that a time would come when an outsider would bring the most danger that Trew had ever faced, and it would be a danger that would be faced by the forces of another one not of Trew."

"I thought no outsiders could get into Trew," said Hamlin. "If these Rogen are doorkeeps, how could anyone without those marks you have get in?"

"All our mother said was that the great battle for Trew would be fought by one who was an enemy, and that the borders would no longer be bound in the old ways."

Starboard nodded at his brother, and they went on mumbling their agreement for some time, speaking in their native tongue.

"That has all come to pass, it seems," said Chellin. "All our borders are being changed by this unseen hand that keeps throwing these raiding parties our way. It's been so slow a thing over the years, we haven't noticed how it's all beginning to be remapped. Old settlements that used to be prominent on our charts are not marked at all, or given a name that ends with 'ruins,' or with a mark that there was once a settlement there."

"Does that tie in with what you saw at the millers' lake? Were the elves a part of all this grand plan?" asked Jeremy. "They didn't seem to be much concerned with anything we might be involved in."

"They left after the Middle Islands," explained Chellin. "The times were already such that they could see their race would not be able to continue on in the old ways. More and different humans came, which brought more settlements, and covered more territory. There would be no room for the world of the dreamers. They have long awaited the call of the High Havens, to go home at last over the Sea of Silence."

"That's wonderful stuff, Chellin. Where did you stumble on it? All we ever heard from you was manual of arms, and repetitions of swordstrokes, and instructions for bow shots."

"Then you are witnessing the rebirth of Chellin Duchin, as he shall be in the future, lads. Old Chellin shall shed his skin like the bush snake, and emerge in a coat of different colors. It is time for that, I think."

Chellin laughed, enjoying some small private joke that seemed to amuse him greatly.

"The signal came at the lake," he resumed, "when I saw the tracks in the mud, and the cask that was come back for. It was said that when the dreamers return to gather their dead, that the time will be upon us when the mountains shall shift their shoulders, and the seas will find new shores."

"Not much to put weight to anything there," said Port simply. "That sounds like the sort of thing our mother was always saying."

"She always was," agreed Starboard. "I never could listen to her without wondering what it was all going to be like."

The Company was interrupted then by a delegation from the settlement, led by a frail-looking old man who wore a band of silver ringlets about his head.

"We beg pardon, Steward, but we thought we had best bring this news straight to you as soon as we heard it. Come up, Elrid, and deliver it to the steward just like you told me."

A young man dressed in light green cape and trousers was coaxed from the midst of the crowd, and came to stand before Chellin, protesting mildly, but enjoying all the attention he was getting.

"Come out with it, lad," encouraged Chellin. "Tell old Chellin Duchin what you've got behind your gums there! Spit it out!"

Chellin's appearance seemed to chill the young man's enthusiasm, and he could not find his voice right away, but after another prodding by the old man with the silver ringlets, he gave his report.

Chellin and the others of his squadron listened carefully, growing quieter and more serious as the young man went on to the conclusion, which took some time to reach.

The stewards of the Line sat up far into the night formulating their plan of action, and adding a new dimension to their line of thinking. It seemed that Chellin's predictions of change was coming to be with a vengeance, and even Port and Starboard found new reason to remember well their mother's words about the storm that threatened them all with a whirlwind of destruction.

Stones from Trees

Owen had waking visions about the hauntingly beautiful girl who stood beside the still waters of the lake he had seen in his dream. He spoke to no one about it, although Emerald had sensed a change in him, and asked him repeatedly if he were ill. Kegin, ever the hard-lined disciplinarian, saw to it everyone kept to the pace of the march, only sparing the horses at hourly intervals, and had taken on the role of assigning tasks at each night's camp.

"We'll have to find our water and food from here out. This is the last of our stores. I don't like it."

"You worry overmuch, Kegin," chided the minstrel. "We're surrounded by game, and there's a river behind us, and another

"Do you think they might have poisoned the river?" asked Owen. "After seeing what the outcast had, I begin to wonder at what black trick they won't try."

"They'll use them all, lad, and then go you one or two more. I've seen the likes of those villains stoop to any depths to rob, or plunder, or kill."

"But they have to have food and water, too," said Darek. "Why would they poison something that they would have need of?"

"They don't seem to think along the same lines as we do," replied Emerald. "For as long as I've been moving about back and forth here, I've come to find that not everyone has the same way of looking at a thing. And I've also seen some poisons that would kill you as quickly as you could blink an eye, then be perfectly harmless in a matter of a day or two."

"Where would these louts be getting anything like that?" asked Kegin. "That sort of devil's brew is difficult to find, and harder to handle. Who would teach them how to use it?"

"I think we may find our answer to that once we're further into Trew. There are many stories of the magical nature of the clans who dwell here, not all of them pretty. Yet the Lord Trew was himself one of the high elders at the Council that went to war and fought in the Middle Islands."

"If that's true, then why have we had only horror stories about those that live here?" asked Kegin doubtfully. "I've been taught all my life that enemies are enemies, no matter what coat they're wearing, if they strike a blow to harm you."

"We have more mysteries in Trew to unravel than that one, Kegin. If Owen is right in the sayings of Gillerman, and if he is indeed waiting in the South Channels, then we'll find puzzles enough to keep us busy for a good long while."

Owen had been slowly revolving the sword in his hand, turning the blade in a circle, as if trying to peer into its depths for an answer to a pressing question that nagged at him whether awake or asleep.

The minstrel noticed this, and tried to get the young man to talk. "Come on, lad! Let's have it! Why such a glum face?"

"Do you ever have dreams?" asked Owen. "I mean dreams that are so real you hardly know if you were dreaming or awake?"

Darek nodded from where he sat beside Owen. "I have dreams like that sometimes. It's always about my father. I'm about to find him, but there is always something that keeps me back. I can ever hear him calling my name, but I can't reach him."

"Do you ever dream about your mother?" asked Owen. "I wonder if there's something wrong that I don't have any dreams about my mother?"

Kegin was laying against the trunk of a tree with the reins

of his horse in his hands, and his legs stretched out before him. He was chewing thoughtfully on a twig as he spoke.

"I don't think I could honestly say I ever had a dream of my mother. She was a good-natured sort who always hounded my father about teaching me his bad habits, but I never thought too much of her tongue. Sometimes she'd bake special cakes for us to take when we went on outings, or for the high holidays of the settlement."

The veteran warrior stopped, shaking his head. "She blamed my father for me going off joining the stewards. Poor old fellow never had an idea in the world that that was what was going on in my head. I never talked to anyone about it before I took my oath."

"Is your father alive?" asked Emerald.

"He was two winters ago. That was the last time I saw him. There was a party of mappers that were sent to the upper regions near the borders of the Reed Plains. My father was a master charter, and headed the column."

Kegin fell silent, twisting the twig about with his lips, and finally removing it to doodle in the soft pine needles of the forest floor.

"You never heard more of him?" asked Emerald in a soft voice.

"Oh, I heard more of him," replied Kegin. "He came back from that journey not in his head. He couldn't remember the simplest things, not even his name. He could quote the legends off any of his charts, but he said he never had a son, and spent most of his time taking apart the pen and quills he used to draw with."

"You mean he didn't know you?" asked Owen, visibly alarmed.

"He was pleasant enough, but said he never married. Couldn't remember my mother or any of his brothers, but he could call out the name of a dog he had as a child. No one could explain what happened to him on that trip."

"Was there a battle?" asked Darek.

"Nothing. He came home after that journey a broken old man. My mother didn't seem to know what to do with him, so they put him with the shepherds. They have a way of dealing with mute, dumb things, and are always kind."

Kegin's voice had trailed off to an uncertain tremor, as if he were on the verge of tears.

"My father was always so stern and proper. I never got over seeing him gibbering about in front of our shelter. That was always the hardest. I think it would have been easier if we had heard of his death in a battle."

Emerald drew small circles in the earth with a stick, nodding. "It would be so much simpler, I agree. I think we would all wish for a quick and painless end. Dragging out the business is such a messy affair."

Darek's eyes began to mist, and his chin trembled. "I wish we could talk of something else," he said.

Kegin sat up, dusting his hands together to knock off the pine needles that stuck to his palms. "Sorry, lad. It's a burden on you, I know, but there's a time when you have to go on and make the best of it, no matter how much differently you would have things."

"And you don't know for certain that your mother and father are dead," comforted Owen. "In all the upheaval the Line has gone through, you may have simply lost them in the shifting of camps."

Darek blinked back his tears, trying to smile. "It's good of you to say so, Owen. I don't know what to think anymore. I wish I were back with them at my old home."

"Don't we all wish something as simple as that," said Emerald quietly. "The world would be an easier place if we could live by our wishes."

"I feel one of your songs coming," Kegin smiled. "I hope it's a cheery one."

"The cheeriest of all," replied Emerald. "It tells of life and death, and the road in between. Gillerman's uncle taught it to me while we were waiting in an eagle's eyrie."

"Gillerman's uncle?" questioned Owen. "Where did you meet him?"

"It was just the usual run of luck, lad. The master had been giving me instruction in the nature of birds, when all of a sudden Ephinias showed up with bundles of drawings and chalkboards, ready to lecture me on what I would need to know about chimney whippets and poppins."

"How did you get into an eagle's nest?" asked Darek, distracted for the moment.

"Flew," said Emerald. "Just up and there we were, as pretty as you please. I wasn't the jaded dollop I am now, and I can tell you that it was an uplifting experience."

"What was his name?" asked Owen.

"The eagle's?"

"No, Gillerman's uncle."

"Ephinias. He said he'd spent a lot of time with the Old Ones at the Middle Islands. Before that, too, I suspect. He had a quick way of letting you know everything he knew by just looking into your eyes."

"Will I ever get to find out how to fly?" asked Darek.

"If we can find Gillerman, then I'm sure we can find Ephinias, Darek. And I don't think he will have forgotten all those good tricks he knew. He was a marvel at peeling apples with his front teeth, and he could stand on one foot for a whole night through."

"Why would he want to do that?" asked Darek.

"Part of his initiation, lad. When he was let into the Order of the Falcon, he had to prove himself worthy by eating a mouse whole, and standing on one leg in his coop all night."

"Ugh," blurted Owen. "I don't think I'd want to join that Order."

"Oh, he wasn't Ephinias the man, he was in bird-form. A mouse isn't so bad a treat as you might think."

"I'd have to be hungrier than I am now," said Kegin, "and that's fair hungry."

"Did you check the outcast mounts? There may be some provisions there."

"I wouldn't want anything they carried," protested Kegin. "It would be hard to tell what they had poisoned from their own provisions."

"We're not that desperate yet," agreed Emerald. "Perhaps we may chance on one of the old settlements before too much longer. I keep having the strangest feelings that we're

being allowed into Trew without a fuss. By all the calcula-
tions I've made, we should have come into the Edges
yesterday."

"Then we would already be nearer the trail to the Silver
Mist Pass," said Owen, his excitement rising.

"If Gillerman's chart proves right, then the next step
would be the South Channels, and Gillerman himself, or
some form of help."

"How can you be so sure, Emerald? How do we know the
South Channels won't be even more dangerous than Trew?
You could put them both in a bag of trouble and not be able
to tell them apart, as far as I can see."

"You'll worry yourself into an early grave yet, Kegin.
Owen has the blade Gillerman gave him, so we shall have a
way to guide ourselves to where we need to be."

"Early grave or not, I want to see some flesh-and-blood
mark that will tell us where we are. If we're in Trew, I want
to know it. There's enough of my superstitious old mother in
me that if I find myself in danger, I can remember the words
I need to say to keep me safe."

The minstrel walked to a tall pine and stood before it,
gazing up at the higher branches.

"You may have a sign quicker than you would wish,
Kegin! I think I recognize something here that has slipped
my mind for sometime past."

"What is it?" asked Owen, going to stand beside his
friend. "What made you look here?"

Emerald pointed to an object halfway up the tree, concealed by the thick branches, and cleverly made to look like
nothing more than a fallen limb, or a bough broken by the
wind.

"Help me search these other trees for any signs! Keep an
eye peeled for anything up a tree that looks like it doesn't
belong."

The minstrel's voice had taken on a guarded sense of
urgency, although the others couldn't make out the half
amused expression on his face.

"But what are we to look for?" asked Darek anxiously.

"Anything that looks suspicious to any of you. If you see anything at all, show me."

Emerald shook his head, his eyes hidden from the others.

"I should have begun to guess what was happening when we couldn't match any of the marks on the chart with our surroundings," he said, half aloud. "Curse me for the fool Gillerman always said I was. It was right under my nose all along, and I failed to see it."

"See what? What are you going on about? I can't see anything has changed so much than what it was yesterday, or the day before!"

"Kegin, you're as blind as I am! But I couldn't expect you to be aware of anything, for you've never had dealings with this end of the wood." Emerald flung out his hands in an exasperated gesture. "Gillerman will have me hided for this!"

Owen stood beside the distraught minstrel, trying to think of something to say to soothe him, when he caught sight of the slight movement out of the corner of his eye. It wasn't a distinct motion, or even something that he could identify, yet there was definitely some object in a place where there had been nothing a second before. He was on the verge of tugging at Emerald's elbow to speak, when the first of the man-sized stones dropped out of the treetops, making a horrible noise as it fell, and landing with a ground-shaking thud right at his feet.

The stone was followed by a high-pitched screech that echoed through the wood, deadening the senses with a cold dread; it was answered by more of the same terrifying voices from the treetops all around them.

Emerald had pulled out his harp and held it before him like a shield to ward off another blow, striking a short chord on the instrument as he did so.

A long, heart-stopping wail rode up the wind, cutting through the filtered light of the forest with a dark edge that seemed to dim even the sun, but Emerald held the harp higher, and struck another chord. The wail faded into silence, and the minstrel strummed a chord, then another, and finally added his voice to the music.

> "In the dark shadows
> of the Darien Mounds
> there are three kinds of dying,
> one is under the damp,
> cold earth, but the other
> two are fear and anger,
> so come out, come out,
> you Darien clan,
> we have not come
> to buy our death
> at your door."

Emerald trailed off, slowly turning from side to side to watch the effect the song was having on the hidden onlookers.

Darek was at Owen's side, the small knife Stearborn had given him drawn and clutched tightly in his hand.

"I don't think we'll need our weapons," hissed Emerald through clenched teeth. "If we were looking for a clue as to where we are on the chart, we have it now."

"What are these things that throw stones from the trees?" shot Kegin, an arrow strung and ready, paying no attention to his friend's advice that they wouldn't need to defend themselves.

"Where else could we be but the Darien Mounds," explained Emerald. "And the mounders are not so terrible as they sound, although they can be dangerous enough in other ways."

"I've only heard the worst about the place," Kegin went on, his sharp eyes scanning the treetops for a movement at which to loose a shaft.

The minstrel saw the direction of his glance, and shook his head. "You're looking toward the wrong quarter if you're trying to find them. This is the ruse they work so well."

"The stones were no trick! If one of them had cracked our skulls, it would have been a far sight more than just a headache!"

"They didn't hit us," soothed Emerald. "I don't think

they expected anyone to come up the back way. We've frightened them."

"We frightened *them*!" blurted Kegin. "By the Sacred Glen of Morlin Tayhe, I think they should certainly be guilty of frightening *us*, what with all the screeching and stones they've thrown."

"Do you know these people?" asked Owen, looking with a new respect at the minstrel. When he had met the musician, Owen had looked on him as a somewhat pitiful figure, for even though he was a strong, healthy man, he carried the leather case with a harp, rather than the stewards' arms, and claimed that he fought the worst of enemies with his music, driving away ignorance and hatred. That did not impress Owen at the time, although he found the tales amusing, and a way to distract him from his anxious thoughts for his mother's safety and well-being.

As time had gone on, and he knew more of the man, he saw that there was a great mystery growing at the heart of the question as to who Emerald really was. It began to appear to Owen more and more that it was not a chance meeting that had drawn them together.

Emerald had strummed another note or two on his instrument, and called out in a strange, awkward tongue that seemed to be made up of wild bird cries, and the sound that the trees would make in a strong spring wind.

There were answering calls after a brief silence, and the screeching was renewed with twice or three times the number of voices as before.

Darek held his ears shut with his hands, his face drawn with pain.

"Make them stop!" cried Kegin. "For the love of our hearing, call them off!"

Owen watched Emerald as he called out again, and saw the strange way his windpipe moved as he gobbled out the odd-sounding language.

"They're distant cousins of the old clans who lived here," explained Emerald. "I should have begun to suspect something when we were so far gone into what should have been the Edges without a sign or clue as to where we were. These mounders have removed all the markers, or mixed up the ones that are still left. It's a trick they've been using for a long time."

"You mean we *are* lost?" said Owen flatly, looking steadily at Emerald.

"No, lad, no such thing. We know where we are exactly! The Darien Mounds! Somehow I must coax them out to meet us." Emerald paused, lost in thought. "Wait! I've got it! Get me that waxed thread from the outcasts' saddlebag! They love sewing. I knew that ball of thread we found there would stand us in good stead somewhere down the road. Look lively, Darek!"

The youth moved hesitantly toward the horses, his eyes still scanning the tops of the trees for other stones to be loosed. He saw the clever rope and pulleys that were rigged in the trees where the large stones had fallen from, and vowed never to be caught so unaware again.

"Hurry, lad! I think I feel one of the fellows coming out of his hiding now."

Emerald struck another chord, and sang in a singsong voice a nonsensical little tune that Owen had heard mothers humming to their infants.

"They like the simple things," said Emerald. "I came on them when I first traveled through here with Gillerman. He told me of their oldest ancestors, and what had happened to them."

"What happened?" asked Owen. "Why do they have such terrible voices?"

"For protection. Much like a beautiful flower that has an odor so dreadful it drives away any who would tear it from the plant. These poor chaps can't get over their looks or their size, so they have devised ways to protect themselves in spite of them. A lot of the dreadful stories you've heard of the Darien Mounds are fabrications by these folk themselves."

Kegin had lowered his bow, and came to stand beside Owen and Emerald.

Darek cried out from behind the last of the horses they had captured from the outcasts of Leech. The next second, he was dragged kicking and struggling toward his friends by beings that were no taller than the youth, although they had hair and beards that were flecked with gray, and grew down to their thick leather belts.

"Help! They've got me!"

"Easy, lad, you're all right. Just hold onto the thread ball."

"I couldn't get it," shot Darek. "They surprised me!"

Owen watched in amazement as the dozen or so small figures marched Darek along in their midst.

The leader, who appeared to be about Owen's height, stood before Emerald, his dark eyes flaring between anger and excitement. He was dressed in pale green with leather cuffs and collar and a cloak thrown back over his shoulders. At his belt was a dirk of some strange shape, and he had what looked to be a longsword, only there was simply the hilt, but no blade.

After a moment or two of hand signs among his followers, the small being turned to Emerald and spoke in a gentle, low voice.

Owen could understand none of the words, although it seemed that from time to time he could almost make out a sound that was familiar. Emerald nodded and shook his head, pointing and gesturing to Darek and Owen and Kegin, and obviously giving the leader of the small mounders an explanation of their presence.

After what seemed a long time, the leader's ancient face crinkled into what might pass for a smile, and he said in a very loud voice, over and over, "The Windameir, the Windameir!"

"It's all right," said Emerald. "They say they have been infested with the vermin from above the Rogen Keep and the Malignes. They have had their settlement here for a long time, but they are being driven to the point of leaving. They thought we were more of the same armies which have been gathering here."

"What armies?" Kegin questioned. "Can he tell us strengths and locations? Famhart can use this to formulate a plan to rid the Line of this scum, whoever they may be."

"This fellow says his name is Luka. He knows where the man is who is the head of these armies!"

"Ask him if we could go there?" Kegin persisted. "Would they take us? Just so we could see for ourselves?"

The other mounders, all dressed exactly like their leader, but without the broken longsword, had moved to circle the comrades, leaning against short pikestaffs and cudgels, and in one case, a stubby crossbow that was armed and ready for action.

Emerald spoke again in what seemed a series of chirps and gurgling sighs, and whatever he was saying seemed to excite the small figure into a fit of nervous activity. Between bellows and short explosions of whistling sounds, Emerald translated the mounder's speech for the others.

"He says this man has come from over the Silver Mist Pass and sits in the South Channels at the head of a warrior band. Luka says this is a man who has the form of a bear."

"A bear?" asked Kegin. "What on earth would that mean?"

"He says it's got the South Channels in a fair state of alarm. They have begun to march in droves toward the borders, and his people here have been having a difficult time keeping their mounds safe."

"A bear," mused Kegin. "I wonder where I've heard of that?"

"Somewhere on the path here," said Emerald. "I remember it too, but I can't place it just now."

"There was talk of bears at the last refugee settlement we passed through," replied Owen. "Someone told a story about a man in the mountains who was able to take on the form of a bear."

"That was it. Well, Luka says that the very fellow is a fact, and has sent raiding parties to attack his settlement on the last three nights. That's why they were so ready to finish us."

"Good timing we've got," snapped Kegin. "Out of one frying pan right back into the fire."

"All we need to do is get through," said Owen. "If this fellow is busy arming and planning attacks, we may be able to get through the backdoor and find Gillerman. All we need is a chance to get the leaf my mother needs. We'll leave the man-bear to my father, and the stewards."

"From what Luka says, there may be more of a threat than the stewards can handle."

Owen shook his head stubbornly.

"The stewards of the Line have held fast through everything. It would take more to defeat them than any of the armies the outcasts have."

"There are more things here that threaten us than the outcasts and the raiders from the borders, Owen. We shall have to find our help in the form of the Old Ones. We must find Gillerman now. Everything depends upon him helping us."

Kegin broke in anxiously. "Is there any way to get through Trew without running across this fellow who has stirred up all the trouble? See if Luka could arrange that."

Emerald spoke again in the odd-sounding tongue, and the small forms of the mounders moved about and talked animatedly among themselves, making sweeping motions with their hands, and pointing away toward the east, where the companions could just make out the taller peaks of the South Channels.

"I think they mean we can get over the Silver Mist without trouble. This bear lord is gathering an army, and the roads are full of recruits that are going to join him. There is another man in Trew now who is doing the same thing. We can blend in with the flow."

"That's well and good, old fellow, but what happens when we get there? Do we march with this bear lord, or this other chap, or do we just say we've changed our minds and want to go home?"

"It's a fair question, Kegin, but one I can't answer now, for we haven't gotten far enough along to deal with it."

"I'd like to give some thought to a road that comes back the other way before I set my course. I've grown highly fond of my hide over all these turnings."

"This bear lord might help us," offered Darek. "If he's as

powerful as these funny little men say he is, he might listen to a plea to help someone in need."

"Not likely, Darek. This chap doesn't sound like the sort to be an almsgiver. I don't like the sound of him."

"But we might try, Emerald. It would hurt nothing to try."

"The lad may have a point, Emerald," said Kegin. "Not about the warlord, but some of the other folk there might be ordinary people who want nothing to do with all the commotion that's going on."

"We do seem to find that lot everywhere, don't we?" asked Emerald. "Thank the High Throne of Windameir for that. It seems its always had the bad apple that turns the barrel sour."

"Then we're going on?" asked Darek, looking faintly uneasy.

"Yes. We've got to cross Gillerman's track before long. We're close enough now to the South Channels that we should be having a sign of him soon."

Emerald had no more than finished speaking, when the longsword at Owen's side began to hum and tingle in its scabbard, and when he drew it forth, the golden-white light began to throb in brilliant arcs that formed halos above all those there, terrifying the mounders and sending them scurrying for cover.

A Riddle Underground

In the cool darkness of the tunnels that wound down into the entryway of the Darien Mounds, Emerald and Kegin talked of finding a way through the South Channels, and back safely again.

Their conversation was halted at intervals by different-colored lanterns, which evidently marked the various levels of the vast underground settlement.

"Did you know of these beings before, Emerald? I mean you speak their tongue, which is not the usual sort of thing to run into."

"Barely, my friend. My master taught me what little I know of it, but I can merely manage to get by with the crudest sort of slang. He is fluent in the tongue, and knows their history all the way back to the terrible time when the Dwarf King Ruka Kar abducted a human girl and forced her to become his queen. From that time on, the Dariens, or mounders, were a clan that was despised by both the dwarfish clans and humankind."

"Yet they don't seem to be of a bad sort," said Owen, his eyes taking in every inch of his surroundings. "I wish I could speak their language. It sounds like birds or wind. I like that."

"Luka says their Querle has the tongue of all kinds. That's where we're on our way to now."

Darek had been walking beside Owen, but began to slow his pace, stumbling a bit, and reaching out a hand to steady himself against the cool surface of the smooth stone.

"Easy, lad!" said Kegin, catching the boy before he fell. "What is it. Darek?"

"What happened?" asked Emerald, turning toward Kegin just in time to see him catch the fainting youth.

"He's out! I don't know why! Can we stop here to see if there's a wound?"

"It would have to be lighter, I think," said Emerald, and he spoke urgently to Luka, who glanced at the stricken boy, his throat contracting and expanding as the strange noise that was their language filled the passage.

The minstrel nodded.

"He says we are almost to the Fourth Chamber. There are healers there, and light enough that we might feel it is day. These lads don't spend much time outside, although they don't exactly follow the dwarfish rule of living entirely below ground."

As Kegin held the lad, a troop of Dariens came and took Darek on a rolled cloak that had been spread between them.

"It's all right," said Emerald. "They will go on ahead. They can make better time down these tunnels than you or I can. And it might be urgent to get the lad help quickly."

Kegin reluctantly let the small strangers take the boy, and seemingly without noise or effort, they vanished into the dim reaches of the tunnel that stretched away into the distance.

Luka spoke again, raising a hand to point out something that was on the wall, although neither Owen nor Kegin could see what the Darien was trying to show them.

"It's the first level," explained Emerald. "These underground digs are broken into levels. He says this is the first time in his life that any of our kind have ever been so deep in his home."

"I'm not so sure I take that as an honor." Kegin laughed nervously. "It doesn't seem to be the sort of place that I would make a point to find."

"These shafts are cut for a person no larger than Luka," said Emerald. "But he says that we shall find room aplenty when we come to the Fourth Chamber. Evidently that's the largest of all the mounds. I think he said it had once been the upper dome for an ancient dwarfish delving. They're pretty tender on that score. If we meet this Querle who can speak our tongue, don't let on you know anything of dwarfs, or any of their affairs."

"I had no idea about any of this sort of thing until I met you Emerald. You've been the harbinger of all my ill-fortune these past days, bless you."

"There were things that would be known by all, sooner or later. Our lifetime has seen a fairly quiet run of events, but I'm afraid it's done with now."

"You call the border raiders a quiet run of events?" shot Kegin.

"It was only a prelude of things to come, it seems. Luka said they have seen armies marching through these parts. It sounds as if there are enough massed troops to deal the stewards a fatal blow."

Owen paled, and his breath grew short as he listened to the minstrel. He tried to keep the fear and anger down, but couldn't, and his voice broke as he spoke.

"My father and the stewards have never been bested," he repeated, straight from all the history of the Line. "We have lost battles, but never a war. The Line is still unbroken!"

"I know it's hard to believe, Owen," said Emerald, trying to reassure the youthful heir of the Elder Famhart. "What has been going on has been far beyond the borders of your home. It would have been difficult to know all these things, if you don't travel as much as I."

"Where do you come from, Emerald? And why do you travel so much? All we know is that you found us when we were camped on the run from Sweet Rock. You never did tell us where you hailed from." Kegin was not openly hostile, but he had the same thoughts churning through his mind that troubled Owen.

Emerald did not break stride, nor turn to look at his companions. "I come from a country that knows war, and has been devoured. Its name would mean nothing to you."

"My mother might have read of it to me," insisted Owen.

"Your mother would have heard of it in a way," replied Emerald. "Your father's father would ring a bell with her."

"What do you mean?" asked Owen, beginning to take offense with the cryptic talk of the minstrel.

"When I came to you, I had been told that the Feast of the Red Bear had been celebrated all across the land. My master said long ago, before you were born, Owen, that I was to find the son of the son of one from Boghatia. It was to be my penance for an old injury."

"Boghatia? You mean you came from the lands where my father's father came from?"

"Not from Boghatia, Owen. The East Ledges. We were at war with the Boghatians until our clans butchered each other down to but a few survivors. Those left, and so the maps show only the ruins of once proud countries that could not abide peacefully."

"I never heard that story," said Kegin quietly. He wanted to ask more questions, but the minstrel's face had hardened, and there was a coldness in the glance he turned on his friends.

"I shall sing of it one day. It still stings me to remember the sorrow of it."

"But how did you find us? You still haven't told us that."

"There is no questions you have of Darek? Did you find that a satisfactory way to explain him, that he came to your camp when his parents were killed by the raiders?"

Emerald turned to answer a remark the Darien had made then, and he conversed for some time with Luka in the alien sounds of the small one's language.

As they had talked, the stonework grew more elaborate, and there was a distinct chill in the air now, as though they had gone far beyond the range of the sun's warming rays. The floor of the tunnel was cut in small squares, which seemed to reflect back a mutual light from the ceiling, and when Owen looked up, there were miniature stars ablaze in that blue-black stone; it was so realistic, for a moment he thought they had surely followed the small figure up through a tunnel, and out into the night beneath a moonless sky.

"Luka has heard of the sword you wear, Owen. That is one of the reasons that we are being allowed into the Fourth Chamber. The Querle has told the story of the sword of light, and that it will one day rise to strike a blow for freedom for all those who have been kept in Darkness."

Kegin looked sideways at Owen, and the cumbersome longsword that had frightened him from time to time by bursting into a dazzling golden white light.

"What do you mean? Now you say that this pup is carrying on with some mystic affair? My stars protect me," muttered Kegin. "Famhart will have my head for this."

Emerald laughed unexpectedly. "Don't fret over it, good Kegin. There is nothing either you or Famhart could have done to have prevented these things from happening."

"I could have followed my instincts, and stayed safely in camp until Famhart returned."

"It would have done no good. We've been dragged into all this whether we want it or not."

"My mother would still need the leaf from the country of the Three Trees, Kegin. Right now, that's all I'm concerned with," said Owen solemnly.

"And to find what has taken Darek," added Emerald. "I hope he hasn't been infected with that vile potion the outcast carried. Sometimes it is enough to simply get it on your hands. I've seen strong men weaken into a fever and lay up for days from a small drop of it."

Owen stopped dead in his tracks. "He was behind the outcast when I threw the vial. I might have splashed him with it then."

"But then you would have gotten some of it on you too, Owen. I don't see how you could have helped it."

"It may have something to do with a sort of protection the sword gives him, Kegin. Do you feel ill, Owen? Any dizziness or fainting spells?" asked Emerald.

"No," replied the youth. "I never would have thrown that vial if I'd know what it was."

"If you hadn't thrown it, Owen, you and Darek would probably be buried in that clearing back there, along with the slain outcast. The man was clever, and he was bound to kill you both, for sport, if nothing else."

"It's hard to believe that, after seeing him with the poison on his face."

"A fate he would have cheerfully subjected you to, my buck. These are hard lads we're dealing with."

"I'll be glad to find out what is wrong with Darek. Maybe these small ones can help us. I hate to think of him without a mother or father, and dragged off by the likes of us into more trouble than he would have had back at the camp."

Owen's head dropped as he trudged along beside Emerald, and he felt the pangs of guilt at leaving against his father's orders. It would be doubly bad if anything happened to Darek, for he was left in Owen's charge, and even though he had gone through a time of disliking the boy for his lack of courage, he did not wish him harmed.

"Luka says we're almost there. It's just beyond the curve in the tunnel," reported Emerald, translating the Darien's speech.

"How far down do you think we are?" asked Kegin.

"I wouldn't think so deep as you might suspect," answered the minstrel, studying a small bas-relief design on a wall, then going on. "These Dariens aren't dwarfs, so their digs won't run as deep as a dwarf delving. I think we may actually be very close to the surface, if truth be known. Remember, it's called the Darien Mounds on the chart."

"You mean to say these things aren't tunnels underground?"

"Oh, yes, Kegin, we're underground well enough, but not as deep as you think."

"How can you tell?" asked Owen.

"The air," replied Emerald. "It still smells like outside."

"Wouldn't they have air shafts?"

"Exactly. If these were dwarfish delvings, we'd be far below ground by now. The air would be good, but it wouldn't have this sweet smell to it."

"Have you been in a dwarfish delving?" asked Kegin, amazed at the breadth of the minstrel's experiences.

"My master took me once, although it was long deserted. A sad sight, all that grandeur gone stale, languishing away there in the forgotten earth. I learned quite a sad song about it."

"Will you sing it?" asked Owen.

"Not here. It would upset the Dariens tremendously. We're off to a good start with them. I don't want to ruin our good will with them now."

Kegin laughed uneasily. "Please, it isn't nice to upset a host in his own cave. We don't even know for sure our way out."

"Will we ever hear the song?" persisted Owen.

"Of course, you reckless lad. At the very first chance I have, I'll sing you all the verses. It's very sad, though. You'll have need of much linen to dry away the tears."

As the minstrel finished speaking, they came to the entryway of a large domed chamber that was lit on wall and ceiling by shining orbs that glowed in powerful spheres, round and silent, and filling the immense room with black and pale gold shadows.

The Darien who had guided them turned and spoke to Emerald for a moment, then hurried away.

"We are to wait here. Luka says he will fetch the Querle, and the rest of the Justins. They are the lawmakers for the Dariens."

"Where is Darek? I thought they were bringing him here."

"I'm sure he's all right, Owen. They would hardly have reason to harm the boy."

Kegin paced uneasily into the room a few feet further, peering about anxiously. "They have something on the walls here! Look, Emerald! Can you make out what I'm talking about?"

On the edges of the bottom of the carved stone walls, just below the orbs that lit the room, were more bas-relief designs of an odd nature that none of the companions could make out.

"I can't tell what it is, but it has covered the walls all along here. Look!"

"Here's more," said Owen, running his hand over the cool smooth figures in the stone.

"If this were a delving, I'd have a bit more idea of what it means, but since we're in the Darien Mounds, I would have to ask Gillerman."

"If only he were here," lamented Owen. "We're in a fine mess, being gone when we weren't supposed to, and now Darek is sick. I don't think we'll ever find the way to the country of the Three Trees at the pace we're going."

The young man's face had screwed itself into a tight mask, and he felt humiliated that he was so near crying.

"Easy, old man," said Kegin, and Owen was grateful to him for not seeing the hot tears that flooded his eyes and ran down his cheek.

"We shall see the end of this together, no matter what it may take to find what your mother needs. Famhart may skin us all alive, but it would be worth it if we could bring Linne back to her senses. I'd let myself be hided every day for a year, if I thought that would help our chances."

"We are off the road," protested Owen. "I don't know

what these Dariens are up to, but I don't like the idea of being down in these old tombs."

"These aren't tombs, Owen," corrected Emerald. "Everyone who sees the mounds thinks they are burial grounds, but they are actually the stairways to Trew. That's what they originally were, and still are, I suspect, unless the Dariens have sealed them off to protect themselves from intruders."

"Can't you ask this Luka? He seems to be free with his replies."

"He's simply awed by the fact that a stranger is familiar enough with his speech to be able to understand, and make himself understood."

The small company had reached a bottom level of the shaft, and they could feel the floor even out, no longer at a tilt. The lights from the shimmering globes had grown in intensity, and now it was light enough in the enormous chamber to see even the top-most part of the ceiling, high above them in the patchy web of darkness.

There again were the miniature stars that Owen had seen earlier, blazing merrily away, and making it difficult for the lad to believe that the bright twinkling lights weren't real stars in a vast blue-black heaven. There were other lights then, deep gold and red, flaring on the horizon of the dome-like flashes of lightening in a nighttime summer sky. A distant sound of thunder rolled through the chamber, making the ground tremble faintly, then more golden flashes lit up the room until a bright round orb began to rise behind them, slowly traveling up the starlit dome until all the smaller lights were faded into the burning glare of the Darien sun.

A slight fanfare played on small horns blared, and a company of mounders entered from what appeared to be a floor that had been sunken into the smooth surface of the chamber. Three Dariens there had on dark blue cloaks and square hats that rose above them another three feet, giving the impression that they were taller than the others of the court. Luka stepped forward then, and, bowing low to his leader, turned and addressed Emerald.

"His exalted Wisdom, the Fire of Age and Courage, Querle Unidan."

As the small Darien bowed to his Querle again, the horns sounded again, joined with a kind of whistling.

A strained, almost falsetto voice came from the old man, who spoke in a jerky rhythm of ancient words, and undecipherable slang from any number of past exchanges with humankind.

"The Windameir eats always," said the Querle Unidan. "Forever may the egg of truth be born to His followers."

Emerald bowed, and struck a chord on his harp. He had been carrying it out of the case since they had been in the shafts of the mounds. He now struck a deeper, almost melancholy series of notes that had the group of Dariens almost sobbing.

"I am called the Blue Wind, O Querle. I have blown from the dark stars and back again. I have heard the song the robin sings when it is not spring and the winter has come to murder his voice. I see the buried ruins of all in the distant eyes of the future, and weep for all that we have been, but are no more. "

Owen and Kegin looked quickly at Emerald, then at each other.

"What about Darek?" asked Owen in a small voice. "See if the Querle knows anything about Darek."

The Darien elder settled his gaze on Owen then, studying him intently, and with perfect innocence, until the youth had to turn away from the unfathomable black eyes. They revealed nothing to him, but he thought he had seen his own thoughts there, which was disturbing and frightening to him, so he turned back to Emerald.

"Do they have healers here?" he asked, trying to rid himself of the uneasiness of the Darien Querle's eyes on him.

"The small one you brought to us is with pain now, but will survive. There was a patch of the black sleep that had spilled on the clothes. That is a deadly burden to place on one so young, and one who does not know how to undo the spell."

"Are you saying there is a way to undo the black sleep?" asked Emerald.

"There are ways. Fortunately this young sapling did not have much of the lethal potion to deal with. Our healer has undone the mischief."

"Our thanks, O Querle. The young one is of special importance to us. We breathe easier to know he will recover."

There was a hurried conference among the Dariens then, and the Querle called Luka to him to confer for a short while in a low, thin whisper. After a time, Unidan turned back to Emerald.

"Perhaps my use of your tongue has grown poor over the turnings, or perhaps we have as yet to match our thoughts. These things are always so difficult at first. We seem to be at odds over the nature of the sapling you brought to us."

"How do you mean, O Querle? What difficulty do we have?"

"You speak of the sapling as 'him,' yet we say it is 'she.' Our lines are far removed from yours as humans, and don't take me amiss, sir, but we do know a female of the form when we see it. Had the child been male, I doubt he would have lived, for the black sleep was made of a potion to harm warriors."

Emerald's mouth gaped open, and he turned to question Owen and Kegin.

"It can't be," muttered Kegin, shaking his head. "We would have known!"

What seemed to be a laugh escaped through the Querle's long, thick beard.

"I see," Unidan said. "Now I can understand what the sapling meant when our healers were at work."

"What do you mean, O Querle?" asked Emerald, turning back to the Darien.

'Don't let them see me', is what the stripling said. 'They will find out!' No wonder there was such a secret of it. But why, sir? Do you travel with such silence among yourselves that you cannot speak freely?"

"No, O Querle, this is a most unusual case. We had no

idea. The boy—," Emerald stammered, then resumed,—
"er, girl, came to Owen and his mother as an orphan. Then
the lad who is with me here, found his mother struck down
with a potion of this black sleep you describe, or something
very like it. From then we traveled to now, thinking of
Darek as simply a boy."

The Dariens talked for a few moments among themselves
again, then motioned for Emerald to come with them.

"Where are we going? Why can't Kegin and Owen go,
too?"

"They shall have their chance to meet their young friend
anew. But I don't think it would be wise to go all at once. We
shall start with you, minstrel."

"Wait," cried Owen. "Don't leave us here, Emerald. We
can't speak the language!"

"He shall be back in time, young sir. Don't fret your
whittles over nothing. The others shall show you to sleeping
cells, and offer you food and drink. You all look as though
you could use refreshment."

"We must see to our horses," said Kegin, not liking the
idea of being separated any further.

"Your mounts are sheltered in our stable. They shall be
quite well tended until you have need of them again."

Kegin and Owen were escorted further down the huge
chamber, until they neared one wall, where they could hear
the faint echo of music and voices, seemingly coming from
the very stone.

The lights dimmed momentarily, and a small arched
doorway appeared at Owen's elbow, startling him into
jumping backward and stepping painfully on Kegin's foot.

Their smiling, silent hosts beckoned for them to come
through the strange doorway, although both Kegin and
Owen were reluctant to follow, putting themselves further
away from Emerald and Darek.

The news of Darek not being who he said he was had not
fully registered on Owen's consciousness. "A girl!" he said
aloud, looking at Kegin incredulously. "How could we have
been so blind?"

"Not hard, old fellow. If a chap says he has blue eyes and

a lame leg, after a while you start believing him, even if his
eyes are brown, and he's got two perfectly healthy pins."

"But we've been with him—or her—for the whole time
since we left Sweet Rock. I don't see how we could have
been fooled for so long!"

"Your mother would have spotted it, sure enough, if only
she'd been all right."

"Do you think so?"

"A woman always knows another woman, lad. Now we
have to find out from Darek, or whatever her name is, why
she hid her identity from us."

Before Owen could reply, the Dariens had stopped in
front of another wall, where a gliding stone door opened
back against itself, and the two friends were led into a snug
study, complete with fireplace and tea table, including a
plate of what looked to be some sort of cakes.

"This looks like they were expecting us," grumbled
Kegin. "Mark my word, no good has ever come of meddling
in another's affairs. We'll see a dark side to all this yet."

"I've still got the sword Gillerman gave me, and Emerald
is a friend of their elder. We won't be harmed here, Kegin.
Look!" He pulled it from the scabbard. "The blade is dark.
It would be on fire if we were in danger!"

Two of the Dariens saw the movement, and fell back a
few paces, keeping their backs to the wall, and drawing
small darts from their belts.

"Hold, friends." Kegin smiled. "This has nothing to do
with you." He laughed, and raised his hands above his head.
"See? All peaceful! We don't want to harm you!"

In a split-second, the Dariens had put back the darts and
vanished, leaving the two startled companions to explore
their surroundings alone for some time, before they bitterly
conceded that there was no doorway that they could find or
open, and after another frantic effort at calling out, they
sunk down heavily in the comfortable chairs by the fire to
ponder this last strange twist of fate.

The Track of the Dragon

In the time it took Largo to come to his senses from the horrendous din that was clattering wildly through his head, he had run from the river all the way to the small settlement, where Elita and the others had provided him with a shelter of his own when he had first come to them, furnished simply in the same fashion as all the rest of the dwellings of Trew.

Slowly his head cleared, and he tried to reconstruct what had gone on at the river, with the blinding lights, and horrible noises. It wasn't anything that the conscious part of him would have recoiled from, but the dark corner that seemed to linger somewhere below his heart had spread an icy terror through his body, and a voice he could not forget warned him to flee for his life. After the voice, it was as though a thousand dead bells clanged against a bitter winter wind, and the frozen air numbed his mind until he had come to, standing in front of his shelter, staring numbly in front of him.

"Largo! What's wrong?" cried a worried voice behind him.

It took him a moment to recognize the face of Elita.

He shook his head, trying to rid himself of the icy cobwebs there, and put a hand out toward the wall to steady himself.

"I must have caught a chill," he said weakly. "I haven't

been feeling up to the mark this past week. I don't know what's wrong with me."

Elita leaned close then, and looked deeply into his eyes. Largo tried to pull back from her inspection, but she held him firmly, and there was something in her gaze that momentarily hypnotized him.

"I can see many strange spells at work. Where have you come from? Is there someone who tried to control you with potions or cants?"

Largo shook his head vigorously. "I don't know what you mean! I know nothing of spells or potions! I come from my old country, like I told you, to try to gain back my rightful holdings."

"There is a strong will evident there, Largo. It's frightening. I've never seen so much power before. I think it has sensed me searching it out!" Elita gave a little cry then, and backed quickly away from him.

A strange look came over Largo's handsome features then, darkening his brow, and turning the corners of his mouth down into an ugly scowl.

"There is nothing to sense, Elita! You've read something into me that's not there." Largo's voice was not quite menacing, but it startled Elita all the same with its harshness.

"I didn't mean to offend you, Largo. It was just something I though I saw there. I was afraid some enemy had worked an evil spell to harm you! I was only trying to help."

Largo's face softened then, although the scowl still lingered at his lips. "I thank you for that, my lady. I assure you I have no enemy but my sister capable of harming me. There are those who follow her, but they won't be able to stand against me, now that Linne is safely out of the way."

"Is that her name?" asked Elita.

"Yes. If your spell has worked as you said it would, there will be no more need to mention her at all."

His face brightened then, but a dark frown lingered at his brow. "What was the cause of the lights on the river? They frightened me."

Elita reached out a hand to him, but he drew away.

"There is nothing to be frightened of from the riverfolk,

Largo. The old stories have it that it is the Evening Clans, come to seek out all their cousins who might be left in the world."

"The clans of what?"

"Some call them the Even Star Tribe, and others have different names, but they are the same clan, no matter what name you put to them."

"What do they want here? You say they always come to your river at this season?"

"Always. I can't remember a time when they haven't. My grandmere once told a story of the time they didn't appear for three turnings. There were bitter snows, and the crops were parched, and then the floods hit. It was a terrible time in Trew. The last of the Purge was still abroad then."

"Was your grande dame alive then?" asked Largo.

"Oh no, that was long before her time. I think it must have happened in my great-great-grandmere's life. There is still a spot at the river's edge where you can see a track of the dragon. It has killed all the plants nearby, and no wild thing goes near it, even now. They told me as a child that you could go blind from even looking at it, but I know there is no truth to that story, for I've looked at it many times."

"Where is this so-called snake track? I'd like to see it."

"It's where you saw the lights that frightened you, Largo. Do you want to go back? We can go in the daylight, if you'd rather. There isn't so much activity from the Evening clans then."

Largo's mind was following a thread of thought, and he barely heard the woman, but he nodded his agreement.

"Yes, tomorrow would be fine. I have heard much about these snakes, but I never thought they really lived. It would be interesting to see what sort of thing left a track there."

Elita paused, unwilling to go, although she could see that Largo was anxious to be alone.

"There is a comet shower later tonight. It comes at the Cross of the Moon and Southern Crescent. They are very pretty to see."

Largo refocused his attention on Elita, and shook his head.

"I'm sure it is a pretty sight, my lady, but I have had enough excitement for one night, I think. Perhaps I'll boil myself some apple-leaf tea, and turn in early. We can go look at the snake track tomorrow."

"Very well. Good night, Largo. May your sleep be protected by the Lord Trew."

"You, too," he returned. Not waiting to enter his shelter, he didn't see how long she hesitated before turning and slowly walking away.

It was dark inside, and he had to search about for the tallow bowl and fire striker, but he soon had a rushlamp and latern lighted, and a fire burning cozily in his small open-faced stove. He drew together a parcel of small parched scales from his knapsack, and placed them on the table next to the lantern.

"This is a stroke of luck," he said aloud. "Finding a track of the snake here in this unlikely spot. I've used up much of my supply of the dragon scale, and it is hard to keep the riffraff in line without the power of my little nuggets of persuasion."

As he spoke, he dropped a small portion of one of the small scales into the stove, which immediately gave off a sickening odor of old scorched wood and dwellings, and a chill spread through the room, in spite of the fire. There was a rushing noise, like a great teakettle coming to a boil, and the rushlamp began a wild flickering dance, casting grotesque shadows on the walls of the ancient shelter. An eerie, wailing cry came from the fire, and a writhing, whirling shape began to rise and take form.

Largo leaned forward and touched the amulet at his neck, which had begun to glow warmly on his skin.

"You have called your master, human! What is it you wish?"

A voice, or what could be passed off as a voice, crept into the room on the hot, seething breath of the fire.

"Do you know what the filthy swine at the river are up to? I nearly passed out from being so close to them before I found out their true nature. They're of an elfish strain, by the Dark One's hand, I swear! I thought there was to be no interference from those cursed meddlers this time. I understood that the dwarf-lords and elfin hosts were all gone!"

"These were the water rats you sensed tonight, captive. They are weak now, and will be no threat to our plan," hissed the voice.

"They almost strangled me! And the woman wants an answer to my strange behavior."

"We will give you a reason. I can give you a fever that will last but a few days. She will think you're dying."

"None of your filthy tricks! I know how that mind of yours works. If I want to be sick for a day or two with a fever, that's exactly what I mean. No lingering effects, either. You make me healthy again day after tomorrow."

"We will make you more than healthy. You shall have need of all your strength, for the time is almost upon us when we shall rise for our vegeance on all those who would have cast us away forever. Once the Lower Meadows are opened again to the Dark One, we can escape the Fields of Light. The Law is plain when it states that there shall always be the guardians of the Lower Gates. That's my brothers and I. We cannot be denied the right of our birth."

"And I shall have my vegeance on the sister that betrayed me." Largo laughed, the scowl deepening into a hard grimace. "She has flourished all the while I lay dead in the dragon's hall, being tended by our Lady of the Darkness. My life was held in the balance until she had gotten my hatred boiling into rage. I owe my life to being able to carry so much ill-will toward another human being."

"You bear up well, captive. There is another in the mountains to the south of here. He has not yet been visited by the Protector, but she won't let him escape from her web. He is powerful, and seeks to avenge himself on Windameir as well."

"What is this one called?" asked Largo suspiciously. "Why wasn't I told of him before?"

"You are told only what you have a need to know," replied the voice. "There is no need to speak to you of everything that goes forward in our plan for the recapture of the Lower Meadows."

"But you say he's in the mountains near here? It would interfere with my plans to have another army so close at hand, and one that would take their orders from a different leader."

"When the time comes, you shall meet this man. It is fated to be so."

The voice in the dragon fire laughed malignantly, and the flames turned a pale greenish color, tinged by hot orange edges that burned fiercely against the gloom of the shelter.

"Then the sooner the better. If I am to deal with the vermin of elf and dwarf, I shall need a strong ally here who can help me rid the country of this scourge. Why are these wretched things still abroad? I was told they had all passed over to the Sea of Silence."

"Many have, captive. My brothers and I have sent many of the scrawny rodents to their fates. It was always the greatest pleasure to fry one of the horrible things. I could almost hope there are some to be left for our return."

"You can have them all for yourself, then. I want no more to do with them."

The fire grew in strength, and the fiery breath licked closely at Largo's face, forcing him to lean backward to be able to breathe.

"You shall have no say at all, captive! The Protector has her reasons for saving you, but I can see none. When we win back the Lower Meadows, I shall take great pleasure in educating you in the ways the doom-snakes have of prolonging your life, while we torment you beyond hope. You will plead for death, but there will be none. It will be a delightful tidbit for my brothers and me to sit and ponder."

"You are a vile soul, you wretched thing! If it were not for the Protector, I would have nothing further to do with you or your filthy kin."

A putrid blast of the fire singed Largo's eyebrows and mustache, and his heart trembled within him, but he knew the dragon spell was powerless to harm him. It could not reach beyond the fire, for the snakes of the lower realms had been taken to the Fields of Light, and would be held there forever, unless the Dark One regained control of the three lower plains of Windameir.

Largo had been drilled over and over by the voice of the Protector while he lay in a state of limbo, between life and death, at the lair of the dragon that had carried him away from his ruin. Time passed slowly then, and it was hard for him to remember how many turnings it had been until he had come forth again. Even after all the time that had passed, Largo had been greatly surprised, one day shortly after his return, to see his young features in the calm pool of a high mountain lake.

It was as though he had not aged a day!

"It will be a great pleasure for me to see my sister's wrinkles, and Famhart's gray beard." He laughed aloud, stirring up the dragon spell again, and causing the fire to sputter and send orange fingers leaping out onto the wooden floor. He stamped out the burning embers, and set a teapot to boil on the stove, while he pulled the charts from his knapsack, and spread them before him on the table.

"Here we shall have a look at the country where my lovely snake says there is a man raising an army. It does not strike me well! I was to have my way here! I may have to pay this one a visit to let him know who is at work in Trew, and that Argent Largo is no one to be tampered with."

He smiled to himself, and full of his wonderful powers, he caused the stove to erupt in another shower of sparks.

A noise beyond his shelter wall answered this last outburst, and Largo leaped to the door to surprise any intruder that might dare spy on him.

He threw open the thick wooden frame, and saw a frightened Elita.

"I thought you might want some of this tea, Largo. You said you were feeling ill. This is always good for a fever."

"You shouldn't sneak about like that, Elita! It makes me think you were spying on me!" Largo's face had hardened, and his handsome features were more threatening than she had ever seen.

"I wasn't spying, Largo! I was worried that you were feeling ill," protested Elita, drawing back a step further.

"Give me the tea," snapped Largo. "Thank you for it. I'll have some before I go to sleep."

She hesitated, then stepped forward to hand him the small teapot. As she neared the door of the shelter, a great hot wind burst forth, flapping her cape, and causing her to cry out in terror. "I knew there was something there! I could see it! Leave it, Largo! It will harm you!"

Largo angrily twisted away from the girl. "You have to leave, Elita. This is none of your affair. I have things I must do before the night is out."

"What have you to do? You told me you were ill."

"You wouldn't understand, you meddling wench! I've tried my best to be civil to you, but you refuse to let me. Now I have to ask you to leave me! Go back to the others!"

Elita was sobbing, but it didn't delay Largo's slamming the door in her face and bolting it.

Sparks and showers of embers were shooting from the chimney. Some of the largest seemed to have a life of their own, and they landed on Elita's cloak in a dozen places, setting the garment ablaze. She shrieked, and tried beating out the flames, but the hot wind caught the cloak, fanning the fire. Her hair and tunic were ablaze, and she ran, a terrible scream tearing from her throat, in an effort to reach the river.

The girl's cries of terror brought Largo to the door, only to see the receding ball of flames going away toward the water. For a brief moment something moved his legs into a half attempt to pursue the burning girl, but then they grew heavy, and he simply watched, his face drawn into an ugly leer. The fire in the stove leaped and jumped about wildly, and the voice of the flames was excited beyond forming words, and simply made sounds that were harsh and grating to the ear.

Somewhere near the river, a floating white flower burst into a thousand petals of intense light, and it began flowing along the ground in the direction of something that was making horrible nosies, and coming through the thin wood directly at the wavering white glow.

A voice, low and melodic, gave an order, and the dazzling

petals formed a soft cloud of radiant golden mist, and as the screaming Trew girl ran wildly toward it, the mist caught and held her gently; it covered the flames and slowly lifted the badly injured Elita and carried her senseless body to the bank of the river, where the other lights were waiting. There stood the tall elf who had spoken, dressed in a pale blue tunic, with golden leaves woven through the fine fabric. On his head, there was an archer's cap, with a thin white plume that dropped almost to his knees, and he carried a silver bow, etched with the figures of animals and birds, and a quiver of silver arrows that matched.

"What has caused the grief to this child of Hamen?" asked the elf, in the same gentle voice.

The petals of light returned one by one to their own forms, and the riverbank was lined with elves who were dressed like the first, but were much younger in appearance, without his lines and the sadness at the eyes.

"There was a fire at the shelter of the one who fled earlier, Camrile. "A fire that smelled of the snake."

The gentle features of Camrile hardened.

"I thought there was something I could not put my finger to. First the Rogen are stirred and loose, and now we see the basic cause of it all, brought back to us by the stench of that nest of fire and destruction from the old days."

Camrile loosened his quiver so he could sit by the stricken Elita. Her face and hands were terribly burned, and her hair was but a molten black char.

"This is not the way this was meant to be, Hiter. Bring me the Second Book of the Realm. We shall ease this sorrow. I cannot bear to look on this child so wounded."

"But Camrile, it isn't for us to meddle in the affairs of these Hamens. We have held neutral for all this time, as is written in the code of the Elboreal."

"I am the elder of the Elboreal now, and I remember the stink of the doom-snake. We have lived so long that it is almost forgotten. That was to be the time when we would see the full circle come, and the ugly head of the Purge raised again."

"We should not meddle with this Hamen girl! She is

almost dead. It will cause the Leighter to call us before the Richlin. We have our orders!"

The speaker was another elf almost as old as Camrile, but less colorfully dressed. In the place of the silver bow, he carried a gilded sword, with many colored jewels and etchwork at its hilt.

"The Leighter will do his duty then, and so shall the Richlin. If we are called to answer for what I have ordered, then so be it. We have stood by for many tournets without involving ourselves. The last of the Elboreal was to have had the job of simply making sure that all the clans returned safely to Altana. That job is almost done. And this child is an innocent harmed by the shadow of the snake."

"She's not the first innocent to suffer, Camrile. Remember our own!"

"All the more reason to correct this now. If this is the one thing we ever right in a sad world so full of wrongs, then it will let my heart sleep easier when it is my time to rest."

Another of the elves had stepped up to Camrile, handing him a tiny gold-covered book, with a small mithra strap that held it shut.

"I will need the star water," said Camrile. "And bring me the dust from the sunflower. We shall have to work quickly."

"Will you fix her face, Camrile?" asked an elfin maid, who had knelt at the side of the unconscious Elita.

"She will be more beautiful than before, Danen. There is nothing in beauty so appealing as that beauty which has been lost."

"There may not be time, Camrile," suggested another elf, pointing toward Largo's shelter. "The Hamen there is working some sort of spell. He's built up the fire, and the stench of the snake is heavy. He is calling out for the Rogen to join him."

A flickering white-hot rage passed over Camrile's fair features, but the soft sadness returned quickly. "Hold the candle and the cup, Danen. This shouldn't take more than a breath of our lives to give her back hers."

The elf then took the candle and cup, and along with the elfin maid, they chanted a line from the book that Hiter held, and in a soft whirling motion, Elita was lifted up from the riverbank and carried away by a floating cloud of golden mist, until she was at the river's center. There, the mist parted, and the girl disappeared beneath the cold, crystal waters, leaving not a ripple behind on the fast-moving current that sang its own song as it wound away toward the beckoning sea.

"Hurry, Camrile! The Hamen in the shelter is coming! He's not alone."

"Our work is done, Hiter. Call the others. Let us put out our lights and see if we can't lure this one closer to us. I would see who this is who smacks so of our ancient enemies."

Without further word, the brilliant lights that had glimmered and shone beside the quick-running river vanished, swallowed up by the late hour of the night.

Largo strode purposefully toward the lights, assured by the voice that spoke to him that there was nothing to fear from the petty rodents that were the elves. They had been totally defeated at the Middle Islands, and had crept off to lick their wounds and count their losses. Never would they thrive again, for that is what the voice of the dragon said, and the voice had never lied. And now there was a job at hand, that even the elves could not stop, no matter what they did, for the Rogen were to be made allies, and turned loose on the lands beyond Trew. The foolish girl Elita had told him that the Rogen could not be controlled by anyone but the Lord Trew. But Largo held the key to it all with the dragon scales, and his ability to call upon the Purge to help him win over the infidels who did not believe his power.

An eerie, greenish light shone from a coal that Largo carried in a pair of fire tongs from the stove, and he was casting his glance about, trying to detect his helpless enemies. The green flames that darted about the lump of coal grew brighter, and then burst into tiny fingers of green flame that whirled and writhed about the tong, and moved up Largo's hand to his arm, until he was at last completely ringed by the green fire. It danced and leaped all about him, and the pale colors turned his handsome face into a death mask. He searched the ground before him then, and the green fire grew stronger as he neared a spot by the river where no living thing grew. The trees and brush that thrived elsewhere were absent there, and even the water shunned the dark-rimmed outline that lay in the slime like a broken piece of shadow flung out into the darker shade of night.

"It's here," gloated Largo. "Just where that foolish girl said it would be. What luck Argent Largo! With it, I can call upon my new allies, the Rogen. Letta! Letta, can you hear your new master speak? There is no place you can go to avoid doing your duty for me! We shall march to a grand tune, your sisters and I! You shall have all the new blood you want, and I shall have the sweet sureness of driving out all those who ever crossed me."

Largo threw back his head and laughed a hollow laugh that sounded thin and broken on the wind that had sprung up, fanning the green fire until it snapped.

There were strange moans then, coming from the wind and the river, and a dark line of hooded forms began to flicker and flare in the greenish black shadows, and a low, wispy voice called out over the hissing roar of the flames, barely audible to Largo.

"You have called us in the name of the doom-snake. Where is our house of flesh? Where are the rivers of blood that you have promised? If we are to forsake the Lord Trew, we must have a promise that is bound by all the bond that holds together the blackest part of fear, and feeds on the sureness of death. Letta won't let the pretty Largo off with a promise. He gave that to Letta before, and the monsters from Trew almost caught Letta in her own form."

"I meant you no harm, Letta! You shall have more than a mountain of flesh and a river of blood! I shall make you as bold and feared as the snakes themselves. There will be no country left below the gates that will not fear and dread the name of the Rogen!"

Letta cackled wildly, and the other hooded forms joined together in a chorus of harsh chants and whirled and flung themselves about by the water, although being very careful not to touch it.

Largo noticed this, and the cunning intelligence that had always been his stored the nugget of information that the Rogen did not like water.

There was another movement along the shore then, and a silver white skiff shaped like a great swan pulled powerfully out into the center of the river, and a dreadful-sounding note from a reed pipe tore against the fabric of the darkness, causing Largo to cover his ears and reel backward like a wounded animal.

"It's the Elboreal!" shrieked Letta, turning an ugly shade of orange, then vanishing entirely, followed by her sisters. The cries and moans of the Rogen continued on, although there were no material forms to give them away.

Largo lurched out into the shallows of the river, brandishing the tongs with the wildly flaring green flame that leaped and darted from the lump of coal, but Camrile held his ground in the skiff.

"You have forfeited your life in this folly, young Hamen. If you give up your revenge and swear your oath to me that you will turn your energy to better usage, I shall release your life to continue."

Gnashing his teeth in fury, Largo leaped wildly at the silver white skiff where the ancient elf stood, lunging foremost with the tongs that held the hissing and sputtering green fire which was erupting from the burning coal.

A flash of fiery red and green sparks filled the air then, and a great explosion came from the swan's head. A waterspout rose out of the churning river, bearing the elf away into a spiraling stairway that blazed forth with blinding colors, flashing one after another against the darkness.

Another explosion of green fire leaped up, then fell back extinguished, and all was pitch black and silent.

Ambush in the Dark

The fires of the watch had been set, and the sentries made their rounds of the perimeter of the camp in noisy efficiency, with jingling spur and squeaking leather harness that held their swords and quivers. All across the high mountain pass were stretched the lines of the waiting army, crouched by the tents and carts and bonfires, awaiting the arrival of the dawn, which would signal the invasion. There were many last-minute details to be seen to, and the milling of men and mounts made a dull roar that carried a note of dread to any beyond the darkness that could hear it. Arnault and Morghen both hurried into the large canvas shelter that had been set up to house Lord Bern the Red. His battle flag drooped on a tall lance at his door, and his horse stood already saddled, clad in a dull gray armor, with a single picture of a bear rampant, painted on the metal in a blood red color.

"In time, Arnault, you will learn to announce your presence before you enter my halls," snapped Bern, glaring with undisguised dislike at the man.

Morghen bowed low, ignoring the remark.

"He means nothing by his rudeness, Lord Bern. It is the ill-breeding of all the mountain clans of the Channels. We are not bred to call any man our master, or to stand too much on manners."

"Then you and all the rest of these rude clansmen will have to be schooled in my greatness! I have been more lenient than I should, but I swear my oath of blood that if it continues, I will show you my displeasure in a way you won't soon forget."

Arnault stood at the end of the camp table studying the charts laid out there, with the plans marked and squadrons shown by pins with different-colored strips of ribbon tied to them.

"We have left a hole behind us, Lord Bern," he remarked sarcastically, pointing to a spot on the map. "If anyone on the opposite side has a single brain among them, they will seize this opportunity without any delay."

Bern glared coldly at his impudent lieutenant, but there was no change of attitude on Arnault's part.

This had bothered Bern for the last few weeks of preparing to strike beyond the mountains, for he could not intimidate Arnault, nor find out what secret information the man had that gave him the cocky air of one who knows something that will spell disaster for his enemies. Bern had twice reverted to using his only hold over the huge gathering of troops, and as Bern the Red in his bear form, he had whipped them into a frenzy of battle lust. They were eager to pour out upon the lands below the South Channels, down the fair valleys that lay between the two great ranges to the east and west, but Bern could not cow Arnault, and he could not be sure of his control over his army beyond a certain point. He had promised them loot and any land they might desire, but it remained to be seen if he could still hold them to his will once they were sated with fighting and spoils. This Arnault who stood before him was one of the keys in how that puzzle would be answered.

"We have no need to cover our tracks behind us, Arnault. There will be no one left to explore that interesting fact."

"Perhaps, perhaps not. We have been getting odd reports of deserters from the Line in these last few days. I find that passing strange, don't you, Morghen?"

"More than odd, Arnault. I have never in all my time as a commander in the border guards of the Channels heard of such a thing."

Bern rammed an angry fist down on the chart table, upsetting some of the colored pins.

"If you have an argument with me, Arnault, address me! If you find this so out of the usual, why? What makes you feel so? Speak up, if you have a suspicion of some of these new converts."

Arnault smiled inwardly at having upset the strange upstart who marched at the head of all the combined armies of the South Channels. It gave him a great deal of pleasure to see this grotesque magician ill-at-ease.

That was the ticket, he thought to himself, always keep the enemy off balance. Aloud, he said, "Morghen has talked to them at length. He doesn't doubt the story they have told him. You offered a great fortune to be made by any who come over to your camp. It's not that that bothers us. It's the way they seem to be taking the whole affair."

"Almost as though they're *too* willing to be going about the business of turning against their own," added Morghen.

"The stragglers we were getting in the early part of this campaign, I had no thoughts about. Now we're getting entire squadrons from the stewards of the Line. They have come in droves these past weeks."

"My thinking was correct then! Give a man something to dissatisfy him, and he will be a willing pawn to your offer."

"Mayhap, Lord Bern. I have often spent my time wandering among these deserters from the Line. They seem to be a well-fed lot, and not our usual run-of-the-mill outcast from the Leech Wastes, or the Bitter Roots. They're orderly and well armed, and full of bitter tirades against Famhart, the Rod of Truth, and all that he and the stewards stand for."

"Those are the sort of men we need for the leadership, Arnault! Would you fill in our command from some of the rabble you see in the recruits we have from the outcasts?"

"I might prefer to trust their groveling anger. Their plight seems more real than the things I hear elsewhere."

"What are you driving at, man? You can speak as plainly as you wish here! If you think these men from the Line are not with us, we shall dispose of them at the outset. All we have to do to test them is set them on the first squadron of the stewards we chance upon. That is a simple way to end all arguments. If they are not to be trusted, and refuse to fall on their old comrades, we will slay them all."

"We shall see, Lord Bern. There are rumors that some of these deserters were of high rank in the Line Stewards."

Bern ears perked up.

"High rank, you say? Are any of these deserters easily reached? Perhaps we might have a word or two with some of them."

"Oh, they can be reached well enough. We didn't want to bother you on this last night of planning. The Rogen Keep is a difficult objective. We have told you how it is defended."

"With invisible blood-suckers? You surprise me, Arnault. As a practical man, I find it hard to believe that such things guard Trew."

"We have seen a man who became a bear before our eyes," went on Arnault smoothly. "So there could be truth to the old tales of the Rogen of Lord Trew."

"How long did your two lands fight?" asked Bern. "Was it something that was ever settled?"

Arnault's face remained frozen in a smile, but his anger burned brightly inside him as he answered.

"The Lord Trew took the best of the settlements there in the corner where you see it marked on your chart. The land was rich with game and water, and the natural boundaries made it a safe haven from invaders. We came through a period of time together, hunting and fishing the same grounds, and a peaceful existence was held to by all concerned. Then the Channeliers began to grow in number, and we needed space. There was plenty to spare in Trew. They seemed to never multiply, so we borrowed what land we needed to use to help feed our hungry. They at first tolerated us, and nothing was said, but as the years passed by, and they saw we were spilling over our bounds, they said we would have no more settlements in Trew."

Morghen took up the story then.

"We never felt our presence on the fringes of Trew would be a concern for the settlements there, but the Lord Trew wanted to hoard the precious water he found in the underground wells there. It was spoken of by our healers as the water of life."

"We wanted to share it," broke in Arnault. "It was only fair. They should not have the only source of healing and long life. The Lord Trew was supposed to be over five hundred turnings, but it was said he looked to be no more than a man of middle age."

Bern watched the two men closely, his eyes dark. The talk of the secret wells in Trew interested him greatly, for a new thought was beginning to stir within him, and a plan began to formulate itself down among the slowly burning embers that remained of his old existence, before he had been consumed by the hatred of his brother and father. With that secret well, he could live on forever, if what Arnault and Morghen said was true.

Arnault continued the story, walking back and forth before the camp table.

"It progressed into bickering and offers back and forth in a plan to share the wells, the Tears of Trona—"

"Is that what they are called?" interrupted Bern.

"Yes," went on Arnault. "No agreement was ever reached. A party from our settlements went out one night to try to locate one of the wells, but they were found out. A battle ensued, and they were all slain or captured. From that time on, it was open warfare, but lopsided. They have the wells, and so don't grow old and die as we do. But now we shall see if we cannot set straight the accounts."

Bern looked sideways at Arnault, watching the man closely out of the corner of his eye.

"Does anyone know the exact whereabouts of any of these wells? What was it you called them?"

"The Tears of Trona. There was the legend of the elfin queen who lost her way on the journey back to the Havens. Some say these wells run underground all the way to the Sea of Silence. Then there are other yarns that say the wells were a curse left to haunt the Darien Mounds for stealing their queen from mankind. It is impossible to escape this world if you have drunk from the Tears of Trona, for you live on and on, even if you should weary of it all and wish to die."

"What fool would waste a gift like that? It sounds as though it is a thing that would be lost on many."

"Oh, it has many properties, Lord Bern. I don't think the only one of interest would be the power it has to give you long life. They say it can heal wounds and drive away arrows, swords, and Morghen heard one story that said if it were poured over stone, it turned it to solid gold."

"No wonder the Lord Trew became a jealous guardian of his boundaries. If that knowledge got out to all the surrounding lands, everyone would be trying to get those wells."

"Then he called up the Rogen. They were a part of the spell woven into the mystery of the wells. I don't know exactly how it was done, but the bloodsuckers who guard the borders there are under the control of Lord Trew. No one knows what has happened to him, or even if he still lives. We, of course, were sealed out, and forced to stay in the South Channels."

"Then it is timely that I came to your aid," crooned Bern, leaping on an obvious sore spot with his reluctant lieutenant. "I bring a power with me that will unlock those secrets for us. We shall drink our fill from these wells. I don't fancy the name, though. Once we have taken Trew, I shall call the wells the Wisedom of Bern the Red. All who I invite to drink of the water shall have endless life and swear allegiance to me, the true ruler of all the land. We shall drive out the traitor and the weakling, and establish an order founded on strength and survival. We will build an empire where all who serve me shall rule like kings, and the weak shall be used for what they have always been used best for, to serve their natural masters."

"You speak of heady things, before their time, Lord Bern," reminded Arnault. "We have yet to set foot in the Edges. We had best remember the wise saying from my childhood that says he who treads a path of dreams would do well to walk soundly on stones."

"What I have in mind will satisfy your plans, Arnault. I

know you are an ambitious man. I have seen that all along.
Some would think you dangerous because of it, but I think
exactly the opposite. You are an opportunist, my good el-
low. The moment you see that I hold these pauper armies
under my control, you will be quick enough in joining my
plan for command of these simple folk and their lands. Your
smart wit and rudeness will become a thing of the past,
because I'll hold something that you'll treasure."

"And what might the Lord Bern have that Arnault would
treasure so?"

"The use of the wells! With those, we will have a free
hand anywhere. No one can harm us, or slay us, and we
shall live on and on, and all those who oppose us will drop
away like leaves on a fall wind."

"You are very perceptive, Lord Bern. That much I give
you. But what assurance do I have that I will ever partake of
the water from the Tears of Trona? Why would you simply
not exclude me along with all the others who you wish to
destroy?"

"Because, Arnault, I dislike you so much, I would like to
bend that stubborn will of yours over to my way of thinking.
It would give me a great deal of satisfaction to see you
grovel before me."

Bern's voice thickened with hatred, but he wore the same
malignant smile.

Arnault laughed aloud in genuine glee. "That's the spirit!
Now we're down to the real way of it! This is the first open
discussion we've had on the subject since you came to
bestow your greatness on us poor devils lost in the
Channels."

"Don't drive me too far, Arnault! I have my limits! You're
nearing the end of my tolerance!"

"What? The magnificent Bern has an end of patience
with his humble servants? They will be sore-pressed to take
that, you know. All your loyal and faithful subjects out
there will clamor for your head if they think you won't
deliver all you've promised them. And if they find out about
the Tears of Trona, they will insist on sharing them as well!"

A terrible change crossed Bern's face then, and his eyes

burned with a greenish fire. His hand was at his sword hilt, and his mouth was forming the secret words which would transform him again into his old form.

"Easy, Arnault," warned Morghen, growing alarmed at the turn the confrontation between the two was taking. "We have an early call tomorrow. The Edges will require more than half our attention if we are to win through."

"You may leave us, if you wish, Morghen," said Arnault. "You can gather our squadrons now. Tell them we will go over the final plans before midnight."

Morghen was reluctant to leave, but was stared down by Bern, and at last departed.

"Your friend is right, Arnault. You drive me too near the edge." Bern was toying with a chart at the top of the stack on the table. "I know there are things that delight a Channelier, whether you would guess I know it or not. I have done my reading on you and the sons and daughters of these mountains. It is always wise to know who you're dealing with."

"I would think you should know that better than most, Lord Bern. You have come from a far-off land with this strange story of yours, and you have no roots to ground you. These mountains are nothing to you! I see the look you give the armies that are gathered to spill their blood for you! They are no more than two-legged cattle, being led to your slaughter!"

Bern laughed, a dangerous smile flickering across his features. "You and I now see eye to eye, Arnault! I've wondered at your motives all this time. You dislike me, yet are willing to go along with my plan for reasons that have eluded me. I do not think it is for love of your countrymen or the sacred Channels that you go on about so much. I suspect I know now what drives you."

"You wouldn't know the thoughts that move my heart, Lord Bern! You and your kind are forever lost in great causes that stir up the maps or battle charts, and create empty lands without people, but you never have the least idea about what it is you really want. You are a powerful warlord here, at the head of a great army. We move tomorrow against old enemies of my homeland, and I feel a sense of joy in trying to right an old grievance. I can face the day knowing that I shall be able to give what I can, and as a Channelier, I will be upholding the honor of my family. If I must die, then it will be a good day to die! I understand Arnault, but I do not understand Lord Bern. I'm not even sure I would want to try."

Neither of the men moved their glance away, and it was Morghen coming back into the shelter that broke the struggle of wills between them.

"I've brought you one of the last recruits from the Line, Lord Bern. He's out here waiting to talk to you."

"Send him in, Morghen. I would like to hear what he has to say."

Morghen bowed, and motioned for a figure who had been waiting outside the shelter to enter.

A tall, heavily armed man came through the low tent flap, pushing it aside with the sweep of a thick, muscular arm. He was dressed in the colors of the new Channelier army, although he still carried the arms of the stewards of the Line.

"Greetings, Lord Bern! Captain Gio Nashet at your pleasure, at the head of a full squadron of seasoned men recently of the lost territory of the Line."

"What brings you to our camp, Captain Nashet? A little idea floats around the back of my head that says you have something more in mind with joining us than meets the eye. I'm good at spotting rotten wood in a plank."

"You've got the right lads for this bit of work tomorrow, my lord. My men and I had a splitting hard time trying to throw off a steward by the name of Stearborn who was chasing us. Near came on us unaware, too, and caught us red-handed, but we finally gave him the slip. It'll do my heart good to be on opposing sides. I'd like to mash his smart gob in a bit, for all the devil's work he's done me."

"Then perhaps you'll get your chance, my good man. I like to hear of grievances! That is a good insurance to the proper performance, is it not? We wouldn't want to hear that the brave Captain Nashet had played at straddling two camps."

"My men and I have lived for all these last turnings with poor pay and little reward, commander. A Line Steward spends all his time drifting up and down the fallen borders of a country which has outlived its usefulness. When we heard of your offers of land and promotion for siding with your colors, we talked it over among ourselves and decided that if the Line was sinking, then we had best find the best road out for ourselves and our families. The older stewards have nothing to lose, so they won't see the writing on the wall. It is perhaps better that they die that way."

"Do you think there are many men of the Line who are as reasonable as you are, captain? That logic is hard to spar with."

"After this last attack, and all the toll that the turnings have taken, you won't have any too much difficulty with the paltry defenses the stewards can put up against this great force. It won't make any difference at all what reason or logic you use, for your armies can more than enforce your word and law. I can tell you for a fact that there are not sufficient troops guarding the Line to hold against what I have seen here."

"That's reassuring, captain. However, there is a small matter of reaching the Line. We have to cross the Edges tomorrow, and find our way through the territory of the ones we have been warned about. What was their name, Arnault?"

"The Rogen, Lord Bern. The blood-drinkers of the Rogen Keep."

"Yes, the blood-drinkers. You see, Nashet, it is to be something of a problem even reaching the Line. Perhaps we can find a place for you at the head of our assault tomorrow. That would set my mind at ease about your desire to join me, and give you every chance to cover yourself in glory. Yes, a splendid idea. Morghen, see to it that Captain Nashet is at the head of the assault on the Rogen pickets."

Bern dismissed the two with the wave of a gloved hand.

Nashet bowed low, and followed Morghen out of the shelter, shaking his head.

"I'm sorry to have been so foolish as to think I would like this man. He may be powerful, and have the ability to deliver what he says he will, but I wish I had not found out how difficult he can be. I'm not used to this sort of treatment."

Morghen talked as he walked, moving quickly through the knots of men engaged in last-minute preparations for the morning's assault.

"Like or dislike have no place in a war camp. The followers of Bern the Red will be rewarded by how well they have served. You are a newcomer, and it's only expected that you shall have to prove yourself trustworthy."

"We had expected that! I don't know what I was thinking of when I tried to imagine Lord Bern. He seems to be a cold one."

"You have not been with us long enough to have seen him take on his other form."

"They say he can take on the form of a bear. Have you seen him perform that trick?"

"Make no mistake, it was no trick, Liner! I saw him transform right before my very eyes."

"Yet you seem doubtful about this arrangement in your camp. Why is that?"

Morghen stopped abruptly and put a warning hand on Nashet's shoulder. "I am a peaceful man, and I go a long way aside to make allowances for anyone, but I want one thing understood between us, and that's that I'm a loyal Channelier, and always have been. If my actions seem less than agreeable to you, look to your own conscience!"

A look of utter scorn crossed Morghen's face, but he said nothing further, and continued on to the fire ahead of them where the lieutenants were mapping out the final battle order for the morning attack.

"We shall see who is left after this fray tomorrow, my good fellow." Nashet grumbled. "There are ways of disposing of obstacles in the heat of battle without arousing anyone's suspicions. It will be, 'poor bloke, served well. A dreadful loss to us all.' You mark me well, Master Whiptongue, Nashet shall have his due. You're almost as bad as that unbendable tyrant Stearborn, with all his high-handed talk of duty and loyalty. I thought I had ridded myself of his likes, but it seems all sides are blessed with the drumbeaters who love to lord it over anyone who shows a feel for common sense."

Morghen cast an inquiring look over his shoulder, raising his eyebrow. "Is there something I need to hear of all that muttering?"

"You'd like it better if you didn't," returned Nashet, not realizing that he had been overheard. "It wouldn't sit well with your soup."

The two had reached the wide expanse of charts laid out on the ground, with lamps lighted at all corners, and men marking off quadrants here and there, assigning duties to some, or sending runners to all parts of the camp with the latest marching orders.

In spite of himself, Nashet had been impressed with the huge, sprawling war camp, and the endless rows of tents and fires that spread away toward the dark outlines of the mountains. It was a camp such as he had never seen in all his life with the stewards, and a part of him trembled with uncontrollable excitement at the fact that he was at last to be with a victorious army. He doubted that even if all the squadrons of the Line were gathered together—and they were scattered on a dozen directions now—that they would be of sufficient force to deal with the troops Bern the Red had marshalled.

"It is time for a change," said Nashet, half aloud, trying to rid himself of the faint leaden feeling that had settled in the bottom of his belly since his conversation with the commander of the invading army.

"A change is always good for what ails you," agreed Morghen, who had overheard the Line captain. "It chases away the boredom and stirs the blood to a fever pitch. Here! Come here, and I'll show you what we wish of you bold men of the stewards."

Morghen leaned closer over a section of the chart on the

ground before him, and pointed a gloved finger at a spot near a rushlamp that was spreading its orange light over the map in strange patterns of melting shadows.

Nashet leaned close to see where the Channelier had chosen for his attack, and it took him some time for his eyes to adjust enough to the poor light to be able to make out his objective.

When he did register the information, it was all he could do to not let the held breath in his lungs out in one explosive protest.

"We have had reports of the Rogen Keep for a week now. It is one of the first objectives in the Edges that we must secure. If there is any truth to this business of the blood-drinking watchers there, I'm sure you'll handle them quite effectively, so that we won't have to keep our forces split for too long. We are using a pincer movement to cross their borders in three places, and to sweep on until we join forces here! By then, we should have no more to do than take prisoners of whoever is left of their army."

"These blood-drinkers are there," said Nashet, his skin cold beneath his heavy cloak. "I have heard of them all my life. They can become invisible, and carry many spells from the ancient rock-dwellers."

"Is that so?" asked Morghen. "Then it will be well to deal with them before we commit ourselves too heavily in the other areas."

Nashet's heart leaped to his throat, and no words would come. He broke out in a cold sweat, and had to swallow a few times in order to keep from choking. Across the large, unrolled battle chart, stood his old commander, Stearborn, looking at him coldly, his huge hands resting at his belt, near his longsword and quiver.

Before Nashet could give the alarm to Morghen, a dozen battle horns pierced the night with strident, sliding calls, and the sounds of ringing steel and fire-torched wood drowned out everything else. In another fleeting moment, the encampment was embroiled in the wildfire suddenness of the ambush.

He whirled, his naked sword in his hand, but where

Stearborn had been, there was now a rushing line of stewards, closing fast with the startled Channeliers and their armies. For a brief moment, Nashet saw the proud red banner of Bern floating on the fiery blast of battle, but it wavered and disappeared into the melee, replaced by the white-and-gold pennon of the Line, carried by what appeared to be a small child in brilliant silver mithra armor, and brandishing a gleaming longsword that flashed through the darkness like the tail of a blazing falling star.

Unexpected Allies

From across the river ahead, Famhart could see the lights dancing in the distance, wavering above the dark water, and disappearing at times behind the trees that came down to the grassy banks. They had traveled many miles that day. The Tybo had run foul with the signs of ruin further on ahead, and on more than one occasion, they had seen dead horses wash by, followed by what was left of human remains. There was no way to tell if it were enemy troops or allies.

"There were two more, sir," reported Alac, reining in his horse beside his leader. "That's more than a hundred we've counted."

"And no telling how many more we may have missed in the dark. There must be some big battle going on ahead of us, lads. Let's press on! The sooner we're next to this question, the quicker we'll have our answers."

"They might not be the answers we're looking for," grumbled Alac. "From the looks of things, I'm not so sure I want to confront whoever has been dispatching all these soldiers."

"Is that a man of the Line I hear?" chided Famhart. "A

steward's job is never to leave a riddle unsolved when you find it in the field."

"I might be a bit more inclined to think that way if I had a nap and something to eat," complained Standin. "I think all the rest of the lads feel the same way."

"We shall have our rest and food, Standin. I fear I drive you young whelps like I used to drive my old guard. I forget you're but youngsters to all this. Call a halt, Alac, and we'll rest the horses and have a hot meal."

"A fire, sir?" questioned Alac. "With all the strange lights we're seeing, do you think it would be wise to show a fire?"

"Aye, and a big one. I think it's time the Line Stewards showed a bonfire the size of an army. Light a dozen, if you can find the wood. Let's set this part of the Tybo ablaze with the grandeur of the stewards!"

Alac and Standin looked at each other with worried frowns.

The others of the group sat quietly in their saddles behind the three, not sure of what to do.

Famhart whirled, and shouted over his shoulder.

"Do we let the beggars know we're stewards of the Line? Or do we continue to skulk on like thieves? What's it to be, lads? Shall we start now to behave like the men we are?"

A smattering of tired voices replied with muffled, "Ayes," but it was a subdued band who remained quiet, looking worn and showing their youth.

"Well, well, lads," said Famhart in a different voice. "I'm afraid I was still trying to go back to my old ways. My old guard would have turned to, but those were different times then, and the world was another place."

"We could camp here for the rest of the night, sir, and start again at sunup. I don't want to overrun whoever those lights ahead belong to before we know if they're friend or foe."

"Alac is right, sir. We're all done up. We've come more than a good distance this day. Even the horses are finished," said Standin.

Famhart had dismounted and idly took a small locket out of his shirt, where he wore it on a chain against his breast.

"I have been driving too hard, my buckos, but I've had this weight riding over my heart. I keep thinking that any day we'll perhaps find the one thing that will help Linne."

"We want that, sir, more than anything, but we shall have to have our strength to carry it back. And to light a fire now would be sheer folly, sir."

Famhart laughed wearily. "Do I hear my lieutenant correcting the commander? Is my upstart whelp already so eager for the job he tries it on for fit before the old dog is ready to lie quiet?"

Alac started to protest, but the older man cut him short.

"I jest with myself, Alac. I can see the wisdom to your words. I am tired, and my judgment seems to find some other place to dwell at times. I have been sleeping in my saddle, I think. Those lights we have been following seem to have gone! Was I dreaming them?"

"No sir, we all saw them. They've been out there ever since we first caught sight of them just after sunset." Alac's voice was strained, and he ordered the others of the small company to dismount and form a defense line. Standin hurried away to make sure all got the order, and whistled from the darkness a few moments later to signal all was well.

The sound of the river seemed to grow louder then, and the silvery light with its broken reflections wavered like a shiny ribbon over the water, curling and turning as it flowed past the horses and riders of the Line. It had grown colder after the sun had gone down, and there were small clouds of white mist at the nostrils of the animals, and from the men who waited beside them in tense silence.

"It can't have been any of the raiders," whispered Alac, straining to see into the darkness. "They never operate this way. They would have attacked at once, if they thought we were here."

"I agree, Alac. If it had been any of the various bands we know of, we would already be up to our knees in gore. That's why I was banking on my bonfires to draw out our elusive

friends. No one can resist a bonfire at night. It's as sure a
draw as a keg of honey to a bear."

"I'm not so sure I'd like to find out who they are, or what
they want until I've had a few hours of sleep, sir."

Famhart was only half listening to his youthful subaltern,
for his attention had been on the change in the water's
sound. There was something familiar to the different timbre, and it reminded him of something. He turned his head
slightly, trying to detect exactly what it was, but Alac spoke
again.

"We have the dried beef in our kit, so we won't need the
fire, sir. We'll know soon enough about who our visitors
might be when daylight gets here."

"You may know before then, lad," said Famhart, dropping the reins to his horse, and easing closer to the icy river.

"What—" Alac began, but another change in the water's
sound came, and a floating bouquet of tiny, glimmering
stars floated toward them, out of the black shadows that
were cast by the taller woods on the far side of the
streambed. There was a very soft reed pipe playing, and the
air it carried was sad beyond belief, and it was all the men of
Famhart's squadron could do not to weep at the fragile
melody.

Alac turned to question his commander, but he saw the
two small streams of tears that glistened on Famhart's face,
and fell back silent, his eyes wide and unbelieving, as the
shimmering cluster of sparkling gold and white stars rose
out of the water into a form no bigger than a half-grown
child. The face was concealed in the folds of a gleaming
white cloak, and there was a small circle of mithra, which
came to a crown of five stars, each one a different hue of
brilliant gold and blue.

"We should have lit the bonfires, Alac," breathed
Famhart, although it was not the lad he was talking to.

A voice, if voice it could be called, for it was so musical,
sounded like the refrain of notes from a haunting pipe or
flute.

"What is it?" whispered Alac, who was joined by

Standin. The horses had begun to stamp and shake their manes, trying to move closer to the shimmering light.

"I never thought I would see their likes again," said Famhart, his voice very soft, to keep it from breaking.

"From the winds of the Sea of Silence, we bring you tidings, O Rod of Truth, ally of old. The Elders sent us out to seek the bearer of the flame that keeps the word of truth and honor. We have seen many things that have saddened us. We are near the end again. But greetings to you, Famhart."

The commander of the Line bowed low to the small, glimmering figure, and unstrapped his sword so he could sit down in the grass at the water's edge.

Alac and Standin stood immobilized, as were the rest of the troop.

Out of the light, there grew another, even brighter and larger, until there was a wall of glittering white and gold that lined the bank of the river in both directions. Across the dazzling, shimmering water, there rode a stately craft shaped in the likeness of an otter, and driven by a small white sail that filled and pulled as though there were a fierce wind blowing, although it was still and calm everywhere beyond.

"What is it?" whispered Alac again, this time louder.

"Hush!" warned Standin. "I've heard of these folk. They're as likely to change us all to stone as not, so be quiet!"

As the small boat came to rest on the shore at Famhart's feet, he stepped forward and knelt, holding out a hand to someone who was disembarking. In all the glitter and reflection on the river, it was difficult for Alac and the others to see, but the general outline of the small figure suggested that it was a woman.

"You have surprised me, Lady Elina. I would have thought you and your clans would have long been gone over the Boundaries."

A small laugh, like tiny bells heard from far away, came then, and another voice that reminded all there of the musical notes of a flute played softly on a still evening.

Neither Alac nor Standin could make out what was said, but their leader leaned closer, and spoke something in return.

"I don't like this," said Standin, keeping his voice hushed not to be overheard.

"Shut up!" snapped Alac. "I never dreamed I'd clap my eyes to anything so strange as this! I always thought the tales from the past were just yarns to keep us youngsters impressed with the wiseness of our elders. Look at that, Standin!"

"I'm either dreaming or gone off my gourd," replied his friend, his eyes wide with awe and wonder at the scene before him.

The lights had grown softer, pulsing now with a golden glow that covered everything with a shimmering reflection. It had a strange effect on Famhart's soldiers, and they began to sway to and fro, as if listening to an unheard melody.

"Your travels have taken you a long way from the shores we met on last, Famhart. I think we both look the worst for wear."

"You never change, my lady," replied Famhart, reaching out to take the hand the elfin queen had offered.

Her touch was at once electric and silken, and Famhart touched her wrist with a kiss.

"I hear from my lendens that there has been a great sorrow upon your house. Our sister Linne is still unrecovered?"

There was a sadness in the deep gray-blue eyes that touched a buried spring of grief in Famhart, and he wept openly, unable to make any reply but to nod.

"I have heard it that the Scourge of the Islands is back to all her old tricks. I did not think then we had seen the last of her."

A small silver tray inlaid with ivory and red and green jewels appeared, and a small tea service was laid out before Famhart.

"My men have had no food or rest, my lady," he began, but she cut him off.

"It is being taken care of. They shall not remember much of this, but it's just as well. We have not a great time left before our hour is done."

Famhart gazed for a long while into the soft, sad eyes of the Lady Elina, then turned to his men, who were all fast asleep beneath a rainbow-colored canopy that breathed above them in the damp night air.

"They will be rested and strong on the morrow. We shall travel by my highway tonight. You shall be where you need to be soon, old friend."

"We are far from where we need to be, my lady. There is another week's march ahead of us before we reach the Edges of Trew, and the Silver Mist."

"You were once shown what an elfin hand could do when it was turned to a problem that seemed beyond hope."

"I remember well that night on the landings of the South Beach, my lady. There was never a braver deed done than what your kinsmen did for the glory of Windameir."

The Lady Elina sighed, her gaze growing deeper still, and Famhart suddenly heard the snore of the ocean as it was that fateful night, and the plash of boat and oar cutting through the waves toward the shore where the elfin army was landing the combined forces of Windameir on the beach called Death's Handle by the Dark One and her allies.

"It wasn't to be the end of the illusion, it seems. Even when Trianion called forth the Purge and carried them away to the Fields of Light, I knew there would come a time of change here in the Lower Shandin. We have seen my kin and the Dwarlicht lines closed away from all. It is a new time for the Black Death to reap her crop of new converts. All the old ones have gone over the Boundaries, and there are fewer here now that know how to combat her."

Famhart laughed wearily. "There are so many holes in our defenses that it wouldn't take a very strong effort to overthrow all that's left of decent beings that still live. I was asleep for so long when we came home from the Middle Islands that I didn't dare let myself think that it would be simply a matter of time before we were faced with all the same dangers as before."

"Perhaps more! This sleep that Linne has fallen into is nothing but the old thrall of the Dark One. We have seen it for as long as we have been locked in the struggle with her on these fields of Windameir. Yet it is written that no one shall be left here. We will not be able to rest until we have called Home all those who strayed or were lost to the Darkness for a time."

"I have always wondered about that, my lady. It was hard to understand why your race ever got involved at all with the affairs of men! That has brought grief and destruction to your kind for as long as we have been lost in this battle with the Darkness."

"You are no different than our clans, Famhart. We shall be able to leave these fields when we have claimed the last fallen Elboreal who have gone astray. Each race is charged with that duty."

"You mean the humans will be here until we have called all the outcasts and bandits and evil ones back to the side of Windameir?"

The elfin queen nodded gently, pouring more tea for the exhausted Famhart. The soothing sweetness of the tea was slowly washing the weariness from his bones and clearing his head.

"There are circles we all complete, my dear old companion. It happens that the lot of my people falls to rest sooner than yours. But you must remember, the Elboreal are much older than your race. We have been at work here in the Lower Shandin for as long a time as even the Dwarlicht clans, or the older races that have long since crossed over the Sea of Silence."

"I would like to make that trip with you, my lady. If only I had Linne at my side now, I think I would gladly forgo everything else, just to know I was bound for rest and an end to this madness that plagues the Wilderness."

"It always falls out this way, it seems. When we are weary enough, and have no desire left to hold us down to the task here, we have some attachment to something that always pulls us back. There is more to your lady's wounds than I have heard from you or my lendens."

"It was her brother," explained Famhart, his voice edged with a rage that burned white-hot against his brain. "We thought we had seen the last of the poor accursed beggar long ago, but the Dark One has evidently seen fit to return him to us for more mischief. He was the one who sent the poisoned brooch. The blackguard is offering a fee for all the stewards of the Line who join with his army in Trew, so my troop and I are on our way to oblige!"

The Lady Elina reached out a hand to touch Famhart. "You shall have your wish there. The Eye of the Elboreal never misses a mark. I have seen it so, just the way you say it will be."

She held up a delicate hand, and the ring on her third finger flashed and spun out a golden ray of light. It seemed to draw Famhart into the color, pulling him closer and closer, until at last he gazed into the depths of the golden pool that lay at the bottom of a great distance, further in and deeper than a mountain lake. It then turned a gray-blue, the color of the eyes of the Elboreal, and there were ribbons of silver run through a black background, and it took him a long while to see that what he watched was a river, seen from above, as though he were floating freely in the air.

"What is this?" asked Famhart, trying to make out the now changing scene that went on before him.

"Look closer, my old friend. You will see for yourself."

In the next breath, the river was full of light and dazzling silver boats that pulsed on the water like wind kissing the silent surface and breaking it into a hundred reflections, all turning and spiraling away like colored glass in front of a fire.

"There are boats there," he said at last. "If we had boats for my squadron, we could be in the Edges without anyone the wiser."

"You shall have your boats, old friend. The Elboreal have been ordered to assist you."

"But how can you assist those of our size, my lady? It is a thought well taken, but I cannot see how all my men would fit into any of your craft on the river. You and yours are welcome to join the march for the Edges, and to join us in whatever adventure we may meet there."

A slight laughter filled the air, and the Lady Elina rose and walked to the bank of the swift river.

"Your men will have no recollection of anything," she said, turning toward the still figures of Famhart's squadron. She waved a hand twice in a small circle, and drew a tiny pipe that sounded almost like the voice he had heard before, but then the silence crept slowly over the glade by the river, and everything seemed to grow so still that he had a hard time keeping himself upright. There was a slight aroma of pine and musky water smell that reminded him of the sea, and then the silver boats were there, pulled up on the shore before him, looming as large as cathedrals in the drawings of the old ruins of Boghatia.

"By the Sacred Blade, where have these giants come from, my lady? I never thought such things could come and go on so small a patch of water as the Tybo."

"You are correct upon that, dear Famhart. We have simply made things a bit easier to transport. The Elboreal have always had difficulty in this world since the Hamens have grown so much larger, and all the other life has gotten so immense as well. Something needed to be done to bring it all back into proportion, so I've just altered you and your men for a short while, until you reach your journey's end at the Edges. Others are traveling there as well, and great trouble is stirring in the South Channels. It will be well to have as many of our kindred there as we can, for a great danger has been stalking us ever since the Middle Islands. It's like a shadow that you can't quite see in the broad daylight, but the dark brings on all the fears and uneasiness. That is the splinter that the Dark One left to all those below the Boundaries."

Famhart looked about him. There were elfin warriors, dressed in full battle armor, climbing over the sides of the sleek watercraft, and helping to pull the boats to even higher ground. In the boats were elfin mounts, the small horses that he had not seen since the days of the invasion of the Middle Islands, which now seemed so many worlds away.

He felt old and tired in spite of the refreshing tea the Lady Elina had given him.

"We shall take your men and their horses aboard these slendils, and deliver you to the Edges by dawn. There you may find what it is you are seeking, my friend. Your wife's sickness had its beginning in Trew, and there is a cure for it there as well. The Tears of Trona may hold the answer for you."

"What are these things you speak of, my lady? How will I know them?"

"They will know you, Famhart. But a great danger lurks about them, for they are guarded by the Rogen. They are dangerous enough, even for us, for although they cannot slay the Elboreal, they can harm us in other ways that are more painful."

"How is that, my lady?" asked Famhart.

"They can sound like the Forgotten Wind, and deafen our ears to the sweet music of the pipe and harp, and cause our eyes to see only dark shades by day."

"I thought no one could reach your secret places, my lady."

"None but a few can. The Rogen were given that secret by the Lord Trew, when he sealed off his country from the outside. He was a chief elder in the war of the Middle Islands, and he knew both the runes of the Dwarlicht and the Elboreal. He knew we might try to keep him from falling prey to the power of the Wells of Trona, so he thought to keep us all locked safely away from him."

Famhart watched silently as the horses of his squadron were loaded aboard the elfin ships, looking no bigger than small fieldmice. One by one, his followers were carried swiftly to the boats and put on deck for the coming voyage up the Tybo River.

"You shall have allies to help you with the Rogen. The Lord Trew was not quite so thoughtful about his own house when he set out the guardians he called up. There are those there who will help you. You must find the ones who have remained true to the Light."

"How shall we know friend from foe there, my lady? I

have never traveled there, or know of anything that would mark an enemy from a friend."

"You will find that easier than you suspect, Famhart. I have seen a great tide turning, and there are more forces loosed this night than what I could explain to you in such short space as we have."

"Then we need only finish the loading of my squadron, and set our course for the Edges! I ache to be doing something. It is always the worst to lie awake at night on the eve of action, thinking of all the things that could go wrong."

"You Hamens have long tortured yourselves with that trait, Famhart. We of the dreamers know what is to be, so we don't dread the coming of the end. That was the hardest part to ever get accustomed to, when we were very young in the Lower Shandin. The Elboreal have always known from the time we first visited the Wilderness that we would spend a long, lonely time here, always aware of every hour and minute that we would have to stay."

"Didn't we humans ever have that curse to bear?" asked Famhart, following the Lady Elina as she walked slowly to the last of the boats that had landed.

"You still have it to bear, although sometimes I think you forget it on purpose. There are never any of those powers taken away."

"I forget them, and all the rest, unless I am with you, my lady. I seem to shut out these things that I am witnessing tonight, just as I chose to ignore my son's stories of the strangers who rode the talking horses. Linne was always the one to believe that anything was possible under the sun. It makes me sorry to think that we quarreled over so many unimportant things."

"You shall have time to mend your mistakes, old friend, with any luck at all. Behind the worst of our sorrow there is the promise that when it is met and dealt with, it can no longer hurt us."

"I hope that is so, my lady. To be separated from Linne has been the worst of it all. We were together through all of our time at the Islands, and our worst dangers and sadness we always faced together."

"That's as it should be," answered Elina, giving the order to launch the elfin craft back into the swift, cold reach of the river.

Famhart stood at the rail of the finely wrought boat, watching as his own horse stood stamping the deck behind him, surrounded on both sides by others of the squadron, calmed and quieted by the steeds of the Elboreal. In another instant, he was listening to the horses talking among themselves, and suddenly he heard a name mentioned that took him back in time to the beginning of this last desperate adventure.

"My lady, do you know of a man who goes by the name of Gillerman? My son met him, and told me of his talking horse. I never suspected anything at the time except an active imagination, but after listening to your steeds just now, I was reminded of Owen and his excitement."

The elfin queen shook her head in answer to Famhart. "But we may know this man you speak of by another name. If he has one of the high animals of the Upper Shandin, then the Elboreal must surely have knowledge of him."

"Speaking of my son has saddened me again, my lady. I have left him to guard his mother until my return. He insisted that we go toward the South Channels to find this Gillerman. His sword was given to him by this fellow, and it has some sort of unusual power, I take it."

"It might be one of the weapons forged in the fires of the Mount of Skye. They were given to all the ancestors of the lost ones who were sent to the Wilderness to find those who had strayed."

"You mean you've heard of these swords?"

"There were many forged, although some have been lost over the turnings. Some, it is said, have fallen to the Black Death. All those she has captured, she keeps buried in a desolate part of her domain. They give her great pain, for they are fired with a spark of Windameir, and their flame of truth cuts her to the quick."

"I have been cut to the quick as well," went on Famhart. "Talking of my wife and son has struck a note inside me that rings like a funeral dirge."

"Perhaps I can cast the Eye of the Elboreal about for news of your young fry. If he carries the sword you say the Mentin gave him, then I might perhaps reach him."

Famhart's hand grasped the rail of the elfin boat in an effort not to stumble backward. "That is very kind of you, my lady. If you could find news of him, that would ease my heart greatly."

Elina turned her attention to the ring she wore then, and her eyes became misty and passed through color after color as Famhart watched. The motion of the elfin boats was almost as motionless as passing through air, but Famhart could see the dark shadows of the wood gliding swiftly by, and there was a soft humming sound that came from somewhere beneath the deck.

In a dreamlike trance, a boy far away caught at the thin edge of a dream that held him captive in a gloomy cave far below the light of the sun, and played strange music in his ear. It was a faint voice, coming from a great distance, but it was persistent, and kept calling softly into his sleep. All he wanted was to fall back into the deep pools of oblivion he had been soothed by before the disturbing dream, but the voice seemed to grow nearer and nearer, calling his name.

For a brief instant, Owen saw the beautiful face of a woman who was not a woman like any he had ever seen, for there was something about the eyes that were older than any human mind could comprehend, and more beautiful than the heart could bear to look upon. There was something that reminded him of his mother, and then after a dazzling display of lights, the sword seemed almost to have exploded out of the scabbard at his side, setting him bolt upright in the confines of the small room, next to Kegin.

THE THREE
KINGS

Collision Course

The dark outline of the trees stood silent and foreboding as the moon rose slowly above the jagged outcroppings called the Marienhalm Slides on Stearborn's charts. The darkness beyond was lurid with the red eyes of the watchfires of the great war camp of the one called Bern the Red.

Stearborn sat silently on his horse and watched for a long while, until his lieutenant cleared his throat noisily, and made a feint at moving away.

"We'll be traveling by moonlight now, sir. We have need of more secrecy than we'll have once the Old Sow is out full."

Stearborn didn't seem to hear at first, although he finally nodded, and reined his mount around. "Have we established contact with the Elm Squadron? Did our messengers reach Chellin Duchin?"

"They have signaled just before dusk, sir. The smoke was from Cobber and Dally. I would make them a day away."

"If they were here, we'd attack tonight," grumbled Stearborn. "By the Sacred Blade, it makes my blood boil to think of these slippery vipers right beneath my boot heel without being able to strike."

"They are too many for us, sir! We would never stand a chance against these odds."

"You grow too cool-headed, Gaide. Too many years of sitting at the council table learning your facts! By the Eyes of Glory, what I'd give to have more of the hot blood I used to have!"

Here the big man dismounted and walked beside his horse as though he were unable to sit still.

"You still have all your hot blood, sir. Nobody would ever say that the leader of the Pine Squadron is any less the man he once was."

Stearborn snorted out a short laugh, then grew more good-humored.

"I wasn't referring to *my* hot blood, Gaide! I wish I had a few more like Chellin Duchin and that rough and rowdy bunch that he holds together with that iron fist of his."

Gaide blushed, and looked away from his commander as he spoke. "You have all the same makings here, if only you'd notice."

The commander of the Pine Squadron stopped and turned to lay a hand on the pommel of the saddle of his lieutenant. "Gaide, you've been a brick, when it comes to hot water and stews that would have sent another man fetching a backway out of the muddle. And the rest of the lads are as good as any that have ever carried the white-and-gold for the Line. Never think that Stearborn of Pine Squadron didn't think his lads weren't the top of the mark in every way!"

He let his reins fall slack, and turned out of the faint trail to look back over the great jagged edges of the Marienhalm Slides, and at the endless line of watchfires beyond.

As he studied the vast dark scene, he saw a movement down along the pale silver ribbon of the river, and suddenly turned his full attention on the new addition.

"What do you make of that?" he asked Gaide.

"I don't know what to make of it, sir. Look! It's all up and down the river!"

"But this side, lad! Whoever they are, it's this side of the river."

"Then we could be in for a bad night, sir, if it's some of the blokes from over there!" Gaide's eyes moved away toward the war camp of Bern the Red.

"Wrong kind of light. I feel something else, as well! And listen! Do you hear the music?"

Gaide tried to quiet his hammering heart long enough to hear what his commander spoke of, but he couldn't calm his racing thoughts or feelings long enough to try to concentrate.

"Roust up the lads! We may be in for it yet! Set out the pickets, and bring Jurin up to me! I want to see how we stand on supplies."

"We'd have plenty if we could win through there," replied Gaide. "I dare say those beggars are having a better supper than we've had in a long stretch."

"You may get your supper yet, lad! Don't count out that idea too quickly!"

Stearborn watched carefully as the lights on the river dimmed, flared once, then all fell into darkness again, deeper and more complete than before. The afterglow of the bright golden white lights burned on in shaded halos as his eyes readjusted, but he could not shake the idea that whoever had shown the lamps at the river had been friends.

A vague echo of a story Famhart had told him long ago began to enter the fringes of his awareness, and he grappled to try to find the thread of the yarn, but without much success, until he remembered it had to do with an old clan, and that they were called the dreamers.

The music had grown somewhat louder, and he strained to pick up the melody, which was somehow sad, but very hopeful at the same time.

Gaide seemed to hear something then, too, for they both fell into a profound silence, listening with every pore of their bodies for the evidence of danger or safety. The hair at the nape of their necks was raised, and the very blood inside their veins seemed to tingle in anticipation.

Further down the slope, right at the river's edge, a swirl of dim lanterns or rushlamps could be seen, although neither Stearborn nor Gaide could identify the shapes that seemed to move through that confused darkness like faint wakes on the face of a dark lake.

"We'd best get the lads ready, in case we have to make a fight of it," said Stearborn, although without much conviction.

He drew out a small, finely carved horn from his cloak, and putting it to his lips, blew a short series of soft notes that sounded no louder than a night bird's call. After a few moments of anxious waiting, there was an answering note from somewhere down the gloomy hillside.

"They're all in place," reported Gaide. "Now we'll see if our visitors are friend or foe."

The rushlamps grew brighter as the last of the horn notes sounded, and there was a flutter of activity that grew more urgent, causing Stearborn to utter a short oath under his breath.

"If they keep this up, they'll have every sentry on the other side of the river up at arms, and the whole of the South Channels will be down our backs before we can concoct a good spiel as to why we're dallying about on this side of the river."

"Maybe they *are* the sentries from over the river," suggested Gaide, although he was feeling none too sure at the moment. "I wish they would make it plain, red or white, as to what banner they fly."

As though complying with the brash young subaltern's wish, the lights flared for a moment into a golden white halo that lit up the water, and cast dazzling reflections that leaped and turned on the deep, serene face of the river. In that few seconds of clear light, the two men saw what was plainly a white pennon, with the golden crest of the Line boldly stitched across it.

"What mystery is this?" cried Stearborn, and he mounted quickly, spurring his horse toward the river.

"Wait! It may be a trap, sir! It might be Nashet or some of his band!" cried Gaide.

"He would never have the backbone to fly the colors so near the war camp there. If it was Nashet, he would have skulked about like a wet rat, waiting for a safe time to bite!"

Stearborn had thrust his horse forward into a brisk trot, and rode boldly forward toward the gathering host that began to show itself at the water's edge.

"Let me call up the afterguard, sir! Don't go down there alone!"

"Come on with you, lad! If you are ever to know what it is to be a steward of the Line, then stop all the thinking and yapping, and feel the blood that runs through your veins! It's the blood of the Line, lad! It's in you because your father and his father before him had a thing or two to say about where they dwelled, and how they lived!"

The older man was riding faster now, and he came down the hill with a clatter of hooves and scattered stones, which threatened an avalanche with every stumbling effort the horse made to keep its footing.

Above the noise of the horse and rider, Gaide heard a war horn, high and clear, but it was cut off abruptly; then there were others, each a trembling, high note, blown once, then again; and another rang out at the end, lower and of such a resonant timbre, that it raised all the hackles on the back of the young subaltern's neck.

He had turned his horse, and now rode back toward the squadron's camp, to draw them into battle order to follow Stearborn's lead.

A tired and restless knot of younger stewards accosted Gaide, wanting to know what the furor had been about.

"Now, lads! We have a rendezvous at the river. Stearborn has us marching to glory across the way. Hop to it, me bucks! Look alive there! We're going to take Bern the Red by sweet surprise, and turn all the blighters back across the borders!"

"Stow it, Gaide!" called a young man with a three-day growth of new beard. "We've been on this patrol so long we've lost count of trying to catch anyone, or to do a steward's job of clearing out the Line! Just point us in the direction the Old Fox has gone, and spare us your blooming second-in-command palaver."

"You can hear which way he's gone, Previn. Just listen to all that hoop-lolly by the river."

Previn and his comrades stopped and listened then, and turned wondering faces to each other.

"That to-do will help tip off anyone across the river that we're here," said Previn, his brow furrowed and troubled.

"Exactly what I told Stearborn," conceded Gaide. "But you know him. He has some idea that if we announce our presence every so often here, all the scouts for the enemy camp will think we're just another renegade squadron coming to join in with the ranks of the invaders."

"I hope he has that right," mumbled Previn. "And if he doesn't, I hope we shall have a chance to at least quit ourselves well in the bloodbath that follows."

"You've a gory way of thinking tonight, Previn! Have you been too long on this little outing? It seems as though we've been waiting and holding off our attacks for ever so long, especially since we crossed over into the territories that are run by that bear master."

"Bear master or not, whoever he is, he's raised an army the likes we've never seen the match of."

Gaide looked away over his horse's head, tightening down his cinch strap.

"I never thought there were so many who held the Line as an enemy. And the rumor runs that there is another hot-brand in the South Channels with an army as big as this.

"We didn't pay enough attention to Stearborn and his tales. Or to Famhart either, for that matter. I always just thought they were funny old men who went off on a campaign once, and liked to tell it all over again when they thought they could catch someone new to tell it to."

A loud cheer had rolled up over the crown of the small hill, and echoed back upon itself.

"Up, lads! Let's see to it! All in a skirmish line, now! Hup!"

The squadron mounted as one man then, and with Gaide leading, the mounted riders cantered noisily across the rocky flat, and descended into the valley where Stearborn had disappeared earlier.

As the troop neared the river, a dim line of rushlamps was lit, lighting the faint bed of the road, and leading the company straight on toward a dark mass of shadows that lingered restlessly at the water's edge.

There was a charge in the air that electrified all there, and Gaide had a brief overwhelming fear that they had somehow all been tricked into an ambush. He was on the verge of drawing his weapon to make a fight of it, when there before him on the path stood Stearborn, feet planted wide apart, and flanked on both sides by Chellin Duchin and his whole crew.

When Gaide looked again, there were also small figures, dressed all in a faintly gleaming silver armor, that took the reflected flames from the rushlamps and burnished the light into a soft reddish golden glow that flickered and moved in the darker pockets of the night like an answer to the signal fires of the war camp that lay sprawled across the river.

"Gaide! Have the lads dismount and stake camp here! Here is the rogue of a Duchin himself, with all his renegade helpers, right down to the twins! I had hoped to be able to see these ugly faces within the space of a fortnight, but we've been lucky, and luck has come in the form of a clan I had only heard tales of."

One of the small figures clad in armor stood beside Chellin Duchin, and spoke something to him that the others could not overhear.

Chellin raised a hand to speak as the elf withdrew, and pointed toward the war camp across the river. "Our good elf here has told me of a new arrival in the camp across the way there! It gives me a good feeling to know that we are to deal with the cream of the crop of all that that rabble has to offer."

"And we want to carry it all on the banner of the Line," reminded the elf. "It has to be done that way, or we shall only muddle it up the more."

"The Hepling has his point," muttered Port, who was echoed twice more by Starboard. "If we go into the camp now, we shall have less to deal with than if we wait until tomorrow to try to deal with all of them fresh and after breaking fast."

"But we have to have an order of battle," protested Jeremy. "There will be no point in any of this, if we get hung up in the river on the way across. Remember the Channeliers have boasted of some of the finest bowmen that have ever been."

"We won't have to fight our way across the river, Jeremy," corrected Stearborn. "You and the good Erases will hold back the brothers, and all the rest of the squadrons, until we have established ourselves into camp across the way, and give the signal. That should be later tonight, when the last of the watch is trying to remember to stay awake."

Judge and Hamlin joined the outspoken faction who favored a more prudent line of approach, but Port and Starboard, ever nodding and agreeing with themselves in endless small signs and signals, stood firm with the older commander of the Line. In the end, Erases, his small fair features troubled by the long time it was taking for the companions to make a decision to move, blew a short, quick note on his reed pipe, and the river seemed to erupt with row on row of the staunch little battle skiffs that the waterfolk of the Elboreal handled so skillfully.

"It is past time to leave these hostile shores, Steward! We have heard many tales from the river tonight, and we must prepare to receive more travelers on the Elverhan Road before this long day is over, so I beg of you, please be so good as to come with me. We will equip you with the best of the old mithra shirts, and our shadow cloaks as well. I don't think this fellow Bern is quite expecting to run into a light show on such unwarranted notice. It might distract him while the others pounce on the rest of the camp."

"Pounce we shall," repeated Port, running his thumb down the keen edge of the blade of his longsword. "I haven't had any good pouncing since the older days before the Line was surrounded by a different kind of enemy than she's facing now."

"A different sort," went on Starboard. "Our old mother used to tell us that it was to come to this, and we should stay in Trew!" Here he shook his head sorrowfully. "Sometimes I wish I had listened to her."

"Then you wouldn't have had the pleasure of being an endless burr under Chellin Duchin's saddle blanket!" chided Chellin. "And think what a sorrow that would have been to you!"

Erases broke into the conversation as he lightly scrambled aboard his lead skiff. "There's work afoot, citizens. Make your peace among yourselves, and let's set to the errand at hand!"

Stearborn bowed low to the elf, and blew a short note on the horn he took from his belt. "Look to it, lads! The Line shall have its reckoning soon! Hop to it! We have elf barges to haul our worthless hides, and a hundred to one odds to keep us sharp!"

A ragged cheer went up from Stearborn's squadron, and that aroused a cheer from the men who rode with Chellin Duchin. As the last echo of the stewards died down, the elfin host gave forth a spine-tingling war cry that made the men of the Line glad of soul to know that they fought for the same cause as the small warriors of Windameir.

In their mithra armor, the Elboreal soldiers looked ten times larger and more fierce than they were, and the steel in their weapons gleamed with a terrible white fire that reflected in their eyes.

"It is the flame of the Elboreal," whispered Stearborn to his young underlings. "The have called it from the old days at the Middle Islands."

"The what?" asked Judge, his eyes wide as he watched the elfin host launching their skiffs and pulling strongly across the swift current of the river.

"The weapons they bear were forged at the beginning of the Troubles. It's on all the swords and shafts they use! See them flashing?"

"I've never seen anything like it," conceded Hamlin. "I thought your old stories of these mystic works were just a play at keeping us in line."

"They were meant to do just that, lad! It looks as though it worked, too! I'm always glad to be able to bear out a story in fact, though. Nothing rubs so raw as a good chaffingstone that has its edge to the skin. We spend a lot of our time swatting at webs that aren't there, and battling ghosts from our own heads. It's good to get down to it, and hear the cold steel ring against steel. We know the way of that."

Jeremy's eyes were alight with the powerful emotions he felt at watching the scene unfolding before him, and the fear was lessened as he listened to this elder of the Line, whose name was known far and wide as one of the true heroes of the stewards.

"I don't know why this is different from any other time we've ever gone into battle, Stearborn, but I feel it's so, and I'm glad that our squadrons are joined together."

"There will be more, youngster," said Erases. "The Eye of the Elboreal has spoken of many things that flow on the back of the river now."

As he spoke, the elf held out his hand, and the gray-blue stone in the ring he wore burst into a brilliant golden white halo of light that flared up suddenly and reflected in the thousands of small mirrors hidden in the dark face of the river.

"It's Famhart!" cried Stearborn, looking deeply into the faint visions that danced in the elusive shadows of light. "And Linne!"

"The Rod of Truth from the Middle Islands," repeated Erases. "It is a time when the strongest are called, and the lines shall be drawn."

"Where is Famhart, master elf? Will we see him in any way except this spell that you weave?" asked Chellin, trying to draw himself back to the solid ground of his own senses.

"You will see him before another sun sets, good Chellin. The Lady Elina has taken his squadron aboard our river-craft, and is on her way to find us even now."

"Three squadrons," echoed Stearborn in an almost dreamy voice. "Three squadrons of the Line together, and a host of the dreamers as well! It will be a fine reckoning, I'll wager! The Devil of Entwender take the hindmost, when we strike out to this skirmish!" The steward elder struck his fist into his palm so loudly he startled Judge and Hamlin into a little frightened jig.

"It will be a fit way for a steward of the old school to close out his books," said Chellin. "After all this time, to be called into duty with the fierce clans of the Elboreal is the greatest crown an old soldier could have."

"You speak of it as a finish, friend, when it is yet the beginning. We have a long path ahead of us in this direction."

Erases held out his hand, and the ring gleamed and shone a bright white orb of light that slowly circled and whirled and finally became a solid image of a great host of men and elves, stretching away in every direction.

"We but begin tonight. There are times yet to come that we shall deliver what we have to deliver, and find an end to the road we travel together."

"Then let it be a long and successful road, and one that gives us victory for Windameir," said Stearborn, raising his sword in salute to the elf.

"Hear, hear!" chimed in Chellin Duchin and the others, and they were joined by the squadrons of the Line, all raising their salute and filling the night with a terrible promise of truth that lit the darkness with their hope and courage.

As the fires of the war camp across the water burned on into the night, a slight edge of a frozen wind began to blow from the forgotten halls of the Dark One, and a bitter fear stung the heart of Bern as he tossed and turned in a fitful sleep beneath the bright banner of the Red Bear.

The Return of the Elerwan

Kegin stood up as though he'd been shot! There was no one else in the close, sweet-smelling darkness, and he cursed himself for having slept. If anything had happened to Owen, he would never be able to face himself again, and in his rage and frustration, he began to pray for an overwhelming number of enemies to strike him dead, so that he could perish honorably.

"That's all I would ask," he said, half aloud, and was surprised to hear it echo dully in the dim gloom of the small room the Dariens had tricked them into.

"Hush," came a voice, from a deeper shadow near the far wall. "There's someone out there!"

It was Owen! Kegin's relief made him, for a moment, giddy, then he was clutching at his weapon as he joined his young ward.

A sticky, sweet aroma filled the room, coming from a crack along the floor at their feet. Neither Owen nor Kegin could place the smell at first, although the lad finally caught at the fleeting images it evoked, and plucked at his memories until something connected, and he remembered the smell that had been in the air the night his mother had pinned the fatal brooch to her cloak.

"It's flowers," hissed Owen. "The same that felled my mother!"

Too late, the two began to seek a way to retreat from the noxious fumes that slowly filled the room, and Kegin had to help the struggling youth to his feet twice, feeling his own consciousness slip dangerously closer to a deep black void that loomed nearer and nearer to him, filling his mind with a cold dread that was the worse for its lack of form.

"It's the flowers, Kegin! They have murdered us the way they snared my mother! And I can't avenge any of it!"

Owen wept with a rage that kept his senses from falling under the relentless fumes for a time, but at last all went dark, and he knew no more. Kegin dragged the senseless lad for another few steps, then fell in a daze.

A faint crack of light shone in at the very center of what seemed to be a solid wall; then widened, until two faces could be seen, peering intently into the gloom.

The Dariens moved boldly forward once they saw the two fallen outlanders.

"It was as easy as Querle Unidan said it would be," said the first, speaking in the odd-sounding tongue that had amused Owen so much. "Even the one with the fire-blade was nothing to fear. We were foolish to have worried."

"And now we have the Elerwan back. She has been gone long," returned the second.

"All will go well for us now. We shall move the Channeliers and the outlanders from our borders, and grow as we once were growing. We shall go beyond twenty hands yet."

"Perhaps thirty or more. The minstrel will make a good seam, for he is thirty hands, at least."

The two small figures rolled their eyes in wonder, and repeated several times the magic number of thirty hands. They stood at the wall near the unconscious companions, and went through a strange ritual that had one mount the shoulders of the other, and walk about like jugglers, reeling like a drunk, and finally facing a wall and making a strange hieroglyph at about the eye level of a human adult full grown. These were the strange markings that the companions had seen earlier, on their way to the Fourth Chamber of the Darien Mounds.

"Look, Lolin! It won't be too many turnings before we shall all have the tall, and be able to frighten the birds out of their very trees!"

With this, Lolin and his friend, Lobe, tumbled upon the shaft floor and rolled with unrestrained glee, kicking and biting at each other like maddened beasts, then turning somersaults backward and forward until they were exhausted with their efforts.

After they recovered somewhat, Lobe sat up and grumpily said they should take the prisoners to the Querle.

"The sooner the better," agreed his friend. "The minstrel won't be happy." Lolin laughed an ugly laugh. "No, no, not not happy at all, when he sees his friends roped and tied and to be fed to the Tears."

"He thought he was such a clever dog! It has been a long and wasted time he spent learning to whisper in the sacred tongue of the mounds. Only enemies were able to break our order and master the low speech. He has said it was one of the Old Ones who taught him, but the Querle says there are none of that race left. None but the outlanders come to the Dariens now, and we know why."

The two mound dwellers had tied up Kegin and Owen, and dragged them to a small opening near the front of the chamber they were in.

"Call for the drudge, Lolin."

"That I shall," replied his friend, and he placed his fingers to his throat and made a slight chopping sound that was half whistle and half screech. He paused, then repeated it again, and waited until he heard an answer somewhere in a lower quarter of the vast underground maze that was the Darien Mounds.

As Lolin and Lobe waited, Emerald sat impatiently at the table of the Querle Unidan, baffled and angry at the evasive answers he had been receiving.

There were a number of strange discs stacked before the Querle. They were obviously some sort of important relics, for as Unidan touched each of them, the other Dariens present all bowed twice to an invisible point over Emerald's head, and touched their hands to their hearts many times.

The minstrel asked again what it all meant, and demanded to know the whereabouts of his other companions.

"You and I have some difficulty in making our meanings exact," explained the Querle. "We must find a way to bridge this."

"My meaning is exact, O Querle. All I ask is to know the whereabouts of Darek, he or she, and my young ward, Owen, and his keeper."

"They are keeping. You will see them very soon. We have to all be present at the well for any of the law to have effect. You are most fortunate, O minstrel, to be the key in so great a moment for the Darien clans."

Emerald looked at the gathered half-dwarfish, half-human faces.

"I would consider it extremely good fortune to know what is going on, and to what honor I owe all this good fortune! You know my friends and I have a very urgent mission that we are embarked upon, and that we have no time to spare in anything other than what roads will lead us closer to our destination."

Here Unidan smiled broadly, and said something aside to his nearest companion, who smiled in his own time, nodding his overlarge, round head vigorously.

"Your destination is not to be what you thought, sir
minstrel. We now have all we have needed, and what was
promised to us when the tide began to run against the
Dariens."

Unidan paused, looking about the circle of mounders.
"We were scorned a long and weary time for the conduct of
the good founder of our realm. He discovered the only way
open to save our race, but it brought shame and disfavor on
our heads that we have borne all these turnings."

"You speak of the first King of Darien, O Querle. What
has he to do with me or my friends?"

"Everything, sir minstrel. We have long known a secret
that is written here on the Code of Sherin. It is the ritual to
free us, that will give us what we must have to be free!"

Unidan's eyes had grown wild as he spoke, and his hands
trembled as they touched the odd discs before him on the
table.

Emerald felt a cold tremor somewhere deep in that hidden place in his mind that warned of danger or madness. He
slowly let himself believe that if he were to emerge from the
Darien Mounds unharmed, and with his friends, he would
have to find a plan that would allow him to do it, for it was
plain the Dariens would not release them of their own good
will.

"We are to be free at last," agreed the others, all nodding
at once, and beginning to grow as excited as their Querle.

"How do you think that I shall be able to help you, O
Unidan? Or my humble compatriots?"

"It is in the Code of Sherin! It is all here, O minstrel. All
the signs have been met, and all the old sayings have come
to be. We will escape the curse of the Darien Mounds yet!"

"There is nothing to escape, O Querle. You have long
been a friend to those of my calling, and to all the Old Ones
who came and went here peacefully."

"They used us in ill-trust," snapped Unidan, a harsh edge
creeping into his voice, but Emerald could not tell if from
anger at an old injustice, or madness.

He looked more closely at the halflings then, and discovered that they all suffered from the wild eyes, and the desperation that comes from being too long shut out of the world. A wave of pity flowed through him, although riding at the tailend of it was a great apprehension for the safety of himself and his friends.

"I don't think the Old Ones would use you ill, O Querle. Let us try to call up one of the masters! We shall lay all this to rest. You have one here who has one of the blades from the forges of Skye."

"We know of him. They are being brought here now."

"Good," said Emerald, breathing a sigh of relief. "Then we can reach a bottom to all this, and set the course anew."

"Oh, we'll set the course anew, well enough," agreed Unidan, laughing his disturbing laugh again. "We shall indeed set the course straight. It has run a crooked path so long I had begun to wonder if there ever should be a way that would lead us out of these dark chambers."

The minstrel began to try to find something in Gillerman's teachings that would be of use to him in this dangerous moment, but nothing came to mind, except the Dariens' hatred and loathing of all things dwarfish.

"If you would like, I could sing you a tale or two of some delightful folk that have a bearing on your situation! It is a catchy tune, too."

Emerald had taken his harp from its case as he spoke, and stuck a plaintive chord or two. As he looked from one mounder to the next, he began to hum along, then he fell into full song, an ancient melody that Gillerman had taught him long ago, of dwarflore, and time, and the ending of the delvings upon Atlanton Earth.

He had gotten no further than a few bars, when he was stopped in midnote by the arrival of a hairy, misshapen creature called a drudge carrying two unmoving figures: Owen and Kegin.

A white-hot rage fired his soul, and it was all he could do to not draw his longsword and run it through the Querle's heart. He subsided a bit when he saw that his companions still breathed, although they were clearly under some sort of spell.

"Now you see what we have in store for saucy minstrels who would mention a certain race in these sacred chambers," said Unidan, his lips drawn back in a sneer. "We shall move on now to our next rendezvous, which will bring us nearer our lifelong dream!"

The other Dariens broke out into excited babble, and hurried to stand beside the drudge.

"May I be allowed to go with my friends?" asked Emerald coldly, but in a level voice.

"They will have no more meaning for you soon, sir minstrel, but you may walk beside the drudge if you have a wish to do so. We are going to the well to cast these two in, and to draw a drop of your blood to mingle with the blood of the young woman you thought was a man-child. Then the Code of Sherin will be complete, and the prophecy fulfilled. We will have tall!"

"Tall, tall, tall," chanted the others, all in a dull monotone that echoed back again from the stone walls of the shafts. It sounded as though the voices were joined by others from above and below, and soon the entire Darien Mounds was a dull, throbbing voice inside Emerald's head, mouthing the one word over and over again.

This, Emerald thought, is where Gillerman should have made his appearance to calm the heated Darien Mounders, but his old master was very strict about never appearing where he was really needed, thereby forcing Emerald to rely upon himself and the teachings that Gillerman had been trying to impart.

There was a strange noise just below the awareness of the Darien's chant, something that was hovering just at the threshold of memory, but it kept eluding Emerald in his nervousness. He had badly misjudged the mounders and forgotten that without his master, there were places in the Lower Wilderness that proved to be unsafe for anyone; yet there was a nagging notion that there was something in his presence that would prove to be of use.

The drudge grunted and shuffled along in front of the minstrel, and he at last noticed the fact that Owen still wore the longsword that Gillerman had given to him, and the gray bag that the lad had been wearing was strapped tightly across his back.

As Emerald walked, it seemed to him that the low, humming noise was coming from Owen's body, or something that was on his body. At last, a turn in the tunnel caused the drudge to shuffle the two humans in such a way that Owen's longsword rattled free of its scabbard. It filled the shaft with a blazing golden white light, causing the beast to squeal and drop its load clattering and banging onto the hard stone floor.

"Now you've done it!" shrieked Unidan, lunging forward to help the guards retrieve the spilled contents.

A weary smile played at Emerald's face when he saw that nothing had happened to the gray bag or its contents, or to the blade of Skye. Almost without hesitating, Emerald retrieved the sword and stood holding it still and steady as though it were something that he had done many times before.

The Dariens fell back hastily, and Emerald eased his way forward to a tunnel that had the runes of a forest and sea emblazoned across the archway.

"Keep him from the well!" screeched the Dariens' Querle. "Don't let them near the well!"

The druge lumbered forward, dragging its long, hairy arms on the stone, but the minstrel held out the sword of light before him, and it pulsed ever brighter, turning away the beast, who let out a howl of pain and confusion.

A knot of mounders tried to rush Emerald to overpower him, but were stopped dead in their tracks by an invisible wall that stretched out around the minstrel and the still unmoving forms of Owen and Kegin.

"They must not reach the Elerwan! Save the new queen of the Dariens! Is there not a mounder among you who will throw down this fiend who calls himself a friend to the traitors of old?"

Unidan had gone red in the face, and his blood vessels stood out in blue lines across his forehead.

More Dariens appeared then, from side shafts, armed and

with blood in their eyes. Emerald held the sword with one
hand, and tried dragging Owen with the other, but in the
instant it took him to look down, a mounder had loosed a
bolt from one of the short crossbows. The shaft had crackled
past the minstrel's ear in a buzzing, snapping sound. There
were more then, and the air seemed to be full of angry
hornets, although none of the bolts found their mark.

He had gotten Owen to the opening nearest to him, and
could see a faint blue light emanating from somewhere in
the distance, although he could not make out any clear
definition to the nature of the chamber. By now, Emerald
saw that the sword was somehow protecting him from the
bolts from the crossbows, for the shafts were deflected away
just as they neared him. He left Owen in the opening of the
chamber, and hurried back for Kegin. The Dariens were
pressing forward now, urged on by Unidan, who leaped and
screeched like a demon gone loose of his tethers, and frothed
at the mouth as though he would grind his teeth through the
very bones of his jaw.

The minstrel feigned an attack on the nearest knot of
mounders, and they flew backward from him in terror,
dropping their crossbows in a panic.

"The Elerwan is by the well! We must save her!" cried the
Querle, leaping ahead of his faltering troops, and rushing
headlong at his hated enemy. At a distance of about three
feet from Emerald, the Darien elder stopped abruptly, as
though he had crashed into a solid stone way, and fell
backward, stunned and silent. A long, low moan swept
through the ranks of the Dariens then, and two of the
bravest of the lot crept out of the crowd and dragged
Unidan back to a safer distance from the terrible radiance
of the sword Emerald brandished. Its light had grown more
spectacular, and changed color, from golden white to an
almost pure blue-white that was so dazzling it blinded even
Emerald. A humming noise continued to come from the
blade, and as the minstrel tugged Kegin into the relative
safety of the blue chamber's doorway, he began to detect a
noise that reminded him of a voice, although it seemed far

away and indistinct. When he recognized who it was, he almost wept with relief.

"Gillerman!" he shouted. "Can you hear me? I hold the sword you gave to the lad! He's been taken by one of the spells of the Dariens! I need your help!"

More bolts shot from the mounders crackled by his ears, and he couldn't make out any reply from the voice in the sword, but the lights had flared up even brighter when he had called out to his old master, and he sensed there had been some connection of a powerful current as he spoke.

Emerald began to make out a soft, blue light that bathed the center of the chamber into which he had dragged Owen and Kegin. The floors were almost a transparent color, making it look as though you could see through the very floor of the rock itself. The roof was so high he could not see the top of it, and a soft plashing of water and the feeling of a damp, cool wind led him to believe that he was in the chamber of the well the Darien elder had called out to the mounders to keep him away from.

As Emerald pulled his two senseless companions along the smooth floor, he felt that he was nearing something older and more powerful than anything of the Dariens' history, and the sword took on another softer color of blue, as if in answer to the blue light of the chamber around it.

"They're trying to destroy the well!" screeched Unidan, come to his senses again, and whirling about himself in frenzied circles. "Let the Rogen take them all! Call up the blood-drinkers! We cannot let these invaders reach the sacred well!"

A chilling cry was heard then, echoing down the chambers of the Darien Mounds, followed by others.

"You should not have spoken of them," shouted one of the Dariens, fallen back, his face a mask of terror. "The Lord Trew said only those of the pure line would be spared if the Rogen were ever called to the Darien Mounds."

"It's true," wailed another of the stricken Dariens. "We have long lived without the threat of that godless lot! This is no time to open ourselves to their treachery."

"You fools," blustered Unidan. "Can't you see the cost of

this? The invaders are at the well! We will lose the Elerwan!
We shall forfeit all!"

A low moan passed over the gathered Dariens, but not
one of them pressed their attack. This gave Emerald a
chance to get both Kegin and Owen further away from the
entryway into the chamber he had escaped to, which evidently held something of great importance to the Dariens.

As he lay back to rest against the wall of the chamber
next to the young son of the elder of the stewards of the
Line, Emerald thought he could make out the shadow of
another figure laying still and quiet, and covered with what
looked to be a funeral shroud. His heart skipped a beat, and
a gray, leaden fear choked him, making his body seem stiff
and old as he got up to go to the terrible silent form. The din
and confusion in the outer hall subsided, or his ears no
longer heard it, and the chilling sounds of the unearthly
beings who haunted the mounds held no terror for him that
was greater than his fear of pulling back the silken shroud
that draped the youthful form that lay beneath it.

With a strength he did not know he had, and by calling
out to the Great Friend of Windameir, and brandishing the
blade that had been fired in the flames of Skye, the minstrel
slowly pulled the soft coverlet back, revealing the familiar
face of Darek, only changed and more beautiful.

With a start that surprised him, the eyes of the youth
opened, and without a further word spoken between them,
two arms flew around his neck, and a weeping young lady
cried desperately at his chest, her shoulders shaking in
violent sobs that struck at the very chords of Emerald's
heart.

Death of a Spy

A long, black finger of smoke curled menacingly along the horizon, blotting out even the higher snowcapped peaks that were the beginnings of the Mountains of Skye, far away and beyond the last of the South Channels. Twice there were ominous rumbling sounds that might have been mistaken for thunder, had not the pale, falling dusk shown no clouds that would signal a storm. There had been other disturbing signs for some days past, and Argent Largo paced restlessly in the shelter, hurrying back outside at every sound. He twisted the ends of his riding cloak, and started up nervously at any sudden noise, although the twilight was like so many others in the strange land he had wandered into, full of lightning bugs and soft evening breezes off the river, and rich, sweet smells from the forest.

Since the disappearance of Elita, Largo had stayed away from the river, for the lights still came to haunt him, and the terrible music of the reed pipes drove him into a frenzy whenever he heard their thin voices, rasping away at his head until he thought he could bear no more. He had managed to scrape and dig out enough of the dragon's track on the deadened riverbank to replenish the small supply of scales he carried in the amulet at his neck. But even that was bothersome to him now, for it burned and galled his skin when he wore it, and frightened him badly when he didn't. He dreaded being without his only protection against the Rogen, who railed at him daily to be set free upon the mountain of flesh and blood they had been promised.

"Curse her bleak heart!" muttered Largo. "Just when I need the wench, she chooses to leave me!" He muttered a foul curse beneath his breath, and entered the shelter once again, although he was unable to sit or eat any of the food that had been set out for him.

"Blast that batch of mullets that call themselves Children of Trew! If they had a brain the size of a pipe stem, they'd see my argument and march tomorrow! Now they've got the rest concerned with the Rogen, and lights on the river, and all the rest."

He jumped up abruptly, and stormed out at the sound of an approaching horse.

"By the Dregs of Sedon, it's about time you've dragged your mangy carcass here, Mouse. Get down and come in! I want you to show me on the maps how we stand tonight."

Mouse, a frail-looking gray man with a drooping gray mustache, touched his hand to his forehead, and bowed a dozen times as he did as he was bidden.

"All saints preserve you, Argent Largo, and your sons and daughters, too. May you see a dozen lifetimes more, all in fair weather with no storms!"

"Silence, you mongrel! Show me on the maps what I've asked you for!"

"Surely, surely, your radiance. The tidings are many, and it has took myself and horse a long and weary hour to traverse all the camps and to find all the news you asked me for, sir. My throat still has the dust caked thick, and my tongue needs a lubricant to carry all the load it must bear to you this night."

Mouse rolled his eyes about, looking for a bottle to ease his pains, and he grimaced openly, as though struck, when Largo waved him to a water pitcher that stood on a side table next to the charts.

"It has been dreadful long of a ramble, sir, and some of the vagrants you calls commanders are rough to the touch, sir, I can tell you in no mincemeat terms."

"I can tell you in no uncertain terms, you maggot, what

I'm going to make of you, if you don't give me the reports that I sent you after!"

Even though he threatened the cowering Mouse, Largo went to a cupboard and returned with a long-necked brown bottle that caused the trembling man to smile and nod.

"Thank'ee, thank'ee, sir, plumb from the dead bottom of my cranky old heart. This here will do the trick, no doubt!"

Without further word, Mouse tipped up the bottle and drank half the contents without a breath, and when he had finished his drink at length, he let out a long sigh, and wiped his mouth on his sleeve.

"You've been took for a bad omen, sir, says some I've heard today! There's dirt abroad about you up at the double fork camp! They says the Red Bear is already at work, and there won't be nothing left by the time we pulls up stakes here!"

Largo spat, and took a long drink from the water pitcher.

"The Red Bear! If I hear that miserable name once more, I shall tear out the tongue of any who utter it in front of me! I have heard his name these past weeks until I grow sick to my soul of listening to the number of troops who have gone over to his banner!"

"They can't be blamed," said Mouse, shaking his head. "Begging pardon, sir, but they can't. All the spies that have found their way in always tells these brigands the same thing! The Red Bear will give them more gold and land than Argent Largo, they says, and Argent Largo keeps to his camp like an old woman, and won't even have so much as a glass of kindness with his lessers."

Largo grew redder and redder as Mouse spoke, but the other man didn't notice until it was too late to soften his speech.

"I would have your tongue, you worm-slime, but I need it to keep on wagging in that vacant head of yours long enough to finish your reports!"

"Well, it wasn't me what said them things," protested Mouse, cowering before his master.

"Not you, but other scum just like you," snapped Largo, his eyes wild and vacant. He had begun to hear the infernal reed pipe again, just below the subconscious level, where it hovered like a mosquito in the darkness.

"And the riverfilth is back again, even though the Protector promised me they were finished," he went on, his voice rising.

"Protector? Begging pardon, sir, but which protector does you mean? The Lady Elita is gone for dead, after all the talk I've heard. There's some what say you was the one done for her."

The bitter young man whirled and struck the informer with an open palm, sending the slightly built fellow crashing backward into the map table.

"It wasn't me what said it," whined Mouse, holding a hand to his bleeding nose.

"Then mind your tongue about your betters! The Lady Elita is on a secret mission for Argent Largo. Let all those scum who wonder where she is be as brave and loyal to Largo as their lady is! Tell them that when you're skulking about on your appointed rounds!"

"I always says only the best of you, sir, you knows that! The old Mouse weren't nothing for a snake to avoid a'fore you come, and he knows it, right well. Why, there wasn't no use in cuffing Mouse! I always makes the very top pitch when it comes to talking of you, sir!"

"Then pray get on with your pitch now! What do the front pickets make of all the business up toward the Edges? How close are the Channeliers to attacking? Have the scouts been able to say which way the push will come?"

The slight informer seemed to grow larger as Largo questioned him, and he reveled in his new importance. "They has come up on two fronts, sir, one up the north side of the Silver Mist Pass, and the other down toward the Edges. Some say they is bent on the Darien Mounds, but old Mouse has his own thoughts about that cursed lump of a devil's business."

Largo's eyes narrowed as he looked at his charts and tried to second guess his invisible, but highly present rival for the control of the Lower Meadows. Ever since he had heard of this man they called the Red Bear, Largo had planned and schemed to snare the fellow by cunning and trickery, rather than risk his growing army. For though he had promised each one who joined great wealth, it was obvious to Largo that the warriors he drew to his camps were of lowly, outcast clans, who could not be relied upon if the element of dread were removed from their hearts. There had been a few more performances since the disappearance of the Lady Elita, and Largo staged each of his appearances to best quell the curiosity of all those who would know more of Argent Largo, the bold avenger who sought recruits in the wilds of Trew.

With the calling up by the dragon-spell of the Rogen, he had been able to open the boundary of Trew to the soldiers he desperately needed, but according to all the scouts' reports he had received for the past days, the army of the Red Bear was vast beyond the scouts' ability to count.

This had ruffled the brother of Linne for a time, until he remembered the dragon's scale, and the deep, dark part of what had once been his heart, opened to a new, more vile plan. It would be perfect vengeance on his sister, and death to this upstart who challenged him for mastery of the South Channels, and Trew, and all the lands beyond.

"Blast his eyes to dust!" snarled Largo. "He's put in to the wrong quarter if he thinks he'll just walk into Trew at his fancy! I've got Letta and her sisters at my beck and call now, full of the blood-lust, and hungry for a morsel or two like the mighty Red Bear! We'll see how well his troops stand up against the Rogen!"

Largo had to stop there to let out a deadly laugh, for the memory of his encounter with Letta was still fresh with him, and he relished the thought of having such allies at his disposal.

"There's been much smoke today," said Largo, off on another tack abruptly. "What do you know of it?"

The informer wrinkled his pale brow, drawing a hand across his face.

"That's frightful puzzling, sir. Some say as its funeral pyres, and others says its the burning of the tithes, as is wont ever year, but it's not harvest time yet."

"I know that, you miserable thorn! What else?"

"Watchfires! They say they can seem 'em from Noodle Dome, plain as if they was right there with 'em!"

The messenger nodded briskly three or four times and took another deep pull off the long-necked bottle.

"Yes sir, I thinks along those lines for myself, I does."

"I don't care a whit about your opinion, but I think you've struck near the truth of the matter. It doesn't make sense to believe they would have fired a settlement. There's none to be fired, as far as I can see, according to my charts."

"Oh, they is out there, sir, but you won't often come on them. When them blood-drinkers you call the Rogens was of a mind to suck all the vigor out of any poor soul that was not pure Trew, there was a covey of settlements all over those parts, and right on out to the Edges. Then the killing started, and anyone who was able left for the better life. Like as not, they was all drunk up, too."

Largo shuddered. "How did they manage to miss you, you poor wretch?"

"They came at me fierce, sir, don't think they didn't! But my old granddam was blue-blooded Trew. I remembered the little songs she used to sing me when I was a cub, and I think that finished it."

"What songs, you wretch? Sing me one!" commanded Largo.

"They ain't nothing to get riled over, sir. They just make a lot of nonsense noise, and you jiggle your throat like this!" explained Mouse, holding his nose and thumping his Adam's apple with the heel of his left hand.

The noise was enough to drive Largo to distraction.

"It was a wise Rogen that shied away from that cater-wauling. I could hardly fault them for it! You may have more use to send out as a spooker toward an enemy garrison! All you have to do is the same thing you've shown me here."

"Oh no, sir, it wouldn't do none at all well for anyone other than the Rogen! They is plumb dried up on any morsels except of the humankind, and if they learns your name, they is said to be able to take over and use your body whenever they please."

Largo was studying his charts again, and paying little attention to his spy. "Do you think this bush bandit from the Channels will be able to break through the Rogen Keep? What is the opinion of those commanders there?"

"Why, they don't say, sir. They know all they have to do is keep back, and let the blood-drinkers do their work. But there is a powerful lot in that army. I don't know if the Rogen are that keen on squeezing their victims so many at a time or not."

"We shall have to go there to find out. Call the others here. I'll have a word with them."

"On the way, sir, begging pardon. I've got to relieve my head of a nagging fear for my missus. She ain't seen hide nor hair of me since I left three days ago to find out how things stood for you. I just wants to stop in to say a quick how is you. I won't take a moment of your time, sir."

"Go, you wretch! Send the others before you forget."

"Oh, the old gray rodent never forgets what's what, sir! I've come unglued of my good senses from too much gourd, but I never forget what's what! You can count on that, sir!"

As he bowed and scraped his way out of the shelter, he knocked against a stack of charts that spilled out across the floor in a jumbled mess, and as he bent to try to pick them up, Largo placed a boot square on the bottom of the spy's spine, and sent him sprawling through the shelter entrance.

"There weren't no use in that rough stuff, sir! I was a picking up your precious charts. Your Mouse is hurt fatal, I can feel it! You've cracked my ribs," he whined, rubbing the parts mentioned.

"If that's all I've cracked, you can consider yourself luckier than most. Now be off with you!"

The frail informer slowly got to his feet, his eyes narrowed and cunning, and his walk the walk of a man who was weighted down with such pressing problems that his poor human frame could no longer hope to keep up the struggle.

Mouse hobbled away, grumbing oaths under his breath, and whenever he came to the good part, where he, Mouse, was put in charge of the punishment of Argent Largo, his eyebrows knit into a perfect arch above his long, fine nose, and he burst out laughing to think of the fine sight that would be.

"I won't have no time to pay no attention to him, though," went on Mouse. "There's work to be done that needs doing, and I is just feeling as fit as a fiddler on Strawday, all keyed up to dance a reel or two."

Here Mouse had to stop to laugh again, and the fit came over him so powerfully that he had to remain doubled over for some time before he was able to go on again.

"Yes sir, there's a sweet job afoot for the sly Mouse. Oh, he's a coney he is, all fat and plump for the taking, but just wait 'til you bite into it, master high and mighty! You'll taste the death of you a little too late!"

After another long fit of laughter, the frail informer went on about his errand, obviously pleased with himself.

Largo still stood poring over his charts, making notes hurriedly along the sides in a small script that was nothing more than a scrawl. Then he would debate in his mind some further confrontation at another locale, going back to scratch through the first notations with other additions, until the legend of the maps were crossed and recrossed, making odd patterns that looked as though they were features on the map as well.

"Here!" he said aloud at last, stabbing a finger at the chart near Rogen Keep. "It even has an ominous-sounding name. Perfect for the snare, should any of the bushrats win through that far."

Largo turned aside to the center of the shelter, where he drew a large chalk circle on the floor with some difficulty, for the white nub kept breaking. He had an easier time of it when he drew the inner figures, all done with a precise coolness that would have frightened Mouse even more if he had seen it.

"Now we call the allies," said Largo, smiling to himself. "The smoke and the nearness of the enemy has convinced me its time! Come to your master, Letta! Bring your sisters with their hunger! We have much work before us, and you shall have your fill of flesh!"

Largo stoked up a small fire in the open stove, and held a

tiny part of the dried dragon track from river in the hottest part of the flames, until the room began to darken, and a foul stench filled the air with a black odor that reeked of decay and rot. As the dried mud of the dragon track melted into the flames, a low rumbling noise shook the stove, then the building, and Largo's eyes rolled with a wild frenzy, and drops of gleaming sweat burst out of his forehead like molten silver running down into his eyes and stinging them until he had to force himself to blink.

"Come, O snake! Your servant Largo calls! The hour is upon us! We must strike our blow now!"

A graveled voice scratched out a reply on the air. So harsh was its sound, it hurt Largo's ears, although he tried to conceal his discomfort.

"You have called to me, O lump of rotten flesh, and here am I, the worm of eternity and destruction! I hear your puny request for my might! I am a worm that has eaten towns in my time, and swallowed woods whole! There is no power that can stay before me! And it was I who carried your worthless hide to the Dark One when you were nothing but a morsel for the cold earth!"

"You can't harm me, you bag of ash! The Dark One has given you your orders to follow me, and that's what shall be! You have to depend on me to burn a scale from those precious hides of you and your brothers, or you wouldn't be able to appear at all. You need me, don't ever forget!"

Largo's voice was full of catches, for the vile smoke made breathing uncomfortable, but he went on.

"Here are the Rogen! You two will be my main force to crush this enemy that has come out of the South Channels."

A hollow laughter erupted in the room, as the voice of the dragon grew louder.

"You lump of human vileness, you talk of a grand scheme which the Dark One has carefully planned and executed over these grim times. My brothers and I are trapped here like flies in amber until the Protector gains her ends on the Lower Meadows again. Then we shall by Law be freed from the treacherous plot that the vile Trianion, curse his eyes forever, hatched upon us when he brought us to these horrible places they call the Fields of Light!"

The voice grew lower and more dreadful.

"It is the most horrible of all here, for the sun never dims, and there are no nights! When all a dragon's soul longs for is a long night to wing his way over a helpless land, to pluck a life here and there as he pleases, or to find some trinket to amuse himself with while he naps."

"My heart bleeds for you," snarled Largo. "All you will do for me is what I ask, and there shall be no holding back, or I will see to it that you stay in the Fields of Light forever!"

A booming roar filled the room then, and Largo's hair began to smolder from the heat that leaped out of the stove.

"You puny mortal! How dare you address me, the Purge, the crafty, the cruel, as an errand knave like your poor lackey there!"

Largo turned at this to find Mouse standing in the doorway of the shelter, hat in hand and eyes wide in fear.

"You have dealt with me for the last time, human! You are going out of your usefulness by crossing the Protector in her designs for the one called the Red Bear. It is not for you to decide how this battle on the Lower Meadows shall be fought!"

"You will do as I say!" shouted Largo, ignoring the informer and the men who stood behind him on the shelter's porch. "The Rogen are called, and I shall attack as planned! Do your worst, but you won't stop me!"

Largo hurled the pitcher of water onto the fire, and a great, searing scream of agony was heard from somewhere just above the level of awareness of ordinary things, and a vast, dark cloud of smoke bellowed out of the open stove like a giant claw, reaching for Largo's throat. He turned with a strangled cry, and bolted from the room, knocking his spy and the men gathered there aside in his flight, finally stopping in the open air outside, and flinging a hand up to defend himself from his ghostly attacker. He had ripped off the amulet at his neck, and threw it down at his feet, where it burst into flames.

"You devil!" shouted Largo, his voice taut with fear. "If you don't help me with what I want, I shall fling this cursed necklace into the river, and that filth of the waterkind will have it forever!"

The voice of the snake blazed in anger through the smoldering amulet.

"The Protector has her plans for you, you spineless toad! She is going to hear of this, and you shall pay more dearly than you thought a poor bag of flesh and bone could pay!"

"You will do as I say!" cried Largo, picking up the necklace, and starting toward the river with it, although the pain of touching it seared his hand, and he fought to control the urge to drop it.

This grim test of wills had so shaken Mouse and the gathered commanders of the varied watches, that they covered their ears to shut out the dreadful grating iron noise of the snake's voice.

"When the time comes for you to hear what I have to say to you, you shall hear it from the words of the Protector. I go now to tell her of this betrayal!"

With a flash of black smoke, and a noise like a clap of thunder, the amulet glowed a dark, ugly red, then lay quiet in Largo's hand. The informer and the others gathered there uncovered their ears, and took a few hesitant steps to see if Largo was harmed.

"Is you all right, your honor?" asked Mouse shakily.

"Of course, I'm all right, you rag heap! Get to your posts the rest of you! We attack tonight at the Keep. We shall have the blood-drinkers loose, even if this sniveling worm won't help. There's nothing he can do to stop Argent Largo now! I shall drive away and slay these bandits who would take a fancy to my new realm!"

Largo stormed past the others, scattering them again like leaves before a wind. The watch commanders sullenly went to their duties as they were ordered, but the informer crept up the porch stair behind Largo, and whispered quickly into his ear.

"You has a gentle way about you, your honor, and I likes that in all manner of them who is my betters. They sees things in a clear light, and knows how the wind blows, so to speak."

"What are you driving at, you miserable leech? Speak out! I have important matters to attend to here! We shall be at the Keep by midnight, and I don't think tomorrow will be a good day to cross me in the heat of battle!"

"Why, I wasn't thinking of getting against your current, your honor, not at all. In fact, I was remarking to myself and to a few friends on my way back here, how much of a cotton we took to your way of rootin' out them who is your enemies!"

"You're getting too clever for yourself, you dullard! Get to your point, or be gone!"

"Why, the point is, and it's a dandy sharp one, sir, that I knows of a certain night back when, when you was all aboggle with this same business as you was just about, and I happened to be out and having a little ramble down by the river to watch all them strange lights that had the river all ablaze like daytime."

Largo's face had hardened, and his jaws clenched as the informer went on, studying his face intently all the while.

"It was a harsh fate, sir, that the lady met! I just get the gray shudders when I think of all that beautiful face all melting down, and them horrible shrieks she was making while she was running past me!"

Mouse spoke in a voice barely above a whisper, and he spoke the words slowly and clearly into Largo's ear.

"You gets my drift, doesn't you, your honor?" he asked, smiling a crooked smile through his uneven, brown-stained teeth.

Largo seemed to be having difficulty with his breathing, and his face went an ashen white. He clenched his fists until the veins were straining through the skin of his forearms, but he didn't speak, and closed his eyes for a moment, as though he were trying to banish something from his thoughts.

When he spoke again, it was the old Largo, oily and full of good cheer toward his informer, and he escorted him into the shelter warmly, nodding and smiling his agreement to the terms the spy had spelled out.

Mouse had reason to distrust Largo, so he kept a safe distance between them, eyeing his master warily. "You can't do nothing against me, sir! I has my witness! They would know it if you was to hurt poor old Mouse!"

"Of course they would, my dear bag of bones, and I assure you I have no intention of touching a single part of your body! For shame to even think that!"

"Well, you knows how the land lies, your honor. A bloke does himself a good turn, and the next thing you knows, someone has took a twisted-up look at it, and then you gets the dirt between folks. Not natural! Never did see no harm in folks trying to help theirselves!"

"You are a philosophical soul, my good fellow, and I shall remember to write that down for your gravestone!"

Largo spoke in a flat voice, low and lethal, and he raised a hand and beckoned to the chalk circle, and pointed a hand at the informer.

"An enemy of Trew!" barked Largo, and a dark, cold wind blew through the room, whispering by the murderer's cheek as it passed, like a bitter night in the dead of December.

Mouse stumbled backward, not yet comprehending the nature of his death, until he half squealed aloud the one word, "Rogen." It was the last breath the spy took, for in another instant he was picked bodily up by an invisible force that shook him like a rag doll, and then drained him of his life blood in the wink of an eye.

It was over in the barest part of a second, and Largo had to steel himself to hear the lip smacking and crunching of bones as the invisible Rogen devoured the impure son of Trew.

After they were finished, Largo pointed to the spot on the chart he had marked, and gave another simple command.

"We shall attack tonight, Letta! Tell your sisters to swill to their hearts content! We shall mow down these invaders like a field of ripe wheat!"

The cold wind blew at Largo's cheek again, and he held

his hand to the small flask he had carried since the night he saw Letta and her sisters were afraid of the water of the river, and prepared to ready himself for the journey to the Rogen Keep, and his appointment with glory.

The Kites of Auroiel

The small gaudy kites flew against the wind's eye, darting and frolicking in the late afternoon breeze. There were hundreds of them, all in the form or fashion of some bird or animal, and they hung in the air like a tattered rainbow that had broken in thousands of pieces. Far below them, resting on the edge of a sheer drop that ran down to the Silver, sat a man with gray hair and beard, weather-beaten and sun-browned, who pulled lazily at an unlit pipe he had clenched between his teeth. In between pulling at the dead pipe, he hummed a refrain or two from some old half-remembered song, then went on to a snatch of another. The man had passed quite some length of time lost in these pleasurable pursuits, when his ears picked up an awaited signal, and he stood up, knocking out the pipe on the heel of his hand.

"Ephinias! Come up to the roost! We bring you a tidbit for your nest!" The speaker was a soaring hawk, gliding down lower than the colored kites. The man nodded, and without the smallest hesitation, repeated over a list of runes to himself, and swept powerfully off the steep hill where he had perched, to all the world a white-tipped hawk on a late afternoon hunt.

"Greetings, Karlin! May your wings carry you down the wind's backroom until you wish to cease!"

"Greetings, Ephinias! All the good days of my life are yours to share."

The two magnificent birds soared away until they hung suspended in the upper rafters of the sky, next to the bright kites that seemed to grow in number.

"We have seen the old water clans, Ephinias. They are on the river now, coming this way. They will see your signal soon."

"It is well they should. The news from my nephew was unsettling, so I traveled as quickly as I could to meet the help that was called for. I'm glad to find I was in time."

The dark feathers of the hawk Karlin shone a muted gold in the high ceilings of the afternoon, and he arched his wings powerfully, and swung away toward a distant green patch of woods that ran down close to the riverbank.

"We can wait for the boats there," he said, circling above the clearing. "It's far enough away from the Edges for us to talk freely. Come on! I'll race you!"

He folded his wings, and plummeted earthward at a dazzling speed, until both speed and sound seemed to be one with the dimming sunlight.

Ephinias followed, although more awkwardly, for he had been away at other chores, and found himself rusty in his flying.

As the two friends neared the river, Karlin suddenly arched his back, and flared his body out into a graceful braking motion, and quietly landed in a gnarled old elm that drooped out from the riverbank over the water. Ephinias settled gingerly down a moment later, winded by the unfamiliar effort.

"Whew," he gasped, "You've worn me out, Karlin! I knew there was some reason that I gave up being a part of your clutch."

The other bird chortled, ruffling his feathers and stretching into a different position on his perch in the tree.

"You do me too great an honor, Ephinias. A humble hawk such as myself would never be able to tire so great a flyer as you."

"I thank you for your kindness, but I must claim nothing, for I had two such teachers that I could not have turned out elsewise."

"Selohan and Tenon were the first to have crossed the Mountains of Skye. To fly at such heights gives you the greatness. It is the same with any who go to those places beyond the tallness of clouds."

"Selohan and Tenon," repeated Ephinias, and the two friends sat turning their heads and lifting their wings for a few moments in tribute to the heroes from the past.

"I think you spoke to me of news," said Ephinias at length, changing his stand from one foot to the other. Even in this unfamiliar body, the old wound to his left knee still troubled him when he stayed on it too long.

"News, my friend, news of a sort that will take the pin-feathers right off you!"

"What could be so pressing bad as that?"

"I've been keeping my coopage in Trew these past seasons, and I've seen all that has come and gone there. I've watched a new leader arise there as frightening as old Trew himself."

"You knew the Lord Trew?" asked Ephinias, trying to remember how long a lifespan the great birds had.

"He was one of the most unsettling fellows a human could be. He kept a hawkery, and I have cousins who flew for him, but they were a dowdy lot, and never spoke of anything without running it to the ground. Always out on a hunt, or in the process of mending. They never were stable birds that could get down to what was needed and do it."

"So you've been in Trew all this past season," urged Ephinias, trying to coax the bird on to his point without breaking good roost manners.

"Yes, yes, I was coming to that," went on Karlin testily. "I get confused sometimes in my way of keeping accounts with things that have gone on. Some seasons I think are made of the stuff we find in snowflakes! They just seem to dazzle your eye with how beautiful they are, but the minute you think you have it marked for memory, it's gone, and you never are quite sure you saw it exactly that way or not. Seasons are the same with me anymore. I've watched a lot of young stout wings take to the sky's stairway, but I've watched as many perish before they've reached an age of maturity."

"It's that way with all kinds, my friend," said Ephinias softly. "It seems to be the way of things."

"Yet you still feel it," replied the hawk. "I feel it terriby when I think of who I was hunting with even last season, down along the Lower Tybo. Good stock, and fast flyers, yet they are all gone, I hear, lost to this horde of outcasts who have come from beyond good sense to plague us all again, like it was in the days when we shared the air with the scaled snakes who flew. That was danger for you! I never dreamed of anything so horrible as that, and it took me a good many turnings not to bend my neck out of joint watching out for signs of them everytime I was up."

"I didn't think you were so old as all that, Karlin! I would never have taken you for one so advanced in turnings!"

The handsome bird ruffled his feathers and preened the skirts on the tips of his wings.

"You never spend enough time with us to find out the full history of our order. We are one of the oldest flights, and we go all the way back to the coming of the wind, and the beginning of trees and water."

"I know your order is old, Karlin! I meant you! You just spoke of the Purge in a way that led me to think you had actually seen one!"

The hawk turned his even gaze on Ephinias.

"I think I have! Or what was something very like it. Of course I was not flying when the winged snakes were abroad! That was long before my egg was dropped. But I spent time here in Trew, as I said, and I have been about up and down its breadth and width, and there is trouble brewing there that is right out of the old days."

"How do you mean? Have you seen something I should tell Gillerman and the others of?"

"I should hope they already know. If they don't, it may be too late to turn the tide that's running."

"How so? Are there so many enemies afoot?"

"Many times many, and they have a firebrand for a leader. I know he is come from the old days. Sometimes we see things that others don't, and I see the brand of the dragon on this one. I saw him call up a spell that set my heart drumming like it hasn't since my mater tossed me out of the aeyrie for the first time."

"This man called up a spell that smacked of the snake?" asked Ephinias anxiously. "Does he have a name?"

"He is called Argent Largo. I found that out by careful listening in a tree in his camp. He is highly rated with himself, so I had no trouble hearing his name, nor that he has a sister that he hates."

"A sister? Why on earth would he hate his sister?"

"He's human, and there's no knowing the end of the mysteries about humans. No offense, Ephinias. You know I don't refer to you."

"None taken. What was her name? Did he say?"

"Never. He also killed a woman of Trew with his spell of the snake. It caught her with its fire tongue, and devoured her."

"I have to tell this to Gillerman. It all sounds too grim to believe, but I trust your eyes, my friend. They see beyond the dimness of the night, and through the brightest day. I have to reach Gillerman, that's all there is to it!"

"Your kites will draw him."

"Perhaps. They will draw all who are in these parts to come see what the news is. It may draw some unwanted guests as well."

"I think they are coming already," answered Karlin. "Look!"

In the distance, a thin plume of dust was slowly raised, and coming in the direction of the kites of Ephinias. It seemed to be a large party of riders, perhaps a hundred or more, and they were coming fast at a brisk gallop.

"What do you make of them?" asked the man.

The hawk's hard, unblinking eyes studied the horsemen for a moment, then turned to reply.

"They are no friends to you or me! I see some there who have flown hawks before, but they are cruel and have no heart for true flying. I think they are in the service of the one I told you of."

"Argent Largo?"

"That is the name. I think he is come from an older time. When he called up the spell of the snake, I was amazed that there were any left who remembered any of that horror."

"It was well you should be, my friend. It was not supposed to be, after a period of time called the Middle Islands. There was supposed to be an end to all this then."

"There is a bowman with the riders there who carries a crossbow that covers his back! We had best find our wings and move to safer ground."

The graceful wings of the hawk lifted and swept him away up a golden sunbeam that broke through the branches of the tree. Ephinias quickly followed, but not soon enough to escape notice from the rapidly approaching horsemen. Horns blared, and a great hubbub broke out among the riders. Ephinias, puffing and blowing mightily, as he struggled to reach the upper altitudes with Karlin, looked around and down in time to see one of the mounted men release a great falcon, all steel gray in color, with a dark russet head.

"Come up! Come up, quickly!" warned Karlin. "It's a Skye falcon! They kill for pleasure!"

"I can't climb any faster," huffed Ephinias. "I'm not used to this."

Karlin hung suspended for a brief moment, then seemed to fold into a lightning bolt of speed and power.

His battle cry followed his plummeting form as he flashed past. Ephinias only saw a fleck of color against the blue sky, and then a great explosion of feathers and a stricken death rattle jarred the afternoon with its chilling finality.

As the feathers slowly settled in spiraling motions toward the ground, Ephinias watched as Karlin surged back toward him, in desperate flight after having slain the great falcon from Skye.

"Watch out!" warned Ephinias. "They're shooting at you!"

The horseman with the huge crossbow had fired a bolt at Karlin, barely missing the bird's wide wingspan as he clawed the air to gain altitude, and to fly out of range.

Another bolt, then another, arched upward in slow

motion, seeking out Ephinias's savior. Karlin seemed to be stuck in molasses, for he could not get beyond the range of the powerful crossbows.

"The kites!" cried Ephinias suddenly. "We'll hide in the kites!"

Karlin heard, and veered to his left abruptly, gaining speed as he went, diving back down toward his attackers, but with a velocity they could not measure with their crossbows. Only another few yards, and he would be safely among the thousands of colored kites, and away from any clean shot the bowmen could make.

Ephinias was there before him, and swooped on ahead in ungraceful movements, although at the moment the hawk was not of a mind to berate his friend about his sloppy flying.

They went on, weaving and darting among the paper throng, and although they heard the occasional hiss of an arrow slicing by, they knew they were safe among the endless lines of tethered kites, for the horsemen would find their way blocked until they undid the strings of all the lofty kites, and that would be a task that would take them the better part of a day.

"Your kites have saved us," shouted Karlin, beginning to slow his pace.

"The Auroiel have come in handy on more than one occasion, I can tell you," replied Ephinias, curving away slowly to his right to better observe what had happened to their attackers. "They stood us in good stead at the Middle Islands, just when the Purge had tried to find where a certain band of elfin cavalry was quartered. There is something disquieting about all these fellows, if you don't know what to make of their meaning."

"I'm glad you had the time to set them out here," said Karlin.

"Oh, they set themselves out," replied his friend. "I'd never have time to do it all myself. They seem to have a real flair for getting themselves up and hanging just right. I learned the trick from a fellow who said he was able to do it with tables and chairs, but that never took my fancy."

"You are a strange one, Ephinias. All the rest of my flight have warned me against having dealings with any so shifty and treacherous as humans, but how could I doubt a man who is able to take on the form of a brother, and who knows the secret color of the wind's eye?"

"I'm not so strange as you, Karlin. You've been who you are this time without a single dart to the left or right! That counts for a lot in the scheme of things. You have been up here at your work for all this time without a single grumble. There is no like story among the lot I've been with before I crossed your trail again."

"They've interrupted my report to you, my friend, but at least you've seen what we're up against here. These men with the Skye hawks were not from a settlement true to the one deep meaning of where we all fit into the nature of the Law. I think I shall have to find a way to change my shape, so I can walk around at human affairs like you, Ephinias, for then I could get close enough to do some damage."

"I'm not so sure you'd like to do that, Karlin. I could teach you everything you'd need to transform yourself, but I think you'd find it as boring as anything you'd ever done. Hawks are born hawks, not man. It would only make you sad!"

The two birds were still amidst the throng of the kites, and turned and glided safely now.

"Sad or not, sometimes it would be a relief to be able to do as you do, Ephinias."

"You wouldn't say that if you knew how taxed my time is. Even as we're here now, I feel the pull of someone who needs me, too. Speak! Tell me your feelings and what has occurred that you needed to tell me of?"

Karlin pondered heavily before me made his reply. "So this is how you speak to your old friend? Not even so much as sharing a morsel or two, with some of the fine talk that brings in the group after a long hunt?"

"There's no time to stand on ceremony, Karlin. These brigands were here looking for any signs of someone coming from the hills to free their slaves from the bondage of the tyrant who has taken hold here. These outcasts have spread like a disease spreads over a body."

"Is that someone coming on the river?" asked the bird.

"Yes, according to the signs. If this Largo is among them, there is still unfinished business that shall have to be worked out between the two of them. It is an old business, and has its roots deep in the old days. My little kite trick is nothing compared to what this Largo has been about, if you say he has touched the fire and brought forth a dragon-spell. Anyone who dabbles with those is too far gone to lock horns with until you've got a rock-steady plan, and you know what you're about."

"Do the people on the river know what it's all about?" asked Karlin.

"The waterfolk, Karlin? They know all there is to know, and now I have to know all it is you know from your time here."

"Then this is the way I have found it," replied the hawk. "I will forgo the rituals this once, since it is you and I, and we understand each other well, Ephinias. It seems a shame to let any of the old ways go, in these times. There is always an absence there when you do."

"We'll make up for it, master hunter of the deadly eye. We shall find time to carry out all the old rituals to our hearts content, once we have met this new challenge."

Karlin paused, gathering his thoughts, then began, starting from the beginning, when he had first hunted inside the borders of Trew, and when he had first discovered Argent Largo.

After a time, Ephinias nodded, and drew up his wings, allowing himself to fall from the heights he and Karlin had been flying, and plunged down toward the river far below, a silver ribbon that wound through the heavy wooded foothills, and reflected back the dying rays of the late afternoon sun.

"I will go now, Karlin! May your wings keep you on the fairest wind from the west! You have been a blessing beyond telling. Farewell!"

The hawk cried his farewells, and watched as his friend

disappeared from view, a tiny speck of dark wings against the blue of the sky, and finally into the greenery of the forest below.

Ephinias landed roughly, for he was older and stiffer than he had been when he first learned the ways of the wind-riders, and after carefully scrutinizing his surroundings, he repeated the runes that would allow him to return to his true form. He shook himself, dusting his cloak as he did so, trying to get the feel of walking again.

"I hate all this business," he mumbled to himself. "Just when you get the hang of how to do something, you're called away to something else. It's no wonder everything is in the muddle it's in, what with all this hopping and jumping about from one thing to another."

He shook his head angrily. "My garden is wasting away for want of me, and I shan't be back to it until goodness knows when!" He paused, shaking his head again. "And the peonies were going to be lovely, too!"

His flowers were forgotten, however, at the smallest hint of sound that announced he was not alone in the wood.

A slight breeze blew through the dim wood, bringing with it a soft scent of rotten leaves, and shaded glades that never saw the full light of the sun. Ephinias slowly eased his way into a position to examine his surroundings fully, and was ready to protect himself in whatever manner he deemed necessary. The mounted horsemen with the long crossbows were heavy on his mind, and he had forged a plan of action for that event, should it come to pass, when he heard the first of the vaguely familiar signals.

"Children of Lemuria, welcome," he said aloud, though not too loudly, for he still had visions of the horsemen with their ugly weapons.

The sounds grew louder, and a fresh smell of the sea was everywhere, along with the tangy crispness of snow on a high peak, frosty and squeaking.

"You may play out my secrets on your silence, but I have no desire to harm you! I am Ephinias, the Second Son! I am an amuser of sorts, and a ne'er-do-well of habit, and a frankly spoken man who lives for the day when someone will find it in their hearts to argue with me!"

"Then we are well met, citizen," came a clear voice, edged with humor. "I have come from a country where it is said that he who can't count his wits with a two-parted cudgel is indeed a dull dog that needs a fair dose of the restorative mentioned."

A small, round figure, somewhat less than the height of a man, yet larger than a dwarf, stepped out of what appeared to be the dead stump of an old oak. He was dressed in the fashion of an older time, although what time Ephinias could not have said, and he carried a great broadax that he now leaned upon to study his new acquaintance.

"You don't seem to be one of that lot I've been hiding from these past days. Are you an outcast as well, stranger?"

"My name is Ephinias. I thought at first I had run across some of the clans that are of an older line."

"You're speaking to a soul of the older clans, citizen, even though you couldn't be expected to know it. I am Third Faronet of the Realms of the Misty Sea. You may call me Aron."

"Forgive me, Aron, but I meant no affront. What I thought I saw was one of the small dreamers who used to roam these lands, and all the lands around."

"They are the very ones I have come seeking!" exclaimed Aron, his features growing animated. "I have been abroad all these past years in search of the seven clans, for only their aid will rid our realms of the curse that has overtaken us."

"What curse is that, my friend? Do you have outcasts and border wars where you have come from?"

"Worse," confessed Aron. "Since the sea has retaken all the land that used to make up a large portion of our livelihoods, we have found a way to tend to our growing communities by reaping our food from underwater farms. There was nothing new in this, for our distant cousins had carried out these operations, and many more, in times of need. What has changed all this are the ones who steal the food we grow, and who turn brother against brother in the off-shot."

"Why do you seek the dreamers, friend? Could not any army help you drive the lawless ones away?"

"Not anyone could help us, because it is a band of the dreamers themselves! I couldn't believe it either, because I have been bread-and-buttered in the myths of the Evening Clans, who dwelled behind the stars, and who held the gates of dawn open for an endless time, before they began to disappear. I guess there is nothing that says anywhere that you have to feel what you are feeling all the time."

"I can't believe it of the elfin clans! Surely you must be mistaken?"

"There is no mistake to it, citizen! I've come along here to try to recruit a true band of the silent ones into service for me. They will be obliged to go, once I get it through their crafty minds that when it involves their kinsmen, they are bound by law to help."

Ephinias shook his head, his eyes hidden. "It is a sad day indeed when the legends die. I am almost sorry to have lived so long."

"Cheer, citizen! I overcame all my lost ideals. I've even come to love the world as it is, for what it's worth. We must never be daunted," said Aron, puffing out his chest as he spoke.

Before Ephinias could reply, another sound reached their ears, and a faint outcry was heard, although muffled, as if it came from a great distance away.

"It sounds as though a battle is joined," said Aron, turning all about to try to locate the source of the sound.

"A battle, most assuredly," agreed Ephinias. "I can't seem to find what point of the compass it's coming from."

"I think it's coming from down here," said Aron, looking at the ground beneath his feet, and tapping the butt of his broadax solidly in the dirt.

Ephinias looked at the small stranger in surprise, then got on his hands and knees to put an ear to the ground.

"I do believe you're right," he said after a time. "There is certainly a ruckus down there now."

Aron joined him on the ground, and the two listened intently for another moment, then rose.

"Do you know anything of these parts, Aron? Is there anywhere we could find a way into this underground settlement?"

"These are the Darien Mounds! I don't think you'd want to find a way into them."

"I've heard a name called aloud! I must find a way down!"

"There are openings to some of the old mounds not far from here. If you're determined, we could try to find out if they go underground."

"Lead on, good Aron! We may yet not be too late! Lead on!"

"Do you know anything about the kites?" asked his new friend, looking up in awe at the colored sky that was strewn with the bright kites.

"They are the wind's army," answered Ephinias. "They've come to help us. But we must hurry."

Aron tried to question him further, but the strange man with the piercing blue eyes led him on at a hot pace toward the ruins of the old mounds. He would say nothing further about the meaning of the wind's army, and muttered something under his breath that sounded to Aron like the word "minstrel."

He tried to ask Ephinias if he meant the sort of minstrel who played and sang, and did amusements, but the reply he got was curt and short.

"This fellow isn't so much on amusements as he is rather prone to be up to his harp-strings in hot water. If this is my man, it sounds as if he is still up to his old tricks."

There was no further time to speculate on the meaning of his words, for the two had found the overgrown opening of an old shaft. It was cluttered with the debris of an ancient disaster—there were scattered pieces of broken furnishings of an odd sort, built for beings of a very small stature, and cast-off weapons, and in a sudden grisly discovery, skeletons that were no bigger than a small human child of ten or so.

Aron held back, hesitant to go any further, but Ephinias

picked up a small rusted sword that had at one time been encrusted with gems of some sort, and pressed on into the open dark tunnel that smelled of a vast undisturbed tomb.

The Red Bear

The braying of the war horns was deafening, and the clash of steel against steel crushed the soft velvet of the night in an iron glove; watchfires became funeral pyres, and the terrible roar of thousands of men joined in mortal combat drowned the senses. Mounted men raced back and forth in the battle camp, trying to rally the troops, and to find out what had happened, and who was attacking. The banner of the Red Bear floated still in front of Bern's shelter, although he had leaped from it earlier, changed into his old form, and brandishing a long, wicked-looking sword, with an iron pommel and a blade that glowed a dull green, and struck green sparks whenever he engaged in combat with anyone.

"Morghen! Arnault! To me!" he bellowed, standing upon the carcass of a dead horse. "To me, followers of the Red Bear!"

All about him, to his left and right, his troops were engaged in a deadly struggle, which angered Bern until his eyes burned in his head. This was the fault of the imposter in Trew, and he would make him pay dearly for his resistance. Bern cursed loudly and ordered no mercy shown to any enemy of the Red Bear. "Off with their ears, lads! Take their hearts!"

He blew a loud, wailing call on his war horn, then whirled to find himself engaged with two stewards of the Line, and only after he had slain them, did he realize they had been part of his deserters' army.

"Curse the fools for continuing to wear their blasted colors," he cried, looking about in confusion. There were others in stewards' uniforms in knots of twos and threes here and there, fighting with both his troops, and among themselves. A slow idea crawled through Bern's fevered mind, which caused him to lash out angrily with the lethal black sword.

"They've been a sly lot, those stewards," he shouted. "Come, lads, come to it! Slay anything dressed as a steward! They are in among us now! Death to all stewards."

Bern's voice was hoarse from shouting and he worked his way through the struggling throng to where he could get an overview of the field of battle.

There before him floated the hated standard of the Line, and he gnashed his teeth in rage, whirling about in a frenzy that lopped off the heads of two unfortunate soldiers who happened to be standing too near their leader.

"To the Red Bear!" growled Bern. "All come to the Red Bear! We will drive these treacherous cowards into the river and drown them like the rats they are!"

Bern blew another frantic call on his war horn, and it was answered in a dozen echoes, from all directions.

A fire had started in a more distant part of the camp, torching a clump of trees nearby, and now the surrounding wood was in danger of becoming an inferno. Out of one of these pockets of smoke, a band of the elfin host appeared, mithra armor glowing an ugly dull red from the fire. The leader of this small party saw Bern and held out a gleaming elfin blade that crackled with a golden white light that shown in the elf's eyes.

"You waterfilth," shouted Bern, and leaped to attack, cleaving the air before him with dreadful strokes of the black sword.

"The dreamers!" cried the elf, and parried the blow easily, sidestepping Bern's vicious attack.

A second elf entered the fray, driving Bern back toward his shelter.

The small warriors were experts with all their weaponry, and Bern could get no advantage, fairly or otherwise. He had a burning desire to get away from the small soldiers with the unsettling grim eyes.

"Morghen! To me!" cried Bern again, and this time a dozen or more of his army were all about him, and set on the elves in a frontal rush. More horns blew, and the air was filled with long-shafted arrows, all of the green feathers of the elfin host, and as the company shielded themselves from the barbed onslaught from the sky, the two surrounded elves disengaged and withdrew to the safety of the smoke and darkness.

Morghen and Arnault appeared at Bern's side, although both were careful not to startle him, and stood at a respectable distance.

"You've taken your own good time in answering my call," growled Bern.

"There is deviltry afoot!" shot Morghen. "We're attacked on both sides of the river!"

Bern whirled, and turned his full displeasure on his lieutenant.

"You were to have seen to the other side! It was planned to not have to deal with those imbeciles! What happened?"

"This is always the way of it," muttered Arnault, coming to his friend's defense. "They'll be cooperative as you could want when the talk is around the campfire, and there's no steel drawn. It's another matter when you get down to looking at it over crossed blades."

"You told me the matter was settled, and that you had the guard of Trew aligned with our cause!"

Morghen smiled weakly at his leader.

"You know that dealing with anyone who comes from Trew is only courting disaster. I warned you of just this very thing!"

"But you said it would be seen to, confound your oily tongue! You push me to my limits, Morghen! I am reaching my tolerance of the lies and deceits! I've had all I can stomach!"

"There is another way into Trew," interrupted Arnault. "It may be the way we have looked for after all this. While the big set-to is going on out of doors here, we could be in the old digs below, and win straight through to the heart of Trew. They might not be so keen on continuing to resist us if we had their beloved throne hall in our hands."

Bern's eyes burned a deeper red, and a snarling smile spread his lips back over his teeth.

"That plan might suit us well, Arnault. I'm glad to see there is one from the Channels who uses his brain for something else besides roguery. Do you have any of the underground ways marked? Are they big enough to support a large party traveling through them?"

"The scouts brought detailed reports back from their survey here. They have seen bands of small dwellers going and coming through certain mounds that are marked above ground, and plainly open for any who might chance along on them."

Morghen started to speak, but caught the look of Arnault's eye, and remained silent.

"Show me!" ordered Bern.

"Round up an assault squadron," added Morghen. "We shall see to it that nothing is left undone across the river!"

The two Channeliers looked at each other over Bern's head, who had lowered himself to study the features of a fallen deserter of the Line.

"Isn't this that fellow that you brought to me?" he asked, kicking the dented helmet away so he could better see the face.

"It looks like it," said Morghen. "I guess the fellow was telling the truth about wanting to join us."

Morghen laughed harshly.

"Now he's got his just desserts."

"Traitor's wages," snarled Bern. "Remember his face well, Morghen! It's a wise thing to never raise a slumbering bear!"

Morghen bowed low to signal his acknowledgment, and to conceal the sneer of fear and loathing he could not hide otherwise.

The plan Arnault had so deftly introduced had not aroused Bern's suspicions, and it went forward unchallenged, which amazed and delighted Morghen. There were

risks involved, but there was also the off-chance that one of
the underground shafts might house one of the Lord Trew's
mystic Wells, and if that were the case, then the long wait
would be over, and the tolerating of the violent, demented
bear lord would be at an end. They could fall on him by
force and slay him below ground! None of the others of the
vast army need know of his murder, and then Morghen and
Arnault could control that huge army to do their own will,
and it would be a thing of the past to have to grovel before
the old elders who had thwarted their plans for so many
turnings.

The battle about them had increased in fury, and the two
men hurried away to gather their handpicked squadron to
make the assault underground, leaving Bern to direct his
army as he would, from whatever vantage point he could.
He ranged back and forth, finally ending up by the water's
edge, where a company of elves had engaged one of his most
elite troops.

"Carry it to them!" he admonished, sensing that the elves
were getting the better of the lagging humans, and he waded
into the river to strike a blow to encourage his followers.

The appearance of Bern in his bear form seemed to drive
the men into a frenzy, which pleased him, and he shouted
aloud his approval as he saw the elfin line falter and begin to
fall back.

"On to Trew! Spare no one! Take no quarter and give
none!"

Bern had waded out into the shallows of the water, which
was full of bodies from both sides of the conflict, and
motioned his followers forward, the battle fever burning
brightly in his red eyes.

On the other side of the river, which marked the boundaries of Trew, he saw an odd combat ensue, which eluded his
understanding, and shook him somewhat, but he thought
perhaps it was the smoke from the fires that had been
started that made the scene appear so grotesque. All about
him, the woods were afire, and the terrible flames seemed to
leap from tree to tree, devouring all in its path. Even though
the forest floor was damp and cool, the army of the Red

Bear had weapons of war that used skins wrapped on projectiles that carried hot oil that would blaze up and spread like a lake of fire over anything it touched. The Channelier army had dragged horse-drawn launchers of these long flaming darts, along with a vast array of other weapons that would enable them to lay siege to even the most fortified settlements.

The flames leaped higher, and Bern saw many corpses of soldiers who had been burned by the flaming oil, and then there was another confused scene on the riverbank directly opposite him. Through the knots of struggling combatants there blew a violent wind, raising them off the ground and shaking them about, and then they simply vanished, leaving nothing behind but their clothing and armor and weapons.

An uneasy fear stole over Bern, and he retreated from the river back to safer ground, calling out for the troops to advance, and pointing the way to victory. He went on a rampage for the benefit of a new lot of replacements that had come up, and directed them straight into the maelstrom that went on across the river, so that he might better understand the nature of the enemies' defense.

Before he was able to find out anything further, Morghen and Arnault returned with their handpicked squadron.

"We're ready to launch our strike," reported his lieutenant. "We have a force big enough here to contain anything we might find in the underground. The scouts have only seen the small ones there, and they will be no match for us."

"Get on with it then!" growled Bern. "We need to end this as quickly as possible. I know the stewards are behind this, but I don't know who else is. Trew was not supposed to be this well defended."

Bern looked menacingly at Morghen, but his underling simply shook his head. "There was no hint that this would be so," he agreed.

"I hope we're not in for more surprises," snapped Bern peevishly. "These upsets make me forget my compassion! If I get too far gone, you had best not be near me, my good Morghen! I have a feeling somewhere inside me that we are devilish close to settling our differences."

Bern's voice was cold and hard, and he held the great black sword in such a way that it accidentally touched against Morghen's leg, sending an electrical shock through the man, which caused him to gasp aloud for air.

"I hope this plan of yours works, my good lieutenant, and that you and Arnault haven't had some other notion in mind about luring me down into some dark hole and murdering me!"

"This plan can't fail," blustered Arnault, in a voice that seemed much too loud, and he tried to cover his discomfort by making it seem that he had to shout so as to have his voice carry over the sound of the ongoing battle.

"It had best not," returned Bern, looking to his two subalterns, and the men they had brought along on the raiding party.

There were faces there that he recognized, and some that he knew were true to Morghen. To add to his own sense of well-being, Bern called forth another handful of faithful warriors who had proven their loyalty to him, and whom he knew he could trust.

"Now we shall set at this work," he said, satisfied at last with his arrangements. He sent messengers to all the watch commanders to rendezvous at dawn at Rogen Keep, and to take no prisoners. When the last of the messengers was on his way, Bern called the attack group together and outlined the plan that Morghen and Arnault had proposed. He broke the party into five elements, each with a specific mission to accomplish, and with what details he could gain from his charts of Trew, he set out the main goals they would hope to achieve with this daring underground strike.

"There is just one question, commander," said a surly, heavily bearded man who was a full head higher than Bern in his human form, and who outweighed him by a hundred pounds.

"What is it?" growled Bern.

"There is stories about blood-drinkers in these holes you're talking about traveling through! What is we going to do about them?"

Bern's eyes were on fire, and he glared at the man a moment before replying.

"Don't let them drink your blood! That's why you're armed!"

The other men laughed uneasily.

"That's the way of it, Rundle! If you don't want to end up drunk out, then don't let no such creature as them bloodsuckers get sidled up to you!"

"There is truth to the rumor," said Morghen, in a voice only Bern could hear. "But if we can capture the throne room in Trew, then we can call them off, or turn them on whoever we want."

"It is a risk," agreed Arnault. "We have weighed that carefully, and find it worth our taking."

"I'm glad you've decided so firmly among yourselves," glowered Bern. "I am happy to have subalterns who seem to have the capacity to make decisions on their own."

"Never without consulting you," went on Arnault hurriedly. "We only discovered the possibility of going through the old Darien digs a short while ago."

"I hope that's true," said Bern cryptically. "If there is any little hint of treason in the plan, then the shafts of the Dariens will be your resting place."

There was another flareup of frantic activity then, and a fast-moving skirmish line of cavalry from the Line smashed through the camp, scattering all the defenders before their unrelenting attack. A larger force of the army of Bern tried to thrust the stewards back, but were repulsed, and had to fall back to regroup again. Another volley of the green-shafted arrows dropped in then, and a new wave of the elfin warriors rolled over the enemy camp, and thrust right up to the river, where Bern and his party stood braced to defend themselves.

Bern saw a Line Steward in the forefront of the struggle, and he called to his archers to fell the man, who rode his horse among the fighting mobs, hacking and slashing as he went, leaving cloven heads and lifeless bodies behind him.

The man was Stearborn, armored in the mithra mail of the elves, and carrying one of the elfin swords that had been forged in the far mountains of Skye, at the beginning of the long history of the dreamers, when they yet remembered how it was to go back to the Silent Halls without the sadness of having to leave once more. A horn touched his lips, and he blew out the pure, high call that had rallied the stewards of the Line for as long as there had been a place called the Line. At his side was Erases, the elf, shining in mithra armor, and looking as grim and fell as death itself. Behind the two rode the elfin squadron that had been at the most crucial battle in the campaign for the Middle Islands, all seasoned warriors who knew their craft well.

Stearborn saw they had split the enemy camp into a dozen or more separate groups, which was the goal he and Chellin Duchin had agreed upon. As Chellin attacked from the south, Stearborn and Erases had come down from the north in a pincer movement that squeezed the huge enemy force into an accordionlike collapse upon itself, and in the confusion of the sudden ambush, and the late hour, and the darkness, the much smaller forces of the stewards had driven a wedge into the army of Bern the Red in three places, cutting in three the superior manpower, and setting many of the enemy troops to fighting among themselves.

Chellin and Stearborn had seen the massacre at the edge of the river on the Trew side of the water, and knew what dread news that meant, for the terrible stories of the Rogen were well known to all who had ever heard of the strange guardians of Trew.

"The whelp has sprung his own death-vise, I think," said Stearborn, turning to Erases before they had begun their attack. "Keep your elves this side of the water! We shall have to find out more of how to deal with that lot!"

"The Rogen can't kill an elf, old friend. They can rob us of our seventh sense, but then that is worse than death to a dreamer! But we have as yet no cause to worry of them. The Lady Elina is on her way with Famhart and his squadron. We shall have news then of how to deal with this old threat from the misguided Lord Trew."

"I, for one, will welcome Famhart and the stewards. And I don't think it will hurt so much having another elfin squadron to lend us a hand at this sticky business here on the Silver. It's bad enough finding the fellow who calls himself the Red Bear, but to come on Linne's brother and the Rogen is a horse of another color. The Line Stewards were not trained to deal with enemies that have no form."

"The Rogen have form," explained the elf. "You must understand the nature of these other beings. They are not so formless, or horrible. If you carry their image in your mind you will be able to avoid them. They cannot slay any who are connected with the Lord Trew, so the elves are immune, except for that foul deed that I spoke of."

"What is this sense they can rob you of, Erases? You said 'the seventh sense?'"

"It is the ability to see the Last Gate, Stearborn. The one gate that must be reached before an elf can return to his own without the promise of a return. If that vision is taken away, my kind can never find our way back, unless another of our kinsmen come to seek us."

"So the cycle is repeated? Always one or another forced to return to fetch the other?"

"Exactly. Some of our other enemies have found out this trick, and have kept us struggling down here in the Lower Shandin far longer than we would have liked. The Dark One has worked her ways in trying to split and isolate the dreamers, for we pose a grave threat to her plans here. I know she is at work to get the Fields of Light opened so the Purge can once more return to their old haunts, but she has too many elfin hosts to contend with before she can accomplish that goal. If we are involved with the rescue of kinsmen, we won't be able to turn our full weight to the problem of dealing with her, and she knows it."

Stearborn laughed to himself in the middle of a sword-stroke as he watched Erases and his elves overrun a large contingent of enemy troops, and send them fleeing for their lives.

"The dreamers!" echoed the elfin battle cry, and a horn and pipe took up the call, rising on the dark night air with an urgency that rang like doom on the ears of those who fought on the side of the Red Bear.

Stearborn wheeled his own squadron around, and set himself to sweep back down the riverbank, when he saw the lights on the water, and heard the glad hurrahs of some of the elfin warriors who rode with Erases.

"The Lady Elina! Famhart!" they cried, chanting together in a voice that rang out as one.

The lights flared and burst into a white halo that hung over the first of the elfin battle skiffs to arrive at the shore, and in the course of a short breath, the skiffs grew in size until they covered the river entirely, and grew larger still, until they were large enough for a gangway to be laid over the bow of the craft, and a horse and rider came down together, both dressed in battle armor that was from another time and place.

It was Famhart, wearing his old colors, that he had worn before he had become an elder of the Line, and he was followed by his young squadron, all dressed in the same manner.

Stearborn dismounted to embrace his friend.

"It is well met this night, Famhart! We have our work cut now! The Red Bear is at his worst against us, and the Rogen are afoot across the Silver! Trew is held captive by that lout of a brother of Linne's, and we now have enough clout between all the squadrons to do some good here!"

"Good Stearborn! Always the brick. Well met, indeed. The Lady Elina has brought enough of her fusiliers with her to see to it that we won't be worried too much by the backway tonight. Perhaps I can convince Largo to help undo the harm he has caused his sister!"

"He will, or we'll have an answer to what he can do with what's left of his head!"

The Lady Elina came ashore next, mounted on a startling white steed with pale blue eyes. All the elves knelt on one knee as she came among their ranks, and men of the squadrons of the Line felt the ache of a beauty that was too much to look full upon without weeping.

There was the other elfin squadron next, and the battle lines were drawn and pickets put out to probe at the strength of the enemy troops all about them.

A lull had fallen over the battlefield when the elfin skiffs had landed, but the pace picked up again. Soon the night was shattered with a terrible wind, tearing at the senses with the howl of death and destruction, and the cries and moans of the dying and maimed.

Ephinias heard all these sounds in the distance, as he and Aron took the first careful steps into the dark tunnels at the ruins of the ancient mounds of Darien.

The Wells of Trona

Even more frightening than the all-out assault by the Mounders, and more disturbing than the unmoving Owen and Kegin, was the total silence that now fell over the chamber where Emerald held the trembling girl who had gone by the name of Darek. The blue light in the cool stone ebbed to a darker blue, and paled somewhat, but the noise and chaos from outside the archway had fallen away until nothing was to be heard but their own breathing, coming in rapid gasps.

The minstrel sprang to his feet, and brandishing the sword from the forges of Skye before him, leaped to the entryway into the high-vaulted hall.

There were no voices from beyond, and the shaft was so dark Emerald could hardly make out the dim outlines of anything but the walls and furnishings. There was no one in sight, and no noise to be heard, except for a sound of water softly splashing against stone.

The sword still glowed a faint golden white, and Emerald crept slowly forward, ready for any sudden onslaught, but none came, and there was a faraway sound that reached his ear then, of something that was vaguely familiar.

A voice behind him almost caused him to jump out of his skin.

"Don't leave me behind, Emerald! I'm frightened!"

It was Darek, with a long braid of dark hair undone and hanging free from beneath the cap that had concealed it for so long.

"Come along, then! But tell me your name, lass. I feel so foolish at how we've treated you."

"My name is Deros. I come from a land far away. You were all kind to me, Emerald. I didn't mind, except when there was the fighting. I shall have to learn to do that."

"I hope not, my lass. If we have any luck left to us at all, we shall have Owen and Kegin out of this drab hole, and find them aid. There is something amiss here, though, for our friends the Dariens have deserted us."

"They were going to make me marry their ugly little leader! He had all the others go to fetch you, because they needed your blood to do something with. I don't know what they meant, but it had something to do with the well where you found me."

"Is that the well the Querle was trying to keep us from reaching?"

"It is a strange place, Emerald. I can smell the sea in the lands where I dwelled. I think this may be one of the channels that cross between our lands."

"A well? It must be such a well as a poor minstrel has never seen the likes of! Before this has all played out, we'll find more about it, I'm sure."

Emerald searched a bit further into the chamber where he had most recently held off the Dariens, but aside from the cast-off crossbows and bolts, and various other weapons, there was no clue as to what had happened to the mounders.

"They seem to have withdrawn in a terrible hurry," said the girl.

"Or been driven away. Come on, let's tend to our two wounded."

"Are they hurt badly?" asked the girl timidly.

"I think they've been put under a spell of some sort.

Owen's mother was felled by the same black business as this."

"Those ugly little people said the water from this well would undo any of their spells. They gave me some to drink when I was first brought here. That's when they found out I was not a boy."

Deros shuddered and clasped her arms tightly to herself as if warding off a chill.

"That ugly elder found my braid and guessed the rest. I was so weak I couldn't struggle. I thought they were going to do something horrible to me!"

The frightened girl shuddered again, and wept.

"That was why my father disguised me as a boy. He knew I would be in less danger if I traveled as a man. I tried so hard not to let you three find me out!"

Emerald laughed and reached out to reassure her.

"You succeeded, young lady. You could have knocked us all over with a feather when those stuffed little turnips came out and told us that we were traveling with someone we had no idea at all about."

"I had seen what happened to all the others along the way," wept the girl. "I knew my father was right. My only chance was to keep my true identity a secret."

"Those two louts there will be sorely surprised to know you now, lass. Let's see if we can't find some way to rouse them. The sooner we are away from here, the sooner I'll feel easier."

"I think if we could get some of the water of the well to them, it might revive them," said Deros. "Then we could find our way out of here."

The minstrel walked slowly back to where Owen and Kegin lay, their features a gray waxy color that disturbed him deeply.

"I don't like the looks of this. Let's hope that something works! I don't like to think of having to go on with this whole business alone."

Deros had knelt by the raised circle of stones that marked the edge of the well, and touched her hand to the water.

"Look, Emerald! See the ripples? They are like rainbows there. And see how dark blue the water starts to turn there!"

"This is the strangest of things." Emerald nodded. "I get the distinct feeling it's trying to tell us something."

His senses tingled like something was tickling his memory just at the edges, and a faint impression of a person from a lifetime ago kept nagging at the borders of his mind's eye, but he could not place exactly what the thought was. A faint image of a large bird crept nearer to his thoughts, although he could not tell if it were his thoughts, or an image that was deep inside the fathomless blue shadows of the mysterious well.

"Do you think they can hear us?" asked Deros.

"Owen?"

"No. Them!"

"I think we are still in their own backyard, and they probably have a dozen other tricks to play. It doesn't seem likely that they would just throw down their arms and desert the field."

"Then let's hurry and find our way clear! I'm frightened, Emerald! I know that ugly little brute isn't going to give up so easily. I saw the way he looked at me!"

"Get something we can use to give Owen and Kegin some of the water from the well. Your cap will do."

Deros took her cap off hurriedly and offered it to the minstrel.

Emerald laid Owen's sword beside the well, and dipped the girl's hat into the water, which had grown more agitated as the two talked. A silver stream of moving shadows curved gracefully up from the surface of the well and touched Emerald's hand as he scooped up the water with the hat, and it felt to him as though a living thing had brushed against his skin.

"What was that?" asked the startled girl.

"I don't know, but I know it tested me. There is a great power here that could destroy us easily, if we don't pass muster."

"Do you think it belongs to the Dariens? If it does, I think we're lost! We'll never be able to get out of here."

"I think this was something that is much older than the
Dariens. They are a relatively new clan compared to whoever was around when the stones were laid around this
well."

The stones were all cut and laid in a precise fashion, and
when examined more closely, were seen to have tiny scenes
carved into the hard surface with such intricate detail, it
amazed them that a hand could have held a tool that would
work in so small a fashion. There was a row of reddish
brown stones, then green, then blue, and the top layer was a
smooth black, which was deep and reflected what seemed to
be distant stars within its shiny surface.

Emerald took the girl's cap full of the mysterious water,
and carried it to kneel beside his two motionless
companions.

Deros was crying as she sat beside Owen, and reached out
a hand to touch the dark, silent brow. "Do you think he will
be all right, Emerald? I have been such a burden to him!
And poor Kegin! My clumsy feet have almost been the
death of him!"

"You had made us think we would have our hands full to
teach you the warrior's trade! I'm glad we won't be pressed
to continue that."

"But I have to learn it! My homeland needs all her
children. My father sent me away to find what help I could,
and to learn any way I could that would help our cause
against the Hulon Vipres."

Emerald wet Owen's lips with the water, which seemed to
grow warmer to his touch. "Who are they? An enemy?"

"The worst of the lot. They have captured much of my
father's kingdom, and threaten to take it all!"

"Your father's kindgom? Is he a great lord?" asked the
minstrel, and saw the girl blush and look quickly away.

"I cannot tell you. It was part of my oath when I left. I
was to renounce being a girl, and any position I might have
held. I am now as you see me, with my oath of secrecy
broken, but I cannot be other than Deros, from the lands of
the Southern Fetch."

"You know I won't press you, lass! You're with your friend, remember."

"I mean you no offense, Emerald. You have been the most kind of all. I must keep to my oath, at least until I can return home with aid for my father."

"I respect that. Help me with this lump's head! I can't get the lad up enough to pour this down his gullet. He weighs a ton like this."

Deros helped Emerald to hold Owen's head up slightly, and the minstrel trickled a thin stream of the well water slowly into the still, parched lips of the young descendent of Famhart and Linne.

"If this only works," said Emerald with a sigh, "then we'll have an answer that will help his mother as well."

"She was a very beautiful lady. I think she knew my secret from the first."

"Linne? You think she knew?"

"I didn't think she would betray me. I was so frightened when she was struck down by the spell! I thought someone in Owen's camp had done it. I was barely in my senses then. The settlement I had stopped at before, in Clover Hill, had been attacked and destroyed by the raiders from the Leech. It was a woman there who saved me from exposure! She hid me in her barn so they couldn't find me." The girl trailed off, sobbing. "I couldn't find her anymore after they were gone. Only a few of us escaped."

Emerald reached over and stroked the hair back from the frightened girl's face. "Poor lass, you've had a time of it."

The compassion in the minstrel's voice made Deros weep the harder, and while Emerald sat trying to console the girl, Owen's eyes opened with a start, and he jumped wildly to his feet.

"It's the flowers! That smell was there when my mother fell under that spell!"

"Owen! Good lad! Good, brave lad!" cried Emerald, and he hugged the revived youth so stoutly that Owen's ribs ached from it, and he was unable to draw a breath.

"Darek!" stammered Owen, looking over the minstrel's shoulders, and seeing the girl, with her long dark hair flowing down her back in the thick braid. "I mean, miss, I—" he trailed off, confused and feeling such strange upheavals inside he hardly knew what to do with himself, so he returned Emerald's hug and sat down exhausted on the edge of the well.

"What did you do to bring me back?" he asked, when he had recovered somewhat. "I could hear something, and I knew where I was, but there was a black cloud that kept me on the other side. I struggled and struggled to make you hear me, but I couldn't get back! It was awful! If my mother is caught like that, I can't stand to think of how she suffers! We have to help her, Emerald! We have to get to her!"

Owen's resolve slipped, and he had to cover his face with his hands to keep the others from seeing the hot tears that coursed down his cheeks.

"Buck up, lad! We have the very thing to help your mother. We're going to wake this other lout now, and then we'll find our way out of this pit we've landed in. I don't think I'll miss not having to use my Darien anymore. It hurts my throat to speak it."

Owen nodded his head. "I once thought it reminded me of birds, but it is an ugly sound now! I don't care if I never hear it again."

"With any luck, we won't, lad. Now come help me with Kegin. All we have to do is get a drop or two down him."

Emerald gave the cap back to Deros to fill, and she hurriedly completed her task and returned, unable to meet Owen's eyes as he watched her.

"Why do you stare at me so?" she asked shyly. "Are you still so angry with me because I'm not a good fighter?"

Owen blushed to his ears, unable to make a ready reply.

The minstrel saw the difficulty the youth was having and laughed, a clean hearty laugh that felt as though it had cleared away a mountain of gloom that had descended over his heart since he had been among the ill-starred mounds of Darien.

"He's not at all carrying a grudge over that, lass, I'll wager! No, indeed, I think he's closer in spirit now to a certain feeling that usually overtakes us all at one point or another, and turns everything exactly upside under."

He laughed again, as he took the cap with the well water from Deros, and administered a few drops to the cold lips of Kegin. Owen held his protector's head up on his lap, and looked anxiously at Emerald as the still form went on unchanged and unmoving.

"It takes a pinch of time for it to work," assured Emerald. "I'm not sure how it works, or why, but you're here before us to prove its worth. All we have to find out now is a quick way back to your mother."

"My father may already be there before us," lamented Owen. "Poor Kegin! I've ruined his life by my insistence on coming here!"

"Famhart will forgive anything, if you have something that will bring your mother out from under this devil's work."

"Look!" cried Deros. "He moved his eyes!"

Kegin moaned deeply, and tried to sit up. His limbs were stiff, and he had to make another attempt, and finally succeeded with Owen's help.

"That blasted foul smoke! I can't seem to rid my nose of the smell of it! Sickly flowers! Ugh!" Kegin sneezed then, and looked about him in a daze. "But what's happened then? Are those little beggars gone?"

"For now," replied Emerald, handing Owen back the sword Gillerman had given the lad. "This blade was our redeemer! They couldn't get near us, or shoot us full of bolts. There was a big commotion in the outer hall there a bit ago, but whatever happened is a mystery. They are all gone now, and I think it's time we made the best of that."

Kegin stiffly stood, testing his legs. "I'm a bit wobbly on my pins, but I think I'll be right enough if I can walk around a bit."

He looked at Deros and smiled.

"Holla, lass! I wondered what it was about you that I couldn't quite put my finger to. All that business with that ugly outcast back to the Edges should have tipped your hand then. That's such a girlish thing to do, falling down like that!"

Deros burst into tears again, which made Kegin feel like he had somehow done something unforgivable. He looked to Owen and Emerald for help, but they simply shrugged their shoulders.

"I didn't mean to," wept the girl. "I've tried so hard to learn all this business of being a soldier. I promised my father I would, for my brother is gone. . . " She trailed off here, and cried for a time, tryng to gain control of herself.

"Was he lost in the wars?" asked Owen, handing her an old piece of cloth that he carried to keep the feathers of his arrows dry in their quiver in wet weather. She blew her nose on it in thanks, and nodded in the affirmative.

"What was your brother's name?" asked Kegin, trying to cheer up the weeping girl.

"Lord Tristan," she replied absently, wiping her nose.

"*Lord* Tristan? Is your father an elder?"

A stricken look crossed the girl's face then, and she turned her glance downward. "I can't remember anything right anymore. So much has happened, I sometimes feel this is all a dream."

"It does seem that way now," agreed Owen. "Waking out of that dark place I've just come from, I can hardly recall what the sun looks like, or what color the sky is."

"Let's find out!" said Emerald. "We've wasted time enough here. I think we can find something hereabouts to carry away some of the water from our well. We must save it to take to Owen's mother!"

After a brief search, Emerald found his harp and case, and their pile of gear the Dariens had stacked aside in one of the branches of a shaft off the main room of the Fourth Chamber. There were their water flasks, and a larger skin or two of Darien make that they filled, and Kegin picked up crossbows and bolts for them all, so they wouldn't be quite so vulnerable if they ran afoul of the mounders again.

"Do you think we could find whatever they used on us to put us under that spell?" asked Owen. "It might come in handy before this is all done and over."

"That's an excellent thought, Master Helwin," said Emerald. "It would be good to have it in our kit, in case we ever needed to play a rough crowd to sleep!"

"How do you think the Dariens kept from going under, too?" asked Kegin. "This place is as tight as a tomb! They would have had to breathed it when they got us!"

"Maybe something to do with the well water," suggested Deros. "I heard a lot about the well. I think they have all drunk from it. It brought you back from the spell, so I think if you were exposed to it again, it wouldn't work."

"You see?" teased Emerald. "You're needed for your brains, lass, not the muscles in your bow and sword arm! Who would have thought of something so simple as that?"

Deros blushed and grew so flustered she rattled a great many bolts for the crossbow she carried, and tried to rearrange the small knapsack so it would accommodate all the things she had gathered in a pile at her feet.

"This well is something," said Kegin, who had stopped to look into the depths of it, and found some small vision that floated in its deeper parts, just out of his reach. "Look! There is some kind of reflection there!"

The others crowded around him to look into the well, and were jolted by a sharp sound that came from above, in one of the upper levels.

"What was that?" asked Owen.

"Boots!" snorted Kegin. "Lots of boots!"

"And coming this way," added Emerald, listening carefully. "It may be the Querle has finally cowed his cronies into coming back to attack again."

"Let's leave," pleaded Deros. "I don't want to face that horrible little beast again!"

Emerald took the girl's arm, and led her toward the shaft outside, that seemed to be a main north-south tunnel that ran from one end of the Darien Mounds to the other, with feeder chambers leading off both sides into other mounds in the group. Emerald explained to the others how the mounds were made up like beehives, and how all the chambers and shafts interconnected at some point, and that they would all lead them back eventually to the fresh air and freedom.

"If we don't run afoul of the mounders in between," corrected Kegin.

They had gone no more than a few hundred steps, when they heard the war horns, and the rattle of steel against steel, and the dreadful din of voices, hoarse and strident, baying out like great wardogs locked in mortal combat.

"That's coming from in front of us," warned Owen. "And moving this way!"

"Aye, lad," confirmed Kegin, beginning to draw back his crossbow, and making sure his sword was close to hand.

Owen mimicked his instructor, and felt the eyes of Deros on him, which confused him greatly, and he had a difficult time getting Gillerman's sword back into its scabbard.

"We can go ahead a bit further before we reach a danger zone," said the minstrel. "If we can, we'll wait this out in one of the side shafts. I don't see any reason to show ourselves unless we have to make a fight of it."

He turned to the others, then looked sternly at Deros.

"Here, lass, put your cap back on and wind that hair up in a braid beneath it!"

Owen was flustered again when the girl handed him her weapons and knapsack, and set quickly to work winding her long hair about her head, then pulled her cap down securely over it, becoming in a few moments the old familiar Darek again.

Kegin had stepped up to the side of one of the shafts, and stood looking upward at it for a time, and at last he motioned to the others to come and look at what he had found.

"What is it, Kegin?" asked Emerald.

"Steps! I think there were steps carved here!"

"There's nothing," argued Owen. "How could you see steps?"

Kegin looked about for something, and he scoured the floor of the chamber, and of the chamber across the main tunnel, sniffing about like a dog on a cold scent. "I can't find what they used, but maybe these iron bolts for the crossbows will work as well."

As he spoke, Kegin took two of the metal bolts out of his quiver and inserted them into a string of small holes that had been drilled into the smooth surface of the stone.

"Look! This goes on up to somewhere above! Give me all your bolts! Hurry!"

"Why, you're right, Kegin! It's like a ladder!" said Owen, much impressed with his friend.

"Hurry, lad! It may not go anywhere, but I have an idea the Dariens have been afraid of their shadows for so long, they may have just put a few escape holes here and there to be on the safe side."

As Kegin talked, he inserted more of the bolts from the crossbows into the small holes in the wall, and climbed steadily higher, until he was but a shadow in the upper part of the chamber roof.

"Be careful!" cautioned Emerald. "We don't have anything soft for you to fall on down here!"

"I won't need it," he replied, sounding muted and far away. There was a silence then, and then the sound of him coming down very fast.

"It's there! I hadn't expected anything so good, but it's there! Hurry, and we'll find our way out of here before any of the Dariens or anyone else knows we're here."

"Can you climb?" asked Owen, turning to address Deros. The girl nodded. "I'll have to, if I want to get out of this."

"Good girl," encouraged Emerald. "Let's see to it we all stay together and go carefully. Keep a tight grip on the shafts, and don't try to do anything fancy."

Emerald was ready to go on with more cautions and instructions, when the tide of battle crested in the great central tunnel outside of where they were, and in the briefest moment before they began to climb for the safety of the secret passage that would take them outside, the minstrel thought he saw what looked to be a bear in full battle armor, with a large, pointed helmet, leading a party of heavily armed men along the smooth corridor.

Emerald shook his head, and promised himself that he would take a long time to rest and study with Gillerman and

Ephinias, if ever he could manage to find them still at work in these Lower Meadows.

Ephinias would know about the bear, he thought hopefully.

Fire and Destruction

As the battle intensified upon all fronts, the night became as bright as day, and the fires that had begun in the wood raced out of control, consuming everything, and raging with a noise that was dreadful to hear. On top of it came the din and racket of the blood-crazed warriors, locked desperately into a wild dance that whirled and spun with a dizzy pace, grotesque in the red glow of the fire, and maddened by the smell of death.

The troops of Largo had held the invaders at the river, although there were those unfortunates who had managed to gain the opposite bank, only to be devoured by the unseen Rogen. Largo rode back and forth on a tall black horse, gloating and throwing his head back in crazed laughter every time he saw the enemy troops gain the Trew side of the river, only to be set upon with an irresistable assault that left no trace of the victims other than the cast-off clothes and armor.

Largo spurred his mount, and guided it carefully past the slaughter of another troop of Channeliers, and stopped right at the water's edge, where he had a good view of the blazing inferno of the enemies' camp. A hatred that burned inside him as fiercely as the fire across the river spilled out of him like a torrent, and he threw his fist out, shaking it violently.

"You see, you scum! You are dealing with Argent Largo, the Invincible! We will leave nothing but ruin behind us because you dared to attack the rightful heir to the Lower Meadows!"

He stopped to laugh again, but his eye was drawn to another light on the river, further up and on the South Channel's side. It was as bright as the red-orange of the inferno which raged through the darkness, but it was different, and something about it struck a chord of fear in what would have been Largo's heart—if there had been anything left of it after his return from the cold instructions of the Dark One, as she carefully brought him back to life to do her bidding once more in the Wilderness.

There was a great deal of horns and pipes, and many chorused voices that rang out over and over, and they seemed to be chanting names, but he could not understand them. Some were so garbled by the roar of the battle that he made little sense of them, other than to feel a wave of fear and loathing at the sounds, but then there was one outcry that caught and held his attention, and his eyes burned in his fevered brow until he felt as though he would be consumed by a fire that was hotter than the one which raged through the woods.

"That cursed name is here to blight my victory," he screamed, pulling at his hair, and striking himself savagely on the mail shirt that covered his breast. "Letta! Rogen! Come quickly! We must destroy this mite that would sting me!"

Largo waved his sword above his head, and spurred his horse into the river as though he would crash forward in a full frontal attack of the entire force of the enemy, but a shower of arrows rained down nearby, and he was forced into a hasty retreat.

"Letta, blast your soul, if you have one! Come forth!"

A whirling gray wind blew up, licking at the river's edge, but staying clear of it, and a damp chill touched Largo's feverish skin.

"We shall rid this world of one of my most hated enemies, Letta! This shall be our crowning glory! We will have ridded the Channels of the infernal Bern, and I shall have the exquisite pleasure of knowing my dear sister's loving husband has fed you and your sisters!"

A shapeless form emerged from the cold, gray wind, and Letta's voice echoed in a hollow fashion against Largo's ear.

"The Lord Trew bound us to these limits, my pretty! You have to lure your unwilling little fly to us, before we can have him up in our web."

"Curse Trew, and all his tribe!" cried Largo. "Famhart is ashore on the other side of the river, and we shall have him up before the night's out! And there will be no protector for the dear, pure Linne when I arrive in the name of Largo to take up my rightful kingdom!"

"We cannot cross the river," repeated Letta, and the gray wind whirled into a cold finger, pointing away toward Trew, and then was gone.

"Curse your eyes!" screamed Largo. "I need Famhart's head! You can have the rest of him! I want to deliver his head to my pure and upright sister! I shall remove the spell long enough for her to see I am returned, and I'll give her her precious Famhart in a sack of ash!"

Largo called again for Letta, but the Rogen was gone, back at her grisly work among the forward elements of the armies of Bern. He pulled the scorched amulet from his neck, and called aloud for the dragon, but without a fire to rouse the beast, there was only a lifeless blackened necklace that stared back at Largo, driving him into a deeper frenzy.

The chorus of voices from across the river began again, carried on the back of the fire, rattling against the sky, and Largo grew more crazed with each renewed roar.

"I shall have you! Your cursed name will ring in time with my victory cry!" shouted Largo, his voice hoarse with hatred. He reined his horse in, and turned the animal with a cruel cut of the bit, and thundered back toward his command post at the top of a slight rise that ran the distance between the ruins of Rogen Keep and the Darien Mounds. On both sides of the rise, the ground sloped away sharply, suggesting that the small hill had at one time been part of a walled moat or canal of some sort. Here Largo had planted his battle flag, and guided the Rogen and the other troops of his army toward the hot spots of the on-going battle. He dismounted and paced frantically about on the ancient ground, slashing his leg viciously with his riding crop.

A plan had begun to formulate itself in his head, and he gave a sudden little hop of glee as he ran it through again.

"Letta!" he screamed hoarsely, "Letta, get your sisters together for a real blood-letting! You shall have the cream of the crop of the Line! I shall fetch you my second-most-hated enemy to dine upon! Look sharply, now! I'm counting upon you!"

Largo laughed then, and mounted his horse roughly, spurring the poor brute with sharp stabs of his spurs. He rode straight to the river, and sought a place where it was shallow enough to ford. As he went, he drew his cloak about him, so that the enemy could not readily tell if he were a friend or foeman. He splashed across into the outer realms of the South Channels, his horse blowing heavily and stamping the ground in an excited dance of sidesteps and pawing movements. The noise was unbearable, and the flames of the forest fire leaped higher and higher into the night, making it hotter than an oven, and threatening to touch off anything in its path.

Largo saw a white banner floating on the burning wind that thundered ahead of the fire, and made directly for it, wrapping a white neckerchief about his sword hilt as he went. Satisfied with his work, he held it out from beneath his cloak as he rode, watching the fire reflect from the steel and the whiteness of his signal flag, expecting any minute to be stopped, but going forward unhindered, until he was far inside the perimeter of the enemy camp.

There were slain Channeliers amidst the bodies of the stewards, and in one place, Largo drew in his horse and stared malevolently at the small bodies of three of the waterfolk, with ugly black bolts from crossbows driven through their throats.

"Good riddance!" he spat, muttering oaths under his breath, and hoping that the bowman who had done the work was no longer around.

Another few steps forward, and he was grabbed roughly

by the knees, and a man was at his horse's head, wrenching the reins from his hands.

"What is it you want, stranger?" demanded a gruff man, garbed as a Line Steward. "Speak quickly, on your life!"

There was a sharp pain at his ribs, and Largo looked to see a younger man standing beside his horse, with a mail-piercing spear lodged next to the open slot beneath his arm.

"Hold friend, I come seeking your leader. I hear we have the great Famhart among us!"

"He is just come! And we have the Lady Elina to stand beside us as well. Are you a Channelier?" asked the gruff Line sergeant.

"Hardly, my good fellow. I know Famhart will want to see me. I have news of a nature that concerns his wife, and her welfare."

"Who be you, stranger? Speak out! I wouldn't feel too amiss if we had to leave your carcass here for the birds' breakfast on the morrow."

"Argent Largo," replied Largo smoothly. "And I know the one thing that Famhart needs to know to help his precious wife."

"Climb down off that animal," ordered the sergeant bruskly. "If you be who you say, then let's have some proof!"

"I think he's telling the truth," said the younger steward, who stood holding the spear to Largo's side.

"Listen to your young friend," cautioned Largo. "This is a matter of life and death. Your cherished elder will make you pay dearly for costing him the information I am prepared to give him."

"Fetch up a messenger, lad," ordered the blunt sergeant. "Find out where we can find Famhart!"

"Now you're beginning to show good judgment, Steward." Largo slowly dismounted, his eyes looking about apprehensively.

"I've heard your name before," continued the steward sergeant. "It wasn't a name that pleased me over much."

"You flatter me, Steward," replied Largo coolly. "I

should like to think that there must be something of great
import attached to my name if you've heard it here."

"Nothing of much import, master, just a word of
caution."

"Caution? I shouldn't wonder. Your elders are trying to
keep you in ignorance of how matters truly stand. I think
you might have heard of my small offer to any of those who
would like to join me, and reap the harvest of plenty that
goes to the strong and victorious!"

"I've heard tales from that quarter 'til my ears fairly
ring," shot the sergeant. "Then there's the Red Bear over in
the Channels been up to the same mischief. Now you two
fellows seem to be hard at trying to do one another in! I'm
glad to report that the squadrons of the Line, and our allies
from the old clans are helping you both to find a quick road
to glory!"

Largo's jaw clenched and he grew ashen white, but he
spoke evenly. "I cannot find fault with you, sergeant, for
you're no more than a lackey! What would your masters tell
you except lies? They have kept you under their thumbs for
so long now, it's no wonder you believe them. I am willing to
share power and spread wealth to the ranks! All who follow
me will have a say in what befalls them!"

"Mighty tall talk for a renegade," said the sergeant. "No
matter what clever words you use to try to color it differently, it all washes out as the same mulhash in the end."

A mounted messenger forestalled Largo's reply. Famhart
had been found, and upon hearing Largo's name was following close behind.

Within seconds, a heavily armed party, which included
both stewards and elves, pulled up. Famhart emerged from
the others of his group, and strode to where Largo awaited
him. A dangerous look flashed across Largo's face, and he
reached up and touched the amulet at his throat, and was
seen to mumble something under his breath, although his
movement had brought the sergeant closer, ready to counter
any attempt upon his leader.

"There you are, Largo! It has been a long hard time
between you and me and your sister! What do I owe this

visit to? Speak, man! I can hardly make myself stop these men from hobbling you to the nearest tree with a length of hemp around your neck!"

Famhart's voice was thick with emotion, but he was carefully under control, and paced to within a foot or two of his brother-in-law. He saw before him a ghost from the past, for the Largo he looked at had not aged a month, although his own hair and beard was shot through with gray.

"Your travels have tired you, Famhart! You look done in!"

"My travels wouldn't be half so necessary, if you were of a more fortunate temperament."

"We shall see who has the more fortunate temperament, my good master! I have a bit of news that might interest you, if you can keep a civil tongue long enough to hear it."

"Your visit interests me greatly, Largo! My stewards are rooting at the ugly sore called the Red Bear and his army, and here I have the very core of the boil in Trew! What would keep me from slaying you now, and having done with half my problem?"

"You cannot slay someone who has yielded to you, master. You well know that!"

Largo knelt at Famhart's feet, and placed his sword down, touching his head to his boot top as he did so.

"I yield, Famhart! You cannot harm me now!" said Largo, looking up with cunning eyes, and a crooked smile that masked his handsome features with an ugly glow.

"I cannot do otherwise than accept your sword, Largo! You shall not be harmed in my camp for so long as you have yielded! It is the law, and must be obeyed."

"I could say he went for his dagger, sir," offered the gruff sergeant. "No one would blame you, sir, if you were to lop his head off in self-defense."

Famhart shook his head resolutely, his eyes a dark shade that Largo couldn't read. "No. The law will be obeyed while he is at my mercy. But I cannot tarry long here. What is it you wish to tell me? The messenger said it was important."

"It is important if you consider my sister's life important!" said Largo, reveling in the sudden stiffness that struck his hated enemy. It was as though Famhart had been struck a physical blow.

"Speak, you miserable wretch! Speak, or by the Hand of Windameir, I'll tear your tongue from your head!"

Famhart had lunged at Largo, and had the younger man by the tunic. The messenger and the sergeant separated the two, and held their elder back from the shaken, but defiant prisoner.

"So this is the way the great Famhart stands by his word," taunted Largo. "I yield, and in front of witnesses, and this is the treatment I get!"

"You are lucky to still be breathing," admonished the sergeant. "You'd best hold your tongue! I am under no duty to spare your life! You haven't yielded to me!"

Largo looked at the steward evenly, although there was a tremor in his voice as he spoke. "I have yielded to the stewards of the Line. That is enough. The code is the same for all."

"I will renounce my oath, sir, if you will it, to rid ourselves of this worm which has come to crawl among us, and throw up our code before our faces!"

Famhart waved the sergeant off. "I wouldn't have your hands fouled with a deed like that, sergeant. Now, Largo. Speak!"

"I know how you treasure my sister, master steward, and if you love her as much as you proclaim, you might be interested to learn of the way she fell victim to the black sleep!"

"Why do you come to tell me this? What could you possibly gain, except your miserable life? If I had met you in battle, or any of the stewards, or dreamers, you would have been a dead man before you had a chance to yield!"

"That's why I took it upon myself to come as I did. I have a proposal to make that might change your mind about me."

All about the gathered men, the sounds of an intensified battle fell on their ears with a dull, leaden roar, and the fire had leaped higher still, touching off the tops of even the tallest trees, and sending explosions of sparks cascading high into the torn and broken blanket of night.

"You can have the mystery solved, if you come with me," Largo continued. "I have the object you need to break the spell my sister is in."

Famhart looked hard at the handsome young man, his thoughts full of Linne, and the pain her brother had caused before.

"And what shall Argent Largo ask in return for this favor? If it's more than for his life to be spared, it cannot be! I cannot offer anything more than that."

"That is all I seek," replied Largo. "But I don't trust your men! If you will have my help, you must come alone with me to fetch the one thing that will save Linne!"

The steward sergeant reached a hand out and held Famhart by the shoulder. "Don't trust him, sir!"

"I thank you for your concern, sergeant. If I accept his offer, I shall expect you to stick close to the rest of the squadrons. Stearborn shall be next in command, then Chellin Duchin."

"Don't talk that way, sir," implored the sergeant. "It don't sit right with me to hear you talk that way."

"I shall be perfectly all right! I have no intention of allowing anything to stand in the way of getting my wife the aid she needs."

"The pragmatic Famhart! Ever the good Boghatian," chided Largo cautiously.

"What is this thing that will help Linne?" persisted Famhart. "If you have such a thing, and want to bargain for it, you know my terms."

"I have heard your terms, master steward, but I don't think they are quite good enough."

"Your life is enough. What else would you have?" asked Famhart.

"Your word that I shall not be harmed! Delivered to all your squadrons."

"You have my word on that."

"Your messenger has yet to tell it to the rest of your men! And the filth you call the dreamers! I must have their word as well."

"I can't speak for the Lady Elina or any of the Elboreal! You trifle with me now, knowing how I feel about my wife."

"Yes, my good steward. I know you would like to murder me, but you can't! You are bound by your stupid honor to not destroy a sworn enemy, and that is why you shall never prevail, Famhart! You and the others are so pure and fine, like my cursed sister! Nothing shall save you, though, no matter whether I reveal to you the spell or not."

Famhart ordered his messenger to him, and looked harshly at Largo. "What proof have I you will hold to your end of the bargain?"

"I shall lead you to the solution you are looking for to save Linne. It shall just be the two of us!"

"Don't listen to him, sir," urged the young Line Steward. "He's drawing you into a trap!"

"Let them all come with us to the river," offered Largo. "If they see anything that resembles a trap, they can ride across and slay me!"

"He speaks fairly enough," said Famhart. "How say you, sergeant?"

"It seems fair enough at the top of it, sir, but I don't like it. It's dark, and this end of the wood is gone up in flames. There's a dozen squadrons or more of the other side roaming about here now, blood-crazed and drawn as tight as bowstrings. There's no sure way to say that anything might or might not happen now! We don't even know which way the tide has turned."

"We know it has not turned against us, so we will be content. Our aim was to divide the camp of the Red Bear. We have succeeded. Now I shall go with this inhuman monster and seek whatever he has that may help Linne."

Largo's eyes flashed, and he clenched his hands tightly at his sides. "You are ever the fool, Famhart! You have been ever since you fell for the foolish woman who called herself your wife! If you had known her more thoroughly before you were bound to her by the nuptial ties, you would have seen what an ambitious wench she was! She was the cause of my father's death, and the loss of the Marshes, and the ruin of all that my father had intended to leave me!"

"Then I am still the fool, Largo, for I want to spare you. It would do Linne's heart no end of good to know her brother had relented, and taken a step to remove her from the spell. If for no other reason, I will go with you, Largo, in hopes that what you have said is true, even if only in a small degree."

"Good! Excellent!" said Largo, barely able to concel his excitement. "Let's go. You'll be able to accompany me across the river, and I dare say you'll be back with your own kind before the hour is out."

"I still don't like all this, sir," said the Line sergeant. "Let some of us come across with your, sir. We'll give our word to you now we won't life a finger to harm this lout! It's just not safe to travel alone through all this."

Largo looked disdainfully at the part of stewards. "If you all give me your word here, then you may feel free to cross the river with your elder. I have no army gathered there, as you'll see, and you'll find I have no other snare set. It's as I said, I have gotten fearful for my life! I'm playing in too big a stake to have anything but my own safety in mind."

"Then let's get to it! Sergeant, round up your messengers, and have all the squadrons made familiar with this operation. Let them all offer any assistance they can to Largo, no matter what becomes of me. As long as he is yielded to us, we owe it to the code to protect him at all cost!"

"Aye, sir! Your wishes shall be followed."

There was a flurry of activity all about them then, and a pocket of stragglers who had been separated from the main body of the Channeliers burst upon the assembled group with a ferocious attack that kept the stewards busy for a few long minutes. When the thrust was beaten back, and the forces of Bern the Red were in retreat, Largo led the way at the head of the procession, with Famhart next behind, followed by the others.

At the river, Largo turned for a quick look to see if he was still followed by the leader of the stewards, and Famhart did not see the evil smile that was concealed in the depths of the darkness and Largo's cloak.

A Snare Is Laid

Ephinias stumbled again in the gloom of the tunnel, and fell forward against a rough stone surface that caused him to cry out in pain. His companion thought he was attacked, and began flashing the broadax about in a whistling circle, coming within inches of the older man's head.

"Stop it, you blasted fool! You're going to split me open with that oversized cleaver if you don't control yourself!"

"I thought you had been set on," apologized Aron sheepishly.

"Not yet, but from the sound of things, we're not far from it."

They stood poised, listening intensely.

From somewhere in front, and slightly below them, they heard the sound of boots scraping stone. There was another confused sound as well, slightly off to their right, but the muffled echoes made it hard to keep the sounds separated.

"I don't like this a smidgen, not a smidgen," said Aron, his voice tight. "If we were to turn around now and find our way out of this lightless bug's nest, I wouldn't be too sorry for it!"

"Nor would I, Aron, but I've got an odd feeling we are in for it above or below. Besides, I think I'm on the trail of an old student who was with me many turnings ago. He was always up to his chin in every devilment that could be devised, and there was nothing I could do to keep him from it. The boy just seemed to be a natural draw to anything of a troublesome sort."

"Exactly who we don't need to run into down here," complained Aron. "I was searching for someone who might be of help to me and my clans, not someone who would be in the way of being my end."

"Oh, pedash and fooh for your worrisome nature! This lad was a draw to everything troublesome, but in a good way. Bright lad, always up on his lessons, and had a keen eye for things as they really were, and not just what they seemed. Had a good ear for music, too!"

"Things as they really are here is a mutton stew of a different flavor, I'd wager. I don't want to try to begin to think of all the good reasons I could give us to back out of here now, and make an effort to find one of the camps of the stewards."

"Oh, we'll be finding them soon enough," assured Ephinias. "They are afoot everywhere now."

"Do you think that could be an answer as to the noise in the tunnels?"

The older man frowned, deep in thought. "It could be, but I won't count on it. If it were only the stewards down this shaft, I wouldn't have this dry taste in my mouth, or these butterflies loose in my stomach."

The two men had continued along slowly as they talked, inching forward with their arms to the wall to guide themselves surely, and turning their heads constantly to try to pierce the dark shadows that surrounded them. There was a general outcry then, and a vague, muffled noise that echoed twice more.

"That was an exchange of blows, or my name isn't what it used to be," exclaimed Ephinias. "I'd give a good night's sleep to know what's been transpiring up ahead!"

"If we were tunnel rats, we'd have no trouble," suggested Aron. "Just scamper up and take a look, then scamper on back."

Ephinias snapped his fingers and shook his friend's hand earnestly. "Thank you, dear friend, for reminding me! Sometimes I think I've been at all this too long! If I don't make myself notes, I sometimes forget most of the old things I've learned."

Aron had pursed his lips to ask his excited companion what he was rambling on about, when his nose suddenly felt it had a whisker itch. When he brought his hand up to relieve the tickling sensation he felt, he was shocked and amazed that it was a fur-covered paw that did the job.

"Squeeeeeeek, squeak!" blurted Aron, terrified, his voice rising still another octave.

"Shhhhhh," came the voice of Ephinias, although the figure that spoke was a large blackish rodent with a pink nose and red eyes, and long white whiskers that bristled on both sides of the long, slightly bent snout. "You'll give us away with that business! Now get hold of yourself, and try to cough out your words from your throat! It's awkward, I know, but you can do it with a little practice!"

"Squeee—I mean—what have you done to me? Do I look like you? Oh, how horrid! I knew I should come to a baffly, dogged end! I was warned by my betters that no good would ever come of my continuing to dawdle about with this sort of thing!"

"Hush up, Aron! All we want is a quick peek at who our friends are in this shaft. It takes a moment or two to come out of this form, and we could be squashed like beetles if anyone caught us before I could change us back!"

Aron made a series of noises that frightened him even more than he had been to find himself in the form he was in. "What will I ever tell my family? They will be mortified to hear that their fine young offspring in the end turned out to be a shaft-rat."

"Now hush, Aron! We must get on with our business here, and that means that you will have to listen to what your new body is telling you! Pad softly, and keep to the shadows! We'll be all right, if we only keep our heads!"

"That's what I'm most interested in," squeaked Aron. "I hope you know what you're doing!"

"I never have any idea what I'm about until I'm about it," replied Ephinias, which did not make Aron feel any the better.

He fell off into a nagging chatter, and did not let up until the two of them were close enough to the other intruders in the tunnel to smell the strange scent of the humans.

"I can smell them," said Aron, testing the air with a wriggling nose that brought his senses so many conflicting messages.

"Of course you can! And from the odor, I would say that we're dealing with someone who has an animal along! Can you pick it out?"

"I don't know what I smell," replied his companion. "I've never used a nose like this!"

"There is definitely an animal down here," went on Ephinias. "I can't quite decide what sort, though. It's not a horse. There's something more dangerous to this one!"

"Well, there's me," sighed Aron. "Maybe you're just getting a whiff of me!"

"I know the scent of a rat well enough. This is something bigger!"

"I hope it doesn't smell a rat," lamented Aron. "If we can smell it, then what's to keep it from sensing us?"

The older rat looked slowly around to its companion. "You really are quite astute, Aron. That would most certainly be the case!"

"Then we'll leave?" asked Aron hopefully.

"After we've found out who is here, and why. Shhhh!" warned Ephinias, laying his ears flat, and pushing himself as far back into the shadows as he could.

Aron started to protest, but there was something in the look of his friend that silenced him, and he followed quickly along behind, careful to be as quiet as possible.

The noise was trebled in intensity now, and there was the unmistakable sounds of a battle closely joined. A shower of arrows rattled dangerously near the two friends, but Ephinias pressed on resolutely.

"We have only a little further to go," he said, turning over his shoulder to reassure Aron.

"A little further might see the end of us, but I'm not staying here alone! Let's get finished with this so we can leave!"

No sooner had Aron finished speaking, when eight or ten heavily armed Dariens ran squarely at the two friends, and it was only the smallness of their bodies that kept them from being trampled by the frenzied mounders. Before they had recovered from that shock, another greeted them in the form of a large reddish brown bear, dressed in full battle armor, and swinging a long black sword wildly about his head. The steel of the blade struck green sparks as it glanced off the smooth stone of the shaft, and rang hollowly in their ears, with a dull throbbing ache. There were humans dressed in battle armor behind this horrible figure, but the two friends had eyes only for the bear.

"To Bern!" roared the plunging form of the big animal, and he lashed out with the sword again, striking green sparks very near Ephinias and Aron, who at first thought they had been discovered. Another shower of bolts fell all about them with a dull metallic clanging. One of the humans in the war band behind the bear grappled violently with a dart in his throat, then pitched face forward heavily, gurgling out his life blood on the shaft floor, making the footing treacherous for those that followed.

"Tall! Tall! Tall!" shrieked the mounders who had counterattacked, and roared back into the passage with a dull low cry like the groaning of a mountain in its darkest breast.

The bear was overrun by the smaller Dariens, but he stood his ground and reared onto his hind quarters, flinging his attackers left and right like paper dolls, his teeth bared and his red eyes crazed with the battle fever which raged through his veins.

"Morghen! Arnault! To the Red Bear! To me, you fiends from the gates of treachery!"

The humans in the party had been beaten back by the onslaught of the Dariens, and now stood locked in close combat with a force twice their size. Ephinias saw that in the meantime, another party of the Dariens had closed off the escape route.

Ephinias and Aron had to dart and duck for their very lives to keep from being crushed to death beneath the wildly flailing feet of the two warring factions. Aron squealed loudly, and his tail was held fast by a large boot that crashed squarely on it, but Ephinias saved the day by leaping up at the man's knee, and biting into the leg there at that tender joint for all he was worth. The man screamed in pain and horror when he saw the large ill-natured rat, but recoiled enough to free Aron. The two fled before the man slashed and hacked wildly with his sword at where they had been but a moment before.

"We have to get clear of here," shouted Ephinias, trying to make himself heard over the frightful roar that became louder still, until the noisy shaft became almost a perfect silence.

Aron chattered his agreement.

"Down! We shall go on the way we were! Down!" cried the older rat, and before Aron could protest, his friend was scurrying for all he was worth through the forest of leaping and struggling combatants, and gone safely on to the other side.

Aron held his breath, said a small short prayer to himself, and closed his eyes. When he opened them again, he was on the other side, free, and running hard after the distant form of his friend, ahead of him by a dozen yards or more.

"Wait!" squeaked Aron. "Wait for me!"

"Come on, lad! We've got ground to cover here! Run for your very life, lad!"

That was exactly what Aron thought he had been doing, but he ran all the harder when he heard Ephinias, shouting breathless and afraid, over his shoulder in the dim tunnel.

And then there was no sign of his friend, who seemed to have vanished into thin air.

"Ephinias!" squeaked Aron, then again, in a louder voice. "Ephinias!"

The noise of the fight in the shafts behind him played tricks on his ears, and he had to remember to focus on his nose. It was new to him, but he slowly edged forward, testing the air every foot or so, and he definitely could sense that his friend was there, and close by.

"Ephinias?" he called out again, a sudden leaden fear

settling over him. A low humming came to him then, and he had only begun trying to fix the sound in his awareness, when an enormous owl landed on the floor directly in front of him, eyeing him hungrily.

"Ephinias, you blackguard! You meddling old fool! You've left me trapped, and I shall never know what was to become of me now!"

Hot wet tears rolled down his cheek, and it took him a long second to register the impression that he was feeling a tear roll down a warm skin that was not covered with fur.

He raised a hand, and rejoiced aloud when he saw his old, familiar hand come up into his vision, and at the same moment, he saw the owl was gone, replaced by Ephinias, who was flushed with excitement.

"There's an end in sight to all our troubles! Hurry! We've got to get down here!" blurted the older man.

"Where? What happened to you? I heard you, and then you were gone! I thought I'd be stuck in that miserable rat's body from now on!"

"No such thing," corrected his friend. "If I had walked off that drop and splattered my brains without having the good sense to take on another friendly form, you would have been released from any spells I had worked on you. It just ends, no more to-do, no explanations, no nothing! Look! See for yourself!"

Ephinias led Aron forward, and against the darker gloom of the shaft, there was a black gash that cut across the tunnel in front of them, which oozed a sense of depth, and the air was even more stale, smelling of a lower level somewhere far below.

"These Dariens were a distrusting lot, as you can see! This was a main shaft, leading you to think all you had to do was bore on, and eventually you would reach the top, or the bottom, depending on what you wanted."

"It looks like this would be a quick way to the bottom." Aron whistled, stepping forward and dropping a button he had in a vest pocket over the edge. After the first few small noises it made as it hit the side of the wall, he could hear nothing else of it.

"Oh, it goes on quite a while," explained Ephinias. "I found where it comes back again, regular as anything. This shaft runs in circles, and it ends up in not a few of these little affairs like this!"

Aron's face fell. "Then how will we ever find the way out? We could be stuck down here until we starve! I'm already hungry, and I can't remember when I had a drink last!"

Ephinias shook his head. "I'm getting so loose in my wit, I can't remember the simplest of things. Excuse me, my friend! You really are good to remind me of these things!"

A simple water flask with a leather cover, and a wallet that smelled of dried jerky lay at Aron's feet.

"Let's have a quick bite and a drink, and then I'll show you what we're going to do next."

"I'm glad you have an idea! I can only think of how we're going to be stuck down here, going round and round until we break our necks on one of these falls!"

"Nonsense! Not as long as you're with me. If Gillerman were here, we could rest even easier, but since he's not, we'd best make do with what we've got! That's always the word I got at the feet of my teacher! Make do with what you've got, and don't regret what you've not!"

"Wise," snorted Aron, unimpressed. "I'd settle for a chart to get us topside of this pit!"

"We shall be there, dear boy, don't fret! We have a task or two yet undone here, though, so you'd best eat up and try to gather your strength."

Aron disliked the older man's tone. "What task?" he asked suspiciously.

"A simple matter of extracting my old student from a good deal of difficulty! I sense his presence strongly now. I wasn't sure at first, but he's reached out to me plainly in this last hour or two. We're very close."

"The bear and those others are very close, too!" reminded Aron.

"Indeed they are. An ugly lot, mark my word! We would be better served to reach the stewards outside."

"Exactly what I've said all along," snapped his friend. He

was ready to launch into a long list of wrongs that had been
done him, but Ephinias closed his mouth with a look.

"Shush! Listen!"

The two companions could hear the distinct murmur of
voices, muffled and excited, but coming from somewhere not
far away. Aron eased carefully to the edge of the abyss
where the shaft ended, and listened for a long while.

"It's from somewhere down there," Aron reported. "And
I can understand a word or two. Someone just said your
name!"

"It's Emerald! I knew I could count on the lad to be in the
midst of all this."

Aron was in the process of speaking, when a strange
transformation made it impossible for his mouth to form the
words. There was a tongue, but his face felt odd, and he had
the definite sensation that his arms had grown long and
hung limply beside him.

"Now, watch," came Ephinias's voice. "All you do is lift
your wings up like this, and flap once or twice. Be careful of
the walls! You'll fly dead into one if you don't keep your
senses about you. If all else fails, just hold yourself open
wide, and you'll be able to glide down."

A series of startled cheeps and garbled fluttering noises
came out of the furry black bat's body that was Aron, but
nothing Ephinias could understand.

"Now slowly, Aron! Think carefully of what you're trying
to say! Just go slowly."

Aron's tongue worked clumsily, and his throat felt full of
something lumpy, but he managed to blurt out a few words,
thick and awkward to his sensitive ears. "What have you
done?" he asked, despairingly.

"I don't have time to teach you properly, but this will
have to do. If I had a proper amount of time, I could have
you using these fellow's native chatter, and how to fly like a
marvel! A shame! Come along!"

The black wedge-shaped figure with pointed wings spread
out like a sail filling in the wind, was gone over the edge of
the tunnel floor that ended in the open chasm.

Aron panicked, then crept slowly forward, struggling to

hold his arms wide. The next instant, he stepped out into empty space, and felt the rushing sensation of the stale air as it sped past him. He flapped wildly then, sending himself crashing painfully into the far wall, which dazed him momentarily, and he began a long, slow glide to the dark bottom of the pit, somewhere below in the deeper gloom.

As he neared the floor of the shaft, he sensed Ephinias, yet there were others, too. He could feel their heat, and there was something else in his head, that was like sounds, only more intense. Aron tried to stick out his clumsy legs to break his speed on landing, but tumbled three or four times, rolled into a tight ball. He secretly hoped that at least something was broken, so he could show Ephinias how wrong and inconsiderate the older man was, but when he attempted to untangle his bat wings to rise, he was sitting upright in his human form, staring at his own vest pocket.

"Aron," introduced Ephinias, speaking to some others who were standing about the older man in a circle.

"Emerald," said the minstrel, holding out a hand to help his new acquaintance up. "I see my old instructor has already had you hard at it!" He laughed, but it was a kind laugh, so Aron was not offended.

"I would like to say I've been instructed," he replied, "But to my knowledge, all that's happened is that I've been both a rat and a bat, and I'm none the wiser for either!"

"Then you are far ahead of the game, friend! I spent time as almost everything Ephinias knew of, or had heard about, and a few mistakes as well! A bat and rat sound fairly tame, when you consider how much more you might have been subjected to."

"*Still* might be," corrected Ephinias. "We aren't out of here yet!"

"This is Owen Helwin, sir," said the minstrel, turning serious. "He has the blade from Skye that Gillerman gave him! We've been trying to reach him since we entered the Edges, for we had hoped he would help us save Owen's mother from a spell she has fallen under."

"Gillerman told me through the sword that we would have to have a leaf from the Three Trees, wherever they are, to help her, but we found some water from a well here that will work." It woke me up, and Kegin! And we have some to take to her!"

"Well, my dear boy? Did you say you got water from a well down here?"

"I heard them talking about it," said Deros, joining into the conversation timidly. "It is very old, and I sensed something in it from my own country."

"Sometimes even the wise and all-knowing nephew Gillerman overlooks things, I see," said Ephinias, looking sharply at the young woman, made up to look like a boy again.

"This is Deros," explained Emerald. "She dresses like this for protection. The Dariens' Querle was all in an uproar to complete the ancient pagan rituals again, by capturing a human from the upside of the world, and doing again what the old Darien king once did."

"The poor fools," muttered Ephinias. "They are still convinced that 'tall' will free them from all their shame! Well met, young lady! You shall do well to account for yourself. I see that you are not from our climes?"

"The Sea of Silence," replied Deros, suddenly shy again, watching Owen.

"I have friends along that stretch. They should be glad to see me, and more glad still to hear I have news of you."

Deros blushed deeply, and could not find her voice to reply.

Ephinias turned to the minstrel. "It's good you have kept her safe. It would be a hard thing to explain to her father if anything should happen to her while she's in your keeping."

Deros pleaded with her eyes for Ephinias to be silent, and after studying her for a few moments more, he abruptly changed the subject, but not before Owen's eyes were wide in anticipation.

"We shall have to go back a bit to rejoin the right tunnel," explained Ephinias. "There are roundabouts, and some nasty tricks along the way. The Dariens' probably are busy with the raiders in the shafts above, but I think they would be happy to rely on these snares, and never have to close with us at all."

"That must be why they left us alone," concluded Emerald.

"Who's this?" asked Ephinias, walking to Kegin. "Yes, that's why they sometimes vanish, Emerald."

"This is Kegin, Owen's guardian."

"You service, sir," said Kegin, bowing.

"We'll need it soon enough," said the older man shortly. "We shall have a deal of a time getting past these clever little bounders."

"There's a way we've found," said Emerald. "We got up to this level by it, and I don't see any reason why we can't go on."

The minstrel showed his old instructor the small holes in the wall, and how they had inserted the bolts from the crossbows.

"That would be jolly fine, my lad, but Aron and I have just come from up there, and the shafts are full of all description of nasty fellows going at it hammer and tongs! We even saw a bear in battle armor, big as a house, and speaking our tongue! There's some ugly medicine afoot, when blokes take on the forms and philosophies of the lower species to gain their own ends."

"The bear!" exclaimed Emerald. "Then you saw him, too?"

"And I imagine we're going to see more of him anon, if I don't mistake my signals," said Ephinias, who had turned his ear to the upper wall, and fell silent, his face a mask of concentration.

In the distance, the others now heard the dull roar, growing louder as though a wave of noise had broken its dam, and now rolled forth to engulf them.

Beyond the Fords of Silver

In the long hours after midnight and into the early morning, the battle at the Fords of the Silver raged on, with the Channeliers of the Red Bear and the armies who flew the flag of Argent Largo, locked into a combat with each other, and with the Elboreal and stewards of the Line. The river ran blood, the corpses were as deep as cordwood in places, and the smell of death hung over the scorched earth like a black pall.

Largo had led the way to the river, and true to his word, there were no visible snares for the stewards to detect, although none of Famhart's men could shake off the uneasy feeling they had. Largo urged the group on, eager to cross, but Famhart sat for a moment longer, surveying the boundaries of Trew by the trembling red-orange light of the battle fires.

A faint movement had caught his eye, the barest of motions that seemed no more than another flickering shadow in the vast shadows of the night.

"What is it?" asked Largo. "Surely the darkness holds no terrors for the great Famhart?"

Famhart did not answer, but peered intently into the gloom, as though reading a strange cypher there. It appeared to him that the vision was of the Elboreal, faint and trembling, and their golden white light that shimmered and shone elsewhere, was here muted and might have been a light that was seen through a dense cloud.

"Strange," Famhart muttered to himself.

They were preparing to step out into the river, when the light began to grow stronger, and the beginnings of the pipe music started, which tore at Largo's ears like a grating of steel on a raw nerve.

"Stop them!" he shrieked. "I did not agree to letting those waterfilth cross with us! I won't deliver the secret of the spell if they are about! I warn you, Famhart! I won't show you how to save your precious Linne if they don't go away!"

Largo had reached the point of hysteria, and Famhart saw that to try to reason with him was out of the question.

"I can't control the dreamers," he said quietly. "I have not asked them to come along, so I don't think they will cross! The Lady Elina is her own commander, and Erases does as he will!"

"Then make sure they keep out of Trew! I swear I won't show you the secret if they step foot on the shore there!"

"Come on, lads," said Famhart, turning to his party. "Let's go to Trew!"

The mounted riders waded their horses into the shallow water of the ford, and started toward the opposite shore, when the pipe music grew louder, and a faint gleam of silver began to brighten right at the water's edge on the banks of the shoreline of Trew. It grew more intense still, and in another heartbeat, it was the shining figure of a woman, beautiful and glistening with a thousand small stars that seemed to be woven into her long hair.

Largo shrieked and fought to turn his mount, but the animal stumbled, dumping his rider into the slow current. He was on his feet in an instant, his sword drawn, taking stumbling, running steps toward the glimmering figure, his weapon raised above his head to strike.

Famhart spurred his mount, and overtook Largo easily, but the younger man dove under his blow, and swam for the middle of the river, screeching in an unearthly voice.

"Letta! Letta, you foul beast, to me! To me!"

He strangled on a mouthful of water and coughed, going under, then coming to the surface again, all the time getting nearer and nearer to the banks of Trew, and his unseen allies.

Famhart had given up the chase, and waited to see what Largo would do once he reached the other side. The shimmering figure of the woman had dimmed, and now stood quietly, watching Largo.

"Come to me, my dear Largo," she said softly. "Tell me why you let your Elita go! If it had not been for my salvation at the hands of the dreamers, I would have surely perished. Now I want you to tell me why you did it, my sweet? You knew I felt a special feeling in my heart for you."

"You're dead, you spiteful witch! I watched you die! You can't harm me. You can harm no one anymore!"

Largo had reached the shore, and took a few trembling steps in the direction of the woman, shaking his fist.

"You shall see what it is now to deal with Argent Largo! Letta! To me! Here is a tasty beginning to your feast! Come ahead and try to stop me if you can, Famhart! I'm here! Everything you need to know is here!"

Largo taunted Famhart, trembling and shaking in a bout of rage that racked his body.

As Famhart rode forward, another voice from the Elboreal reached him.

"Tread carefully, O Rod of Truth! The Rogen await you on the banks of Trew!"

Famhart could see nothing, but he believed the urgent voices of the Elboreal. "Can you protect the woman?"

"She is protected. The Rogen cannot harm her, for she is a child of Trew."

Largo raged and flung himself at the shining form of the woman Elita, but she disappeared, only to be somewhere else, just out of his reach.

"You are like all the rest," he shrieked, diving at her again, without getting any nearer. He stooped and picked up a crossbow that had been dropped by one of the unfortunate ones who had been devoured by the Rogen, and aimed it at the woman. He loosed the bolt with a curse, and watched as it flew through empty air, until it embedded itself in a thick tree trunk not far behind the spot where she had stood.

Famhart was still in midstream, watching as his wife's brother went mad before his eyes.

"My sister is doomed now, Famhart! You will never know how to save her! She will waste away slowly, right before your eyes, and there's nothing you can do! Argent Largo was the one who felled her! I am the fate of that wretched girl, and I'm glad I've done it!"

He had rearmed the crossbow as he ranted and carried on, and he brought the weapon up swiftly, and loosed the bolt directly at his hated enemy who sat before him on his horse in the middle of the river.

Frightened by the sudden movement, Famhart's mount reared just as Largo released his dart, which caught the animal high in the neck, just below its ear. There was a terrible, agonized scream, and then the horse was on its knees, toppling into the water on top of its hapless rider. A dozen men had leaped from the steward side to reach Famhart, but Largo was there before them. The elder of the Line had hit his head on a boulder as he fell, and was stunned, unable to defend himself as Largo swarmed over him, pulling him away from the mortally wounded animal, and dragging him ashore in Trew by the collar of his cloak.

"Back, you swine!" he screamed. "I'll cut his throat and gut him on the spot if you come any nearer!"

The stewards halted, milling about uneasily, torn between their duty and their love of Famhart. "We'll spare you, Largo, just as Famhart said! Release him to us, and you will have all the protection of the Line!"

"Too late, you fine, pure Steward! I am going to feed him to my ally, the wonderful Letta! But I shall keep his head, to take to Linne as a trophy. That will please her!"

The steward sergeant saw that the fine line had been crossed, and that the man before them had been pushed beyond any hope of recall to sanity.

A cold wind had risen out of the darkness, and the stewards watched helplessly as a gray form began to take shape in the area where Largo stood triumphant over Famhart. There seemed to be flickering capes, and hints of hideous figures in the gray fog, things that set the mind recoiling in terror, and all the while it moved nearer and nearer the still unconscious Famhart, who lay helpless before the dreadful enemy.

Largo's face was contorted into a grotesque mask of hatred, and his eyes rolled wildly in his head as he watched the Rogen come for their prize. He turned to laugh at the paralyzed stewards, when beside him, next to Famhart, was the woman, Elita. She touched Famhart's brow, then held tightly to his hand.

"He is a child of Trew," she called aloud to the horrible forms in the gray wind. "I am the Lady Elita of Trew, and I call this man Famhart a child of Trew. You cannot harm him."

"Hurrah! Hurrah for the Lady Elita!" cried the stewards, making a rush toward the shore to retrieve their leader, but they were driven back by the hideous moans and growls they encountered close to the shore from the Rogen, who had now begun to manifest in various foul forms, driving the horses of the men into stark terror. Some of the mounts threw their riders and bolted away, and others simply turned and fled, oblivious to their frightened masters.

"Back, you wretched fools! Stay away from him, Elita! He's mine!"

Largo drew a short dirk from his waistband, and leaped at the woman, but there seemed to be a solid wall about her which he could not penetrate.

"Save yourself, Largo! I know your secret now! You are doomed, but you don't have to return to the Darkness of the Black Death! Renounce her, and you shall find peace!"

A green fire blazed in Largo's eyes, and his mind had slowly been clouded by the presence of his old mistress who had saved him before. The amulet at his neck burned his skin, and he could smell the seared flesh.

"Curse you all!" he cried in a strangled voice. "I shall not call this quits until I am the victor! You have bested me this once, but I shall hound you until I am like a tidal wave crashing over your puny defenses! I shall be back with more of an army, and we shall see who has the last laugh here!"

Largo shook his fist angrily at Elita, then threw the

dagger at where her heart beat against her bodice cloth, but the blade clattered away harmlessly, as if the knife had been thrown against stone.

"Letta! Keep them at bay! Hold them from Trew!" he cried, running down the top of the old moat wall that ancient maps called the Ditch, which led toward the Darien Mounds. Largo would have gone toward Rogen Keep, which he felt was more formidable, but he reasoned to himself that he could hide in the mounds until he could regroup his forces and call up the dragon again. He knew the failure of his plans was all because of the presence of the dreamers, the wretched waterfilth who the Dark One had promised him would no longer be around to trouble him, or stand in the way of his ambitions.

He ran hard, keeping low to the ground, should any of the enemy archers try to shoot at him, and darted from side to side to try to throw off any who might have aimed at him.

The fires across the river had flared up tremendously, then began to sink, having exhausted all the fuel in the nearby woods. The shadows started to lengthen as the silent part of the morning crept nearer to sunrise. Largo was chilled to the bone despite his exertion, and he shivered beneath his mail shirt. "Wretched traitors! They'll all pay for this night's work!"

There was a troubling voice in his head, amid the noise and clamor of all the jumbled thoughts there, and he tried to keep it at bay, but he couldn't drown it out. It did not take him long to realize that it was the old soft voice of the Dark One.

"You have failed me, Largo, and caused my servants to suffer at the hands of the Light! You know the cost of failure. I told you then what I did to those who were untrue to me!"

Largo argued inwardly with the voice, for it was not a thing that he thought existed outside of himself. He hurried along now, nearing the welcome havens of one of the open shafts that led into the first of the ruins of the old Darien Mounds. He knew there was a sort of stunted clan that was a mix of the dwarfish and human lines, but he was unafraid of them, sure that he would be able to call the dragon back soon, for all he needed was the makings of a fire. And then he knew the Rogen were the best watchdogs of all to keep the hated stewards from crossing the river and hunting him down.

"That unlucky shot," he cursed to himself. "If that blasted animal had held its peace for a split-second longer, I would have been rid of Famhart for good, and all these high and mighty stewards would be carrying their dead away to bury him, and I would be free, and rid of these foul sores that plague me. Bern can't be faring much better than I, although I'd like to have a good report on his status."

He thought that might be the way to appease the voice of the Dark One, and was pursuing another idea along that line, when he reached the entrance to the Darien Mounds, and plunged headlong into it, hardly taking the time to think what he did, or check his forward momentum.

After a few steps, his feet touched only empty air, and he had the sinking sensation of having stepped out into thin air, tumbling slowly forward and to his right. He landed painfully on his shoulder on an outcropping of something soft a dozen feet below the surface. He kept pitching forward, unable to stop himself, and as he rolled, he registered the fact that what had broken his fall was the lifeless corpses of more than a hundred soldiers, all hacked and slashed beyond recognition, and all wearing the uniforms of his own army.

A shudder tore through Largo's limbs like a high wind rustling leaves in late fall trees, and his heart hammered heavily in his throat. At last he gingerly lifted himself free of the pile of murdered men, stepping aside into what appeared to be a faintly lit chamber at the bottom of the long winding stairwell that he had missed in his headlong flight.

As his heart calmed, and he began to sense that whoever had killed all the soldiers was no longer in the tunnel, he drew a breath of relief and tried to take stock of his surroundings.

He could hear the distant sounds, once his heart stopped

hammering so heavily and the blood wasn't pounding in his ears. There was the muffled sound of blows and chants, along with some other noise that reminded Largo of the Elboreal, which sent a shudder of disgust through him, but when he turned and looked back at the stairwell littered with the bodies of his soldiers, he knew there was nothing for it but to go forward. He tried to remember what it was Elita told him of the mounds, but couldn't concentrate. He clenched his fists and gritted his teeth when he recalled seeing her, more beautiful than ever, and most assuredly brought back to haunt him by the miserable waterfolk who seemed to stalk him like a curse.

Angered by the thought, he called aloud to Dorini.

"You have tricked me, O Protector! You told me I would have my old territory all to myself, without having to deal with any of the older clans. Why do you send this wretched fate to me? Why do I have to contend with this Bern for territory?"

There was no outward answer, but Largo felt a stabbing pain beside his heart, and his head felt as though it were caught in a vice.

"Enough!" he cried pathetically. "I yield. Only give me strength to slay the wretched Famhart! Give me that, and I will do anything you please. And the Red Bear! Give me the Red Bear!"

Largo's eyes had grown wide and wild as he raved on, and the green fire again blazed dangerously.

Almost in answer to his heated plea, there was a great outburst of battle horns, and the strident cries of desperate men locked into deadly combat. Somewhere in the tunnel in front of him, Largo heard the rallying call of the Red Bear, and his eyes glistened and seemed to see something amusing far away, then went as dead and cold as a vast winter night.

"My service," muttered Largo, and he began to cast about for a weapon. He remembered the slaughtered soldiers, and returned quickly, holding his breath as he did so, and making himself think only of the Red Bear as he stripped a slain man of his arms. Largo strapped the long-sword tightly about his waist, and armed the stubby crossbow with one of the ugly iron bolts, and drew on the man's helmet, which concealed his features, except for his mouth.

"Now we shall see who will inherit the Lower Meadows," he said to himself, a strange light burning menacingly in his eyes. "If Largo is overthrown, then they shall all be overthrown! Death to them all!"

Largo went quickly forward, hunched over and keeping to the wall to conceal himself, hoping that he would be able to strike a fatal blow without revealing his hiding place.

The shaft which ran downward into the deeper part of the Darien Mounds descended slowly, at an angle that made it easy to walk, then dropped abruptly into a steep stairwell, which was carved from the very rock. Water from some unseen source had wet the stone, making it treacherous to walk, but Largo went slowly, with only one thing filling his mind. He had checked and rechecked his crossbow, and paused to count the darts in his quiver, and drawn the longsword to determine its heft. Satisfied with those preparations, he was thinking long fulfilling thoughts of the Red Bear dead, and the stewards safely out of his way.

"It will be that way, O Protector! I have not failed you yet! Give your servant one last chance to prove his mettle."

At the foot of the stone stairs, the tunnel branched into three directions. Over each of the shafts was an archway covered with intricate carvings and many runes that baffled Largo. He tried to listen carefully at each of the entryways, but the sounds of battle that reached him could easily have come from all three.

"Guide me, o Protector!" cried Largo, waiting for a sign to reveal to him which of the three doorways to choose. When no voice came, he risked moving off on his own, choosing the middle tunnel, which had the carvings of a giant pyramid surrounded by small pyramids, all arranged in intricate patterns, and looking as though someone had tried to clean off the finely wrought hieroglyphics.

Largo was well into the tunnel, when a noisy tramp of feet made it clear that someone was approaching rapidly, and there was no place to hide in the closed shaft. He glanced all about him nervously, then cursing under his breath, ran back toward the stairwell, hoping to avoid discovery, until he was ready to strike.

Turning the corner, Bern the Red gave another mighty blast on his war horn, rallying the few troops not slain by the persistent, provoking, pint-sized Dariens, who would dog their enemies until the foe could no longer keep up a guard, then the small mounders would fall on in an overpowering force that simply wore their opponents down. Bern had slain so many of the hateful halflings that he'd lost count, but he wished to kill more. They came in endless streams, and even his strong bear body was beginning to tire. If only he could change back to his human form for a flash, and get the renewed strength of his human form, he might be able to fight his way clear until the threat had been met and overthrown.

Morghen and Arnault had been cut off from him at the height of the battle, and he had no way of knowing how many of his assault party had survived. There were stragglers with him yet, but it was plain to Bern that the Number-one priority here was survival. He felt he would be all right, once he could reach an exit which would deliver him from the beastly small Dariens, with their tall battle helmets, and who Bern knew to be crazed and malformed in their thinking, for all their life was led in the dark tunnels and chambers of the mounds.

It was with a hammering heart that Bern slowed, and drew himself into a quiet cul-de-sac, waiting to see if anyone had heard his call for help. The horn was at his lips again, but he hesitated to blow, thereby betraying his cover.

"I am not so young as some of these who dwell here. My arms are weary hacking at these tiresome little beasts. I shall let my good Morghen and Arnault and the rest of their lackeys deal with this trap, since it seems to smack of a plot gone bad! Welcome to it, if it is the death of those two!"

Bern was breathing easier as he stood resting, and the shaft seemed to be immediately free of Dariens, so he lowered himself to his hindquarters, and sat heavily down, laying his bloody sword beside him. It had been a vicious, brutal fight, and he discovered that his body was covered with a hundred cuts and bruises, and there were wounds that could have only been caused by bites.

"Ugh!" he shuddered. "I have been poisoned by those ugly mites!"

He stood then, and repeated the ritual that allowed him to change back to his human form, which was more comfortable, for there were no wounds in that odd, furless body, and he was well rested once more.

"Now we shall have a little surprise for them, if they should stumble across me!"

He laughed quietly to himself, then began planning how he would find his way out of the underground horror chamber. He tried to recall all the marks of the shafts he had come through, but that was all before they had been set upon, and he couldn't remember how far he had come in his struggle to be free, or how many turns he had made. There were still sounds in the network of tunnels, and he could hear the noise of battle still raging, now closer, now farther away. He decided to wait until it was quieter, and then explore about to see if he could find a clue as to a way to the outside. It was his only plan, but at the moment, Bern the Red had no other card to play. Once above ground again, he could regroup his Channeliers, and withdraw to plan another strike. And there might be a chance that he could still murder the leaders of the Dariens, or sneak into the throne room of Trew, as was their original plan. As he thought of that, and as the sure calming effect of having come through a close encounter with death washed over him, he became thirsty, and being thirsty, he thought of water, and thinking of water, he thought of the Wells of Trona.

"Of course! All I have to do is reach one of these wells, and I can no longer be harmed! My whole thinking has been thrown off by Morghen! They were using this ploy to come underground so they could find one of the wells, and slay me! Two crows with one stone! Curse their eyes, I hope their bones rot in this stinkhole! But I'm on to them now. The wells can't be hard to find. I can smell water!"

Bern immediately changed his form again, and tested his

nose. There was a musty, still stale smell about the shaft he hid in, but there was the faintest trace of the damp feel of water somewhere, although it was not close.

"Now I have it," he said, rising and picking up his sword. "All I have to do is go carefully and slowly, and I will be invincible! Once I've drunk from the well, no one can stop me!"

The huge shape of the bear created a strange sight moving slowly down the shaft, and it seemed to have a shadow, as another large form followed along behind, silent and watchful.

At the first juncture of the tunnels, Bern hesitated, lifting his head to test the air in the three directions, shuffling and snuffling back and forth a few paces into all the shafts, but he at last chose the most promising one of the three, and went on, pausing every few steps, yet unaware of the trailing shadow that crept along behind him, moving forward when he moved forward, and pausing when he paused.

This had gone on for many minutes, when Bern detected a strange, musty odor that confused him, for it wasn't really a smell of the mounds, or any of the things that belonged there. He rose on his hind legs and turned around very slowly, trying to get a bearing on whatever it was, but it was so vague and faint, he gave up and went on, feeling a growing nearness of the wet sensation that clung to his nose.

In the next tunnel, the scent of water grew stronger, blotting out the other vague smell that had bothered him, and as he hurried on, he detected the presence of humans, and soon began to hear their voices, ringing clearly in the still air.

"I'd vote for that," said one. "If we go on this way, there's no telling where we're going to end up. Ephinias said they had just come from up there. It sounds like our escape route is blocked up with both the Dariens and the bear!"

Bern's ears picked up, and his eyes formed malevolent slits as he crept forward silently, listening.

"The well would give us protection," argued another voice, a younger voice, for it was softer, and higher pitched.

"I had a good feeling there. And if Owen's sword protected us once, then it would do so again."

"I might call up Gillerman," said an older man. "The well would be the perfect place to do it. I don't know why I become so forgetful. Sometimes I think I must have too much furniture in this old attic!"

Bern was within sight of the small group now, and he flattened himself against the dim shaft wall to watch, and to hear the rest of the discussion of the well.

Behind him, the other large shadow did the same, and beyond the smooth floor of the tunnel, on the other side, and in a niche placed in the wall to house an ancient Darien statue, stood another figure, sword poised and ready to strike.

WINDAMEIR'S
DREAM

Cross and Shield

Famhart came to from a horrible nightmare, where he was frozen in time as two huge fanged beasts closed in on him to drink his blood. He could see their dead eyes glaring at him balefully, and could hear their low growls as they smacked their lips and drooled hungrily for his life.

There was another figure then, that held out a warm white beacon of light to him to hold, and it frightened the gray forms away. They fell back in terror, although they didn't run away, but seemed to lurk at a safe distance, and content themselves with watching.

"You're safe now, Famhart! The Rogen cannot harm you as long as I hold your hand. My name is Elita, and I am a child of Trew."

Famhart stood, groggy and dazed, and tried to clear the cobwebs from his throbbing head. "The Elboreal told me," he mumbled, feeling his jaw ache as he spoke. "I must have taken quite a crack."

"You did! Largo dragged you here into Trew to turn the Rogen loose on you."

"He's never been the one to let an opportunity pass! His sister has wept many a tear over the poor devil. We thought he had found some sort of peace, but even death was not to release him from his hatred."

"I had fallen in love with him when he came to Trew. I was so simple in my beliefs. It did not occur to me that he could be lying, or that all that he said was only a cover for his real purpose." Elita's beautiful face darkened, and she looked away from Famhart, unable to meet his eyes. "I helped him do a deed that I wish were otherwise now. I can only plead with you for your forgiveness."

"What forgiveness could you ask of me, my lady? You have saved me from a fate that sends chills down a grown man's back, and you speak to me of some forgiveness that I might offer you?"

"It was I who helped Largo to snare your wife into the black sleep! He told me all his dirty lies, and I believed him. Now your wife is under the spell of the black sleep and will perish if we don't free her soon!"

Famhart's handsome features clouded, and he started to withdraw his hand from Elita's grasp.

"Don't," she warned. "I can't let my hold go of you until you are safely on the other side. As long as you are in Trew, I have to shield you from them."

He struggled with a code that ran close to the bone, but in the end, he let the woman hold to him, and he tried to understand what she must be going through.

"Do you know how to break the spell my wife is under, my lady?" he asked at last, hardly daring to hope.

"Yes," she replied. "And the dreamers have gone to bring her here, so that she will be delivered from that horrible prison she has been in. I am so ashamed, Famhart. I don't know if my heart will let me live if anything has happened to her!"

The leader of the stewards softened to see the distress Elita was in, and he squeezed her hand reassuringly.

"You did what you did not knowing," he said. "And if the dreamers are bringing Linne here, then you shall be able to bring her back from that false sleep that has trapped her in its black depths."

Famhart's attention was drawn back to his squadron by their repeated calls and war horns signaling to him. He rose shakily, and used Elita to steady himself, for his head spun in dizzy circles for a few moments while he got his feet back under him.

"We have a new mount for you," shouted the steward sergeant. "We'll send him across!"

"Where did Largo get to?" asked Famhart, his voice at first unsteady. "Did you see what happened to him?"

"He must lead a charmed life. The last we saw of him, he was heading along that old rock wall toward those ruins yonder!"

Elita nodded. "He has gone to the Darien Mounds. I watched him disappear there."

"Can you take me there?" asked Famhart, his mind slowly beginning to function again.

"The mounds are very dangerous now," replied the woman. "I have traveled there in the past, but the Dariens were not aroused."

"I must find Largo. We have been ill-starred since Linne and I were together. We had thought him finally at rest long ago, so I must try to make certain of his fate this time."

The darkness had begun to nibble at the flickering orange light of the fires that burned slowly down all along the river, and the sounds of battle had died away somewhat. Faraway calls of signal horns and the distant drumming of sword-strokes on shields fell more softly, and the unwholesome smell of blood and death and scorched earth became more pronounced as the silence continued to grow.

Across the Silver, Famhart's squadron eagerly awaited his orders, and rode nervously up and down at the ford, hoping for an opportunity to cross without being set on by the Rogen, who still swirled about in the dense gray fog that seemed so full of the fearful forms that had frightened off the horses in the aborted attempt to reach their leader. The horse they had for him was dispatched, and sent forward with a slap on its flank. It shied away from the gray figures that lingered by the bank, but soon was near enough to Famhart for him to coax the animal into standing still long enough for him to get a shaky hand on the bridle, and with Elita's help, to calm the animal into allowing the two of them to mount.

"Show me the way to the place you saw Largo," said Famhart, turning to speak over his shoulder. "I must find him before he gets away."

"You would do better to leave Trew now," replied the

woman. "Await the arrival of your wife on the river. The dreamers will be coming any time now. Be there for her when she is awakened!"

"I shall be," answered Famhart resolutely. "And with her brother either alive or dead, but at peace! I can't be this near to confronting him and just let him go."

"There are things that are better left alone," said Elita softly. "I have no wish any longer to see him harmed. He is a poor lost soul, just like those misdirected ones in Trew who believed what he had to promise them. We all wanted to believe whatever dream we needed to believe in."

"I can't leave this alone until it's finished. It's too old. He is too dangerous to remain unchecked. The Dark One has branded him as her servant, and it is plain that he must be caught and freed. He still looks exactly as he did before the Middle Islands. There is something there that is so unnatural that it can't be left untended. If the Black Death finds a foothold now, then the worst of times will be again."

"Then I have to go with you," said Elita evenly. "The Rogen will never rest until they are freed from their tasks, or until they have slain every living thing that is foreign. You couldn't get more than a small way into the mounds without running afoul of the Rogen or the Dariens."

Famhart spurred the horse forward, and followed the woman's pointing arm toward the entrance to the mounds where Largo had disappeared.

"How has Largo managed to escape the Rogen?" he asked, as they were dismounting. "He is not a child of Trew."

"He has the amulet of the dragon. He was a servant of the Dark One. It was one of the old tales. It was said that one day a man would come from beyond Trew, who would not be devoured by the keepers, and that he would be the Redeemer. The Lord Trew had been gone for so long, everyone wanted to believe it, for we have been trapped here all this time since Trew disappeared. He had set all the destructive watchers into motion, then left us at their mercy when he was gone. It seemed a natural thing at first when Largo showed up and was not destroyed by the Rogen. I think that was what enabled him to gain such a hold over my countrymen."

"Well, so much for the poor soul, and all the misery he has caused you and yours. His fate seems to have been to be the root of everything painful and evil, and to bring ruin down about everything and everyone he touches."

"Leave him for the others," argued the woman. "Soon it'll be light, and the mounds are full of the Dariens. They don't take well to those who invade their chambers."

"I can't leave it to chance! If Linne is to be freed, then finding Largo is a part of that freedom. She would never rest easy if we were to pull her back from that hellish place where she is trapped, only to tell her that her brother who did the deed has not been caught and dealt with."

Elita saw that it would do no good to argue further with the determined Famhart. "If we must go in, then at least let us wait for some of the dreamers! It would be foolish to try to go alone. The ways are treacherous, and even I don't know all the secrets of the mounds."

"The Elboreal can follow along when they can. I will try to mark our way, so that they can come after us."

Famhart had handed down the woman, and dismounted after her. He checked his weapon, and took a small shield off the horn of the saddle, slinging it over his back.

"I wish I had a crossbow, but it might be of no use in these shafts! It shall come down to blows at last, and it is always the steady hand with the longsword that lasts in the end."

He turned to the stewards who were still lined up along the river, and raised a hand in salute to the fluttering white banner that bore the Cross and Shield of the Line. They returned his gesture, and kept their hands raised until he and the woman of Trew had disappeared into the dark mouth of the openings that led down into the secret vaults of the Darien Mounds.

And below, far ahead of his father and Elita, Owen Helwin watched as Ephinias stood at the edge of the well that had brought him back from the shades of the spell he had been under, and that still held his mother fast in its grim deathvise.

They had made good time back to the chamber where Emerald had found Deros, and where he had administered the water to Owen and Kegin. The shafts were still all eerily quiet, except for the now distant sounds of battle, which seemed to echo faintly from farther away each time they came.

"I don't like the feel of this," said Emerald. "It is always the silence which bites the hardest. If there were only a few of them about, I'd feel better for it."

"There is no few of them," replied Ephinias. "These little devils run in packs. You'll never find one without two dozen more close at hand."

"It would still be easier to take than this," argued the minstrel.

Deros was silent, standing very near Owen, her face drawn with fear and tension. "It still smells like the sea from my old home," she said quietly, trying to reassure herself.

"That's strange, child," said the older man, who was peering intently into the depths of the well as he spoke. "It does seem to have odd properties. We shall have no trouble calling for Gillerman from here. I think this is one of the old doorways that are spoken of in the lorebooks we grew up on."

"Doorways?" questioned Emerald. "How could that be?"

"You always wanted to know the most difficult things," Ephinias laughed. "It would take too long to explain all the ways of it to you, my young jacksnipe, but it is easy to understand if you think of all these planes here in the Lower Meadows as being full of shafts, just like the tunnels we're in here in the mounds. Room connections, if you will! Leading from one part of your house to another, only some of them concealed so that you could move back and forth without someone always seeing you."

Ephinias had drawn breath to continue on with his lecture to his old student, when a slight movement out of the corner of his eyes caught his attention, and he turned to the archway that marked the entry of the hall to the Well of

Trona. There outlined in the dim light was the vague silhou-
ette of a bear, dressed in full battle garb.

"If you stand aside, and swear your service to Bern the
Red, you will be allowed to live," boomed his voice, powerful and frightening, and he held aloft a black sword that
glowed a pale deathly green.

Ephinias held out a hand to hold Emerald back, and stood
before his small group in a protective way.

"I think we shall swear no service to Bern," replied
Ephinias coldly, his voice matching the power of the bear.
"And I might say that if Bern the Red yielded to us, we
would grant him mercy and fair dealing!"

A low rumble of laughter echoed about the stone walls.

"You are even more foolish then you look, old one! Your
wits have deserted you before you've lost your hair! I surrender up the well? I am Bern the Red, and I will have it!"

He struck out with the sword, making a vicious sweeping
arc in the air before him. As he did so, another form behind
him seemed to pounce forward, a large, dark massive shape
that seemed to have no beginning or end, and it now fell on
the bear, who fought savagely to free himself.

"It's the drudge!" cried Emerald. "That's the thing that
had Owen and Kegin before!"

"It will give me time to call Gillerman," said Ephinias,
and he turned back toward the well to complete what he had
been doing when Bern interrupted.

"Watch out!" shouted Kegin.

"Deros! Duck!" Owen yelled.

As the drudge and Bern fought furiously about the chamber floor, another figure had erupted into the room, sword
flashing, and made straight for Owen.

Largo's eyes were turned back in his head, and a shrill,
chilling cry came from his distorted lips. He was in range
then, and before Kegin or Emerald could intercede, he had
fallen wildly upon the overwhelmed youth, who was still
struggling to draw his longsword from its scabbard.

A pale blue light from the well had been glimmering
faintly before, illuminating the chamber, but it now flared
up into a darker intense blue that rose out of the water,

growing into a band of blue-white stars that began to drift upward toward the ceiling of the chamber, lighting the scene until the drudge began to wail with pain. Bern had taken that advantage to strike a blow or two at the unprotected underpart of the hairy creature he was battling, which drew a low groan as the thing eased off momentarily, then collapsed unmoving, wheezing in a sad, oddly musical way until there was silence at last from its vast shape.

Bern whirled again, this time seeing his opportunity to fall on Ephinias, still deep in his repetitions of the runes which would call Gillerman.

"Watch out!" cried Kegin. "Keep back!"

He leaped forward, but too late, for Bern had brought the wicked black sword down with a stunning blow across Ephinias's head, and the old man fell into a senseless heap at the well's edge. Before Kegin could move further, the bear whirled to engage him, and in turning so quickly, he tripped over the fallen form that lay at his feet. He quickly sidestepped and tried to regain his balance, but faltered once, then caught his hindpaw against the stones that rimmed the well, roared out in a dreadful voice that froze the hearts of all there, and toppled over with a resounding splash into the waiting Well of Trona.

Deros leaped up from where she had fallen behind Bern, and moved quickly to Owen's side, where he clumsily tried to keep the maddened Largo at bay. Kegin then joined in the fray, and Emerald brought up the rear, while Aron knelt beside the unconscious and bleeding Ephinias.

"Yield!" ordered Kegin. "Yield, or you die! We outnumber you, friend. Don't drive us to slay you!"

"You cannot slay Argent Largo," he raved. "I have come to avenge myself on my wretched sister! I shall slay her husband and her son! She shall pay dearly for what she has done to me!"

"You're mad," said Emerald. "They have done you no harm."

"I am mad," echoed Largo. "I have my madness to protect me, and the Protector to strike you all dead!"

As he spoke, he edged nearer Owen, who seemed mesmer-

ized by the name of his mother's assailant. A slow fire had
begun to blaze up in his chest, and he gripped the sword in
his hand so tightly he thought he must surely feel the cold
steel cutting through the flesh of his palm.

With a ringing cry that echoed through the chamber of
the well, Owen sprang forward. Their swords struck sparks,
and the air was filled with the metallic clamor of the blades
as they clashed against each other, jarring both Largo and
Owen to the bone, and numbing their arms. Deros had
screamed as the young man attacked, and it distracted
Owen just enough so that Largo was able to recover his
balance first, and struck another blow before Owen could
fully parry it.

A thin geyser of blood spurted from the wound in Owen's
forearm, which caused the girl to scream again, although
she was quickly hushed by Kegin.

Largo struck again, narrowly missing Owen's head, but
his blade cut the gray bag strapped to Owen's back, and
split the flask spilling the water from the Well of Trona.

Owen's face contorted into a mask of rage when he saw
this, and he whirled madly, slashing the air in front of Largo
with ineffective strokes that were spent before he was within
striking range.

Kegin shouted to him to close nearer with his opponent,
but the youth heard nothing. He was full of a blazing hatred
that blanked all else from his mind. All he could think of
was to smash the handsome, smirking face of his adversary,
and to hack him into small bits with the sword Gillerman
had given him.

For an instant, and it was an instant only, he thought of
the ancient man, and wondered why the sword hadn't
showed its usual light, or made any noise, or did any of the
other things that he had known it to do before. Then Largo
lunged forward, hacking and slashing in a powerful back-
hand stroke that hurled Owen's sword out of his numbed
hand, and sent it skittering wildly across the floor to land at
the well's edge.

Emerald engaged Largo then, deftly leading him away
from Owen, and placing himself between Largo and Owen,

so the demented assailant could not get at the disarmed youth, who was scrambling to retrieve his lost weapon. His ears burned with shame, and he trembled as he bent to pick up the sword.

"You've let him get to you," cautioned Kegin. "Keep your mind on what you're about! Watch Emerald!"

The minstrel, although he was trained as an entertainer and a poet, had been well versed in the handling of weapons, and he easily held his own against Largo, who seemed to be tiring, and slackening his attack.

Largo broke off the engagement with Emerald, and fell back a few more steps, reaching his left hand into his short jacket as he did so, and bringing out a tiny vial, which he dashed to the cold stone floor at the feet of the minstrel.

"Run!" cried Kegin. "It's the flowers!"

"Don't breathe it!" shouted Owen.

Emerald fell back, covering his mouth and nose with the tail of his cloak, and hurriedly crossed to the well and scooped up a handful of the water to his mouth and drank.

The sweet, heavy smell of the flowers had slowly filled the room, and Deros felt her eyes growing heavy, and her breath coming in short spurts, until Owen sprinkled her lips with some of the water from her flask, which brought her around, although she felt woozy and unsteady on her feet.

"So you have found out the secret of the black sleep," Largo said shrilly. "I have other spells you don't know of, and can't guard against! See what you can do with this one!"

He had pulled another small box from his coat, emptied its contents on the floor, and ground his boot through the ashlike substance until a low guttural rattle came from the crushed gray pile. A dim shape grew into view, wavering and fading in and out hazily in the bright blue light that emitted from the well.

A darker cloud rose from the ash next, and behind that cover, Largo vanished into the doorway of the tunnel behind him. By the time the minstrel had groped his way through the thick gray smoke, there was no sign of him. The crazed youth had called out for the Rogen, but they were busy at the riverbank with their own blood feast, and did not heed the summons of the outsider.

Emerald searched both ways in the next tunnel for as far as he dared, then hurried back to check on the condition of his revered old instructor, Ephinias, who lay pale and breathing shallowly in Aron's strong grasp.

"Is he alive?" he asked, his heart pounding with a slow, leaden beat as he looked upon the drawn, pale features of his old teacher.

"He lives," replied Aron, "but I don't know how! It's a miracle that blow didn't cleave him from head to foot." He nodded his head angrily. "If I only had my broadax, I'd bring some mischief to that murderer."

Aron had lamented the loss of his broadax since Ephinias had first changed their forms, and he had been forced to leave his favorite weapon behind.

"You'll most likely have your chance yet," answered Emerald wearily. "I know we haven't seen the last of Largo yet."

"Not likely," said Kegin. "I have a feeling that he's not gone far! There are too many strange things at work here!"

"Look! The bear is gone! He's disappeared."

Deros had leaned over the well, and peered intently into its depths.

"That was good work, lass," said Kegin in an attempt to be cheerful. "Your timing was perfect."

"It's the only thing I seem to be able to do well," replied the girl. "Falling down appears to be my best defense."

"In this case, it was exactly what was called for."

"Put some of that water to his lips," suggested Emerald. "Ephinias is a tough old goat. I've seen him weather a graver blow than this."

The older man's eyes slowly opened, and he addressed his student in his best authoritative voice. "There may have been blows that were graver, but I don't recall any that were less painful," he said. "And I know you may not think so highly of me as I had hoped, but I thought you might refer to me in more gentle terms than 'old goat.' "

"Ephinias!" The minstrel laughed. "I knew it wasn't like

you to get yourself killed in some out-of-the-way place like this!"

"Not convenient, and I have so many things left to tend to," the older man went on, and tried to sit. His head spun wildly about, so he slowed down a bit, and eased himself up more gingerly.

"Is the bear gone?" he asked, finally in an upright position, with his back against the cool stones of the well.

"Gone. The well has taken him!" replied Aron.

Ephinias frowned. "I'm not so sure that bodes good for any of us," he said. After a moment his features cleared, and he seemed to remember something that made him smile.

"At least the Red Bear has been dealt with here! We shall see what it all means in due time, I'm sure. I never can remember how it is all supposed to be, but I'm certain that we'll know it all soon enough."

Kegin looked puzzled. "We won't have to wait long to hear from Largo! Listen! I can hear him screeching out there again."

Emerald and Owen leaped to their feet from where they had knelt beside Ephinias, and raced away toward the shouting, which seemed to come from the shaft behind the Fourth Chamber, and at no great distance.

"Stay behind me, lad! He's full of those devilish tricks of his. And don't attack until I say to!"

Owen nodded, concentrating on not getting ahead of himself. His anger and inexperience had almost cost him his life, so he vowed to remain calm, as he had seen Kegin do. The lad tried to remember all he could recall of Kegin's instructions on longsword handling, but his thoughts were all cut short again when he and Emerald turned another corner in the branching of the tunnels, and came face to face with Famhart and Elita.

Fathers and Sons

"Father!" cried Owen. Forgetting himself, he flung himself on Famhart, his heart bursting. It was hard to hold back the tears, but then Owen saw his father's eyes were wet too, so he stopped trying to hold back the flow.

Elita embraced him as well, and Emerald waited until the two, father and son, had had their greetings, and he extended a warm hug to the elder of the stewards.

"Well met, minstrel! I remember your amusing tales from a campfire long ago, on a long and weary patrol. You were with an older fellow then, but his name slips by me."

Famhart stood still embracing his son, although he had noticed that the lad had changed, and was no longer the mere boy he had been when he left him behind to seek help for Linne.

"Ephinias! He's here, but wounded. We just this moment came out to find Largo! We had him a moment ago, but he escaped."

Famhart's eyes clouded in a mixture of rage and pain.

"It shall end here, one way or other," he vowed, then turned to Owen. "But how came you here, lad? I left you to tend your mother! What of Kegen and Darek?"

The questions tumbled out one after another, and Owen blushed and fell silent, suddenly losing his voice.

Emerald laughed. "It is a long and complex story, sir, and one that will take some time in telling. The young sprout here had little to do with going against your orders, and he also has a way to redeem your faith in him, by having about him the answer to your problem. The key to the spell that has laid your wife low is in our grasp, and we can have her back and fine again as quickly as we can reach her side."

Famhart listened, elated, his features growing younger as the deep furrows of concern melted away from his forehead.

"All that remains here then is that we find our man, and try to repair what we can that has been the wreck of the Line."

"Darek is a girl," blurted Owen, realizing as he said it that it all came out wrong. "I mean, we thought Darek was a boy, but he was a girl all along. Her name is Deros."

Famhart's face was blank.

"The lad doesn't carry a tune very well," said Emerald. "I shall have to coach him a bit on spinning yarns. He has no sense of timing or suspense."

"There seems to be an abundance of suspense here in Trew," remarked Famhart, beginning to tire, and aching from his fall from the stricken horse at the river.

"The Dariens have been busy with two invaders tonight," said Elita, taking his hand again. "And the Dariens are clever and tenacious. They fear only the Rogen, and let them alone, for they know they aren't pure children of Trew. We must find a way to the heart of Rogen Keep, to still that spell that the Lord Trew stirred up when he closed the borders of our country."

"Can we do that?" asked Famhart. "I don't think I've come across anything quite like them since the Middle Islands. It smacks of the Dark One."

"The Lord Trew fought on the side of Windameir, but he began to lose his sense of things as he grew older. His daughter married an outlander, and left him alone in his old age. I don't think he ever got over that blow. It did something to his mind."

"Maybe that's what happened to Largo," said Emerald. "From all I've heard, it sounds as though he were weak in a way that would be easy for the Dark One to snare him."

"Linne was the strong one of the family," agreed Famhart. "That threatened Largo, and I don't think he has ever forgiven his sister for her courage, for he never had any. It was as though the Great One mistakenly put the wrong souls in the opposite bodies."

"Like Deros," stammered Owen. "She said her brother was gone, so she had to learn all the warrior's ways, and to try to bring help to her father! She's an awful lot like my mother, and all the stories you've told me of when you and she were on the campaigns in the Middle Islands."

Famhart laughed, and slapped his son on the back.

"I must meet this Deros, or Darek, whoever she is now. It sounds as though she has won your heart."

This made Owen blush the more, and he looked away to cover his embarrassment, turning just as the fading figure of Largo disappeared from his view into the chamber they had just left, where Deros and Aron and Kegin were tending the wounded Ephinias.

"It's Largo!" shot Owen, and dashed for the door after the vanished figure.

"Wait!" shouted Emerald. "Don't engage him!"

Famhart was ahead of the minstrel in a flash, with Elita at his heels, the tail of her silver gown floating out behind her like a fleeing ghost in a high wind.

Deros had looked up just as Largo entered, his sword brandished, and she leaped to Kegin's side, picking up the crossbow that was armed and lying at his feet. Kegin crossed the floor quickly, and engaged the ranting youth, who rolled his eyes back in his head until the whites showed clearly, and there were white flecks at his lips, and blood, where he had bitten his tongue through.

"Yield, Largo," coaxed Kegin. "There is no point to going on with this!"

Largo answered with a vicious blow at Kegin, who parried it, and stepped away.

"You need a healer, Largo! Look at you! We can find you a healer in the stewards' camp. We can take care of you."

"Like you take care of all the others who oppose you," snarled Largo. "I've heard how my precious sister and her pure-blooded Famhart treat those they distrust or dislike, or fear! No one can fool Largo! He knows how the ground truly lies!"

He circled Kegin, picking his time carefully, then lashed out again, causing the swords to ring out loudly, echoing again from the chambers that opened off the one they were in.

Largo attacked again suddenly, and as he did so, his hand flashed into his cloak so quickly that Kegin never saw it. The hand with the throwing dirk snapped back out like a snake striking, burying the small steel blade to its hilt in Kegin's shoulder.

He cried out and fell back against the stone wall, but he never dropped his guard, and parried another swordstroke by Largo, even as he felt himself weakening from his wound.

Largo prepared to finish his wounded opponent, when the iron dart from the crossbow caught him in the forearm that held the sword, and he fell back, screaming in pain. Deros was struggling to draw back the heavy pull of the weapon again, but without success. Largo saw his attacker clearly then, his mind focused by the bright electric intensity of the pain in his arm. He pulled an ugly, carved dagger from under his vest, and threw himself at the frantic girl, screeching in his maddened rage.

A bat came from nowhere, and dug its clawed talons into Largo's back, and the vile, ugly mouth with the rows of tiny sharp teeth clamped onto his shoulder right where it met his neck. Largo screamed again, and struck frantically at the soft furred body that he could not quite reach, giving Deros time to escape. She ran straight into the arms of Owen Helwin as he entered the chamber, fearing the worst.

"Owen," she cried. "Kegin is hurt! Largo is mad!"

She burst into tears and was unable to go on. A moment later, Famhart and Emerald were there, and she felt their strong arms around her.

"Easy, lass! It's going to be all right."

"Come on, son," said Famhart. "This is our score to settle."

Owen nodded, although he felt sick to his stomach to see Largo writhing against the wall, still trying to rid himself of the black demon that had attached itself to his neck. He screamed and twisted, but to no avail, for the bat clung to him tenaciously.

"Help me!" cried Largo, seeing Famhart and Owen coming across the chamber toward him. "Get this filthy thing from me! It's bitten me! It's bitten me!"

Almost as quickly as the bat appeared, it was gone, and Ephinias was back in his old place, propped up beside the well. Largo slapped twice more at his back, then laughed, his eyes wild and his mouth trickling blood from his mangled tongue.

"You had your chance to help poor Largo and make him into a good boy, but you missed it! Now he's going to be bad, and hurt you all! No one loves Largo. His sister hates him, and made his father hate him, too! His bad sister will pay, for she's going to sleep for a long time with the black sleep."

Largo had begun to back away from the two who neared him, his eyes bright with pain and madness, darting about for any weapon or avenue of escape. He did not see the woman behind him, nor did he have a chance to turn before she touched him with her outstretched hand that held the small vial of dark blue water from the well. He cringed backward when he saw who it was, but his eyes were already closing, and his tormented consciousness was being covered by a soft blue-black blanket of night, full of stars and a pale moon, and then there was nothing more.

"What was that, Elita? What did you do?" asked Emerald, as they all crowded around the quiet form of the lunatic that had raged before them but a moment before.

"It is the Tears of Trona," replied the woman. "If it is given by someone with no evil thoughts, it can work cures on even the most malignant souls."

"Will it help Kegin?" asked Deros, kneeling beside the injured man, who still had the throwing dirk embedded in his shoulder.

"Quick, lad! Let's get this out," said Famhart. "I hate to see an old comrade used for a pincushion like this."

Kegin smiled weakly at his commander.

"At least you can't dress me down for being out of pocket

from where you left me," he managed. "I was in the clear, too, for Owen and I had the good luck to come upon what will save Linne from her trouble!"

He paused, looking at Deros.

"Then we found out everything wasn't exactly like we thought, which confused us all a good bit. Thank the Stars of Rionde that she turned out to be clumsy of foot, and a passing shot with a crossbow, or old Kegin would be pushing up clover by now."

Deros was wiping away tears from her eyes, looking helplessly on as Famhart tried to ease the throwing dirk out of Kegin's shoulder.

"That hurts, friend! I think it may be pinned to the bone. You'll have to put your foot on my chest to get it."

Famhart nodded, and wrapped his cloak about the blade handle so he could get a good purchase of it, and put his boot against the wounded man's chest, and gave a big heave. Kegin cried out in pain, and his head drooped to his chest.

"He's out, poor devil! Quick, lad, we must clean this and stanch the bleeding. If this was a poisoned balde, we don't have a chance to save him, but if it was clean, then we're in luck."

Deros wept more loudly, holding to Emerald.

"It's all right, lass! We'll clean it with the well water. It was even enough to bring around Ephinias, and that in itself is a feat that would make the properties of this water most unusual indeed."

"Watch your tongue, whelp! I may be under the weather, but I still have my ways of dealing with a saucy pup like you."

Elita came to examine Kegin, and after looking at the bloody wound on his shoulder, declared that it was not poisoned.

"All the spells he learned here were from the Rogen, and the old books that were the downfall of Trew. He had no chance to treat the dirk with any of the poisons. And you can always smell the old ways! It always carries the faint smell of flowers."

"What of Largo! How long will he remain like that?" asked Famhart.

"Until I free him, or until he is called back by someone," replied Elita. "The dreamers could carry him back with them when they go, and he would be freed from the Dark One. The mark of the dragon is on him still. Look!"

Elita pointed to the amulet that he still wore about his neck, and she reached out to take it from him.

A clap of thunder resounded through the chamber, and the smell of scorched earth and flesh burned their nostrils, and Largo sat bolt upright, his eyes flat and lifeless, but gazing at each of them there with such a terrible emptiness that their hearts stood still for a moment as they looked upon the dreadful sight. One of his hands snaked out with a speed that escaped the eye, and wrapped itself grimly around Elita's neck with such a force that her face turned blue, and her eyes began to bulge from her head.

"The Protector has yet another dance to do, and another act to play before the curtain falls. You, my pet, will not escape now, and even the dreamers will have no luck returning you from the dead this time!"

Largo's head flew back and he cackled with a tinny laugh, squeezing the hand around the woman's neck tighter and tighter still. The amulet had begun to glow a dirty orange, and emitted a foul gray cloud that began to fill the close chamber with the ominous presence of the soul of the dragon.

Emerald was in action in a flash. His sword flashed once, and Largo's arm was lopped clean from his shoulder at a blow, but the arm still remained attached to the hand, and that hand had become a claw at Elita's throat. She had lost consciousness, and her tongue protruded from her mouth now, and she had begun to grow a dark, bruised bluish purple about her mouth.

"Quickly! Someone help me here," cried the minstrel, and he tried to pry off the hand from its iron grip at Elita's throat. He could not budge the dreadful claw, and as the gray cloud had choked him, he felt his strength began to falter.

Deros and Owen were at his side then, and Owen held the sword from the forges of Skye poised to strike, but he hesitated as to where to place his blow. Largo had raised himself on his remaining arm, and with his bloody stump at his shoulder spurting blood, he propelled himself toward the woman from Trew, and reached out to pull his severed arm back to his body.

Deros reached into her bodice, and pulled out the small knife Stearborn had given her at the fire when she was not long in Sweet Rock, at the beginning of her journey with Owen and Kegin. She began to pry at the convulsed hand that strangled Elita, while Owen waited, still unsure as to what next to do.

"Strike, lad!" ordered Famhart.

"The sword!" cried Ephinias. "It is from Skye! It will put the light into that dark heart!"

Largo turned at that instant, and looked directly into Owen's eyes, his face a convulsed mask of rage.

"Turn away, coward! None of you can harm Largo! I shall strangle this wretched woman, and I shall come for the rest of you. Nothing can stop the chosen one of the Protector!"

A dangerous green fire had burned slowly through the dead gray of Largo's eyes, and it now flashed in a sickening pale halo of light above the maimed man's head.

"Strike, lad!" shouted his father. "It is your only chance to free your mother!"

Owen's hand seemed to be held fast by Largo's stare, and will it as he might, he could not get it to follow his own command.

"Please, Owen," begged Deros, who had tried desperately to pull the hand away from Elita's throat, but all to no avail, for the woman had lapsed into unconsciousness and was no longer breathing or struggling against her attacker.

Owen tried very hard to remember how to contact Gillerman. A part of his mind that was not controlled by the forceful will behind Largo's eyes, focused on the older man, and his wonderful talking horse, when he had first come to the sleepy settlement of Sweet Rock, so long ago now that it seemed to be another lifetime. He struggled to remember the horse's name, and cried it out aloud when he did.

"Gitel! It was Gitel and Seravan!"

And the thin line that had held him back from Gillerman broke, and the sword erupted into a blue-white flame that cleared his mind of the Dark One's will, for it was no longer Largo's. The blade shot forward with a strength behind it that was not his own, and ran itself through the mail shirt and pierced the body of Largo cleanly. A great wail went up in the chamber, and the cold breath of a winter storm raged about the companions for a time, and then with a sigh, all was gone, and the body slumped forward, still impaled by the sword from Skye. The severed hand that had been wrapped about Elita's throat fell away as well, releasing the woman from its deathgrip.

"Is she breathing?" asked Emerald, at her side at once.

Ephinias held her head up, and Deros poured out a few drops of the Well of Trona onto the still, blue lips. Owen's heart hammered inside him like a wild drumbeat, while his father crossed to him and laid a hand on his shoulder.

The eyes of the slain Largo were calmer, and looked confused, but the facial features had relaxed from the horrible contortions that had been the cruel mask that frightened Owen.

"He's at rest now, son. The Dark One had kept his soul captive, and brought the poor devil back to attack all those who had helped defeat her at the Middle Islands."

"The sword," muttered Owen. "I couldn't strike! It was the sword that did it! I tried to think of Gillerman."

"Then that is what has freed Largo. The Light set him free from the bonds he was held by. The Dark One cannot face that."

Owen turned away, trying to quiet all the raging thoughts that had come to him as he faced Largo.

"Will my mother be here soon?" he asked, trying to think of something other than the elation he felt at killing, followed by the deep remorse that would not let him look again at Largo's body.

"Elita has said as much. The dreamers have her now. All we need do is get topside."

"She's coming around," said Emerald in a hushed voice. "Praise the Sacred Harp!"

"I believe she's going to be all right," concluded Ephinias. "The Tears of Trona is a powerful medicine to those in need."

Elita's eyes opened, fluttering, and she did not register at first at who she was looking. Emerald was the first one she saw, and a strange connection was completed between the two, and she laid her head on his chest and wept until all the fear and horror was gone, and a quiet serenity had come to take its place.

"You have had a near thing, my lady," said Emerald, his eyes gone a darker shade of blue.

"This will be worth a song or two, or I'll miss my mark," Kegin chuckled, shaking his head. "It never takes much to get him going with that music box of his, and we'll never hear this one out."

Owen was relieved to hear Kegin joking, although his friend was stiff from the pain in his shoulder.

"Can we think of trying to find an exit from this bugs' roost?" asked Aron, looking from one to another, tapping his foot nervously. "We're still not free of these little blighters that run these dingy shafts, and I've had all the excitement I can use for now. If I have to die, at least let it be beneath a clear blue sky, with a breath of wind to blow my soul away. I don't want to be trapped like a rat in a dark hole like this!"

Owen looked at his father.

"Do you think that happened to Largo?"

Famhart gave his son a hug and shook his head.

"I don't think that happened, Owen. You have to remember that sometimes we are used in ways we may not understand, but it is still the way of the Law. It takes a very long time to begin to see all these unpleasant things with an untroubled heart."

"Were you sad yet feeling a great power all at once when you killed?"

"The best and worst of it," replied Famhart. "It came very slowly to me that if I was to continue on as steward, and not to become an outcast or bandit, I would have to be merely a channel for the Law of Windameir. It is the only way I managed to survive that crossroad unscathed."

Deros put her hand on Owen's shoulder.

"You slew Largo, but you saved Elita," she reminded him. "That must make a difference."

Owen nodded, feeling very close to tears, and a warm sensation around his heart responded to the touch of her hand.

Ephinias interrupted his thoughts then, pointing upward. "It's time we are gone," he reminded them.

Elita had recovered her strength enough to stand, and she whispered, for her throat still hurt from Largo's attack.

"There is a straight way from the well chamber to the old throne room of Trew. Lord Trew had it done in the final days of his madness. He had drunk of the well and couldn't die as a mortal, so he had tried to find a way out elsewhere. I think he was finally taken by the well."

"Like Bern?" asked Deros.

"Yes."

"Where have they gone?"

"No one seems to know exactly," answered the woman, her voice low and husky. "Yet they will find themselves upon the world again somewhere, to finish their lessons."

"I hope they won't be anywhere near wherever we are," snapped Kegin. "I've had all I want of this business."

There was a faraway sound of rocks being pounded together, making sharp clicking noises that echoed dully in the well chamber.

"We must go quickly," said Elita, her beautiful face grown anxious. "The Dariens are returning."

"Lead on, my lady," said Emerald. "Are you strong enough?"

"I have to be," she replied, and hurried to a sunken niche in the stone wall near the well. She touched a small dent in the gray rock with a short tapping movement. As the surprised companions looked on, an entire wall slowly revolved, revealing a wide, well-lit shaft on the other side.

"This is how Famhart and I were able to reach you. We heard the sounds of your voices, but the other tunnels were so confusing, the only sure way I knew to reach here quickly was Lord Trew's escape hole."

"We'll make good use of it then, and bless his heart," snorted Aron. "But let's don't dawdle!"

As quickly as they were all in the new shaft, Elita touched another spot on the stone, and the entryway was sealed off.

"Won't it be wrong to leave the Dariens with the well?" asked Kegin. "They might use it for no good!"

"They can't misuse the well," replied Elita. "It is impossible to do anything with it. They have lived here for all this time, and they are still the sad little people they have always been."

"I guess you have a point, at that," conceded Kegin, nursing his hurt arm, which he carried in a sling he had made for himself out of a spare bowstring.

The shaft began an abrupt climb soon after they entered it, and within a few paces they were at the foot of a long stairway that had been hewn out of the solid rock. As they neared the top, there were odd markings on both walls, and strange numbers and figures which ran on for as far as the friends could see.

Emerald walked beside Elita, concerned that her brush with death might have left her weakened, but she never faltered in the journey, although she did, from time to time, reach out a hand to steady herself on the minstrel's arm. Ephinias noticed these occurrences when they happened, but he said not a word, and busied himself instead with the conversations he was having with Owen and Deros.

"Gillerman can be most aggravating," he was saying. "He's always one to be forever going on about some detail or other, but if he's with that friend of his, Wallach, there's no telling what the two of them will be up to! I've had tales of the two of them that make me look tame by comparison, and I don't mind telling you, I don't think of myself as a tame fellow."

"He's not," confirmed Emerald, grinning. "You can count on it."

"I'll stand by that," agreed Aron. "I thought I had seen my last days on two legs when Master Reckless here decides to give us a go at being rats! Of all things! Can you imagine my horror to find out that I was this horrid thing with dark gray fur and red little eyes that would burn a hole right through you, and a bent snout to boot!"

"You made an excellent case of it," soothed Ephinias. "You really were a quite handsome rat."

"Ugh," complained Deros. "Can we talk of something else until we can get out of this shaft? All this talk of rats and Dariens has made me think of that beastly little elder! I still can't get his eyes out of my memory. He looked as though he could see right through me!"

"We're almost there," said Elita. "There's the entry to the throne room at the top of the stairs."

As the woman from Trew was pointing it out to the others, the stone that hid the concealed doorway slid slowly and silently back, revealing a soft golden white glow that flowed into the darker shadows of the shaft. A ballooning ray of hope sprang from their hearts as they saw the elfin host emerge from the archway of the Darien Mounds that led to the world above ground.

The Shadows Lighten

Erases and the Lady Elina led the cortege, accompanied by a guard of honor, all dressed in shining silver mithra armor. Behind them came the pipes and, although they were not visible to the companions in the secret shaft of Lord Trew, there were many others behind, in a line that wound to the river like a shining silver ribbon.

Camrile, who had taken the mortally injured girl from the river, was there, and he held out his arms to her, his face forever young, yet with the deep blue-gray eyes with the unbearable sadness of all the race of dreamers, the children of the dawn.

"You have done well, my child," he said, after the two parties had exchanged their greetings, and after the companions were over their shock at meeting the Elboreal in such an unexpected fashion. The elf turned to Famhart, and touched him gently on the arm.

"We have brought the Lady Linne," he said quietly. "We await you."

Famhart's eyes were glistening with tears, but he held himself erect and went forward, pulling Owen along beside him.

"I'm ready."

"There is a chance that we may be able to do no more than free her from the black sleep, citizen. I don't know if we can bring her back to this vale of life."

The elder of the stewards shook his head. "If that be the case, then I would like to crossover with her. I couldn't bear to stay behind without her."

Camrile looked at Owen. "What say you to that, lad?"

Owen's voice was uncontrollable, so he merely nodded, wiping away the tears with the back of his hand. Deros was there, and she handed him the same quiver cloth to keep arrows from the wet, and he took it automatically.

"Owen is past his trial now. He has moved from a child into manhood. He has known the sting of defeat, and the horror of taking life, and the beauty of being in harmony with the Law. There is nothing left that I should be able to give him."

"You could chose to go too, Owen," said Erases. "That would be allowed."

As the elf spoke the words, Deros grasped Owen's hand so hard it brought him back to his senses, and away from the maudlin self-pity he had been entertaining.

He shook his head again.

"Then let us prepare ourselves, and see to it that we shall be ready when the sun rises. It will be the best time to free her, whatever the outcome shall be."

The Lady Elina came and walked between Famhart and Owen, and Camrile escorted Elita. Erases brought up the rear with Deros on his arm, flanked by Kegin and Aron and Ephinias, who was quite excited by all the splendor, and who engaged in a lively conversation with Erases as they went. At the river, the battle skiffs of the elves were drawn up to the shore, and the dead and wounded of the Elboreal host had all been tended to, or brought aboard for their final journey back to their homeland above the moon and stars. A line of the honor guard stood beside a platform that was covered with flowers, which filled the air with an eternal spring, for the blooms had come from where the dreamers stayed for as long as they were bound to Atlanton Earth. On the platform was a silver mithra bed, with four posts that had gleaming balls at the top, all shaped in the likeness of the nine-petaled Flower of Windameir, and on the bed was Linne, pale and distant, but dressed in radiant blue and gold, which made her seem all the more drawn and colorless.

Owen then noticed the other stewards there, from all the other squadrons that he had heard about since he was a tiny child. Stearborn, subdued and awkward-looking as the heat of battle wore off him, and burdened with the sadness of the losses he had suffered by the deaths of his young soldiers. Port and Starboard were there, nodding and repeating their grief, and Chellin Duchin stood supported by Hamlin and Judge, with Jeremy carrying their commander's armor.

And suddenly, from behind the platform where Linne lay, stepped Gillerman and Wallach, looking exactly as they had that long ago night he had met them first in the settlement hall at Sweet Rock.

The shock at seeing them was so sudden and overwhelming, that Owen burst into tears, then quickly fought to control himself and looked even graver.

"Welcome, brave stewards! Welcome to you, clan of the

Evening Star," said Gillerman. "We have had some sadness between us this day, but we shall rise above it, if we set our shoulders to it. Much has been gained by our sacrifice, and the Dark One is yet held at bay."

Wallach nodded to Owen, and the lad saw Seravan nudge his master from behind, in his own fashion of saying hello. So much flooded through Owen's mind that it was hard to remember how it had all begun that night in the wood, talking to the two steeds, who spoke of deeds and mysteries that had grown ever deeper as time had worn on.

"Come," said Famhart, and he took his son's hand, and they approached the raised elfin platform by the water. For as far as their eyes could see, the banks of the river on the South Channels side was scorched by the fires of battle, and there were many graves' details picking their way among the fallen of both sides. The smell was putrid and almost gagged those there, but at the platform where Linne lay, the Elboreal blossoms filled the air with a fragrance that made the heart think of spring, and better times to come.

"We tried to call you," managed Owen at last, when he had drawn close to Gillerman.

"You did call me, lad. I heard you every time. The sword you carry has never failed to reach me, no matter how far away I was, or how busily engaged."

There was a sparkle in the old man's eyes, hidden down beneath the sadness and the fatigue there. His face was the same as Owen remembered, but like the elves, there was a curtain of sorrow that covered their features, and left those who saw them torn between laughter and tears.

From behind Gillerman, Owen heard the horse, Gitel, speak his greeting, very dignified and formal.

Owen turned to his father, with that small item that seemed to loom so large in the face of such dire circumstances. It was like the random thought of who would water the flowbeds as one lay at death's door.

"You see! Gitel and Seravan speak as plainly as you or I!"

"I see, lad," replied his father. "Poor Bristlebeard won't see it, for he has gone on to his rewards, I hear. He was a man outgrown of his time."

Chellin Duchin and his band stepped up to exchange greetings with Famhart, and the brothers, Port and Starboard did the same.

"I knew we should have listened to our old mother," said Port. "She always said we'd come to a bad end if we left Trew."

"Almost did," echoed his brother. "The last louts in front of us were gobbled by that bunch of meat-grinders the Lord Trew called the Rogen."

"It was a surprise for them, I'd say, to find they couldn't lay their choppers on us," snorted Port, looking to his brother for agreement.

"That's how we got to you so quickly," explained Stearborn. "We were stuck across the river watching that bunch from Rogen Keep devour everyone who made an attempt at crossing. Then these two louts said they knew how to dispatch them, and off they went, and no stopping them."

"The Rogen couldn't touch a pure-born child of Trew," explained Starboard, "and my brother and I are Trew through to our core."

"And then some," added Port, nodding.

"The key to releasing the Rogen was to turn over the cup that Lord Trew kept in the old throne room of the keep. His word was that for so long as that cup be empty and upon the king's table, then for so long would the Rogen be needed to protect the boundaries of Trew."

"The Well of Trona filled the cup with water from its secret source," said the Lady Elina. "It was fetched by one of the older clans, and given to the hands of these two to deliver. They have done their job well."

"You mean the Rogen are gone?" asked Famhart.

"Gone," said Starboard simply. "The hex has been removed, and those poor lost souls have been released from that dreadful duty. There is no more danger to crossing into Trew now than there used to be in the older, better days."

"Better days," echoed Port. "Trew was a proud beauty then, just like our sister Elita."

The woman blushed deeply.

"I am only here because of Camrile and the dreamers," she said shyly. "If they had not pulled me from the river, I would have perished at the unfortunate Largo's hand."

"Even he is better off," said Camrile, his smile playing across his clear features like a wind across a still pond in summer. "The clans of the dreamers shall carry him back with us when we go, and he shall not have to return again."

"Come along," said Erases. "We must see to Linne. We have kept her waiting with our lengthy gabbing long enough."

Owen's heart began to hammer, and he thought he would not be able to walk, for his knees seemed to have gone to water. Deros handed him her flask, and had to thrust it at him twice more to get his attention.

"It's the water from the well," she whispered to him. "They may need it."

Owen nodded blankly, and took the small leather-covered flask, holding it tightly to his chest.

"You and Famhart come and stand on either side," instructed the elfin queen. "She will be guided by your thoughts, and perhaps she will be able to see your auras when she is released from the darkness. If that is not to be, I will go myself, and will find her, and take her to a safe place in one of the other havens on the other side of the Boundary. You must not grieve if that is to be, for she will be safe, and all will go on as before."

"But we won't see her," protested Owen, feeling a great wave of grief overtaking him as he looked at the still, forlorn figure of his mother, so cold and lifeless, and her beauty so distant and forgotten.

"Not as you know her, or have known her," answered the Lady Elina. "You must not try to pull her back if we are to go on. That would be very cruel to your mother. If you see that she will not return here, you must make your peace quickly, and let her know all that you would have her understand, then release her to the Light. It is Windameir's Dream that we all go home to, and it is to be looked forward to, not dreaded."

"Windameir's Dream is what we have all been searching

for so long, lad," Erases went on. "It is the one true beacon that lights our way. These other lives are but small stops along the way. We play one role, then another, until we know enough to let go and go on."

"Even Largo and Bern? Have we been like them?" asked Deros.

"Worse, my lass. We have done it all, and that is the one way we learn it."

Erases had drawn back a veil that covered Linne's face as he spoke, and Elina stood beside him, holding a tiny urn that seemed to glow a dozen shades of golden shadows. She held it out to Owen, and instructed him to fill up the small container with the water from the well that he carried in the flask.

A sudden thought flashed through Owen's mind that it might not work, and his hands trembled as he began to pour, causing him to spill a few precious drops on the floor of the platform where Linne lay as though in state for her friends and family to come to mourn her.

Elina turned to Erases with the urn, and Camrile joined the other two, and together they knelt beside the soft bed of fragrant flowers where Linne lay, and bowed their heads as one. A high, thin reed pipe began to play a lilting, haunting tune, and there were changes then that happened to the faint, fragile peach-colored light that painted the underside of heaven near the horizon where the new day was in the process of being born. Bright shades of a golden white light began to glow from the urn, and as Erases touched the water to Linne's cold lips, a faint tremor passed over her, as though an echo of life had passed through some memory that lay locked within the deep bleakness of the prison that held her captive.

"She moved," said Owen excitedly, hardly daring to let himself hope.

"We're not through the wall yet," cautioned Erases. "This is as deep as I've ever seen the Dark One's hold. Even the edges of her dreams are frozen."

The elf placed more of the water to Linne's lips, and

again, a faint tremor, barely noticeable, rippled over the platform, stirring the stricken woman's eyelids.

Famhart knelt at the side of the bier, and clasped Linne's hand tightly, his face screwed into a mask of anxiety. Owen watched his father, and saw him go from old to young, and back to old again as he waited for Erases and the Lady Elina to complete their ritual.

A slight tinge of color, like the first blush of spring after a long winter, touched Linne's cheek, and Famhart felt the hand he held warm to his touch.

The elfin queen placed a small flower on Linne's bodice, and the petals seemed to grow more luminous as she spoke, and a wind sprang up from the south, which smelled of the sea and ancient tides, and all the deep secrets that were tossed about in the dim regions of the great ocean's heart.

Owen found the nerve to reach out and touch his mother's hand, which seemed to make a feeble attempt to return his grasp.

"I think she can hear us," said Erases. "There is something getting through to her."

"Speak to her, Famhart," instructed Camrile. "Sometimes it takes only an old, familiar voice to draw them back."

Famhart leaned closer to his wife, and whispered something in her ear that the others couldn't hear, but which had a startling effect on the motionless figure of Linne.

Her lips began to tremble, and a low moan burst forth, followed by a slight trickle of tears that started from her eyes. After another small sob, the dam burst, and Linne wept as though all sadness had been touched in the deepest recesses of her heart. Her shoulders shook, and the long, frantic sobs racked her weakened body until Owen could stand it no more, falling to his knees at her side.

"You're safe, mother! We have Gillerman and Wallach here, and all the rest. Father is here, along with the stewards. You don't have to worry anymore! The dreamers are with you, so you can't be lost again. We know the secret of the spell, and you'll never have to worry about being trapped there again."

Linne wept bitterly, but her eyes did not open, and it seemed to Owen that there was some great struggle going on within her, as though she fought for her very life with the soul of the Dark One. Once or twice, Famhart heard his wife curse violently, which she never did, and it was as though there were two powerful enemies going at the fray with every weapon they had.

Owen clutched his sword tightly, and prayed that its strength and light might help guide his mother through the dark chambers that she was in, and to deliver her from whatever enemy was attacking her there. It was very frustrating to have to sit helplessly by while she faced such dangers, and in a place where he could not go to her aid in any other way.

The elfin queen's face had hardened, and her eyes were clamped tightly shut. She seemed to be confronting some unseen power that wracked her body, and caused her to rock back and forth on her feet as though she were in intense pain. Camrile and Erases both stood with eyes closed too. For the next few moments, Owen watched as all three of the elders of the Elboreal faced the terrible might of the Dark One's will, trying to free Linne from that frozen palace that lay in the heart of terror and despair.

It was then that the grizzled and limping Chellin Duchin stepped forward, taking something out of a worn leather wallet that he had concealed in his cloak, and he placed a small brown leaf on the silent form of Linne.

As the deadly unseen combat went on, the sun peeked over the horizon at last, and a long golden ray of light came sliding down the rolling hills behind the Rogen Keep, spreading a warm glow to all it touched as it crept nearer and nearer to the raised platform where Linne lay surrounded by the flowers of the dreamers. Even the harsh scorched land that lay burned and withered, seemed to take on new life in the light of the brightening dawn. As they all looked on amazed, the broad finger of light slipped through the last of the early morning shadow, and fell across the sobbing form of Linne, trembling on her bed of fragrant blossoms.

With the sunrise, the powerful battle that raged within the three elders of the elves seemed to abate, and after another heartbeat or two, Erases opened his eyes, and bent down to touch Linne's cold forehead with a kiss.

Owen at first thought his mother had departed, so calm and still she lay, but her eyes opened then, and she seemed to be staring at something far away and long ago, or at the pearl-colored sky that had begun to lighten more into an oyster blue, tinted with gold and pale green down along the edges which topped the trees that were left standing in the woods of the Edges of Trew.

After another pause, Linne turned to Famhart, and the two clasped each other closely in a long embrace, weeping until Stearborn coughed nervously, and said in a very shaky voice, "Welcome back, Linne. We've all come a long road since you smiled at us last."

"Has it been so long?" asked Linne, her voice faint.

"Long enough to do a fair piece of traveling, and to have dealt with two of the worst villains that ever threatened the stewards of the Line, or anyone else left down here below the Boundaries," replied Stearborn.

He was stopped from going on by Famhart, who signaled him with a glance to be quiet.

"Here is a drink for you, my lady," said Erases, offering Linne a drink from a tiny crystal goblet that he held out to her, filled with the water of the Tears of Trona. "You will feel a small bit jumpy at first, so don't try to overdo anything just yet. You've spent a long, nasty time in that dreadful place, and you should just relax and enjoy your freedom for a while."

"I don't remember anything very much," said Linne, her brow furrowed. "It was so awful, because most of the time I remembered that I was in a place I wasn't supposed to be. That made me so angry, and so sad all at once, because I couldn't remember where it was I belonged."

She paused then, and her eyes dimmed.

"But then there were times that I was very afraid, and someone told me that I would never be free again."

Famhart took her in his arms and held her close.

"It's all right now. You won't have to worry about it again. The stewards and the Elboreal have ridded Trew and the South Channels of the threat that has caused so much grief and destruction among our clans."

Linne seemed to remember something then, and she raised a worried face to her husband.

"I had a terrible dream about my brother. He was alive again, and he tried to hurt me."

Owen met his father's gaze over Linne's shoulder, and he shook his head very slightly, trying to signal his son not to speak.

"It was a sad dream. I don't know why I thought of him after all this time. I guess I must have been grieving for him somehow."

"You don't have to grieve for him without hope, my dear. The dreamers have said that they will carry him home. Largo will never have to come back again to the Wilderness."

"They also have offered you a choice of what to do, my lady," said Camrile. "If you like, you may join us when we depart the Lower Shandin."

Linne looked about her, and held out her arms to her son, no longer the little boy he was when last she had seen him.

"Owen!" she cried, and took him into her arms, brushing back the hair from his forehead, as she had done when he came to her in the evenings after their meal, waiting for her to read him a story of the exploits of the Line Stewards and all their glorious history. "You've changed! You're all grown!"

Owen blushed and made a feeble attempt at withdrawing from her overlong hug.

"Will you go with the dreamers?" he asked at last, not sure of what his reaction would be if she said yes.

"We would all go with them, if we were in our right minds, and had a healthy outlook about having a few tomorrows to look forward to," grumbled Port. "But I don't hear any offers for old Port to be going anywhere, with or without these fine folk, so I guess I'm stuck in my same old rut, dug and furnished."

Deros stepped up to Linne and bowed low, with tears glistening on her cheeks.

"I hope you feel recovered, my lady. My name is not Darek, as I told you when first we met. I am Deros, from a country beyond the Sea of Silence. I have come seeking help for my father, and I have hopes that you will spare your life, and not make the crossing with the elves. I have much to learn, and I feel I must learn it all from you."

Linne smiled weakly, and held out a hand to the girl.

"I had wondered at you, child! I knew there was something that I felt off-kilter when you came to us, but I had not time to think on it much before I was struck down."

"Will you stay, mother?" persisted Owen. "We shall all be able to help Deros if you do! Kegin can teach her her arms, and Emerald can see to it that she attends to her music."

"Old Ephinias can make sure she doesn't overlook any of her finer education when it comes to his vast experience with the animals and their nature," added the older man. "And I think Gillerman and Wallach might add the weight of their considerable experience, from time to time."

Ephinias looked through shaggy lowered eyebrows at his nephew and his friend.

"To be sure." Gillerman laughed. "I think there shall be a need of all our assistance before too long. The young lady has come on a mission that I believe I am familiar with, although it is difficult to say exactly when it will come to a head."

"Hurrumph," muttered Wallach. "Not in my lifetime, I hope. I should like to tend to my garden and fishing awhile, before I have more to do with all this beastly affair down here."

Seravan nudged his master roughly, pawing the earth as he did so.

"You'll have your own good time trying to get us to come back with you with a droll attitude like that. Gitel and I did all the work this time, and here you two lugs sit enjoying all the rewards as though you were the heroes."

Gitel neighed in agreement. "Let's see how quickly they can get themselves home if we decide not to budge."

"You two will do nothing of the sort," said Gillerman. "I'm familiar enough with your sassy ways to know you better than to believe you'd leave a young lady in distress, when you know you would be of great service to her."

The older man stroked the horse's soft velvet nose lovingly, in spite of the gruff tone of his voice.

Famhart had stood near Linne all the while, and spoke for the first time as he watched his wife and son.

"There seems to be yet a further need for the stewards. With Bern and Largo out of the way, there will be a time to help this young lady with her trouble in her homeland. I have no doubt that it is all stirred up by the awakening of the Dark One. She does not lie in wait for long."

He paused, looking at Linne.

"Do you feel up to the task of preparing for another campaign, Linne? It isn't exactly the life I promised you when we moved to Sweet Rock, but those times seem far away now. It's almost as though we were never in the Middle Islands, and that all the time in between never happened."

Linne nodded, her face beginning to gain more color as she got up slowly and moved around, stretching her stiff limbs.

"I told you then I didn't want to raise Owen in a world that seemed intent on tearing itself apart, and I didn't believe we should have turned him into another heir to the stewards. I'm afraid I was rather silly then, and thinking too much of my own childhood, and the grief I felt at having been raised in a time of war and troubles."

Linne raised her eyes to her husband's.

"I know Largo was the weak one, and I often thought that if he had been born a woman, he would not have had the trouble he did. Our father always threw me up to him for my courage, even though I was terrified, and he never ceased to find a means to chastise my poor brother for his lack of manliness."

Here Linne looked at the small figure of the young girl from the distant land.

"I saw the two of you with Kegin and thought it was a repeat of all I had gone through. I didn't want to believe that the danger to the Line was so great. In a way, being struck down as I was by my brother was the best thing that could have happened to me. It has finally opened my eyes to the fact that I had lost him long before he died. I don't want to lose you, Owen, to a foolish whim of a mother's heart. You must stand for yourself, and follow your own dreams now. Your father and I will do everything we can to help you."

"Then you're staying?" asked Owen, his voice choked with a wild runaway surge of emotions.

"If you'll have me, and if the kind, wonderful friends I have among the dreamers will allow me."

Camrile bowed low to Linne, as did Erases. The Lady Elina came and embraced Linne, calling her little sister, and holding her closely for a long time, her eyes shining.

"There is always a place in the Upper Shandin for a warrior as true as you," she said, holding her back at arm's length. "We of the dreamers have long been used to the strange mix of the beauty and horror that is a part of these Lower Meadows. I think that must have been what attracted us in the beginning. It is hard to reconcile these things. I don't think we are released until we know all of the heart of Darkness, as well as the secret of the Light."

"Then I shall have to stay a bit longer to try to reconcile all these things in my heart I can't seem to accept," admitted Linne. "I seem to be needed, as well,"

Her husband clasped her tightly to him, and Owen and Deros quickly embraced her.

"We shall need a long season of the fall to rest, and a winter to redo all our new settlements," said Famhart. "Kegin can teach the youngsters their weaponry, and you and I will entertain all our good old ruffians at feast days, and try to recoup as best we can."

"A good long siege in front of a fireplace with plenty of

onion soup will have you fixed up right as a hawk's eye in no time," rumbled Stearborn.

Gillerman and Wallach then held up their hands, clapping to get the attention of the others, and mounted the fragrant bed from which Linne had arisen.

"Now that we're so cozy, I think I'd best announce the news! There will be a feast this evening, in honor of us all, at the old Rogen Keep! There will be plenty of cause for Trew to celebrate her liberation from the Rogen, and from Largo, and I think we shall all have a deal of stories to exchange, and a list of our fallen to hold wake over. Let us prepare them for their memorial, and to host our own feast to the living."

Wallach nodded, his old eyes misty.

"It's a fitting thing. Like the bygone days. I seem to miss them more, at times like these."

The great gathering of the dreamers and the stewards, began to break up then, led by Famhart and Linne, who came down from the raised platform to the noisy cheers of all who were there. They waited for Port and Starboard and the Lady Elita to lead them to the imposing-looking fortress which, for as long as the Rogen had lived, had served as their bloody feast hall. Chellin Duchin was helped along by his young lieutenants, and Stearborn walked alongside Ephinias and Aron, marveling at the destruction of the battlesite across the river, and at the scorched land that bore mute testimony to the brutal fighting that had taken place there but the night before.

The elves brought up the rear, with their queen in the vanguard, flanked by Erases and Camrile. They marched to the haunting refrains of a single reed pipe, which played dirges for all those lost, and seemed to weep at the very edge of all sorrows. No one in that vast cortège had dry eyes.

Gitel and Seravan had fallen in behind Owen and Deros, and talked to the two young people as they walked. Their singsong voices had made the girl laugh.

"We weren't supposed to let the secret out, but our two lumps are going on a special errand, and they won't be taking us," said Gitel.

"Couldn't," confirmed Seravan. "After all these turnings, the two of them are finally going up to see how it's done on the other side. I never thought it would come to this."

"Well, we're needed here," snorted Gitel. "These two will have a need of a steady mount and a true friend, even if someone else of our acquaintance doesn't."

"You mean you're going to stay with us?" asked Owen, incredulous.

"I'm afraid that's the way of it," replied the horse, nodding his handsome head.

Before Owen could react to this news, Starboard and Chellin Duchin had blown the recall on their signal horns, and all the rest of the stewards of the Line who yet lived after the great battle began to muster in ordered rows along the route of march the elfin procession was taking toward the still imposing hulk of ruins that was Rogen Keep. On shields and on their own mounts, the honored dead were brought gently on toward their last rest, to lay in the gray hills of Trew.

The Lady Elina sent out a small white dove from her hand, and a rainbow-colored light trailed out behind the small bird, as it flew high up into the new morning, circling the grim walls of the old castle, spreading the reds and greens and golds and blues over the fallen walls and turrets. After a few more spirals, the company below was astounded to see a broad green lawn appear before the broken gate, dotted with shrubs and trees that were decorated with colorful tinsel and ribbons that reflected back the sunlight, and a moment later, the gate was renewed once more to a golden ivory-colored wood that gleamed in well-oiled splendor. There was green ivy at the turrets then, and a fresh smell of new-mown hay began to tickle the noses of horse and rider alike. Behind Rogen Keep, a vast broad field was revealed, with bright tents and pavilions, and great long wooden tables covered with the finest feast the court of the Elboreal could place before such honored guests.

The solo piper struck up a lively air then, and was joined in that joyous song by all the stewards and the elfin host. Emerald, holding Elita's hand, joined in with a strong voice that rang out clearly above the others, a pure tenor note among the deep rumble of the stewards, and the bell-like notes of the elves.

Next to the minstrel, Famhart and Linne smiled at each other with an old secret, and held hands as they had done when they were first together. Owen saw this, and very shyly offered his hand to Deros, who blushed, but covered her own discomfort by kissing him quickly on the cheek.

Behind them, Seravan and Gitel snorted and pawed the smooth turf, and laying their ears back and tails up, they pranced and raced about the green sward to the amusement of all there, until all the company had found a place to sit or stand. Gillerman and Wallach, flanked by the queen of the Elboreal, raised their hands, and blew a short note to get the attention of that vast throng.

The celebration of victory was ready to begin, and the saying of their farewells to their lost comrades-in-arms. The afternoon and evening and far into the night was spent in tears and laughter and joy and grief, all mixed together until in the end, only the sweet soft arms of sleep were left. The winds of war and destruction had blown past and left the survivors there with a strength they had not had before, and a new hope born in their hearts that one day there would be a time when it would not be necessary to raise their weapons in anger, or to have to carry forth the sad burdens of old friends left behind.

Owen and Deros sat long at table that night, full of the wonder and sorrow there, and full of another wonder that had happened somewhere when they were not looking—the love they felt for each other had steadily grown into a bright flame that promised to burn much more brightly in the coming times.

When the last note was sung and the parting glass was taken, Emerald had made them all weep again with that haunting air. The companions all took their new oaths of loyalty and service to each other, and bade the fair host of the Elboreal a long, moving good-bye, with promises on both sides that the parting would not be long.

And at long last, after the stewards had regrouped and

held their silent service for their fallen comrades, Famhart and Linne began the journey back to their old home in Sweet Rock, where they planned to winter and recover from all the many adventures they had been through. Seravan and Gitel carried the young couple, Owen and Deros, filling them with wonder as the two animals spun them yarns of all their travels with Gillerman and Wallach. They had had a quiet parting with their old masters and, although somewhat subdued and lonely but not wanting to admit it, they settled in to their new duties with a passion that seemed bound to make the errand their masters had sent them on as pleasant a one as they could make it.

The coming spring would bring another tide, and beyond was the Sea of Silence, already beckoning to the young Lady Deros and her new champion.